A Fool and a Whore

John Peter Fer

1

This book is not intended to supplement or replace professional or personal suicide prevention. If you are having suicidal thoughts, please seek professional help. The point of the story is that people, especially men, are not able to talk openly about their mental health. They will go to great lengths, discussing anything controversial, vulgar, or inane to avoid their true feelings. They find redemption (at least Trey does) if/when they realize they were never alone.

Thanks to Victoria, my parents, Derek, Darcy, Ken N, Helaena W, Amy S, Kerry W, Paul C, Chris O, Donald A, Dina, Maureen, Tracy S, Rachel Rowland, Jill S, Chris M, Chris Bright, Sophia, Brian, Phil, Mike, Matt, Gabe, and Jeb.

If you have questions or commentary, please email me at treyciuri@gmail.com.

Cover design by Christine Horner

For Rachel Stiffler, Mike Harwell, Oneil Cannon, and Blake Butler

"Wolf?" a woman cried sympathetically.

Ivan got angry.

"Fool!" he yelled, trying to locate the woman. "What's Wolf got to do with it?"

—Mikhail Bulgakov

Chapter One: The Second Suicide

It was the time of the Columbine High School shooting. Wade and Trey, new lieutenants fresh out of the Air Force Academy, walked in late to their first day of space and missile training at Vandenburg Air Force Base, California. Wade was sweaty and disheveled, his right cheek wore a smudge, and Trey's arms were full of fast-food bags.

"Sorry we're late. Someone had a flat in the goddamn Burger King drive-thru," said Wade. The paunchy major gave an involuntary grimace, first for their tardiness, and then for the image they burned into his classroom: Wade, a square-jawed mountain man; and Trey, his wiry, Roman-nosed sidekick, the smell of fried food their aura. From the nametags on their empty desks, the Major read, "Lieutenant Herndon…"

"Yes sir," said Wade, tucking in his shirt, making room for Trey to share the spotlight. Trey heard one of the other lieutenants whisper, "Burger King drive-thru?" with a chuckle.

"And you—how?"

"Ciuri, sir. Kee-yoo-ree," said Trey with a slight Italian singsong. "We got these tater tots for fixing the tire." He passed out the bags and greeted each person before finding his seat. The class braced for the major's reaction.

"Sorry again, sir," said Wade.

"Yes, sorry sir," said Trey still chewing.

The other lieutenants, all of them commissioned through ROTC, had heard of Academy grads, mostly in exotic, amusing ways. "Zoomies" were book smart and spoon-fed, they hung out in herds and told inside jokes while trying to not admire their class rings. ROTC guys were warned to keep their distance until their Academy counterparts had a chance to adjust to the real world, where one had to pay rent and didn't wear a uniform every hour of the day.

But Wade and Trey defeated Academy stereotypes. Their stories of military school rebellion and hijinks played beyond the usual pranks and after-hours jaunts. Where typical grads told "there I was" ego tales, high-fiving at sneaking girls into their rooms, Wade and Trey delivered fables that had nothing to do with the selectivity of their university or college-boy thrills that arrived by way of calculated risks at high speeds. Many came with hard lessons and tragic outcomes, seasoned by Wade's Midwestern practicality and Trey's Sicilian idea of karma.

Vandenburg training was the least of their concerns. While the other lieutenants took serious notes, Trey and Wade daydreamed through the first day, first week, and most of the modules. Space and missile class was to them decaffeinated Academy, joyful freedom, a pair of silicone baubles to slap around. No one cared what time they went to bed or if they marched to breakfast. They just had to learn "this orbital mechanics shit"—which they did anyway at "the zoo"—and sign a paper promising they'd launch nuclear weapons if commanded to.

Instead of class, Trey studied his classmates, their disparate hometowns and ROTC programs. He shared his background as an Air Force "brat," rolling his eyes to admit he was born at the Academy (and baptized in the chapel basement), then dragged around the world by his father. He put the lieutenants at ease, made them curious, and mined commonalities from them one by one.

If someone in the class was from Texas, Trey talked football; Mississippi, he moaned of the money he lost gambling in Biloxi and

Shreveport, inviting them to correct him. (That's *right*, Shreveport *is* in Louisiana! But they still took my money.) To Chicagoans, he was a Cubs fan. Michiganders found out about his love of Iggy Pop and the Detroit Pistons. Those from Virginia discovered that Trey's dad was stationed at the Pentagon, and if they were Catholic, he shared that he did his first communion there. It was all mostly true.

Trey's parents grew up in Los Angeles, but as an Air Force family they only visited in the summer, and when Colonel Ciuri's career ended they moved to South Carolina. Nonetheless, in front of the new lieutenants, Trey talked about L.A. as if he owned a place on the Sunset Strip, never mentioning that his family was from San Pedro, an unglamorous port town far from Hollywood, where his grandparents still cooked pasta for everyone on Sunday.

Lompoc, which surrounded Vandenberg, was to Trey a prison town where the families of inmates lived in the alphabet streets, subsisting on service industry jobs and welfare. He saw them strung out on one drug or another, wearing wristbands with barcodes, fresh from their latest AIDS tests. They had innumerable kids by prisoners; they had almost as many pets as children; and they bowled frequently, which Trey discovered because he too liked to bowl.

In the alley bar, he sang karaoke and wrote poetry on napkins, hoping girls would ask him to read it to them. But only his classmates asked, and when he read, he got emotional and sang karaoke again. He and Wade often closed the night with a duet.

To their classmates, Wade and Trey were the allure of a road trip, the horizon of the American West. They wore their uniforms like postal workers, like they couldn't wait to take them off and drive fast to somewhere new. They stretched their entry-level salaries to fund cartons of smokes on road trips to Vegas, sustaining themselves on gas station coffee and microwaved burritos. They explored the California coast with Wade driving and Trey reading—aloud at times: Fante, Shepard, Highsmith, and some scattered beat writers. The radio going too, their cigarettes molten.

The other lieutenants ogled the pair as they told their weekend tales on Monday, embellishing by Thursday, vowing to top whatever they'd done the next time. Trey, it seemed they'd met over and over, so it was his way to treat classmates as if he was greeting them for the first time. He made them feel like they were cool individuals, sharp officers, and the most included they'd ever been.

That they were learning how satellites and nukes worked—that they were frequently tested on such subjects—meant nothing to Trey in comparison to what he was learning of the lieutenants as people. He loved his new home at Vandenburg because, unlike the Academy, no one was a smarty pants, no one pretended to be a fighter pilot, and no one cared that his dad was at one time a prisoner of war.

What Trey embraced in their personalities, Wade brought to life by photographing the lieutenants and their families at barbecues, by teaching their kids piano, fixing their cars, spotting them in the gym, and giving hugs to their wives. (He gave teddy-bear hugs with the slightest hint of sensuality that made the wives curious, made him confident, and made Trey jealous.)

Everything Wade touched got fixed. He banged the dents out of fenders and sewed seat cushions shut whenever they drooled stuffing. He drove his truck through the rain without using wipers, navigating by the moon with the headlights off. He parked before the Pacific and sketched sunset at minute increments. He had an eye for useful garbage—rusty springs, copper wire, pillow foam, and driftwood—which he turned into furniture, toys, and tools. Trey often asked with tinges of disbelief and jealousy how Wade learned to do so many things. Wade answered, half ashamed, that he'd worked at his old man's body shop since he could turn a wrench. "You learn shit 'cause you have to."

Wade had six inches and more than a hundred pounds on Trey, and yet Trey frequently borrowed his clothes, making Wade-me-downs his look: flannels that hung like women's bathrobes, and pants held up by belts cinched to the last notch. And on his feet a pair of black Velcro shoes on which he wrote "R" and "L" on each heel.

In college, no one told Trey that he looked ridiculous, mostly because he and Wade hung out in places and at hours where and when no one cared. They spent the wee hours at the Waffle House off I-25, at poetry readings in downtown Colorado Springs, and at Pikes Peak Community College, where they audited evening classes on emergency medicine because they felt it was missing from their Academy curriculum.

In Wade's truck they were kings. Riding shotgun, Trey felt like he was being escorted past a violent mob, into an exclusive club, closer and closer to the vanishing point of the horizon. High above worldly pitfalls, Trey's mouth and mind rambled dangerously while Wade's massive hands cradled the truck like an origami bird. Trey spat ideas, feeling confident that together they would figure out ways to beat the Academy, to beat the Air Force, to make their minds better without using drugs. (The Air Force often tested for such substances.)

It was the best time in history to join the military, and here they were in the safest of services. As far as their memories reached, it was a time of peace and opportunity. The most dangerous event the lieutenants could recall was the outrage in the headlines over Bill Clinton's blowjobs. They forgot the attack in Oklahoma City and the Embassy bombings in Africa. Columbine too would pass. The lieutenants hadn't the slightest inkling that things could end badly.

During the year they spent at "Vandy," Wade and Trey conquered their ROTC classmates with adventurousness, wit, and kindness. One by one, they fell in love with the other lieutenants as two men fall in love with the same woman; and by way of such a competition, it drove the best friends apart. Wade would take refuge in his Air Force career and dreams of retiring at 40, while Trey would fall into despair and again be lured toward suicide.

Months later, hours before Wade shot one of the other lieutenants, he and Trey rode to the bowling alley as they did most Saturdays.

"We have such a diverse class!" Trey smacked, rolling down the window just enough to let the air suck ash from his cigarette. Wade lit up but rolled down further and drove fast, making it too loud for Trey to speak.

He shouted at Wade's right ear, "Bruce and Michelle are from Louisiana! Near where they make Tabasco! Vinchenzo's dad played football at Florida—the Gators! Ken is from Tennessee—he's trying to have a baby with his wife, but he's so used to pulling out that they can't seem to do it right. Harm-wah is from Texas!"

"His name is Harmon."

"But I call him Harm-wah," laughed Trey, making a French *mwah!* with his fingers and his lips. Wade laughed.

"Reminds me of Braz-wah," said Wade. "That grizzled cocksucker."

"He should have kicked us out."

"He tried."

"You know what I thought was the funniest thing about old Braz?"

"There's a list."

"He knew full well that everyone called him Braz-wah, you know, like some refined Frenchman, precisely because that neanderthal wasn't."

"He just wanted to fly. He wife was leaving him—banging that other guy. Plus, he was chasing us like Wily Coyote the whole time."

"I guess it's sad when you think about it. You think we were his white whale?"

"His white what?"

"Braz used to tell me all the time that I didn't deserve a commission. I still can't believe I wasn't kicked out."

"Believe it, why question it? So what if your dad is your dad?"

"I hate to think that I shouldn't be here," Trey said, rubbing his throat, a gesture understood between them as a defense mechanism against crying.

"You shouldn't be where? In my fucking truck? Trust me, even if Braz-wah's psycho ass kicked you out, you'd still be in that seat. What do they call the last graduate of med school? Doctor. What do they call the last grad at USAFA….lee-yoo-tenant!" Wade said the last part like a drill sergeant, and Trey smiled.

"How's your mom?" Trey asked.

"Getting better, doing rehab."

"Seems like yesterday we were back there."

"Where, the zoo?"

"The Zoo. Southern Illinois. Visiting your mom after the accident."

"That was scary. Mom still talks about how much it meant to her that we came."

"Why'd you say that shit to Braz-wah when we got caught coming back?"

"What shit?"

"The shit about emergency leave."

"I don't even remember. I just remember Braz sitting on your bed waiting for us to walk in."

"He asked you why, if your mom was in such a bad accident, did you not take emergency leave. You surely would have gotten permission."

"Still don't remember….what'd I say?"

"You said, 'Sir, if had had taken emergency leave, Cadet Ciuri couldn't have come with me.'"

"I guess that's true," Wade said. Trey punched the cigarette lighter on the truck's console.

"Well, that was the closest we came to getting the boot."

"It was never in the cards—getting kicked out—you got nine lives, Yuri."

"What about you?"

"Me? I'm your guardian angel." They lit cigarettes, passing the coil.

"I feel a meat-beater coming on," Trey said.

"Christ, well you better hold off on that meat-beater till we get home. We're going *bowling*, man. Where you gonna put the afterbirth?"

"C'mon, man, I'll do it in the jump seat, 43 seconds, I'm already halfway there," Trey begged and motioned behind them.

"Wouldn't you prefer to do that with a girl? You just lit a smoke."

"I only need one hand to smoke. Come on, masturbation is a necessary defense against feminism."

"You don't even know what 'feminism' means."

"Feminism is when girls control you, when they get you to do what they want."

"And that's a bad thing, how?"

"It's a weakness to be so attracted to girls that you alter your behavior, spend all your money, and generally make a fool out of yourself just so they'll give you attention. Not even sex. They know they have this power over us! I've found that if I'm shooting chalk dust, women are far less attractive. And they are certainly less interesting. What's that saying, 'if women didn't have vaginas…?'"

"There'd be a bounty on 'em."

"You said it."

"I repeated it. So who do you beat off to? A girl you know?"

"I don't know her yet. She's a librarian or a teacher, someone who cares about her patrons, her students. She dresses super conservative and she works out all the time, and because of that, not genetics, she has an incredible body. She's a 32 B/C cup—depending. When she's in the gym, she's so busy working out that even if dudes approach her, she looks at them like 'hey dickhead, don't interrupt my workout.' She laughs at those broads who parade around with a full face of makeup—at the gym no less—and spend more time stretching than they do exercising.

"Her bras never match her underwear! She thinks of her students and her patrons all the time, totally takes their learning strategies or quests for information to heart. She loves her family, she's frugal with money, her parents are still together…and happy. She wears baseball caps and stuffs her ponytail out the back. She drinks beer and other things but never lets herself get drunk. The drunkest thing she'll ever do is pull me outside of the bar on a cold night, switch her baseball cap with mine, and then kiss me in a way that will make me blow chalk dust down my leg."

"Jesus, you think of all that?"

"Dude, that was the quick version. And the Disney version. You want me to get freaky? Oh, and she never complains."

"A girl who doesn't complain….*right*. Don't beat off before bowling. It'll affect your singing…and your poetry."

"One should never write poetry on a full seminal vesicle. Who do you imagine when you're strokin' it?"

"Allison"

"The vegetarian? You didn't even sleep with her." Trey climbed into the back seat. Wade muttered "goddamnit" in resignation, but also took it as a strange compliment that Trey would do something so private in his truck.

Wade pulled into the bowling alley parking lot, shining the truck's lights on a couple of their classmates walking inside. Trey zipped up and assured him that none of his "kids" were back there. He swaggered through the alley in a Wade-me-down flannel that hung to his thighs, sweatpants with the drawstring tied like an altar boy, the word "stinky" in pink letters sewn into the bum, and his Velcro shoes, which he wore accidentally when he bowled the first frame. The other lieutenants lost themselves in laughter at his irreverence.

But Trey soon grew quiet between his rolls and began to write a poem on the Styrofoam of his beer cup. Four drinks later, he had a sonnet, and it was time to sing karaoke. He charmed a townie into singing the female half of "Love Shack," and she gave him a kiss on the lips when they finished. He pretended like a seventh grader to wipe it off, then hugged her warmly before they walked away, and she eyed him the rest of the night.

The lieutenants orbited Trey and Wade. As they stopped by, Trey made a point to ask each one about a recent class in which the squadron commander brought in a chaplain and a judge to explain why the United States' use of nuclear weapons was and could be justified. It was the day they signed the paper saying they'd launch if ordered.

Wade, recognizing a swing in Trey's mood, checked on him periodically, noticing that he was consuming alcohol faster than his body could process it. He was just about to warn his best friend (of an ass kicking if he puked in the truck) when their classmate, Xavier Bendike, joined the group.

Xavier's jeans were short of his ankles, made more obvious by his personal pair of bowling shoes and white socks. A T-shirt grinned around his neck under a charcoal sweater, and he smelled like detergent. The lieutenants loved him for his aw-shucks demeanor, and then for his engineering mind, his dedication to military service, and his spirituality. He came from the South but laughed at anyone who carried a rebel flag. He went to church twice a week but never tried to save souls. Trey lit up.

"Where were ya, X? At church?"

"Hey, Trey," he said and sat. The second game was midway through, and Trey in the last swallows of his fifth beer.

"I was just thinking, EXelente…."

"I see you've been writing as well."

"That too, that too," Trey slurred, twirling the cup around on the table.

"May I?"

"You may. But only if you have a beer with me." Bendike obliged and bought a cup. Trey watched him rotate the Styrofoam as he read, the cosmic disco lights of the alley clowning his face.

"You're thinking about some rough stuff, Trey."

"Yeah, that nuke session really got to me. Made me sad."

"Made you mad."

"That too, that too."

"Why?"

"It seemed insincere that they brought a chaplain in for that. Man, and a lawyer? To talk nukes?"

"Would you rather not discuss it?"

"I do want to discuss it, but with you guys, not with lawyers and priests. We're the ones that have to launch these fuckin'—sorry, these damned things."

"It's ok."

"I figure that if we do get the order, politics has failed, and they don't need a bunch of enlightened guys who are well read in the Uniformed Code of Military Justice or church ethics. It's gonna be the book of Revelation, am I right?"

"I just don't know," Bendike began. "Yes, it's serious, but the Cold War is over and I don't think anyone wants to go back to those times."

"And these missileers who teach us," Trey went on. "Half the time they're trying to convince us how important the job is. The other half they're making jokes about our boring checklists: 'Read a step, do a step, eat a banana.' I wish they'd just be honest and say, 'Look y'all, we tested these things on our own people—now go out there and fry some Chinamen!'"

"Yeah, I don't like it when they get sarcastic like that. It is a serious job. I don't worry as much about our training as I do about the future. They're downsizing us so fast, and I've got a lot of cousins and family who work for General Dynamics, Northrop, Texas Instruments. I worry about them losing their jobs. They're smart, but they don't know anything else, and they don't want to do anything else. It's funny, we're a family of engineers, working in defense: my brothers, my dad, and me. We all had a hard time in the classroom. But when it came to building stuff, we loved it."

"Sounds like Wade and his brothers and their dad. Wade just understands how systems work. I'll give you an example, and I love telling this story. You'll get it, Bendike, but most people don't. So Wade—that dude could sleep through…well, a nuclear war—good thing he's going to be in charge of nukes, huh?

"And at the Academy, he used to sleep through all kinds of shit—formations, breakfast, class, everything. Guess who got blamed? I tried everything to wake him up—cold water, loud music. One time I threw a tight spiral on a two-liter jug of Sprite from across the room right into his nuts. Know what he did? He grabs his crotch—still dead asleep—screams 'Oh fuck! Oh fuck!' And then rolls back over."

Perked by the staccato mentions of his name, Wade leered over their conversation. Bendike smiled and Trey popped to attention. "Hey, I'm telling the two-liter Sprite story."

"Oh fuck, oh fuck," Wade said, trailing back to his lane.

"So, I said to him one morning, 'Wade, I swear to God, one of these days I'm going to shit down your throat while you're sleeping.' Wade thought about it for like two seconds and was like, 'Well, if I wake up and taste shit, I'm whippin' your ass!' And you see, Bendike, you see? Wade's mind could perfectly calculate how coordinated I was, how deep his sleep would be, and the angle at which I'd have to drop a turd down his throat and massage his big-ass jowls to masticate it, and how the aftertaste would clue him in. I have no doubt that he would know!" Bendike laughed while filtering the curse words.

"There's one thing that scares me about missiles," Bendike said. "I think the people in charge think the systems and the equipment are just fine, or if it isn't that *they'll* be the ones to fix it. I can force myself to learn all these equations, but I'm going to be in trouble if my whole career is spent operating a system that doesn't work the way it should. I mean, we're surrounded by vacuum tubes from the 1950s. Only my crusty old uncles know how those things really work. We're really putting our faith in this."

"'A system designed by geniuses to be run by idiots.' Ben, another beer. For the wisdom you bring to this bowling alley."

"No thanks, I drove."

"Ben! It's a Dixie cup of Coors Light! There's more alcohol in Lompoc tap water."

"That's the one way to get passed over for first lieutenant, Trey, a DUI. It happened to a friend from my detachment."

"Well, I'm not driving tonight, so I'll have another one if you don't mind. Hey, by the way, you said you'd bring me to church with you one of these days," Trey said.

"Yeah, I did. And I meant it, but did you?"

"I did! I go to Mass every week almost. What makes you think I wouldn't want to go with you?"

"Well, I'm not Catholic. It's different, I think, at Christian services."

"You guys always pull that shit, man! Christians! Like Catholics don't believe in Christ? All you Christians have some Catholic in you!"

"Oh, sorry, I didn't mean it that way. Now that I think about it, I can see how you would take it that way. I was raised to believe that Catholics were different. It's the South."

"Yeah, no shit. Try being Catholic in the middle of Sumter, South Carolina. There was an actual high school there called Sumter Christian, and they wouldn't play us in sports because we 'weren't Christian.'"

"I keep forgetting that you're from down there. You talk like you're from somewhere else."

"What, like a Yankee?"

"No, not necessarily. I mean you use words like fixin' and reckon and y'all, but you say them in a different way than we—Southerners—do."

"How different? Like the difference between Catholics and Christians?"

"Ha, maybe so. Trey, tell me, if you're not driving, who is? Wade looks like he's enjoying himself tonight, too."

"No, Wade's driving. I mean, it's his truck, so I reckon he's driving. He says he has a lot of practice driving drunk, so not to worry."

"Y'all could hurt somebody, or yourselves."

"Nah, not Wade. Me, yes. I would be driving on sidewalks, mowing down baby buggies, but Wade has the hands of a surgeon. Shit, Xavier, even if Wade got pulled, he'd be able to convince the cop that being drunk was just the natural cycle of things, and that he was taking me on the slurry, safer scenic route, the only way to make it through this Central California fog. I can't even imagine what he would say, but he would get out of it by lying his ass off."

"Dangerous."

"Yeah, Wade calls it 'protecting people from the truth.' He's been that way since we were 17 years-old in basic training at the zoo. It's funny; he doesn't give two shits about this nuke stuff, that stuff we were talking about. He just wants to work until he's 40 and retire."

"Sounds relaxing."

"Well, Herndon men don't live past 53 or 54 as a general rule. They're all super strong and smart, but they work so much and smoke so much and they….you know, Wade, understands so much, he just knows how the world—at least the mechanical part of it—works. We were watching that Titan IV go up the other night. Did you see it?"

"No, but it knocked me out of bed. When was it, 3 in the morning? I thought it was an earthquake."

"Yeah, it was the biggest rumble I've ever felt. Wade was sitting there in the cab of his truck drawing the rocket as it left, and I was watching his hands predict the movements and the trajectory. He was actually ahead of this huge rocket. He even drew the ripping sound it made in the air. He switched from color to color, and rubbed in the dust from his pencils, and it wasn't at all about art, it was just the way shit was. That's how he would get away with drunk driving—he'd be way ahead of any cop. And to be honest with you, X, that's why you should have another beer with me. I *will* be at church with you tomorrow morning!"

"Ok," Bendike agreed. Trey smiled and raised his cup.

"Here's to your Catholic first name!"

"That's true. My dad really liked the name."

"Did your family vote for Bill Clinton?"

"You know, we did. In '96, too. But most of them are starting to regret it. They thought he would grow up when he got to Washington. Me, I can't say anything negative about our commander in chief."

"I don't care myself. Everyone acts so shocked that politicians do bad things. They're *politicians*. That's their nature. What about Hillary, what do y'all think of her?"

"Everyone thinks she's smart and successful, but I think it's strange that people call her a 'feminist.'"

"My dad calls her a femi-NAZI."

"Well, to be a feminist you would have to care about other women, right? You'd have to fight for the rights of *all* women, I would say. But Hillary doesn't seem to do that at all. And sometimes it's quite the opposite. All in all, we've never seen anything like the Clintons come out of Arkansas. Senator Fulbright was smart, even political, but Bill and Hillary, it's as if they were from somewhere else. I wouldn't be surprised if they didn't come back to the state after his term is through." Trey swished beer from cheek to cheek, then bugged his eyes out.

"I don't know, Bendike, I'm drunk. And I'm thinking about Wade. I hate him at times, because he makes the world better and bigger than it is."

"He exaggerates you mean."

"Yes. In college we invented a thing called 'the Wade factor,' which meant you had to divide every claim he made by 2.2. But as I've gotten to know him more, and especially now—outside of the zoo—I think he actually believes his tall tales."

"Are they serious lies? Do you think he would stretch the truth while minding nukes?"

"Probably not to get anyone killed. He's in control of his embellished world."

"Wade told me a tale once, not sure if it's true," Bendike said. "He explained the origin of coffee, how humans discovered it."

"Oh God, what did he say, that a monkey fell out of a tree and pestered Juan Valdez into peeling those beans?"

"No, he talked about an Ethiopian farmer, a shepherd. Said he had a heckuva time trying to stay awake, but his sheep…."

"His *goddamn* sheep?"

"Yes, they stayed up all night. I admired how he impersonated the shepherd: 'I can't stay awake and my 'goddamn' sheep keep eating these berries and they're up all night—what gives?!'"

"Watch that mouth, X! I hadn't heard that Wade story before, but I can imagine him spinning it. He's a good guy."

"He's your best friend."

"Yeah, I guess you're right. You know something, Ben? Wade loves family. I'm Eye-talian, and I thought *we* were all about family, but Wade goes a step further. He values all families, not just his own. His parents even shower together."

"Trey, c'mon."

"They don't have *sex* in the shower. They just don't shower alone. His old man, I've seen him, he'll be filthy after a day slingin' Bondo and banging out dents at the body shop, and he'll wait for Wade's mom to get home so he can clean up. That's something!

"His mom visits every October for his birthday. She couldn't come this year because she got into an accident. But when she does, she takes us out, takes our picture, and just as we're about to cheese for the camera, I scoop Wade's big ass up like a bride across the threshold. It looks ridiculous because, you know, he's got me by at least a hundo, and his mom laughs every time.

"And in Anna, Illinois, where he's from, they really took me in. They accepted me like another son, fed me, and laughed at my dumb jokes. I felt so at home there, that last summer, after we graduated, on a crisscross-country road trip—I put 10,000 miles on my truck….which I actually bought from Mr. Herndon….he's got a dealer's license.

"Anyway, one night, I snuck in real late, under the crack in the garage door. Their dog knew me, so he didn't bark. It's a good feeling when a dog knows you, you know? Anyhow, I just wanted to sack out on the couch, but Wade's mom heard something, and said 'who's there?!' I was so tired that I just laid there and hoped she'd go back to sleep. But the next thing I know, a goddamn laser sight hits the wall above the couch, and I was like, 'Holy shit! Goddamn, it's me, Trey!'"

Bendike laughed gently, then said, "It must be nice for you to have your family so close. In Los Angeles."

"Yeah, they really like Wade too. Especially my grandfather, Papa, we call him. Papa calls Wade "Dave," but no one corrects him."

"And they're 'eye-talian,' as you say?"

"As the day is long! Every Sunday, Papa cooks pasta….man, I'm hungry for it! But I'll miss it tomorrow because of church with you—just kidding. Anyway, my cousins and aunts live within like 30 minutes, so we all crowd in the house. Papa and Grammy have to set up card tables in the living room for us kids, which is fine because we watch the Dodger game."

"Sounds great, Trey."

"It is! My cousins make fun of me for bringing Wade…for wasting the aphrodisiac effects of pasta on a man."

"I don't follow."

"My cousins bring their girlfriends and boyfriends, who are floored when they meet Pop: a retired fireman in an 'Eat California Cheese" apron, who tells them one-liner jokes. And then Grammy sits with them for what seems like hours, listening, talking, hugging. They fall in love with the whole familial experience. My cousins bring girls, I bring Wade."

"It's nice that he could fit in so easily."

"Ah, yeah. Papa loves him for how many meatballs he can eat, and how he fixes stuff around the house. The other day, he had Wade's big ass on the roof patching a tile up."

"You can skip church tomorrow, really, it's fine. Pasta sounds special."

"Maybe you could come sometime, Bendike."

"Won't your cousins think you're cheating on Wade?"

"Ha. Wade has his place at the table. Though my cousin Denise might notice…I think Wade digs her." Trey looked at the cosmic lights. The music made his head throb. "One time we were leaving pasta, and right after Papa gave him a huge bear hug, Wade told me some stuff about his dad. He talked about working at the body shop and catching ass-whoopins with whatever his old man could reach."

"Whoa."

"Yeah. And imagine the kind of shit just laying around a body shop."

"Part of me understands that part of growing up in the South. Part of me wants to forget it."

"One time, Wade told his dad he wanted to learn piano, but his old man said he could only practice at the shop. So Wade and his brother loaded a secondhand in their truck and drove it to the shop, and Wade practiced every day, before and after work, on breaks, sitting on an old can of Bondo."

"I heard him play the other day! He's very good."

"Yeah, well, one day the old man was pissed and he backed his truck into it. Fu…messed up the tuning. But Wade kept on."

"He's got very strong qualities," Bendike said, then noticed Trey's face darken. "Trey, are you ok? You look like you're gonna be sick."

"Jesus, Bendike, I just shared Wade's secrets with you. It's a betrayal. Am I too drunk to be a good friend? Is that it? Pray that I won't do it again. I'm sorry."

"I think it's ok, Trey. You were lifting him up, not bringing him down."

"Oh-k," Trey said in an exhausted stupor. "Hey, are you going to the Chumash with us after this?"

"No, thanks, I never have much luck gambling. Plus, there's service tomorrow—will I see you?"

"You will."

Wade and Trey went into the bar to sing the last song of the night. Wade talked Bendike into another cup of beer. The townie gave Trey her number. The lieutenants exchanged goodbyes, and Trey and Wade hopped in the truck to continue to the casino. As they smoked in the cab, Wade slapped himself until he felt sober, and then started the truck. Trey sang jingles about how much money he was going to win.

"Choo choo, Chumash! First you get paid…and then you get laid!" As they cruised down the road, Wade noticed the cop lights a few seconds before Trey, who continued to sing.

"Get yo' stash at the Chumash! Get yo' cash! Let da flashbulbs flash at the choo choo Chumash!! Simon says, Santa Ynez! Simon's stash is at the Chumash! Simon gonna go…to the Ka—Seen—oh!"

Wade moved Trey's arm from the center console and pulled out a socket wrench, which he handed to Trey.

"What's this for? To whap you in the goddamn melon?"

"Kind of," Wade said as he pulled his gun from under the seat, and then touched the clip in the side compartment, ready to marry the pair. He pressed past the cop at the speed limit, giving ground by moving closer to the center of the road. Trey's reactions were slow as he processed the image of Bendike's white sedan, his hands hanging limply out the window, the cop waiting in his car, aiming a flood light at their friend.

"Fuck no! Bendike!" Trey shrieked. Wade's headlights coughed into the fog. "Shit, man, fuck! What can we do? We made him drink, goddamnit, we fucked him! He's fucked!" Wade pulled into a parking lot and waited for a car to pass.

"Get out and break the lights above my license plate."

"Why?" whined Trey.

"Just do it." Trey got out still asking why and yammering about Bendike. He rapped the wrench upward, shattering the first lamp, and then lightly tapped the second like it was a hard-boiled egg.

"You done?"

"Not yet." Wade cocked the gun, put the truck in gear, and then growled out the window:

"Break the motherfucker!"

"S'broke," Trey mumbled. Wade killed his headlights and drove back toward Bendike. Trey heard four gunshots, tires squealing, and then cop sirens. He ran the opposite way for as long as he could and stopped in another parking lot. He bent his knees and mashed his palms into the gravel. Wade was long gone.

****

Two miles away, at 1 a.m. in a prison town, the alphabet streets lay between Trey and home. He thought of hitchhiking, but then remembered the signs planted along Lompoc's freeways warning not to pick people up. Besides, he thought, and almost laughed, who would dare pick up a guy wearing an oversized flannel and Velcro shoes? And a pair of sweatpants with the word "stinky" sewn into the ass? He may as well be wearing an orange jumpsuit and shackles.

As he entered the ABCs, Trey felt quickly sad that he hadn't kissed the townie goodbye. She probably lived in the alphabets, on D Street or something. She could escort him through this miserable neighborhood, the worst in a prison town. He walked fast into the smell of cheap dryer sheets mingling with fog, imagining bras in laundromats swimming through tangles of townie clothes.

This was truly a dangerous neighborhood. As that fact sunk in, Trey lost his nerve to joke about it, forgot about the townie, and prayed ceaselessly for Wade to emerge from behind a liquor store. He remembered a time in high school when he and his best friend took a wrong turn. They were greeted with meanness and profanity, but it had a desperate tone, a worrisome inflection.

"Y'all muthafuckas better get out," the gang said, almost pleading. Trey and his friend left quickly, but they knew that nothing bad could happen to white kids in Sumter, South Carolina. If it did, the authorities would terrorize every black family in the county. He was nearly sad that he was safe that day.

People from the alphabet streets of Lompoc gave no such warnings, nor did they consider the race of their intruders, and they certainly didn't worry about the police. ABC folks would likely not utter a word before striking with ultraviolence, while others cheered as if watching a video game. At the end, they would think of the worst beatings they'd witnessed and endured, placing this one somewhere on the continuum. They'd say a prayer for the man on the ground, and scavengers would come to rob him of what was left. Even compassionate neighbors wouldn't call 911 because they knew no difference between the police and the ambulance.

The street letters passed. Trey's legs burned. Idle wires hung from power lines, bikes lay like bodies, and old and new trash mingled in the gutters. Dark and foggy. The socket wrench wobbled in the too-big pocket of Trey's ridiculous sweatpants. He thought of Bendike and hoped that somehow Wade was able to fix the situation, saving their friend from a DUI. Then anger welled up in Trey that Wade would leave him alone—not just in the alphabets in the middle of the night—that he didn't bring him on the mission.

Trey remembered his visits to Illinois, how Wade's brothers delighted their guests by giving the family Great Dane a raw egg. "Dudley," who was a 150-pound blue, took the oval in his mouth and carried it around for the rest of the day, guarding and nuzzling it, sometimes whimpering if it rolled slightly on the carpet. Trey wanted to be that egg, a passenger in Wade's truck, under the moon, barreling toward Gaviota, U.C. Santa Barbara, Los Angeles, and San Pedro. But he was excluded from the adventure, left to walk through the alphabets, to speak Spanish with the strangers he encountered, to humor others who asked him threateningly if he was lost, and to absorb the laughs from those who mocked his clothes.

On F Street, Trey came upon an unconscious man, his wallet torn inside out, sparing only a library card and the photo of a girl likely taken in another country. He remembered his EMT classes from Pikes Peak, making sure there was no severe bleeding, and that he was breathing. The man had a strong pulse. Trey carried him to the H Street IHOP and called an ambulance. The neighborhood slowed as he went up H Street, which was Pacific Coast Highway, and considered less dangerous than the alphabets.

Trey felt safer but his obedience to Wade made him sick. *Wrench, lights, gun, drive.* He couldn't imagine coming up with such an algorithm, much less executing it. Trey remembered the first day of space and missile class, in the Burger King drive-thru, the minutes lolling away as they waited to order. In the same manner as the wrench, Wade handed him a $20 bill and said, "Go in there, and buy 12 bags of tater tots." When he returned, Wade had just finished tightening the lug nut on his spare tire. He lowered the jack, tossed it in the bed, and then wiped a greasy finger on his cheek. And like that, Wade created the truth: someone had a flat tire in the goddamn Burger King drive thru.

Pop, pop, pop, pop. Four shots at a cop. Did Wade have a gun? Trey had rummaged through the truck a million times—surely, he would have known of a weapon. But maybe Wade built a secret compartment. He certainly was capable. Trey, who was as mechanically inclined as a trophy wife, would have never found it. He thought of the poor cop, bureaucratically muscling through Bendike's ticket, scared shitless by the shots. And then the chase. He'd seen Wade do it a dozen times, when there was enough moonlight, switch off the headlights and follow the road, never slowing down, and sometimes speeding up. Riding shotgun, Trey remembered feeling terrified, and yet still in good hands. Wade may die at 53 years old like all the men in the Herndon species, Trey thought, but at least he was in control, at least he was an activator.

When Trey made it home, the fog was muffling sunrise, colored like stained glass. His bones were damp but invigorated. He found Wade's bedroom empty and imagined him sleeping in his truck on a cliff facing the sea. Trey paced and smoked. He hung his head, fighting weary tears, killing time before Bendike's church service was scheduled to begin.

Trey saw Wade again on Monday in class. Bendike hobbled in on crutches. Wade blurted, "Ben, you ok? You slip in the shower?"

"Hey Wade. I got shot if you can believe it." The lieutenants who overheard began to buzz.

"Shot?! Didn't Trey tell you this was a gangsta town?"

"Ha! Yeah, he did. Just grazed me though, thank God."

"I missed you at church, X," Trey said.

"Oh, hey Trey, sorry. But I'm glad you went, I hope you got something out of it."

"You bet. Everybody there said I got saved."

"Really? That's a big deal. I'm happy for you."

"Who shot you? Christ, I've never asked *that* question to anyone before." Trey glared at Wade who looked on.

"Nobody knows. I don't think he was aiming at me. I was in the process of getting a ticket. Right after bowling. The officer was fixin' to give me a Breathalyzer, then out of nowhere a truck cruised by and squeezed off a few shots. One of 'em grazed my foot."

"That's nuts, Bendike. Really, what happened? Didn't want to go to church with a Catholic, so you jumped off your roof, right?"

"Trey, it was the craziest night of my Southern Baptist life. I didn't even know I was shot until after the cop took off. I used my T-shirt as a bandage, and I waited."

"You waited? Man, I'd have gone to the hospital."

"Well, the officer—he was pretty keyed up—he shouted at me to stay put and then he tore off."

"Sounds like a donut-eater to me, Bendike. Was he a fatty?"

"I got law enforcement in my family, Trey. I'm respectful. He came back an hour or so later and told me to go home."

"Well, at least he let you off," Wade interjected.

"I took it as a sign. I'll never drink again."

The lieutenants sorted themselves for class. Trey shook his head at Wade.

"What?" Wade asked laughing. "Oh, Papa and Grammy say hi."

"You went to San *Pedro*?!" Trey blurted. Wade leaned into his space and whispered.

"That cop chased me to damn near Santa Barbara. I kept expecting a roadblock, and I lost him in the foothills. I had to keep going to get distance between us. I stopped for pasta, so what? You still have my goddamn wrench?"

"I can't believe you went to pasta."

"Can you believe that Denise and I watched the sunset at Royal Palms?" Trey's vision blurred in anger, imagining Wade impaling his petite cousin in the bed of his truck as waves crashed on the ruins of the Japanese bathhouses at Royal Palms. He didn't speak to Wade for some time.

After three days of silence, Wade asked him what was wrong. Trey said nothing.

"Nothing, my ass. Just tell me what I did."

"Nothing," he said walking away.

"You remind me of a woman, saying that shit. Just fucking yell at me or kick me in the nuts or something. If I fucked you, I'm sorry. But say something."

Trey softened enough to analyze their interaction. His instinct was to shout, "You should fucking *know* what's bothering me!" But he knew that would sound like a woman.

He remembered a time in college when his girlfriend was angry with him, and as he stood bewildered at the top of the stairs, he asked her finally, "What. Is. Wrong?"

She looked crooked up the flight and bleated, "You should listen to the 'City of Angels' soundtrack. Then you'd know how I feel!" Trey squinted back at her, reliving the ridiculous way he felt in many of his Academy classes. It was the same dumbfounded state he imagined his father in, after realizing the waste that was the Vietnam War. Six years as a POW. Truly a formative experience, one which led to the colonel's marriage and Trey's birth. Could any Ciuri say that the conflict never should have taken place?

Memories bowled over Trey's lid, seizing him like a man electrocuted. *Don't be a fucking woman, Trey. Tell your best friend how he hurt your feelings.* The urge to speak with Wade felt so peaceful, and yet the pride fencing him away was as vicious as barbed wire. He walked out of the room with Wade shaking his head behind him. The pair stayed silent until Christmas break when class rankings were released, and the lieutenants had the option of taking a week off. Wade finished fifth, Bendike first, and Trey last.

On the first day of Christmas break, Trey waited at the picture window, ignoring Wade, who asked, "Don't you care that you were last in our class?"

"No."

"Why?"

"I was last at the zoo, too."

"I thought you wanted to change that."

"For missiles? Congrats, Bendike. You get to spend the next four years of your life in Minot, North Dakota, breathing recycled air a hundred feet underground!"

"Didn't you want to compete with him? Don't you want to beat me?"

"No."

"Who are you waiting for?"

"My parents."

"The colonel's coming?!" Wade put his hand on Trey's shoulder. "Hey buddy, whatever I did, I'm sorry. Really. I don't want us to go off on bad terms."

"That's fine," Trey said and continued to look out the window. Wade removed his hand and started a Nintendo game. Colonel Ciuri burst through the front door a few minutes later.

"What's up, Lom-pukes?!"

"Hey Colonel C!"

"Wade!" he said while hugging Trey. "We used to call it 'Lom-puke' when I was in the Air Force. I'm sure it's a garden spot these days, eh?"

"'Garden' is such a strong word…maybe compost pile? How was your trip?"

"Eh, we got stuck behind a caravan of foo-foos on their way to 'taste wine.' Smooth otherwise. How's life? You keeping Trey out of trouble?"

"He's doing great on his own. He tell you about the poor kids he tutors?"

"No. Where is this, Trey?"

"It's ok."

"He's tutoring kids, immigrant kids, inmates' kids. And their parents in English."

"That's ok," Trey insisted. "You guys ready to go?"

"Ready? We just got here, give me a second. Got any coffee?"

"Yeah, sorry."

"Wade, how's class? Where do you think they'll send you?"

"Almost over, thank God. We only have three choices: Minot, Malmstrom, and F.E. Warren. I think I want Montana."

"Trey tells me that he's dead last—guess they'll pick for him!" Wade eyed Trey's mom who shuddered at the colonel's joke.

"Can we go?" asked Trey.

"Yes, ok. Let me use your bathroom."

"Wade, what are you doing for Christmas?" Trey's mom asked.

"Nothing, just staying back here." Trey's heart broke quickly then repaired itself. He was in shock that Wade's parents were not visiting. They always came out for holidays or shipped him back to Illinois. He began to regret giving Wade the silent treatment for the last few weeks.

"You're not going home? Your folks aren't coming here?" Trey relived the warmth of Wade's mom's hugs, even from a wheelchair. He tasted her cooking, took pride in how she could tame the auto-body animal in Wade's dad.

"Nope. Mom has rehab in Cape Girardeau, and the old man is going with her." Trey's mom looked lovingly at her son. The colonel peed with the door open.

Trey's thoughts drifted back to an abandoned bathroom on the Academy terrazzo where he and Wade smoked. One April, during a blizzard that closed the base, Trey decided to have his ear pierced. In the bathroom, Wade numbed Trey's lobe with Icy Hot, held his head, and then guided a sewing needle through. Trey laughed demonically at the popping sounds and the surprising amount of blood. A cadet with an earring, he mused, that'll show 'em.

He returned from the daydream, touching the scar tissue on his ear. Trey's mom looked approvingly at her son, expecting him to ask if Wade could join them. The colonel tapped his foot, ready to go, but also preparing to cede the front seat to the man his father called "Dave." Trey knew he should save his best friend from a lonely Lompoc Christmas. He knew Wade would do the same for him. But he couldn't escape from the alphabet streets where Wade left him, an unwanted accomplice.

Trey's clothes burned his skin. He imagined bringing Wade to Christmas and loathing him on the ride down the coast, his parents lapping up tall tales during the entire holiday. Wade would change every light bulb in the house, and then eat meatballs with Papa before pasta was served (a forbidden act for grandkids). And when Denise arrived on bronze legs, green eyes alight, if Trey saw an ounce of fairy dust between them, he'd have to play in his mind every Wade story he could conjure about plowing his cousin!

"Ok, well…." Trey said and headed to the car. Colonel Ciuri followed the hint and shook Wade's hand hard. Trey's mom gave him a hug.

****

The new year came with assignments to missile bases: Wade to Montana and Trey to Cheyenne. By then their charisma had long fizzled, and the other lieutenants were careful not to make references to the old times, when Wade and Trey held court, sang duets, and seemed on the verge of leading a revolution. Many chalked up their falling out to the natural run of things for spoiled Academy guys.

At home, they remained speechless save for caveman grunts concerning due dates for utility bills or whether or not there was a roll of toilet paper in the hall closet. Beyond their squabble, Wade saw that something had changed in Trey. The sparks of mischievousness that drove him to seek the few corners of creativity that Colorado Springs hid from the mega-church establishment seemed snuffed. The tender receiver of every character flaw and personality quirk in those who surrounded him had hung up, or was left off the hook. His bright eyes and listening ear under wraps, Trey was palpably sad, which was tragic and confusing to his acquaintances, but it also brought out the best in Wade Herndon.

Classes finished and their lease was up. Trey packed a mattress, seven boxes of books, and a pawn shop desk lamp in the bed of his truck. In the cab he placed a record player, 30 albums, his uniforms, and civilian clothes. Wade tried once more to get at what ate Trey, but his friend remained inward.

Trey asked Wade, "Can you drive me to the beach?"

"What beach? Ledbetter? Santa Barbara?"

"No, Jalama will do."

"Why there? It's fucking freezing."

41

"Just wanna see the ocean. Quick."

"Gonna dig for sand crabs?" Wade asked, repeating an allusion to a childhood memory Trey once shared.

"My mom caught hell for moving away from San Pedro," Trey said. It was the first "Trey" type thing he said since their fight. Wade answered silently. "She really did. Her family was super close, typical Sicilian. She married the war hero who came back from Vietnam to parades and TV spots. Mayor Yorty gave my dad the key to the city of Los Angeles, Major League Baseball gave him a gold-plated lifetime pass to see any game. He got autographed pictures of John Wayne and Frank Sinatra. Their wedding was on local TV!"

"I didn't know that."

"Yep, and my dad's cousin got drunk and yelled, 'Jane Fonda is a cunt!' into the camera."

"Why'd he do that?"

"Because she went over there during the war and said the POWs were treated well….or if they weren't, that they deserved what they got."

"Cunt."

"So, my mom married the Air Force and moved away. They loved my dad, but I have a gut feeling that they—in typical Sicilian fashion—never forgave her.

"She moved with him to Mountain Home, Idaho, where I was conceived because they said there was nothing else to do. Then they moved to the Academy where I was born."

"Baptized in the basement!" Wade yelled. Trey continued.

"We went to the Pentagon, then South Carolina, to Germany, and back to Sumter." Wade knew these facts. He stayed quiet. "My Mom one time leveled with me that what she missed most was not pasta Sunday, or L.A., or even her family, but the water. I just want to be near the water. I'd like you to take me there."

"Sure. But do me a favor: bury these somewhere where no one will find 'em." Wade reached deep into a kitchen cabinet and pulled out a FedEx envelope.

"License plates?"

"My old ones, from that night. Bendike's."

"How did you get new plates? How did I not notice?"

"You were too pissed off to notice. I had the old man FedEx 'em to Grammy and Papa's house. He back-dated the registration in case that cop got my tags."

"Sure, I'll bury 'em."

"Thanks. Hey man, I'm sorry again for whatever I did," Wade said.

"Eh, I'm no fuckin' good anyway, don't worry about it. I'm last in the class."

"Then why am I wasting my time driving you to the beach?" Wade asked. "C'mon, man." Trey grew teary. "You think I'm going to stay mad at you? I can't. You're my best friend." Trey tried to muffle the sounds of his crying. "You talked me into seeing and doing shit I never would have by myself. You taught me to laugh at the Academy. I may be the one who fixes shit, but it's more fun watching you break it first. You keep me in business, goddamnit." Trey sensed Wade was stretching the truth in his compliments and wiped his eyes.

"Did Denise tell you what happened to her dad? My Uncle Tim?"

"She never mentioned him. I just assumed they were divorced."

"No one knows what happened, really, but it was no secret that Uncle Tim was abusive to Auntie Donna."

"Verbally or physically?"

"Verbally in front of the family and physically behind closed doors. One day, probably 10 years ago, Uncle Tim chased Auntie Donna down the hall with a telephone that he ripped out of the wall. He whizzed it at her and barely missed. It hit the wall and exploded in a million pieces. She fell down and he stood over her, wrapping the cord slowly around her neck."

"Fuck."

"Denise ran to Papa and Grammy's—it was like 25 blocks—she was so scared and out of breath that she could only write down what happened. She told me the story a couple years later, one summer on a walk back from Royal Palms."

"So, Uncle Tim is in jail?"

"Maybe. All anyone knows is that he disappeared soon after. The romantic in me hopes that Papa and my dad cut him into pieces, and Cousin Steve used him for chum on his boat."

"Well, at least he's not hurting your aunt anymore."

"Yeah. He was only good for one thing anyway: rooting through Bukowski's trash."

"Who—kowski?"

"Charles Bukowski, the writer. Remember the guy who copied John Fante, but made it nasty? He lived right across the street from them."

"Oh, Fante. I like him."

"Bukowski is much more popular. Denise told me about the time Sean Penn and Madonna picked him up in a limo for the Oscars. She said he used to give licorice ropes for Halloween."

"Your uncle rooted through his trash?"

"Yeah, and if you can imagine the kind of nasty shit that didn't make Bukowski's cut, it was crazy. Illegal. Crazy illegal, like kids raping babies. My cousins sold the greasy pages at Pedro High and Mary Star for weed money."

"So, are you pissed that Denise and I went to Royal Palms?"

"No, but it reminded me of what happened to Uncle Tim. Papa used to tell us about the Japanese bathhouses down at Royal Palms. He said they were beautiful, but no one kept them up after the internment camps. Funny, Pop seemed sad when he talked about what happened to those bathhouses, but he said, 'the Japs' deserved it, said they caught 'em mowing arrows in their backyards pointing to Fort MacArthur."

"So, what's bothering you? C'mon."

"You remember when James Earl Jones came and spoke to us at the Academy? Arnold Hall was packed. We used to skip guest speakers all the time, people who'd actually done shit, like John McCain."

"You skipped McCain, too."

"Yeah, but that was because he became a politician."

"Of course he's a politician, he's a goddamn senator."

"He got lucky to escape that savings and loan shit."

"Whatever, man. You hold grudges like no one I know. I'm surprised you still talk to me."

"It's because I'll always hurt you more than you can hurt me. And I'm not saying that as a brag. I'm ashamed of it."

"I was there for James Earl Jones, so what?"

"He gave a great speech, focused on how much he loved aviation, how he overcame stuttering to be an actor. He even stuttered in his remarks if I recall right."

"He did."

"The cadet wing, the 'elite' citizen-soldier-scholars that we were, what questions did we ask him? 'Uh, heh-heh, do you like use the force, you know, when you're alone?' That was our best. That was your next generation of leaders, at least in the Air Force. That's why I don't take missiles seriously, and that's why I don't compete with you. And in general, I think we're in trouble. I think that most of us are a bunch of losers, starting with me, and we're going to fuck it all up."

"That's not a reason to give up."

"Arnold Hall, man," Trey said, sounding exhausted. "You remember when Big Head Todd came?" Wade nodded. "We were their only Colorado date that tour. A band from Boulder, and they only stopped at the zoo! Tony Odette came down from CU, and we kept rubbing it in that his band chose us instead."

"I remember, ok! I want to keep remembering! Fondly, man. What are you trying to say?!"

"It was the *Resignation Superman* tour! Those silly fools, you and me and everybody, we sang along, and we didn't bother to read the lyrics." Wade shook his head.

"We're about to start new lives at new bases. Comon, Trey!"

"You know when I lost my faith? When I *really* stopped trying?"

"When?"

"When I found out that Air Force football cheated the same way as any other school. Remember freshman year, when the team 'advisor'—Colonel Jones—held a 'study session' in calculus? The players came back to the squadron bragging that he read right off the test. He was the *head* of the Math Department! Remember Karl Penn, the offensive lineman? The Monday after he blew out his knee, when we beat Notre Dame, he found an envelope with hundred-dollar bills in his room. He said it wasn't the first time. And how many guys did you know who were on some kind of steroid cycle? Pretty much everyone.

"I was *raised* watching guys like Dee Dowis and Carlton McDonald. I remember my old man jumping around the living room in his underwear when Air Force beat Ohio State in the Liberty Bowl. He always bragged to me that other schools cheated, and their players didn't have to study, that 'only the service academies did it right.' What a crock of shit. Remember when the quarterback got caught cheating? And during his honor hearing, all the players crowded into the room—it was like a sweat session. They mean mugged that girl who was testifying and she lost her nerve. And he got off. They won their bowl game that year, too." Trey paused. "And you know those dicks are going to eventually 'find Jesus' and come to the reunions as holy as old Ted Haggard down the way."

"Why are you so nice to the people in our class?" Wade asked. "You treat them like they're the smartest, funniest, most goddamned interesting people in the world. But they're the same type of dipshits who would ask James Earl Jones if he uses the force. I'll bet you've had them over for pasta Sunday." Wade flicked his cigarette and tried to subtly rub his throat.

"I don't know. I guess because I sensed that they needed it. I feel sorry for them. I don't think they really know what's going on. I'm sorry I didn't bring you down for Christmas." They let mile markers pass.

"You hold grudges against yourself the worst of all," Wade said as he parked the truck.

"I deserve it."

"No one does. And you may not be suited for this regimented military shit, but you do good things."

"I don't want to hear it."

"You tutored all those immigrant kids. You did that every Saturday and some weeknights. Did a lot of it in Spanish! You took that night class at Allan Hancock College, and you wrote a poem for that girl pregnant by that inmate and she said it made her give up the kid for adoption instead of having an abortion. You volunteered at the base library and read to all them kids. You connected the people in our class like probably no one could. Hell, you probably would have finished higher if you weren't doing all that extra shit."

Trey thought of their Academy days, the perfect crisp of early autumn, and the way the sun shone after a big snow—not that Breckinridge foo foo powder, he liked to say, but a Neal Cassady Larimer Street gutter slush. He thought of how dumb he was in high school, how much he didn't know, how it was stupid to commit suicide then. It was different now. Wade's compliments were tall tales. This time it would be better. He told Wade:

"You know man, that Columbine shit still makes me shaky. I keep seeing those Colorado kids—we may have met them at a Rockies game or at the Tattered Cover or something—getting shot in the face. Or worse, catching a bullet that didn't kill them, but makes their nerves all zappy. I can see 16-year-old girls dying like snakes. You ever beaten a snake to death?" Wade nodded.

"During their last movements, they open and close their mouths, trying to defend and bite their way out. But inside they're shredded. I see the cavitation of the bullet doing things the kids can't see but they definitely feel. And this is a TV generation, a video-game generation. They realize that they're not dying like people who get plugged on screen. There are no hit points, no cheat code, and no restart button. They're surprised and drowsy, and those feelings don't happen together unless you're dying. They don't go together, man…." Wade clenched his jaw. The waves came in on cold foam, like spilled beer. Trey imagined kelp and driftwood, and what a nuke would do to the beach.

"One of the killers was an Air Force kid, man, just like me," Trey whispered, then raised his voice. "Whaddaya say you and me hijack this whole missile business? You do your intel at Malmstrom, I'll do mine at Warren. After a few years….you know where I'm going with this…." Wade nodded and blinked. "You come down to Warren for TDY. By that time, I'll have cultivated a few cops who will let us in the capsule together. We'll gen up our targets quick, then put in our codes, and show those Columbine chumps how mass murder is really done. Whaddaya say?"

Wade breathed to the depths of his coffin-like chest.

"Whaddaya say?" Trey hoarsed. "With your patience and technical expertise and my planning and people skills, we could launch at least ten nukes anywhere in the world! We could go out like Butch and Sundance."

"Alright, man," Wade said, "I hope you find your happy place." Trey got out and walked toward the beach. As Wade reversed, he asked Trey how he would get home, and Trey told him that he would find his way.

Trey spent considerable time digging far enough from the tide's reach that future beach goers would not likely find the plates. He smoothed the sand with his hand and walked into the surf. He felt just as useless to the world as he did before his first suicide, only then it was an impulsive act, this time he was bolder and better informed. Water soaked his Velcro shoes. His sweatpants yanked down by waves, he tightened his stomach muscles and leaned forward like walking into a blizzard. Chest level and off balance, Trey felt like he was in a washing machine. Wade's voice tried to come back into his mind. He refused to swim.

His last thoughts were the sounds and sights of an Air Force childhood: the squeaks of his dad's crude-colored shoes as he wiggled in his feet without untying. The clinks of the colonel's belt buckle knifing through the loops of his trousers. The crunch of an English muffin during the 6 a.m. news, then the sound of a man leaving the house when he presumed everyone was asleep. The purple dark. Birds diving into the lawn as the sun rose. Brown butter on the English muffin, its crumbs loitering on the trapdoor of the rusty toaster. The black-and-white TV in the linoleum kitchen of base housing. The sound of jets churning up butterflies, driving Trey outside to catch a glimpse; and the first time he understood that his dad's plane was once shot down.

Chapter Two: An Air Force Town

Had it not been for Hurricane Andrew, which flattened Homestead Air Force Base in August 1992, Trey Ciuri would have never met his best friend. As such, Tony Odette blew into Sumter, South Carolina like Dorothy Gale, while eleventh grade was in full swing. His sneakers were shiny, he had a head full of questions. Trey, meanwhile, was the shyest kid at Saint Jude High School.

On Tony's first day, as the guidance counselor assigned his classes and explained the bell schedule, Trey cut into their dance, assuring her that he would take it from there. Impressed by Trey's assertiveness, and proud that he would seek to be part of Tony's welcome, she raised her arms as if Trey held a gun, then left the boys to walk the halls, bookbags slung over their shoulders.

"Jude's is one of three Catholic high schools in the state," Trey began. "The diocese doesn't care about us, not like Cardinal Newman in Columbia and Bishop England in Charleston. Buncha rich kids." Bystanders in the hall, after giving Tony a curious look, fashioned their faces into genuine surprise at hearing Trey not just speak—most had never heard him complete a sentence—but expound. Their shocked mugs only encouraged Trey, who took the reaction as a validation of his first two years in relative silence.

"Saint Jude is the patron saint of lost causes. That's who we are. Forgotten on the south side—the poor side of town. This used to be Lincoln High School, before integration. Sumter didn't get around to *that* until 1969. We're Catholic rowboats in the middle of a Protestant sea.

Are you Catholic?" Tony nodded. "I figured. We're also half black and half white. And that's something that just doesn't happen in the South."

Saint Jude's lockers were as thick as hulls, the paint old and leaden, adding to their stroll the drone of a submarine's bowels. For the moment, Trey was the Captain, Tony his new first mate, his face shining with self-confidence, and yet colored with gratitude for Trey's narration: a personal tour from an instant friend after being displaced by the hurricane.

"I'll drive you around, dude," Trey continued. "As soon as I get my license. We'll check out Sumter's 'academies,' the all-white outfits. You'll see the facades out front—they were all founded around the time of the Civil Rights Act."

"*All* white?" Tony asked. "Doesn't everyone have tokens these days?"

Trey thought for a second. "Williams Haven does have these two Brazilian brothers on the basketball team. They dance in front of our bench when they make shots. And they call us the 'N-word,' even the white guys. Quiet so the refs don't hear."

"Jesus," Tony said.

"You said it. I've never lived in a place like this. So in-your-face racial, you know? Is Florida like this?"

"Maybe in the panhandle, not Miami, though. I mean, you kind of have to stay in your neighborhood." Tony paused. "But I'm half so I kind of float."

"Half what?" Trey asked.

"Haitian."

"Haitian! That's where Odette comes from, huh?"

"I guess."

"Well, I guess we're like that too. It's not strictly black and white at Saint Jude," Trey added. "There are shades, if you will. We've got your standard-issue rednecks, your everyday white dudes, and we've got *richnecks* too." As Trey said the word, some richnecks within earshot raised their eyebrows and sent him and Tony a scowl.

"Richnecks?"

"Yeah, local Sumterites with money. They're still backwoods, but they wear those boat shoes with no socks and Duck Head pants. They play golf. Their families have houses at Lake Santee or down on Edisto Island. Can't miss 'em. But you wanna miss 'em, trust me."

"How did they end up here?"

"Good question! Usually, one of their parents married Catholic. They go to Methodist church on Sundays, but on the weekdays, they belong to Jude's."

"Are there a lot of air force kids?"

"Quite a few. I'm one, kind of. My dad retired here, but I was a brat all my life. Is your dad a pilot?"

"Yep. Squadron commander," Tony said proudly.

"Cool! F-16s or A-10s?"

"Sixteens."

"Awesome. Is that what you're going to do too?"

"Yep, gonna go to the Academy—hopefully fly fighters," Tony said, strutting a bit.

"So, anyway, those are the whiteys," Trey continued. We've got normal black dudes, mostly air force kids. Then there's gangstas—dudes who sell drugs and live deep in the cut, on the south side. And we have

Pan-Africans—people call them PA's—guys who wear red-black-and-green medallions and talk like Spike Lee or something. For the most part, everyone gets along. But we did have a huge fight last year—right after the Rodney King riots."

Before Tony could enquire further, a voice gurgled into the PA system, hijacking the hallways. Trey's eyes rolled into the back of his head. Tony grimaced. And the voice shoved its way into their minds.

"Boys use love to get sex. Girls use sex to get love." The woman repeated her mantra half a dozen times.

"What the hell was that?" asked Tony, laughing. "*Of course* boys use love to get sex!"

"Mrs. Braniff," Trey answered. "She's a large woman, if you couldn't tell by the voice, with like ten kids. Three of them go here, the rest are too young. Every month we have to listen to her say that shit in the auditorium. The Braniffs, Wyeths, and Mahoneys are the most influential families at Jude's. They're *better-than-you* Catholics. They think they're imitating Jesus . . . they see his face in every knot of wood."

"What am I getting myself into?" Tony joked.

"Don't worry, man. We'll get through it," Trey said, offering his hand. It was the first time he shook hands with a peer. He led Tony outside, where they sat on the steps until the bell rang, discovering with shared joy that they lived a few blocks from each other. Trey told Tony everything he knew about Jude's, save for the crush he had on Prudence Diehl, who was a year ahead of them.

They reminisced about being air force kids, living in Germany during the Cold War, both pretending to miss those days, both claiming to know more of the language than they did. Trey, who was at Rhein-

Main Air Base when the Berlin Wall came down, told an awed Tony about his junior high class receiving chunks of graffiti-splattered concrete, which unimpressed students whizzed at one another during recess.

After school, while shooting baskets in Trey's driveway, the boys reveled in the sound of jets above Sumter's red baseball diamonds, skinny pines, fields of soy, and ripples across Swan Lake. They chuckled at the usual gathering of tattoo parlors, pawn shops, and strip clubs leading to the gates of Shaw Air Force Base. They dreamed of going to the Air Force Academy, though, in Trey's mind, he was stuck there as a duty to his father. In Tony's, he was a fighter jock like his old man.

What began as an introduction to Saint Jude during Tony's first days, matured into a release of Trey's high school angst, a reservoir broken, never to be repaired. Despite Trey's observations, collected as silently as a spy's over his first two and a half years, he had trouble understanding why people behaved the way they did: why white South Carolinians were such uncreative louts, why the Catholics who ran Saint Jude were so condescending they couldn't possibly have a relationship with God—and why a girl like Prudence didn't recognize the love Trey carried for her.

Trey's quandaries were foreign to Tony, whose philosophy was "fuck it, let's *fly*." He hustled at everything he did: sports, school, girls. Name the requirements to enter the Air Force Academy and that's what he would produce. What was right was right, wrong was wrong. People along the way either behaved well or badly, and to hell with the latter. Even events like Hurricane Andrew existed to rearrange the world.

Two years before Andrew ripped through Miami, Hurricane Hugo menaced South Carolina. The Ciuris, newly retired from the Air Force, arrived in Sumter to a pine tree in their kitchen, which forced them to stay in a motel for two months. They moved into their new house on a Friday night. Mrs. Ciuri ordered pizza. The colonel fired up home movies.

Trey sat quietly as images from the late '70s splashed against a bedsheet tacked above their fireplace, the projector rattling like a toolbox in the back of a pickup truck. In the movies, most of which were filmed while they were stationed in Colorado Springs, Special Olympians raced and competed in field events. The colonel and Mrs. Ciuri cheered for "their guys" as if it were live.

"Go Max! Go Joey!" they shouted as kids with Down syndrome rounded a turn and neared the finish. In the winner's circle, Mrs. Ciuri handed an infant Trey to Max.

"You remember that, Trey?" the colonel asked. "You remember Maxy?"

"He was just a baby, John," mumbled Mrs. Ciuri. In the frame, Max goo-goo'd Trey and passed him back to his mother.

"He could. This kid has a memory like a steel trap. I'll bet Maxy remembers you, Trey." Trey said nothing, which was common during the Ciuri film sessions, and even more common after one of their many moves, though this one was promised to be the last.

The colonel had become a mister. Their Air Force life finished, there would be no more shopping at the commissary or base exchange, no military doctors, no more "permanent changes of station." Mrs. Ciuri adjusted the easiest. She made close friends at Mass and spent most days delivering meals-on-wheels on the south side of town.

She explained to a despondent Trey why they decided to retire in Sumter instead of San Pedro; though she did promise they'd visit every summer. California, she said, was no longer a golden paradise. There were too many "kooks," too much pollution, drugs, sex, and crime. It was Nixon-less, Reagan-less, Godless, and full of immigrants who did not share their values.

"When I was a boy," the colonel added, "even the zoot-suiters had some respect, a code. They went to church with their families. Now, they've trashed California. They don't even learn English."

"When your great-grandparents came to this country," Mrs. Ciuri continued, "they forgot every word of Italian. They didn't even speak Italian—Sicilian was their language. It was only English in their new home. They worked like dogs and *still* kept the neighborhood clean."

Trey paced through freshman year with a perfect GPA, which drew Mrs. Ciuri's praise, but made the colonel suspicious of Saint Jude's rigor, as he hardly studied. Trey's creativity came out after school in their driveway, where he set up sawhorses, ladders, folding chairs, and even a chainsaw to test his basketball skills. Sometimes he wore a blindfold as he practiced his moves, luring the colonel to stare at his son for extended periods.

When the school year finished, the Ciuris returned to San Pedro, and Trey came back wearing a scowl as a souvenir.

"What's wrong?" the colonel asked.

"He's fine," Mrs. Ciuri said.

"No, I'm not," Trey said. "Why don't we live in California? Why are we going back to Sumter, where we have no family? What kind of Sicilians are we?"

"Sicilians that don't want you to grow up in LA." the colonel said.

"My cousins are growing up there. You grew up there."

"It's a different place."

"Seems the same as anywhere else. Not much different than Sumter," Trey said.

"Oh yeah? They got vatos and gangbangers in Sumter? Stoners? Porn stars? They got all that? They got all those Hollywood kooks? How many people you know at Saint Jude do drugs, Trey?"

"Let's talk about something else," Mrs. Ciuri suggested.

"What's a 'kook?'" Trey asked. "What does that even mean?"

"A kook," said the colonel, "is a rich person who pretends to care about poor people but doesn't want to see them." He paused. "A kook is also a poor person who can't imagine living without the government doing everything for them. Both rich and poor kooks have drug problems." Trey looked confused, surprised that his dad had the definition so ready on his lips.

Before school resumed, Colonel Ciuri brought Trey to see Thad Mooneyham, a lawyer with close ties to Senator Thurmond, someone who could help him with a nomination to the Academy. Mooneyham performed a boisterous welcome, walking them quickly from the area where his secretary sat, making sure to thank her, to his inner office, which was less air-conditioned, a carpet-to-ceiling enclosure of books on hard wooden shelves.

"Do you speak any foreign languages?" Mooneyham asked Trey, who mumbled something in German as Mooneyham handed him a book. "This is the biography of General Thomas Sumter, who, among his other talents, was fluent in Cherokee." Mooneyham smiled until Trey looked uncomfortable. "So versed was General Sumter . . . that he translated for Chief Ostenaco when he visited King George in England, before the revolution, of course."

"That's interesting," Trey said.

"Learn languages," Mooneyham said while looking at Colonel Ciuri, who nodded vigorously.

"Do you play sports, Mr. Trey?"

"No, sir," Trey muttered. "Only by myself, in the driveway." The colonel flinched, but Mooneyham pressed on.

"The US military is the greatest team ever assembled. You see what we did to those Iraqis? You join some teams, son." He handed Trey another book, *The Bobby Richardson Story*.

"Ole Bobby," Thad said, "was one of my heroes growing up. My friends and I would crowd around the box and listen to those Yankee games." He stopped himself in the middle of the memory and asked,

"Do you think it's strange, Trey, the idea of listening to sports on the radio?"

"No, sir," Trey said. "When my grandfather visited us in Germany, we listened to the Dodgers in the World Series on Armed Forces Radio. When Kirk Gibson hit that homerun, Papa danced around in his underwear!" The colonel cringed again at Trey's revelation. Mooneyham flashed an amused grin.

"More than baseball, ole Bobby was a hero because he lived his faith. To be a Christian was more important than anything to Bobby Richardson." Colonel Ciuri kept nodding and saying "yessir, yessir," like a Southerner, making Trey blush. "Shoot, ole Bobby'd go out to dinner with his teammates . . .and the Yankees had some rough boys in those days: Mantle, Tresh. They'd drink and carouse all night and Bobby would preach with a glass of milk in his hand. He's still like that. I'm not going to ask you if you've accepted Christ, son, because I believe that's a personal matter between you and the Lord. But I will say that where you want to go to college, it is *very* important." Mooneyham held up a signed photo of a middle-aged man wearing a blue polo shirt and headphones. "Do you know who this is?"

"No, sir."

"This is the head coach at Air Force!" Trey blushed. "A *strong* Christian!" Mooneyham ogled the colonel, who ogled right back. "Service academies are the only ones who play fair—no cheating, no paying players, no steroids. I'm sure your daddy knows that better'n I do."

"That's right, yessir," the colonel said. "In most cases, the Academy can't recruit guys above a certain height or weight, because they won't fit in a cockpit after they graduate."

Mooneyham piggybacked, "Ole Bobby, he was a hero to Sumter—but your daddy—he was a hero to this country. And it was his faith that got him through, am I correct in saying that, Colonel Ciuri?" The colonel agreed, and the two men shook hands as if they'd made a deal. Mooneyham shook Trey's hand softly before they parted and told him to read the books.

****

The first time Trey noticed Prudence Diehl, in the Saint Jude cafeteria, she was doubled over in a coughing fit, her spine jutting from her like a stegosaurus, pulsing under her bra, threatening to crack her ribs, shaking her so violently that her hair looked like a wig. He became filled with concern, pity, and slight surprise that no one had rushed to her as the hacking intensified. Surely, someone at her table was waiting to rub her back or dab her forehead. She grabbed her calves, still hammering away at the phlegm stalactites stabbing her lungs. Prudence raised her head as the whoop retreated, and Trey ambled toward her. He offered his water glass, which she took like a boxer between rounds, and then resumed chatting with her friends. He didn't speak to her for years. But every day after school, he pretended that she could hear his thoughts as he shot hoops alone:

Dear Prudence,

Half the school thinks Lucy Braniff will become a nun, the other half calls her a hypocrite "ho" behind her back. She nods along with her mom during those chastity lectures, but rumor has it that she meets Terry Smith in the USC chemistry lab, where her dad teaches, and lets him do "all kinds of stuff."

"Boys use *loooove*. Girls use *seeeecks* . . ."

To me, the Braniffs are kind of funny, like that joke about religious groups who think they're the chosen ones? "*Shhh*. Quiet when you're passing the Braniffs," says Saint Peter while giving a tour of Heaven. "They think they're the only ones here."

Jude's is a boll weevil deep in these Protestant fields. Our textbooks are older than we are. The Catholic parishes, even Our Lady of the Skies at Shaw, take up collections for us twice a year. But we're not poor mice scurrying through their sanctuaries at hours when Father Mackenzie is donning his socks! We don't even like the bishop, who is probably doing uncatholic things far away in Charleston, coddling his pricey pets, Cardinal Newman and Bishop England. We are Jude's!

You wouldn't guess I'm proud of it. I don't say anything at school beyond what I have to. People call me a nerd, or gay, if they're mean; if they're kind, they say I'm shy. But I love the fact that everyone at Jude's acts lucky to be here. Not because it's a very good school. It's pretty "bush league," as the rednecks say. It's because none of us could imagine going anywhere else.

Where could we go? The richneck "academies?" My dad always points out the founding dates on the facades, how sickeningly close to the time of the Civil Rights Act they are, when they were forced to integrate. But with the price tags at places like Williams Haven, the only minorities who can afford to go there are tokens who play sports, like those two Brazilian brothers. I see them in church with their mother. My mom hugs her during the exchange of peace. The Brazilian lady pronounces it *"peesh."*

I feel bad for Seneca Washington because he sweeps Saint Jude's floors to pay tuition. People say his mom sweeps too. But then, in a way, I don't feel bad for him, because at least he can work for something. When he shuffles past my locker with his saggy pants, two voices compete in my mind. One says, "Poor Seneca! Lives on the south side, doesn't have two nickels to rub together!" And the other, "He doesn't need your pity, Trey Ciuri. You don't even keep the school clean. You just sit there and blend in and turn in your homework."

This driveway is so far from the south side, where my mom does meals-on-wheels. I went with her once. When we crossed the tracks, the houses turned into shacks with rusty roofs and plastic covering the windows. I met my mom's "friends," including Mr. Ford, whose huge hands swallowed mine, whose blind eyes made me not want to look at him, so instead I stared at a picture of him in a World War II uniform. Mr. Felder's legs were covered with ants running toward the food we'd just delivered. Mrs. Geddings's dress was unbuttoned. My mom fixed it as she ate.

I also feel bad for Tracy Morrow because the Pan-Africans make fun of him for being light-skinned. They call him "rett bone." That really scares me, the fact that black kids fight each other. Over shades of skin? That's what the Williams Haven kids want. That's why they call us the N-word, even white people, during basketball games. That's why when Jude's cheerleaders decorate the players' lockers during Williams Haven week, they paste up obscene Ns, to remind the guys what they're up against. We always lose, though. I'm thinking of trying out next year.

The other day, I heard someone in the hallway talk about their "best friend," and while it's a common term, I was suddenly sad to think that I don't have one, that probably my best friend is my cousin Denise, but she lives in California and she's going through hell right now because her dad beats my Auntie Donna. But stuff from San Pedro feels farther away than the war in Kuwait. It's info-tainment, like *The Simpsons*, or, worse, it's people doing a sketch, like *In Living Color*.

If not a best friend, how about a girlfriend? Do you notice me? I notice Toney Chastain, such a proud, bumbling redneck, with his NAPA hat on backward, a fishhook jammed into the bill like an antler in a Christmas pageant. He stumbles into the hallway as only a seventeen-year-old sophomore could, looking for his girlfriend, Alicia, who is the proper age for a tenth grader.

She remains in class because she's the smartest kid in school. I read her editorials in *The Daily Item* and *The State*, hear teachers talking about her with astonishment at how she could be so advanced—taking trig already at USC Sumter?—but also that she could date such a dolt as Toney, who's been held back so many times, who skips class to fix cars in the parking lot, who uses his NAPA wages to pay tuition for both of them, with whom Alicia has a child. Between the bell and Toney's bumbling search, some richnecks call him "T-yo," and rib him by asking him if he works at NASA, which he corrects as they laugh and move on.

The bell rings and Alicia presses pause on her brilliance. She stalks Toney in the hallway as if he were a gazelle on the savanna, and for a good ninety seconds, they engage in a style of physical affection I haven't even seen in movies, moving in ways they must have practiced for years, their clothes practically steaming, students hyena-laughing. I leer with a dry mouth until a teacher comes to shoo them. I'm glad that Alicia is in your grade and I won't have to compete with her for valedictorian, which my dad says will help me get into the Academy.

Everyone gravitates to you, Prudence. Is it because of your disease? No one says the name of it, that which makes you hack more often than the school's bells ring. Kids who know you shake their heads in disbelief; those who know of you bow their heads in prayer; people like me, who don't know you but wish we did, pledge that we will seek you out and say something nice. But you're not as depressed about your future as your fan club. You finish coughing yourself silly, laughing in tiny gasps, and you make jokes about death. You tell people to "enjoy the reunion" in your absence. Those around you wilt. Prudence, I think you're going to teach me something, if only telepathically, as I imitate Isaiah Thomas on this driveway, where I shoot baskets until the sun dies.

One evening, I stayed out so long I didn't notice the difference between my blindfold and the dark outside. I heard trick-or-treaters in the street and felt sad that I didn't remember Halloween. It is a miserable predicament to be too old to dress up and too young to give out candy.

I kept the blindfold on and quickened my routine, thinking of something Isaiah said: "If you can dribble the basketball, you can go anywhere." Then Mrs. Braniff's voice bullied itself back into my mind: "Boys use love to get sex . . . girls use sex to get love."

Suddenly, headlights slapped me in the face. I ripped the blindfold off and jumped between my house and an azalea bush. A dark figure behind the wheel killed the lights. I could see she was black, which is rare in my neighborhood. Then I could see her kids up the street twirling pillowcases full of candy. After they knocked on our door and continued down the road, their mother started the car, got out, hiked up her skirt, and peed in our pine-straw bed. She made a hissing sound in the cool evening, and then she drove away. I thought about why she would come from "her part of town" to ours, probably because it was safer, because white people gave out better candy? I told my dad what happened, and he said, "Well, when you gotta go . . ."

****

The Rodney King riots began in Los Angeles on the Wednesday after Saint Jude's spring break. The next day, when the lunch bell rang, Tracy Morrow, a light-skinned kid who darker students ridiculed, lay on the floor outside of the cafeteria. Richnecks with baseball bats then reenacted the King beating, with Tracy playing the victim, flailing along and yelping like a minstrel.

"He's on PCP!" Thomas shouted with laughter.

"We the man. You just visiting," growled Will as his bat cut through the air, stopping just short of Tracy's body. Some onlookers thought it was funny, others stupid. Pan-Africans Greg, Lonzell, and Denard saw red when they realized what was happening.

Greg ripped a bat in midswing from Strat's hands, wound up, and crushed a homerun into Will's chest. His bat fell to Lonzell, who jabbed it into Will's chin, breaking three of his teeth. Thomas ran and Strat pulled his bloodied friend away, his uneven wheezing spraying blood from his gums to the floor. As teachers arrived, Tracy looked like a patient in shock. Denard shook his head and told him that no beating would be bad enough for a sellout like him.

At the same time, Trey was sitting in Mrs. Smith's room, finishing some work for another class. He cherished the solitude amid empty desks, on which students left their books and bags instead of taking them to lunch or their lockers. To Trey, being alone in the classroom felt like sneaking into a foreign country. He noticed Lucy Braniff's notebook, imagining a demonic wind blowing open the pages. He turned to the last entry and read until a roar came from the cafeteria, driving him to the hallway.

Prudence had also skipped lunch due to the grinding indigestion associated with her disease. Her guts swollen with mucus, body exhausted from a half hour in the bathroom, she made for Mrs. Smith's to get ready for class. She and Trey met in the doorway in an awkward collision, every part of their bodies touching like amoebas in a lab dish. Trey smelled her shampoo, saw her freckles, felt her energy, and spastically blurted something that sounded Middle English, "A thousand apologies, me lady!" to which Prudence simply said, "whoa," as she found her seat.

"Are you OK?" he asked?

"Fine. What's going on over there, a fight?"

"Looks like it. A ton of people standing around."

"I'm too tired to look," Prudence admitted. "You like to come by Smith's too?"

"Yeah. I had some work in another class."

"You didn't read my journal, did you?" Prudence joked.

"No, but I read one of Lucy's reflections."

"You spy!" she giggled. "What was it? A bunch of psalms on safe sex?" Trey walked to Lucy's desk, opened to the page, and handed it to Prudence.

"Smith would crack if she read this."

"Well, at least she would know what kind of person Lucy is."

"You should slip it in."

"I should," said Trey, who realized, as he ripped the page from Lucy's notebook, that he would have done anything she suggested. He put it in the ungraded folder on Smith's desk and sat with Prudence, whose eyes were closed as she battled more pain, while the skirmish outside climaxed and then died down.

The fight over Tracy Morrow's body sent Will McElveen to the hospital for a couple of days, and got the other participants suspended, including Tracy. Both the richnecks' and the Pan-Africans' parents threatened to change schools, and as a result, Dr. Moner visited each kid's house to show how seriously he took the situation. All were surprised by the house calls, save for Greg's mother.

"I am ready to defend every swing of that bat, Dr Moner," said Greg's mom. "I mean, how was my son to know it was fake? It looked real, and I taught my son to never stand by and do nothing." Greg nodded at his mother, who went on. "That boy who got beat—who they were pretending to beat—he's been over here. He's their friend. They call him 'Red.'"

Dr Moner asked Greg, "Why do you call him Red?"

Greg whispered nervously, "Short for 'red bone,'" which enlarged Greg's mother's eyes.

"You call that boy 'rett bone!' Oh, no! I thought he was your *friend!* You make fun of that boy like that!"

"Cuz he light-skinned," Greg whispered. His mother slapped the back of his head and Dr. Moner folded his hands.

"You told me that boy was your *friend!*" She slapped him again and he looked like a little boy as he left the room. "I'm sorry, Dr. Moner, that you had to see that."

"I understand," he said.

"No, I don't think you really do, but it's nice to say. I'm sensitive when it comes to complexion. I was kept out of a sorority for being 'too dark.' They used to hold up a grocery bag against our skin. They called it 'the test.'"

"Oh my." Dr. Moner said. "I'm sorry."

"Don't be sorry. Greg'll be back next year. You can count on that."

Over the summer in San Pedro, Trey played basketball at Point Fermin, even while others were using the court. He shed his Saint Jude shyness during pickup games, chumming with the other players, who taught him Mexican curse words while he tried to explain to them where South Carolina was.

On Sundays, after pasta, Trey and Denise walked to Royal Palms as she recounted the horrible things Uncle Tim did to Auntie Donna. On their way back to Papa and Grammy's, he noticed for the first time, a mural of a three-eyed fish on an old concrete bunker at Fort MacArthur.

In church, Trey contemplated the golden virgin atop the steeple of Mary Star of the Sea, her arm stretched toward LA harbor, interceding to protect longshoremen and fishermen. As he knelt during the consecration, it sunk in that he was in the place where his parents were married, where they received their sacraments.

One Saturday, as he prayed next to Grammy, a Serbian man left the church screaming at Father Nikola, a Croatian, who would not hear his confession. Trey's dad later explained the war in "Yugoslavia," mentioning that there were a ton of "Croats" in San Pedro, but also admitted that Italians called them all "Slavs," and didn't understand what they were fighting about, but it was probably over something from centuries ago.

The California images Trey was used to taking back home—beaches, pasta, church—had evolved into real conversations with his wounded cousin who missed her abusive father; pickup games with Mexicans who called Trey a *cabron*, joking that he couldn't find Guanajuato on a map any better than they could South Carolina; and

Slavs who were fighting over something no one cared about. It made San Pedro a city from another time, no longer home, especially while Prudence lived in Sumter. He prayed for her to have a great summer, and that they would grow closer next year.

Before school resumed, the colonel dropped Trey off at Mooneyham's. The office seemed smaller, less intimidating without his dad, though, when he entered, the air-conditioning made him shiver so hard that beads of sweat jumped off his arms and his neck. Trey caught the scent of "ole Thad" the closer he came to his office. The books, from floor to ceiling, were mostly legal in nature, Trey guessed. He tucked the two loaned to him by Mooneyham like a football, then handed them back.

"Thank you, Trey. I wonder what you thought."

"I appreciate you sharing them with me, sir. Bobby Richardson seemed to go against the odds to become a ball player. He admitted in the book that he 'worked hard,' but I got the feeling that he held back because he was humble. I mean, you don't become an all-star for the Yankees by just 'throwing the ball against a house' for hours on end."

"You're right, Trey, you know you're right." Mooneyham's eyes were lively, almost green behind his glasses, which he removed. "Bobby has always been a humble servant. But a *fierce* competitor! Even when he was coaching over there in Columbia, those boys had that ole *Bobby-fire*, like we saw when he was with the Yankees, but they never bragged about it. And you better believe they were in service every Sunday."

"Well, Bobby Richardson seemed to really love this town," Trey said. "And speaking of Sumter, *General* Sumter was a real adventurer. Thanks again for the recommendation to study languages. I'm taking Spanish."

"That's fine, Trey. I hope I wasn't too preachy."

"No, sir. Spanish is very useful. My family is from Los Angeles, after all."

"California. I've never been, too far. I have grandkids now."

"Congratulations."

"Trey, what do think about this presidential race?"

"I think Bush will get reelected. That's what my dad hopes anyway."

"And you care about pleasing your daddy. That's why you're here, isn't it?" Trey felt sick at the insinuation. He had allowed himself to consider attending a civilian college but couldn't imagine it. The Academy had been betrothed to him for too long, and now Trey wondered if Mooneyham was in on the plot.

"Who will you vote for, sir?" Mooneyham paused for a spell.

"Well, I think Clinton is a joke. He's smart, but he'll only get in if Perot steals votes from Bush, which could happen, because George Bush is *not* his daddy. Ole Prescott Bush was a true 'damn Yankee.' He was a Republican when that was a dirty word down here. Of course, things have changed, and Senator Thurmond has since switched parties. But I don't have as much faith in Bush's kid as I did his daddy. People feared that man."

"Why do you think Clinton is a joke?"

"Oh, just look at him. With his red nose and that granddaddy stroll . . . those pregnant pauses in his orations. I could go on, Trey, but here's the real joke with 'slick Willie.' He's gonna convince all them liberals, and I ain't talkin' deep thinkers, I mean the Hollywood types, that he's one of 'em when he ain't. He's gonna try to sell those charms all the way to the White House. That's what my friends over in Little Rock say. Hell, he charmed them into the Governor's Mansion twice! What my friends and colleagues tell me is that ole Bill is as smart as they come, but he's not capable of serving anyone but himself. A complete narcissist."

"Do you have any books for me this year?"

"That depends on you, son. You come in here, and you haven't expressed your opinion to me yet. All you did is repeat what your daddy said. If you go to the Air Force Academy, they're going to expect *your* thoughts, not your daddy's." Mooneyham paused. "How did school go for you this year? Saint Jude still hangin' on?" He let his teeth show as his finished the question.

"Well, there's a lot of racial tension here. Not just at Saint Jude, seems like everywhere."

"You hit it on the head, Trey. It *ain't* just at Saint Jude, or in Sumter, or in South Carolina, or even just in the South. It is *everywhere*. People who pretend otherwise are fooling themselves."

"But it seems like here it's a lot worse. I did meals-on-wheels with my mom on the south side, and . . ."

"And what, Trey? You saw poverty? I can take you to sides of Sumter where *white* people live in the same kinds of shacks, with cockroaches the size of mice runnin' across the floor in broad daylight. This is a poor county. A poor state in many places. Hell, I can take you to some of the housing on Shaw *Air Force Base*, in the 5,000 area— drug-ridden, got babies runnin' around with days-old diapers, guns laying on the table for any youngin to pick up, no food in the house, husband's 'in the desert somewhere' deployed, mama's pregnant again by God-knows-who." Mooneyham put his glasses back on, his eyes fierce.

"We had a big fight before school ended. Black and white."

"Those things still happen. The important thing is that we all live together, cheek to jowl."

"But how can black students afford schools like Williams Haven? Would they even be welcome?"

"They don't need to go to an expensive academy like that when they can go for free to Sumter High, which is a good school, by the way, and integrated. Again, most *whites* can't afford Williams Haven. You know, Trey," started Mooneyham, his face redder, eyes less green, "I got just the book for you. Help you understand the history of this area and the thinking behind segregation and its aftereffects. It was written by Strom Thurmond, the man who *may* nominate you to the Academy.

"Some people called it 'The Southern Manifesto.' More than one hundred members of Congress signed it." Mooneyham ran his fingers over his forehead and then furrowed his brow. "But I'll tell you who *didn't* sign it! Al Gore Sr., who was a Senator from Tennessee before his snot-nosed son ended up in his seat. People never forgave ole Al for that." He handed him a copy of *The Declaration of Constitutional Principles*, which was more a pamphlet than a book.

Trey walked home slowly enough for the heat to strip Freon from his limbs. He showed Mooneyham's pamphlet to the colonel, who said, "You get your nomination next year and then leave Thad Mooneyham and his inbred state in the dust."

Trey returned to Jude's as a junior with more confidence, buoyed by his new acquaintance with Prudence, to whom he said awkward hellos in the hallway about five times a day. He began confirmation courses at Saint Jude's Church, and, to his dismay, found the Brazilian brothers from Williams Haven in his class. He made the basketball team.

Across town, Ray Allen was as close to a superhero as Sumter County knew. He arrived like all air force kids, a student with no past, save for the names of the bases on which he'd lived, and the job his mom or dad had. Hillcrest High, which became the de facto "black school" after Lincoln closed, dominated South Carolina basketball with Ray on the squad, winning the state title in 1993. Boys in Sumter clipped Ray's stats and photos from the paper and pretended to shoot like him in their games. They repeated true rumors, such as the one that Ray had lived in England, that he was quiet, almost shy, and wild tales—that at the start of every game Ray stole the tip-off and calmly dunked on his own goal. If anyone could put Sumter on the map (and expose its problems to the world), many hoped it was this soft-spoken man-child from nowhere.

Mrs. Smith, a student favorite, retired over the summer, leaving an address for anyone who wanted to write. Dr. Moner read her goodbye over the PA and announced that he would cover a few of her classes until they could find a replacement. In truth, the school couldn't afford to hire anyone, even at the nominal rate Jude's paid. The diocese would decide on the school's fate by the end of the year—a notice Moner shared with no one.

Alicia Brown and Lucy Braniff were neck and neck for valedictorian. Alicia bet her and Toney's future on the full scholarship given by USC to every South Carolina topper; while Lucy simply wanted the status of being number one. She said she'd never attend "a state school," even though it would be free because of her father's professorship. She was likely headed to Steubenville, a small Catholic college in Ohio. In October, Alicia found out that she was pregnant again, but waited a few weeks to tell Toney, who would not be able to hold the secret.

Dr. Moner led the "Tracy Morrow Seven," as they were now known, through American history, in which he threw out the recommended textbook for one on his shelf: *Who Speaks for the South?* by James McBride Dabbs. Dabbs, an early crusader for civil rights and integration, and mentioned by name in Dr. King's *Letter from a Birmingham Jail*, was an English professor from Sumter County, but no one had heard of him. His family owned a plantation called Rip Raps, which the class visited after reading a few chapters. They also bused to South Carolina State's library in Orangeburg to watch Dabbs's 1958 interview with Mike Wallace. Then they visited the site of the Orangeburg Massacre, in which three black students were killed in 1968 outside of a bowling alley that refused to integrate.

When word got around that the Morrow Seven were reading an alternative text, many hunted down Dabbs's writings and shared photocopies, thinking they held secrets the state wanted to bury, creating a subcultural buzz around Jude's. Some black air force kids even wrote "Dabbs" on walls and stalls, but tensions flared again when they started tagging the richnecks' lockers.

Prudence's disease worsened, forcing her to miss school at least once a week, during which time she barred her girlfriends from visiting the hospital or her home. The girls gained weight and grieved in the hallways. They skipped class to kibbitz in the library for half days when she was absent. Beyond those who felt closest to her, the rest of the school missed Prudence's wit and gumption, and they noticed that without her cough, the halls' normal noises loosed ghoulish echoes between lockers. Trey felt paralyzed because he had little right to openly miss her. In his mind, he drew, erased, and drew again her smirk surrounded by freckles, animating himself, mouth open, to suck the mucus from her lungs. He still didn't know exactly what was wrong, but he prayed for Prudence at night, in Mass, and during daydreams of her in confirmation class.

It was difficult for Trey and the other juniors to understand that confirmation meant, as their teacher said, "becoming an adult in the church." Most of them behaved well in class, with the goal of getting it over with, and hopefully receiving some holy cards with a couple of dollars pinned inside. Aside from class, students enjoyed the opportunity to socialize with Catholics from other schools in the county.

One Sunday afternoon, the older Brazilian brother complained to a girl from Laurence Manning High about a police officer who gave him and his brother trouble, just because they "weren't from Sumter." He flogged the point, his accent growing thicker as he counted and recounted the episode, as if the girl would be more drawn to him the more passionately he explained: cop pulled them aside at the mall, asked them what they were doing there, which shops they visited, and if they had parents.

With an innocent twang, the Laurence Manning girl asked, "Do you think it's because y'all 'er not . . . white?"

The Brazilian reared back, his head like a stallion's, his hair bouncing like a mane, teeth grinding, and hissed, "I *am* white!" Trey laughed to himself, knowing the Williams Haven kids probably called them spics when they weren't around.

Just before Christmas break, Dr. Dre released *The Chronic*, which sold out of every store in Sumter, driving crazed kids to Columbia to buy it. Even the Pan-Africans were entranced enough to push pause on their militant tracks and rap along with Snoop and his crew. Because of the busyness of the season, few people noticed when Saint Jude added a new student, Tony Odette, whose family had to leave Homestead Air Force Base a few months back because of Hurricane Andrew.

But Tony came in with swagger and wasn't ignored for long. He wore a Hurricanes sweatshirt and said he was from Miami, spurring kids to call him Vanilla Ice, though his complexion was darker than the average white guy's. His father commanded a squadron of F-16s at Homestead and now Shaw, and Tony told everyone of his plans to go to the Academy and fly fighters.

After two days at Jude's, and less than a week before the Williams Haven game, Tony asked the coach for a private tryout, then made the team for his hustle and positive attitude. In practice, he threw his body all over the court, saving loose balls and snatching rebounds, and his voice soon rivaled the captains' in trying to pump up the team.

Tony liked Trey from the jump, nicknaming him "Yuri" without asking if it was OK. They paired up at school, on the basketball court, and even in confirmation class, into which Tony was able to "transfer." Every social convention of Jude's Trey had absorbed from afar, each character sketch he narrated for an imaginary Prudence while shooting hoops alone, every inkling he had that Sumter brewed a racist stew that most accepted or ignored, he fed to his new friend.

They shot hoops on Trey's driveway until darkness drove them to toss a baseball between streetlights. They talked about girls, but never Prudence, which suited Trey fine. As the two grew closer, Trey dreamed of the day he could tell Tony about the freckled angel of Saint Jude, the mermaid who guided teenage ships by the courage in her cough. Until then, the duo exchanged Led Zeppelin lyrics and quotes from Chevy Chase movies, and each boy felt lucky to know the other.

Jude's students didn't know what to make of Trey now that he had a date to the dance. Tony was instantly popular for his brash but friendly swagger, his mysterious complexion and French surname (he was half Haitian, half Italian), and teen-TV good looks. He was olive-toned but not greasy, his hair full but not shaggy, his clothes fit like they were tailored, and he smelled of a strange brand of detergent. His teeth were straight but not by orthodontics, and he sometimes put on sunglasses when he went outside. He laughed like a child, but always at the right moments, and never at anyone who didn't deserve it.

He drew hangers-on and suitors like a bug zapper, and Trey was happy to whisper in his new friend's ear which students were worth keeping around and which he should cold-shoulder. When skanky girls tried to lure Tony, Trey passed him a quick cut symbol and a quote from *Spies Like Us*. When the richnecks tried to recruit him to their clique, Trey let him know that they were to be humored and nothing more. Some students resented Trey, who reveled in his new nickname, playing ambassador to the new kid. But as their junior year went on, most recognized his and Tony's as a true friendship.

The Williams Haven game began well, with the Padres' home crowd rocking the bleachers while Colonel Ciuri videotaped. Saint Jude avoided its usual mistakes, running a simple offense to create high-percentage shots, and a dogged defense that won most loose balls. Williams Haven's players, unaccustomed to being down, lost some of their swagger and were not able to talk their usual trash, and even the Brazilians seemed to have forgotten their dancing shoes.

"Now, who you callin' 'nigger!'" screamed Will McElveen as the Padres entered their locker room up ten points, feeling momentum from the first half. At first, the spirited bunch processed Will's cry as any other whoop to keep the energy level high, but then the black players considered the way he said the N-word, with a bit too much familiarity.

"What!" yelled Greg from across the locker room. Will pretended to ignore him. "Hey, Will," Greg said with a growl, beginning to stand up, with Lonzell and Denard ready to follow his lead. He sat frozen as they approached, looking like someone who'd fired a gun, not realizing how quickly it could take a life.

Tony, his uniform pristine, as he hadn't yet played, and a tad too tight due to limited supplies, snuck over to Will's side of the locker room. Trey tried to warn him to stay out of it but couldn't in time.

"Will, Will, Will!" he said in a rhythmic way unfamiliar to most, something Trey incorrectly attributed to Tony's Haitian roots; something voodoo, he thought. "Will!" he said again, but louder, keeping Greg and the others in his periphery as they continued to bubble, wiping sweat from their foreheads and reapplying lotion to their legs.

Tony looked Will in the eye, and with little time to spare, he said, "Do you know how bad that word is? Say 'yes!'"

"Yes," Will said quickly, his voice hoarse and mouth dry.

"And is this something we ever want to call *anyone*? Ever?"

"No," said Will with a downward glance.

The Pan-Africans' muscles were knotted, prepared to be worked as weapons, their eyes squinting at the target. Tony stood on the bench in the middle of the floor, pausing the PA's advance, and said, "I'm new on this team. I walked on in the *middle* of the year before the *biggest* game, against those *assholes*, who I guarantee right now are getting their *asses* chewed. And they're going to come out *hard* in the third quarter." If we ain't *tight*. Right *now*! If we don't come out of here *as one*, we may as well go home. We're going to lose. Now, *Will!* That word ain't got no place on our team, in our school, in our house, does it?!"

Will said "no" with tears in his eyes as he felt the caps now covering his front teeth. "Greg, Lonny, Den, are you tight!" They nodded. "And y'all don't even worry about me. I'm lucky to be on this team, lucky to have a home after everything got blown away down in Miami. I'm asking y'all, the Saint Jude's Padres, are you tight?!"

"We tight!" they boomed. "We tight!" they screamed and then mobbed Tony and Will, rubbing their hair, slapping their triceps and pushing their shoulders to build energy, a sense of rebellion, and grit. Trey removed himself from the moment and thought of Prudence coughing in bed, praying that they would wheel her in for the second half.

Williams Haven caught up by the fourth quarter, through little fault of Saint Jude's; however, the Padres were feeling deflated for losing the lead, their home crowd anxious and expecting a letdown. With the game tied and thirteen seconds left, Trey was in at point guard for the starter who'd fouled out. He brought the ball up, his man harassing him until half court, where Williams Haven came with the trap. There were eight seconds left as Trey lunged to pass around the double team but found Denard covered. He pivoted to his left to look for an open man, and just as Greg came free, the referee whistled Trey for traveling. The crowd burst into boos, and Trey stood in disbelief. Williams players set up their inbound play, demanding the ball. Jude's coach was on the floor and the ref warned him that he would get a tech if he continued, so he backed down. Trey continued to hold the ball. One of the Brazilians called for it forcefully, and when Trey wouldn't oblige, he dragged him by the ball to the ground. Before Trey could get up, Tony was on the Brazilian, punching his face and trying to choke him. A Williams player pulled Tony off and held him, and the other players restrained each other. The other Brazilian shot two free throws for the technical foul and they killed the clock on the inbound.

****

When school resumed after Christmas break, Tony was more popular than ever, but his hyperactivity confounded the student body. Just when he'd finish one head-turning feat, he was on his way to attempt something new. He petitioned the school to let him do meals-on-wheels three times a week, for which he got credit in social studies. He tutored immigrant kids in English and organized regular cleanups at Swan Lake, again getting points from his impressed teachers of religion and English. He got a job bagging groceries at Piggly Wiggly and used his first $250 to buy a 1979 Mustang from a guy on the south side.

At "The Pig," he was mayoral in his ability to remember customers' and coworkers' names. From the little old lady who counted out her change from a jar, to the undercover cop who Tony kidded about "guarding the doughnuts," he connected with most everyone. After work, he drove to Trey's, where the Ciuris enjoyed having him for dinner, and afterward the boys shot hoops. A few weeks into the job, he confessed to Trey in the driveway that many of his coworkers depended on their wages to pay rent and feed their kids, and he felt guilty that he spent his wages at McDonald's and to put gas in the 'stang.

After Tony got the hang of meals-on-wheels, he wrote letters to the VA on behalf of Mr. Ford and Mr. Felder, who were World War II veterans but for some reason could not get free care at Tuomey Hospital. He wrote to Dick Riley, the newly appointed Secretary of Education (and former governor of South Carolina) to provide funding for adult education on the south side for residents who either had to attend segregated schools or did not go at all. He welcomed his classmates to add their names to the petitions, which many did.

85

After Easter break, Dr. Moner approved the showing of *The Last Temptation of Christ* in religion class, drawing the outrage of the Braniffs, who called a meeting of the more influential families at Saint Jude, Colonel Ciuri among them. When Dr. Moner reversed his decision, Tony submitted a petition signed by nearly every student, which did not change the principal's mind.

At the next sexuality session, without raising his hand, Tony asked Mrs. Braniff, "Why did you cut *Last Temptation of Christ?*" hissing the last word like a champagne spray over the crowd. She scowled, ignoring the question. "You should answer me," he said and stood as the room began to stir, some teachers moving toward him. "What, you afraid your god ain't real? What are you afraid of!" Students started to laugh, albeit nervously. The Braniff girls, sensing their mother's peril, hissed at Tony, encouraging their friends to do so as well. "Don't you shush me, Branz!" Tony shouted. "I know your dirty secrets! Maybe we should tell your mama right *now* how *pure* you are!" He winked at Trey, who had shared rumors of the Braniffs' lustful encounters.

The student body burst from the session as if after three days in a tomb. Kids rattled lockers, stomped their feet, and mocked the Braniff hisses. They looked for Tony, but he was long gone, doing something else, so they settled for Trey, who embraced the role as his best friend's spokesperson. They circled him like paparazzi, and he nervously shouted something like "down with the hypocrites!" in an Old-English-like accent and walked to class.

Later in the evening, Tony parked half on the Ciuri grass, half on the gravel shoulder, and came in for dinner. The colonel made it a point to mention the meeting he'd attended with Mrs. Braniff about *Last*

Temptation, that he agreed the film had no place at Saint Jude, and he'd heard of some sort of student uprising. Trey and Tony winked at each other, feeling sly, and ready for more disruption.

During hoops afterward, Tony admitted that he'd taken the SAT every Saturday since Christmas break, and he'd yet to achieve a qualifying math score for the Academy. Trey told him not to worry, that he would beat math like he beat the Braniffs.

"I want us to be classmates," Tony said somberly. "At the Academy."

"Dude, we'll be wingmen! At least I'll be yours," said Trey with a slap on Tony's shoulder. "Hey," Trey added, "You should seduce Lucy Braniff. Get her to do some dirty things. I know you could." Tony grinned and launched a jump shot.

****

The boys were confirmed in May. Trey took the name Isaiah, after Isaiah Thomas, though his teacher said it was technically illegal because Isaiah was a prophet, not a saint. Tony took the name Jean Bertrand, after the Haitian priest, which the teacher also cautioned against because he was not canonized, to which Tony replied, "Not yet."

At the reception in the parish hall, the boys were dying to shed their ties for baseball cleats and caps. Colonel Ciuri handed Trey a mug and told him to get coffee for Mrs. Basso, the Brazilian's mother. As he poured in the kitchen, he noticed a jug of bleach beneath the steel sink. He filled a cap and was about to dump it in Basso's cup when Tony stopped him.

"What the hell are you doing?"

"I've wanted to get these motherfuckers back for two years. Their mom is gonna pay."

"Are you stupid?" Tony asked as he slapped the cap away.

"What the fuck!" Trey yelled, nearly pushing Tony. "They deserve it. They called us the N-word and danced in our faces."

"They'll get theirs."

"When," Trey said, a statement more than a question.

"I don't know, next year, when we beat them."

"Yeah, right. Look, man, you don't understand. I made a promise to myself that I'd get them and here it is."

"Then beat them in basketball. Don't poison their mom, seriously, dude. You would throw away the Academy for this? They'd kick you out of Jude's, maybe put you in jail."

88

"No one will know!" Trey said angrily, turning to bring the coffee to Mrs. Basso, who thanked him with a heavy accent. He was embarrassed to be caught by Tony and then told what to do. The whole idea made him sick, as if he had taken the bleach himself. But his desire for revenge was filling inside him to the point of being sexual, the thought of closing a loop around an enemy's neck; he wanted it sometimes more than even Prudence's perfect skinny body.

In the last month of school, Mrs. Perch let it slip in math class that Alicia had earned the highest GPA and would represent Saint Jude as valedictorian for the class of 1993. The students clapped, and even a sour Lucy Braniff walked over to shake her hand, for which Alicia stood up, though seven months pregnant, and gave her a hug. She sat down, smiled, and then cried, holding her belly from the sides.

At the end of the day, however, Dr. Moner announced that *Lucy* would be valedictorian, generating outcry in most classrooms. Students rushed to find either girl to verify, but both had gone home early. Toney, who was confused about how he would get to work that afternoon, was no help to Trey and others who asked him what happened. Some students proudly yelled, "Oh, hell no!" through the halls. Tony offered T-yo a ride to NAPA, which was just down the street from Piggly Wiggly.

"Oh, hell no!" screamed T-yo in Tony's car once he understood, squishing his hat in one hand and grabbing a tuft of hair with the other.

"I'm sorry, man," Tony said. I don't know what's going on. We'll find out, though, I guarantee it."

"I know what happened, Trey," he growled. "Alicia said they'd do it!"

"Who?"

"The fuckin' Braniffs, Trey! God damn!"

"Tony."

"What?!"

"My name, Tony."

"What?! C'mon, goddamnit, oh, I can't go to *work*! Alicia's got the baby and Clayton and she stayed up late studying all them nights, and I wasn't no fuckin' help to her."

"That's not true, T-yo. She brags on you all the time. Shit, you're the father of her children." Toney stared into the windshield.

"You know, Trey, or, what do they call you, Yuri?"

"Yes."

"You can't even wanna get mad or get even with the Braniffs, because they have all that holy shit on their side. It's like they get more out of Mass than us regular people. All I can do is bow when they ring the bells for the bread and wine. That's all I got. Braniffs got somethin' else."

That night, at the dinner table, Colonel Ciuri confirmed that Alicia was disqualified as valedictorian because she was "living in sin" as put by "many concerned parents."

"That's bullshit, Mr. Ciuri."

"This is a Catholic school, boys. What kind of message are we sending, especially with the diocese breathing down our necks, if our valedictorian is pregnant with a baby out of wedlock?"

"She earned it," was all Tony could manage, suddenly looking exhausted and sad. Trey had not seen him so daunted, even more so than at the thought of SAT math.

"Dad, Lucy Braniff is a conniving hypocrite. Her whole family is a bunch of judgmental assholes," said Trey.

"Bill and Jane Braniff? And those girls? You guys would be *lucky* to marry girls like them. *They're* the example, boys, not Alicia and that kid who works at NAPA. They live together!"

"They have a son, Dad! Where else would they live?"

"We can't condone it, we can't promote it. Plus, we need Dr. Braniff to help keep Saint Jude open. You *do* want to graduate next year, right?"

"Not from a hypocrite joint like Jude's," said Trey as he grabbed the basketball and bid Tony to follow him outside.

Just before the Ciuris were to fly to San Pedro for the summer, Trey and Tony visited Mooneyham's office. Trey talked up the lawyer as if the two of them had been fishing buddies for years.

"Mr. Ciuri, a rising senior! And a guest," said Mooneyham with pleasant surprise.

"Yes, sir," said Trey, "This is Tony Odette. He's new at Saint Jude, but he's also looking to go to the Academy."

"Well, that's fine! Each congressman gets ten nominations, I believe, so there should be room for one more. Assuming you got the grades, boy. You qualified?" he asked with a playful gesture toward Tony.

"Almost, sir, just waiting on my SATs."

"Well, good," said Thad. "What's your ethnicity, Mr. Odette? You're not Italian like our friend Trey, are you?"

"Half, sir, half Haitian."

"Haitian! I've never met someone from Haiti, and I wouldn't have guessed that all day! That's something! Sit down, gentlemen." They talked politics—national and in South Carolina. Mooneyham tested Tony to see if he knew his representatives, and Tony asked the lawyer who he thought would replace Strom Thurmond.

"Here is your book, Mr. Mooneyham," Trey said. "I can't say I agree with what they wrote, those congressmen, but I appreciate you loaning it . . ."

"You can't agree, Trey, because you don't understand. And you can't understand because you ain't a lawyer."

"Uh, sir, I don't think you need to be a lawyer to know that segregation is wrong," said Tony, who'd read it quickly in the car and gotten the gist from Trey.

"Can you *tell* me what the fourteenth amendment says, Mr. Odette?"

"No."

"Do you know what it established?"

"I assume something to do with civil rights."

"You assume. Well, I assume that your friend Mr. Ciuri here assumes the same thing. Am I right, Trey?"

"Yes, sir."

"Here's the story, fellas. You can disagree with segregation all you want, but if you don't bother to learn the facts about the case in question, then your opinion doesn't hold much water, does it?"

"Mr. Mooneyham," Trey said with a shy smile, "I brought *you* a book this time."

"You did. What do we have here? Oh, Trey, you *didn't*. Dabbs! I've got every one of his books—just over there on the shelf. This book is from the Sumter County Public Library, Trey. Were you going to come get it from me in three weeks?"

"Well, I . . ."

"No, I think you're just another kid who discovered Dabbs, and wanted to use him as an example of a Southerner who supported civil rights, or as Martin Luther King said, wrote about 'our struggle in eloquent and prophetic terms.' You know ole Dabbs kept Confederate muskets on the wall right above his honorary membership in the NAACP?"

"Are you saying that he was playing both sides?" Tony asked.

"You could put it that way. Let me ask you this: where did Mr. Dabbs and his family live?"

"At Rip Raps."

"And Rip Raps is what? A house? A farm?"

"It was a plantation."

"A *plantation*! Hallelujah! And who do you think *worked* that plantation?"

"Dabbs wrote in the 1950s, there weren't slaves then," said Trey.

"You think you need *slaves* to generate disposable time, son? Just because it ain't free no more, don't mean. . ." Mooneyham stopped himself for a second. "You just think about what enabled ole James McBride Dabbs to have so much leisure time to write so 'eloquently.' To go up to Columbia University and study 'Eng-lish,' and then come back down here and teach it to us. One thing Dabbs's writing *will* tell you— and he tried hard to escape this truth, but he never could— everybody has their place, boys! Everybody! The sooner you learn your place, the easier life becomes."

"This is crap," said Tony. "I can't believe guys like you have survived."

"Not just survived, Odette, *thrived*. I know you won't forget it."

"General Sherman should have taken every nickel you guys stole and put the freed slaves in charge of it all."

"That's a great idea, Mr. O-dette! Let's turn North Carolina into Liberia! And Virginia—we can rename her Sierra Leone! Oh, and South Carolina, just for you, Odette, we'll call this state 'Haiti.' Ha! That's what a bunch of freed slaves would do to a place if *they* were in charge—make it a third-world country! Heck, look at most major cities in America!

"Why do you think the Jews got reparations—heck, they're *still* getting paid—for the Holocaust? Blacks never got a nickel for slavery—why? Hell, slavery lasted a hundred times as long, killed probably ten times as many people as the Holocaust, and created a permanent underclass in the Americas. Surely, we oughta right that wrong, shouldn't we? Know why we don't? Know why even liberals laugh when the topic of reparations comes up? Know why Jews get paid and blacks don't? 'Cause Jews are smart, fellas! They didn't get sold by their own people! And when they got forced into ghettos, they didn't start killing each other!" Trey was sweating.

"Do you not think we'll have a black president someday?" Trey asked.

"Oh yes, most certainly," Mooneyham said. "But it ain't gonna be no dance-around, fleece-the-flock preacher like Jesse Jackson or Al Sharpton. The president will not be descended from slaves. He'd have to be an islander or something, someone like General Powell."

"What about Ray Allen?" Trey asked.

"That boy over there at Hillcrest?" Mooneyham thought for a moment. "Nope, not him. I've seen him play, and he's a monster on the court, truly a man among boys. But he's a quiet leader. He's gonna need more vocal guys around him in college and the pros, if he makes it."

Mooneyham paused, then asked, "Ray's an air force kid like y'all, right?" The boys nodded. "Air force folks are by and large wonderful people—and the base supports many things here in Sumter—but y'all always get a little sideways when you figure out how we run things. With respect to the races." Mooneyham let his face round into a wide smile.

"Look, Mr. Mooneyham, we just want to come at this from a Christian perspective," said Trey. "And we don't think that Christ would condone slavery, racism, and segregation."

"But y'all ain't Christians, are you? You're Catholic. And if you want to talk slavery, ain't nobody did slavery and 'oppression' better than the Jesuits! Y'all convinced *your* slaves that their reward was in heaven! Got 'em to work even harder! I've got one final book for you, Mr. Ciuri. A book and a secret." Mooneyham grabbed *Wise Blood* from his shelf and handed it to Tony, who held it away from his eyes. "This here is the best you're ever gonna do, Trey. Flannery O'Connor, a Catholic as strong as Bobby Richardson is a Christian. A great Southern writer. And a 'racist,' as you would call her. When you read this book, I want you to count the 'niggers,' the number of times she uses the word, and how she uses it. I helped you by underlining them, and there's quite a few."

"What is that supposed to prove?" asked Trey.

"That 'this land was made,'" Mooneyham sang, "'for you and me!' And half for Mr. Odette," he said, chuckling. "This is our promised land, Trey, accept it. You go to the Academy and represent the Palmetto State!" Mooneyham's taunt buzzed in Trey's face like a stinging bug.

"Well, I think we better be going," Trey said.

"Oh, yes, it's time, isn't it? Before you go, you want to know the secret?"

"Sure."

"You didn't need me or Senator Thurmond to get a nomination!"

"Excuse me?"

"Three years you been coming here! You get an automatic nomination because your daddy was a POW!" The secret sunk like nails into Trey, and both boys left bruised. Tony parked the Mustang in its usual place at the Ciuri house, and they turned to the basketball, hoping a game or two would cleanse them of the experience. Every clang on the rim or rush through the net was a chip away at the ugly barnacles of the country lawyer's ideas.

Tony dribbled for a while, practicing behind-the-backs and between-the-legs, looking at Trey, who was quiet, still ashamed for bringing his friend to the king of the richnecks. Tony grew an impish grin and began to impersonate Mooneyham.

"Who's gonna replace ole Strom Thurmond, you ask? Well, first of all, boy, perish the thought! Ole Strom, the granddaddy of the Dixiecrats has a good twenty years left in the tank!" Tony sounded like the cartoon rooster, Foghorn Leghorn, which doubled Trey over. "But I'll tell you fellas . . . and it stays in this room . . . he's got his eye on a young buck in the statehouse. An air force man too, just like y'all." Trey gained confidence and found his inner Mooneyham.

"The only trouble, you see, with this here air force boy, is he ain't *married*. And that's just plum strange for a man his age and means. Now, I don't think he's a homo*sexual*, my Lord, perish the thought! But he don't seem to 'like' the female species."

"He even has a woman's name, if you can believe it. Which of course don't help his case none," Tony cut in.

"He needs a *man's* name," Trey whined, trying to keep from laughing, "a good strong name like 'Thad.' Boy, the name Thad is so manly, it sounds like . . . it sounds like, like—like . . ."

"Sounds like a dick slappin' you right in the forehead, don't it!" The boys fell on the driveway laughing as the basketball rolled into the pine-straw bed.

"What's wrong?" Trey asked Tony, whose face had fallen into graveness.

"The day I drove T-yo to work—when they announced Alicia didn't get valedictorian. It's sticking with me. He kept calling me Trey, and I didn't correct him after like the third time."

"Funny that you two have the same name," Trey remarked.

"And the same SAT scores."

"You'll get it, dude, don't worry."

"Hope so."

Trey asked him, "You know who I'm gonna miss?"

"Who?"

"Prudence Diehl."

"Why? Were you guys friends?"

"No, but she's . . ." and then Trey realized he didn't have any way of describing Prudence outside of his internal monologues on the very driveway where they now stood. It made her feel less real, dulling the sheen of the "conversations" he'd had with her over the last three years.

"She's dying," Tony said. "Sad."

"What?!" Trey blurted and threw up a wild ball, which clanged and then hid in the pine straw. Trey knelt when he retrieved it, bewildered.

"Cystic fibrosis, man. You didn't know? I mean, I didn't even know what the disease *was*, but Alicia told me. She was in school with Prudence since like third grade, said she was always coughing, always messed up in the stomach. I don't think she's expected to live much longer after college." Trey held the ball and walked back to the driveway with his head down.

"I'm sorry, man. I figured you knew. You know everything about Jude's." They let a minute pass. "I mean, at least she enjoys herself while she can—drinks, smokes, has sex . . ."

"What?!"

"I heard she has a boyfriend at Sumter High." Trey was devastated but knew he had no right to be jealous. He was ashamed that he was sadder that she had a boyfriend than at the news she'd die soon.

"You liked her? I'm sorry, dude." He patted Trey's shoulder.

"Eh, I never talked to her. Except once. I wanted to. It seemed like she had a force field around her." The boys continued shooting into the night, sometimes missing the backboard in the tangy dark, their laughter defiling the Sumter suburb. Summer lay ahead and then their senior year, an epic span that would be colored by calculated rebellion in the form of community service, sports, and cruising Sumter's streets with Dr. Dre rattling the windows.

As he dribbled, Trey told Tony, "Everyone loves Michael Jordan and the Bulls now, and when I tell people I like the Pistons, they laugh, and when I say Isaiah's name, they laugh even more." Trey paused, Tony waited, and Trey finished, "I *like* that feeling of being laughed at by the majority, the sheep. Not sure why I just shared that."

"Eh, Jordan is overrated, mostly hype," Tony said. "You see what the refs let him get away with? He practically tucks the ball like a football to make his first move. Guys like Isaiah had to learn to cross people up, to be quick to get in the lane. Every time Jordan drives, he's guaranteed to get fouled. Basketball is a lot easier when you don't have to worry about finishing most of your shots. At least the Pistons had the balls to drop an elbow on Jordan's punk ass. He has all the privileges. None of the burdens."

"Would you say he's the Mooneyham of the NBA?"

Tony smiled and again became Thad. "You said it, Mr. Ciuri! Now come on over *heyah* and sit on ole Uncle Thad's lap. Lemme know the first thing that comes up!" They fell over laughing, then sat up on the concrete.

"I can't believe I almost poisoned Mrs. Basso," Trey said.

"Yeah, dude, that was close."

"I can't believe I have those thoughts in me."

"You have a lot of good stuff too."

****

On the last day of high school, Trey tucked his valedictory into the waist of his jeans, aimed a ladder at the gutter framing the roof of the Ciuri house, and began to climb barefoot. The midday heat, the emptiness of his neighborhood, and the impending transition to the Academy had him as nervous as the cicadas in the pines. Shingles burned his feet, but he walked quickly to the pitch in the roof, where it was cooler. He took inventory of the chimney, the bubble covering the kitchen skylight, and two spinning vents that looked like Christmas ornaments. The speech he was about to deliver to the neighborhood had not been approved by Dr. Moner.

"My grandfather, John August Ciuri, who we call 'Papa,' is a retired Los Angeles City fireman, and a proud Italian. He still cooks pasta every Sunday for the extended family, asks instinctively if my cousins' boyfriends and girlfriends are Italian, and when we walk through his front door, he jokes, 'How did your day go . . . dago?'

"After thirty-six years of running calls in one of the most diverse cities in the world, Papa developed a set of stereotypes for pretty much every group of people. One summer, while I was visiting, he took me and a cousin aside and said, 'You can't trust Armenians. They're the only ones who can outslick a Jew.' Before we could ask him for clarification— neither I nor my cousin knew any Armenians or Jews—he continued, 'A Jew won't sell his kids. An Armenian will.'

"As random and disturbing as that advice was, it stuck with me until a few years later, when an earthquake hit Armenia. My dad was stationed in Germany at the time, and many Armenian kids were medevaced to Frankfurt's military hospital. Our base collected toys and

102

organized a trip to visit them. I was hesitant at first, but, once engaged, I saw that the kids were sweet and thankful, and I wanted to stay longer. I had no friends in school at that time, and I missed those kids on the bus ride back.

"I'm only seventeen years old, but I've learned that, from Los Angeles to Sumter, you're going to meet people with stereotypes, and you're going to have to accept that a lot of them are shortsighted, a little ignorant, or just lazy. But if you give yourself a chance to live, if you are patient and kind, you'll come to a more accepting place as a citizen and a Christian.

"Now, to my parents. My parents are scared of MTV. They're scared of most of the music and movies coming out these days. Maybe they don't like it because today's styles are so different from what they grew up on? The *content* sure hasn't changed since they were in high school. Dion's 'wandering,' The Beach Boys' fondness for 'getting around,' and Mick Jagger's moaning about 'satisfaction' all mean the same things that Boyz II Men and R. Kelly mean when they sing 'I'll make love to you,' or 'I wanna bump and grind.'

"Regardless of my fondness for the entertainment of this generation, however, Mom and Dad wouldn't have it in their house. MTV was evil, they said, Hollywood, amoral. Family night at the Ciuris, if it wasn't our own home movies, featured Audrey Hepburn or Cary Grant, Jimmy Stewart, and probably some Humphrey Bogart. At school, it was tough for me to fit into conversations about *Wayne's World* and *Terminator 2*, but I was full of quotes from black-and-white movies no one my age had ever heard of.

"I'd like to share with you this evening one quote from a pretty famous movie that I imagine we'll all watch in college and have to write a paper on: *Casablanca*. In it, the main character, Rick, tells one of the villains, 'I don't mind a parasite. I object to a cut-rate one.' Most people watching the movie forget this line because it happens early in the film, and just a few seconds later, the villain is killed by local police, and the plot heats up. To me, though, Rick warns us, in a joking way, against hypocrisy, and then, in a very serious way, says that hypocrites deserve what they get.

"Let's not beat around this bush. Saint Jude will close its doors after summer school this year, possibly for good. And when did *we*—the students, parents, and teachers—find out? After Easter, when it was too late, after our principal, Dr. Moner, concealed the news—like a father who hides a terminal illness from his loved ones. For nearly a year, he *knew* that the diocese would cut us off! He said that he was working behind the scenes to save Saint Jude, that he had to keep things quiet and marshal support from the community, but I've heard people talking, and none of them believe that is true. *I don't mind an inept savior. I object to one who says everything is fine.*

"And what did the community do to help save the school? I would like to ask one of Saint Jude's most prominent families, the Braniffs. Braniffs! Hello, any Braniffs here? No, you won't find them in the audience tonight, because all the while they were pledging their support in Sumter, they were building a home in Columbia and planning to enroll their kids at Cardinal Newman! Like that school needs any more money. *I don't mind a deserter. I object to one who says he has your back.*

"Oh, but let's think about the *good* things the Braniffs did while they were among us. What about all those lectures Mrs. Braniff gave us on chastity? How many hours did we sit there and watch the Braniff daughters nod like puppets, knowing that, when their mom wasn't looking, they were doing things that would make Mick Jagger and R. Kelly blush! And let's remember last year, almost to the day: who stood up here on this stage and represented the class of 1993? Not the *true* valedictorian, Alicia Brown. No, the Braniffs underhandedly forced her from her rightful place—costing her a scholarship to USC—so their daughter could take the prize. They said it was because Alicia set a bad example as a Catholic, but that's sinners throwing stones. *I don't mind a sore loser. I object to one who cheats to change the outcome.*

"These hypocrisies make me think of Sumter in general, all the 'Christianity' we see here. Would Christ want his name on the lips of the white residents of Sumter? The ones who make sure that the south side stays on its part of town? Oh, and let me tell you how proud I am that Saint Jude is located on the south side! These Sumterites claim to have love and charity, kindness and compassion, in their hearts! No, the ruling class here likes to keep people 'in their place.' It's simply a lie if you think that everyone in Sumter gets a fair shake. *I don't mind a racist. I object to a racist who pretends he's not.*

"I don't want to end this speech with negativity, so I would like to highlight some of the great things we did as the class of 1994, and I must say that much of this is due to the leadership of our classmate, Tony Odette. We taught English to more than a hundred immigrant kids; we petitioned the VA to bring care to elderly veterans who lived on the south side; we did the same for adult education through Secretary Riley's office. We cleaned up Swan Lake probably a dozen times. We also, and I saved the best for last, beat Williams Haven in basketball for the first time since anyone could remember. And that could be our saving grace: it could be God's way of saying, 'OK, Saint Jude's work is done, he can shut his doors now that he beat the evildoers from Williams Haven.' Who knows? I do know that I and my teammates, coaches, and everyone who cheered us on—in *their* gym, by the way—will savor that win forever, because it truly was a victory of good versus evil.

"There were two boys in particular on that Williams Haven team, two brothers from Brazil, who I hated more than anyone else. I was so mad at how good they were, and how they would showboat around the court, that I wanted to not only see them lose, but get injured in the process. That's wrong. Talk about unchristian sentiments! It took me a long time, but I forgave those brothers for hurting my feelings, and I actually feel freer because of it. And that's the point of my speech tonight: forgiveness.

"I pointed a lot of fingers this evening, and I hope none of you will blame me for doing so. But I only mentioned these things because I don't want to hold the grudges in my heart any longer. I forgive Dr. Moner for selfishly going down with the ship. I forgive the Braniffs for their hypocrisy, their judgments, and their malice. I forgive the white residents of Sumter for their racism and the actions to oppress their fellow men. A Catholic who can't forgive is the worst kind of hypocrite. Congrats to the Class of 1994. Good night."

Trey climbed down from the roof, still nervous, but feeling a bit prouder, having let his speech out into the world. He drove to The Pig, where Tony had arranged with his manager to buy beer for the evening, which they loaded into Trey's trunk, to be dropped off at the party house. He passed NAPA on his way home and thought of T-yo, who would graduate with them, thanks to tutoring from Tony, Trey, and others. Alicia now had a full ride to USC Columbia, where they were planning to relocate with her mother in the fall, and T-yo found a lateral transfer to another NAPA. Trey dropped off the beer, went home to change clothes, and paced the floor until his parents came to take him to the ceremony.

In Patriot Hall, the renegade valedictory burned in his pocket as he waited with his classmates. Mrs. Perch, their homeroom teacher, came in to shake each student's hand and then asked Trey to speak with her outside.

"Are you nervous?" she asked.

"Yes, but it'll be fine." Perch and the guidance counselor had OK'd the speech that awaited him on the stage. Trey touched the other one in his pocket.

"Tony told me you're planning a surprise," she said. Trey squirmed, looking past her into the waiting room, trying to lock eyes with Tony, feeling betrayed. Perch's husband flew in Lieutenant Colonel Odette's squadron, so maybe that's why he told her? "It's OK," she said, "Your secret is safe with me." She put her hand on his shoulder. "But I do want to share a story with you. It may change your mind, or it may harden your resolve." Trey nodded.

"I was in my senior year at the Academy," Perch began.

"Wait, you went to the Academy?"

"Yes, Trey, you knew that. Didn't you?"

"No!"

"That's where I met Rob. I'm still in the reserves. I talked about flying all the time in class! We worked out equations based on my jet! Should I reconsider the grade I gave you?"

"Too late," Trey smiled, wondering how he could have overlooked it. He feared it was because she was a woman. Colonel Ciuri told stories, which Tony and Trey laughed at, about the Academy's class of 1979, the last one to be all male, which called themselves the "last class with balls." They whooped around the terrazzo before formation yelling, "L-C-W-B!" and some even had the acronym engraved in their rings. Trey felt ashamed.

"OK, take this for what it's worth. It was my firstie year. We had all gotten our assignments and most of us were coasting in second semester, breezing through classes, skipping formations, wearing our uniforms without the usual attention to detail—that kind of stuff. The commandant, who was a real hard-ass, started taking away privileges: first no weeknight passes, then no weekends. After that, he scheduled extra trainings, including parades, on Saturday and Sunday, even in bad weather.

"One Monday, some enterprising and artistic cadets built this amazingly lifelike penis, I mean with veins bulging and everything, which they hung from the comm's balcony with a sign that said, 'You can make it harder, but you can't make it longer.' We thought he would get the point, laugh to himself, and throttle back a bit, but he went at us harder. He said that no one would graduate until the perpetrators came forward. They did and were disenrolled immediately, their lives completely changed."

"Are you telling me not to do it?" Trey asked with a swallow.

"No. But I am saying that if you do, you should be prepared for people you piss off to come at you with everything they have. And they may try to ruin you. It would not be beyond some of these folks to make calls to the Academy and have your appointment delayed or rescinded. Just know what it means to go all the way."

Trey blurted, "My dad says that it's better to fail for the right reasons than to succeed for the wrong ones."

"That's a nice proverb, what your dad told you, and I'll bet he had to show a lot of courage in his day. But you can only act on it once or twice in your life. You want to be real sure before you fall on your sword, Trey." She paused, started to walk away, then turned back. "Are you ready to be so impulsive? It comes with a ton of ripple effects."

****

"Pomp and Circumstance" guided them to the stage. A priest said a prayer. Dr. Moner gave his introduction and the guest speaker said something that none of the students heard. The salutatorian gave his speech, and then the students received their diplomas. Trey entered a blurry consciousness as Dr. Moner introduced him, and he walked unsteadily to the pulpit, where the vanilla speech lay crisp in a folder.

Trey thought back a few weeks, April 6, to the day, when the phone rang extra late at the Ciuri home, and his mom woke him to take the call. A woman's voice asked if he was free, then began coughing. Trey's pulse quickened. She told him to meet her at Swan Lake, mentioning which entrance he should park at and how to squeeze through the gate.

He waited for his parents to go back to sleep and left a note in case they woke while he was gone. It was near midnight when he arrived, his nerves buzzing on the surface of his skin. Prudence stood one hundred yards down the path, strangely illuminated, though there were no lights and Trey saw no moon. He walked to her, internally flogging himself about what to say, but as he got closer, he found the look on her face to be more lustful than conversational.

When he leaned in, she turned gracefully and offered Trey her right arm, which confused him until she guided it to his mouth. He began to kiss and suck as if it were a neck, long like a swan's, he imagined, and then he tasted the salt and almost coughed himself. Prudence laughed and said, "Salty, huh?" He smiled, licking his lips, looking at hers. "It's the disease."

He kissed her hard. Prudence unbuttoned her shirt and Trey fumbled for the belt around her jeans, noticing they were a couple of inches too big for her waist. They fell to the dirt and she pushed him down, the moon behind her, the water making sounds of disturbance, alarm. She smiled, flattening her body to his, his midsection aching, and he fumbled for the condom in his pocket. But she pinned his arms against the shore dirt and let her hair, which smelled like leaves, touch his cheek as she talked at his ear, while he tried to kiss her salty throat.

"He killed himself yesterday, I knew it would happen, the most genuine thing in the world," she said a bit breathlessly.

"Who?" asked Trey, playfully, thinking she was getting kinky, perhaps for something satanic at Swan Lake. He didn't care if she wanted to dip his genitals in hot wax and invite swans to nip at them, for everything was right.

"Kurt Cobain. He shotgunned himself in the garage."

"Yeah, I heard about that. Sad."

"Honest. He said he was going to do it, and he did it. Control, honesty." Trey momentarily fell out of the trance.

"Wait, he had a wife and kid. I guess he was in pain, but a lot of people are going to miss him."

"He had his reasons," Prudence said. "Everyone who suicides has their reasons." Trey grabbed her head and turned it forcefully toward his mouth, enveloping lips that did not kiss him back. He looked up at her, then down at her bra, from which one small breast had been dislodged.

"Are you happy he died? That he did this? I know you always compared him to Eddie Vedder. Is this the end of the comparison?"

"Eddie Vedder would never have the guts to kill himself. That's probably not even his real name. He's going to release a hundred albums and tour like The Stones until he's seventy years old."

"Prudence, I am really happy to be here with you," Trey said and ground his erection into her middle, which turned out to be her hip.

"Kurt gave people an example, an invitation. A way out," she said. She looked at the water. Trey stopped touching her. But she pressed her lips to him, reached into his pants, and then took off her bra with the other hand. Trey opened the condom with one hand and held her shoulder steady with the other. She reared back and opened his pants. Trey tried to raise up, but she pushed him down, again offering her right arm, which he moved up and down his mouth. Prudence swallowed him. She began to cough as she moved, the sensation like a vacuum, bringing Trey closer to climax, which he prayed to put off. She lurched toward him, then arched her back as the cough grew more violent.

"How does it feel!"

"Like a fucking hacksaw," she said as he came, and she fell on him, the cough now dying as faint echoes lived among the irises and whispered in the ears of curious swans. They dressed on the shore, saying nothing until Trey asked her if she was considering suicide, trying to sound professional, yet caring, and not at all preachy.

"Not considering, *doing*," she said as she took a prescription bottle from her purse and shook it at him.

"Oh, Prudence, please, don't."

"Why? Are you going to miss me any more if I hang on until I'm thirty-three and die in my own mucus?" She started coughing. Trey waited.

"I'll miss you either way. I love you," he said, looking down.

"Dude, I just made you a great memory, losing your virginity on the banks of the lake while swans checked us out. *Booyaah!*" She laughed and coughed.

"That's all it is?"

"I have a boyfriend, Trey. This was nice, I could see how you touched me and looked at me and talked to me that you're really sweet and that you care. This was nice. Maybe you'll find out what 'love' is one day, but not with me."

"Give me those pills, Prudence." He surprised himself with his conviction. She, in turn, surprised him by throwing the bottle in his lap. He held her for hours, recounting the conversations he'd had with her while shooting hoops, sometimes making her laugh and sometimes sighing with nostalgia.

Trey stabbed awkward silences with silly questions about her favorite food: "whatever doesn't clog me up;" her middle name: "Ophelia;" her father's occupation: "engineer."

"My mother is an engineer too," she mentioned, and Trey felt guilty for not asking.

He learned more about her thoughts on suicide and was, in some moments, swayed into seeing things from her perspective. But then he felt like a ship drawn to a false lighthouse, one surrounded by reefs. His zeal to protect her returned, and the thought of Prudence erasing herself did not compute in his mind, especially when he now knew her body, and was beginning to know her as a person. After four years of his near-idolatry of her, Trey felt as if a suicide would be an act of theft—that she would be stealing from him.

However, Prudence was convincing when she told him what kind of pain she was in for, that she really had "something like" fifteen years left on her "meter," that she indeed would cough herself to death until mucus consumed her "like a slow sink into your own mud." She assured him that she would be no fun, not to anyone, in her last few years. She wouldn't be able to make anyone laugh or listen to anyone's problems. She'd just run up medical bills and go through tests. Most importantly, she said, until this point in her life, she'd never made a decision for herself.

"People tell us," she said, "that we get to choose things like our clothes, and the music we listen to, the college we attend, but those things are already set by a bunch of companies, people who sell things. I know it seems whiny that Kurt suicided, but it's not. He knew."

When Trey's libido returned, he tried to initiate sex again, which she refused. When they left, the sun was coming up and they made no plans to meet again. Before he got in his car, Trey asked her, "How did you get my phone number?"

"Oh, Tony Odette told me to call you. I'm glad I did."

Trey returned from his memory engorged with sexual confidence, but also dispirited to think that the tryst with Prudence was arranged by his best friend, who'd also revealed the alternate speech to Mrs. Perch.

Patriot Hall was dark and muggy. Dr. Moner called Trey's name.

After the ceremony, Tony found Trey who, looking away, confessed, "I couldn't do it, I'm sorry."

"Whatever, dude," Tony said. "I thought you would at least try. You were the *valedictorian*, man. You're going to the *Academy*. People would have listened to you. You would have changed things. Don't you *want* to change things?"

Tony's words brought him back to the humiliation of Mooneyham's office, to the feeling that everything that was happening in his life was the script of a movie about the son of a POW, and all he could do was watch. He didn't want to go to the Academy. He didn't care about being first in the class. *This wretched state isn't even worth trying to change things in!* he bellowed silently. *Isn't it enough that the Braniffs and those like them are going to hell someday?* Trey just wanted to be with Prudence, to read to her, listen to her cough and hold her until it subsided; stick around until she died from her horrible disease. But that's not what came out of his mouth.

"No, Tony, I *don't* want to change things. You know what I want?" His voice rose, attracting others, including adults, who'd loved his valedictory. "I want to get a job, a normal office job, and I want to have coworkers named Eric, Luther, and Tim, just three guys, and just those names. Except in the office, because we're tight, we nickname Eric 'Eazy-E,' and Luther is 'Luke,' and Tim, he's 'Tim Dog.' And every morning, I'll call them out, just like Snoop does at the end of "Dre Day." I'll bust in the office, same time every day, and I'll say, smooth as hell, just like Snoop, 'Eazy-E, Eazy-E, Eazy-E can eat a big fat dick! Tim Dog can eat a big fat dick! Luke! Can eat a fat *diiiick*! Yeah!'"

Trey rode home with his folks, absorbing their praise for a classy, intellectual speech. He felt like a failure, numbly flashing neon letters in his head: "Moner Wins," "Braniffs Win," "Richnecks Prevail." Suddenly, the memories he had of Saint Jude were as dark as the school's halls after hours, when guys like Seneca Washington were getting done sweeping, and as blank as Jude's listing would soon be in the phone book.

The Academy was in his mind, but only as an old photograph, tattered and floating in a puddle: the picture of an infant with a "Beat Navy" button on his onesie, sitting on his father's lap in 1977, then passed in a home movie to Max, the Special Olympian who has no idea that he's holding a coward. Trey was nothing before his speech and he deserved nothing after. He changed his clothes and said goodbye to his parents, telling them that he would wait outside for his ride to the grad party.

In the pine-straw bed, where the woman from the south side once peed, he swallowed Prudence's pills and sat with his back against a tree. In the dusk, his consciousness followed the earth's turning away from the sun. As he drifted, slightly scared, he heard what he knew was God's voice, which said, "I want to see more of you, Trey."

Chapter Three: Trey's Gospel

Reggie knocked hard on the phone booth, felling loose plaster, which speckled Trey's hair as he spoke with his host father. He spun around with a bloodless face and guilty eyes, his hand gripping the receiver so tightly it spasmed away from his ear. Reggie held up a joint and a dopey smile. Trey exhaled and returned a grin.

The lobby of the Yak and Yeti, where soon-to-be-evacuated Peace Corps volunteers now stalked, was an assembly of wooden furniture and cracking leather, all kissed by a smoky residue. Trey and Reggie, though they came to Nepal in the same group of twenty-one English teachers, didn't know each other well; however, the evacuation seized in them the desire to become better acquainted before leaving the country.

It was a somber time, though most volunteers were unsurprised when the civil war brought an end to their service. Some openly wept, but most kept their feelings to themselves or among close friends. Some criticized the U.S. Ambassador (while he spoke) for giving the order to leave (when Nepal needed Peace Corps most), for selling guns to the King (a murderer himself, they said), and for being part of the Bush administration (as a career Foreign Service Officer, he wasn't). "Shame, Shame!" some of them whispered as they'd seen Michael Moore do at the Oscars. The Ambassador handled it diplomatically.

Reggie and Trey just wanted to get high. They were sad to leave, but they'd served less than a year, and because Peace Corps had halted new groups, theirs was the freshman class—new enough to dream of what came next, and free enough to not care what it was. During the evacuation, they skulked through the hotel, visiting friends and meeting volunteers from other groups, finding dark corners to smoke dope, and pulling a slot or two in the casino.

Reggie wore a walking boot on his right foot, which he earned two days before when he fell from a bunk bed at a preliminary evacuation site in Pokhara. Trey and his colleagues in the Western half of the country were sent to Nepalgunj, where they staged until accommodations could be made in Kathmandu for them to out-process. Volunteers in the East, when they got word that the gig was up, staged in Biratnagar. In total, more than one hundred people were told to pack a small bag and await further instructions, all ending up at the Yak and Yeti.

Reggie's service was easy for him to forget as he spent little time training teachers or teaching English as he was brought to Nepal to do. The Maoist rebels called strikes across the country, freezing businesses and government offices, including schools for days at a time. That, coupled with the weather in the foothills and the relaxed attitude of his partners, led him into a life of self-directed adventure, which meant visiting his fellow volunteers.

To leave site without permission was called "stealthing," and to do so, Reggie had to catch one of two buses that left Jomsom each day, then hop another in Baglung, heading either West or East depending on where his friends were posted. The first person he visited was Minnetonka Will in the town of Raj Biraj, which was in the *Terai*, a hot, fertile plain where most citizens of Nepal (and consequently, most volunteers) lived.

Will was suffering from dysentery and announced via email that he was too sick to get on a bus to go to the capital for treatment. His site-mate, Visalia Sandra called him a whiner as he sat naked under the shower, his butt wedged into the open drain, too swollen to move, blood and shit trickling. Will was vivacious despite the circumstances and sprang up to give Reggie a wet hug as Sandra left still talking trash.

"You don't have to wipe this way," he grinned, toweling off, then led his friend to the roof where they smoked a joint. He told Reggie about his local Maoists, and they joked that every town seemed to have a chapter, like the Lions Club. Weeks back, two sixteen-year-olds with guns slung over their shoulders interrupted his third-grade lesson and ordered him to stop teaching.

"We were just learning the verbs 'to go' and 'to come,'" whined Tonka.

"Next week, gerunds," said Reggie, choking and laughing on an inhale, imagining Will's class of 86 eight-year-olds gawking at his long, sweaty aura. They smoked just enough to relax without being lazy; to affirm one another without embellishing; to ridicule the Maoist conflict without dismissing it; and to understand that Park Ridge Reggie's visit would end after a night of good company.

From the roof the sun went down like a coin into a slot, and they felt as if they could be somewhere between Milwaukee and Madison, swatting mosquitoes, counting fireflies. They were both raised in *Wonder-Years*-like suburbs outside of Chicago and Minneapolis; however, they were self-aware enough to not claim to be from the cities themselves, slightly ashamed that middle class white kids were *never* from the cities, even if their parents worked there. Tonka credited Reggie's visit with a sudden improvement in his bacterial infection, though antibiotics had arrived by courier two days prior.

The next day, Reggie walked across town to Visalia Sandra's, crushing her with the same filial verve he released on Will. He put it out of his mind that Sandra and Will hated each other; that Sandra would leave laughing while Will oozed blood in the shower; and that Will would likely push her in front of a rickshaw if he could make it look like an accident. Reggie loved them both, which was a miracle of geometry.

He and Sandra hugged often. The way she held him, Redge knew she wanted more, but the way he held her left no doubt that she was a sister to him. His talents for platonic touch were legendary in their Peace Corps group. He had the superpower of inducing small bits of palpable electricity into the fingers of those he high fived, shoulders he brushed, backs he palmed. His love was gentle, accepting, and always on, as if it were current running through a blanket or illuminating a noble gas. It sometimes got him in trouble with his female Nepali colleagues, who were repulsed by physical touch from anyone other than their husbands.

Reggie noticed a letter on Sandra's desk, which besides her mosquito-netted bed, was the only other piece of furniture in her concrete room. The paper lay like Bathsheba, with pen strokes as pretty as knees bent, curves all around, and ink flow inlaid eyes, nipples, pubis and toes; a breeze from the fan and the open window keeping her cool. He couldn't take his eyes off it.

"It's from Trey," Sandra said. "Where is his site again?"

"Out west. Indian border. Good letter?"

"Strange letter. You can read it. He's so open when he writes. So different than in person! And I can't believe he remembered all those things I said." She smiled bashfully.

Reggie took the paper and lay on her bed, feeling the familiar Peace Corps-issued linen under him. Sandra nestled into his shoulder as he read while the fan chunked through the morning air. Sandra's host mom knocked on the door to offer them tea, which they refused.

Dear Sandra,

I thought about the story from your father's restaurant back home, and I could visualize the man begging for a job after he was fired from the dairy. I tried to imagine it objectively, but it was impossible. I saw how short he was, how dark his skin was. I could see the desperation in his eyes when he said, "I have a visa!" in Spanish, while your dad, even though he spoke Spanish himself answered in English. Would immigration even care in a farm town like Visalia?

My dad romanticizes the California lore of Cannery Row, Grapes, and Travels with Charley, but he misses the misery of the people who inspired it. I don't think he's ignorant, but he does choose to ignore sadder cases in favor of the glory of the Golden State….he accepts that a lot of miners died in the gold rush, a lot of workers never made it in other industries as well. He would love you and your dad as "self-made, first-generation," though I fear his praise would seem patronizing.

In between the Air Force and P.C. I worked in a bakery in San Pedro. My Grammy had just died, and I moved in with Papa who was confused without her. Six days a week, I got up at 2 a.m. with a cigarette on Pop's porch, staring at LA Harbor. It gave me butterflies that people never stopped working down there, that I too was working while the streetlights changed though no traffic passed. I wasn't making very much money, but after four years of babysitting nuclear weapons underground in my pajamas, I embraced the idea that 6 hours x 9 dollars minus taxes equaled pay. In the nuke business I had no idea why they paid me.

It was a small miracle for our family that the Air Force had a thing called "stop loss," which made us wait a certain period of time before fully separating from active duty. Though I was one of hundreds of schlubs who watched nukes, it took them six months to realize I wasn't needed for the war in Iraq. So, in that half year between Air Force and Peace Corps, I was available to move in with Papa (my parents live on the East coast, so they couldn't help).

At the bakery, I worked with Armando and Antonio, who were brothers, and Felix, who was older. They called each other "cabron" in a chummy way, and even the owner got in on it, calling Felix "pinche Felix," which I thought was hilarious. But those guys took it way too far. Armando and Antonio would sneak up on Felix to sodomize him with carrots and rolling pins, and sometimes they held him down and simulated rape. Felix resisted as if it was real, while Armando bit his shoulder as he pumped, and Antonio laughed while trying to hold him. Armando told me how many times he had sex with his wife the night before, usually about a half dozen, which seemed superhuman considering he got to work at 230. He also bragged about his "girlfriends," and asked me how many I had, expressing disappointment when I said, "solo una." When work was over, they shouted, "Vaminos! A la verga!" which was the only way I knew it was time to go.

Bill, the owner, yelled at them like dogs. When things were going well, he laughed and called them putos in a friendly way, even let them play ranchero music (Armando replaced every other word in the songs with "chingada," which annoyed Felix, who was old school). When things were bad, Bill cursed in English and threw pots and pans. I only cleaned and did odd jobs, so I usually avoided his wrath, though I knew he didn't like me.

After the Christmas rush, during which work began at 7 pm and went till noon the next day, I got really sick, so bad that I couldn't even smoke. The illness lasted through the new year. Bill called every day, sometimes at 2 am, but every day I felt sicker and sicker, until I realized I was sick of working at the bakery, sick of Bill, sick on behalf of the guys I worked with (even though they seemed perfectly happy). By then stop loss had ended and PC had given me a country and a departure date, so I quit. When I dropped by to pick up my last check, one of the girls who worked the front said, "We heard you were the only one who didn't get the Christmas bonus, sorry." It was the least of my concerns, as I was getting ready for Nepal, but hearing it from her made me a bit sad. "White guys just aren't suited to working for Bill," she said, trying to cheer me up.

Felix, Armando, and Antonio had been in the country off and on for years, but they were "mojado" as they described it. Bill exploited it in the way he talked down to them. It wasn't just seniority. I could recognize that kind of hierarchy from the Air Force. Bill had something more, something unsaid over them. Armando and Antonio worked to support their kids, to woo women, and to support the mothers of their kids. Felix, who was in his fifties, had a son, but it was a long time ago, and now all he did besides bake was drink and drive his Mustang Cobra.

Boy, could he bake. With flour in his mustache, he rolled challah ropes, squeezed macaroons, split wedding cakes with fishing line; he cranked donuts into the grease bath and flipped them with huge chop sticks, whisked up chocolate and custard as fast as any machine. He could smell cookies when they were done, and he'd shout at us, "guyetas afueras, cabrones!" He was grizzled, but always kind to me, never called me cabron, only guey, which I took as a compliment.

One day, I pumped custard into the eclairs when they were still too hot, curdling them, and Bill got so pissed that he threw one in my direction. I laughed to keep from crying. "Not fucking funny," I think he said walking away. Felix saw how distraught I was and came over to me and said, "This is not good," some of the only English he knew. My eyes locked with his and….then Armando bent him over, screaming "Tome es! Tome es!" while Antonio held Felix's face into his crotch. As Felix squirmed and said cabron, the éclair slid down the wall like brains in a gangster movie.

That morning, I went home and had an early lunch with Papa. He was diabetic, but I always brought him his favorite lemon danish, which I told him was sugar free. We ate hotdogs and sauerkraut, which reminded me of when I was a kid and we'd visit Pedro in the summer, and he called hotdogs "puppies" and barked like a medium-sized dog. In my memory, it was a perfect im-animal-ation, and I asked him if he remembered those days. In the middle of the meal, he started to cry about Grammy. It was the first time. I thought of the paisley apron she wore on Sunday when we all came for pasta, I smelled her hairspray as I got one of her hugs, and I heard a Sicilian word she used to call us that meant "precious." I think Papa thought of all those things too.

Well, I just wanted to share with you what came in my head when you told the story about the man in your dad's restaurant. I think there's a ton of dumb white guys like me who live in states with lots of Hispanics, who try our hands at manual labor without risking the same things as the real working class.

Sorry if I rambled. I never told anyone in our group about Grammy. Glad I could here. Write when you can,

Trey

"Is he into you? Is this a love letter? Are you attracted to this?" Reggie nearly pushed Sandra off the bed as he asked her. He thought of his own grandmother who'd passed so recently the memories still hurt.

"I hope not!" she semi-shrieked. "It doesn't seem *real* to me, his story. Even though I know it is. That's weird, I know. Trey is super-genuine, I think, but the way he describes the people in that letter, just doesn't seem real to me." She stood and walked to her desk, resting against it. Reggie noticed the gray bottoms of her white socks. "I don't find him attractive, no way. He's kind of—no, he's not—I don't feel anything physically for him. I'm not going to write him back, either. I don't know what to say." Reggie tried to hide his grimace at her speech.

"I was embarrassed to tell that story about my dad at the restaurant," she said. "We help the *braceros* all the time, but he couldn't do anything for that man."

"I don't think Trey was saying you didn't do all you could."

125

"But what could he mean by telling me about the bakery? And his grandma? It's so random."

"That's why I asked if there was anything romantic between you."

"Not that I know of, not from me," Sandra said. Reggie folded the letter with care to notice the kind of paper Trey used, which was unremarkable, probably bought at a local *pasal*. The ink was black gel, splayed across the page like he did it in one take: first thought, best thought. Why was it more appealing to Reggie than to the person to whom it was written? Was it something Sandra cherished but pretended not to? Would *he* keep a letter on his desk for all to see? He wished he had a letter from Trey. Maybe one waited for him at his post, where mail took longer to reach, where he seldom was.

"I'm not the only one," Sandra said. "Will got a letter too. In the same courier package." The way she mentioned Will made Reggie consider again their relationship. She *did* care for Will as her fellow volunteer, her site mate; but she wanted him to stop complaining like he was being watched on a sitcom. He should take his antibiotics—and not with alcohol or drugs. And he should put his many talents to better use, especially in the classroom. In Sandra's world, strong men could do anything, and Will was failing to be one for her. None of these observations, Reggie knew, was Sandra herself aware of.

He left her after a long hug and hurried across town to check on Will, who he found reading comfortably and "back to brown poo." Reggie had little time before the last bus to be coy about Trey's letter, so he simply asked if he could read it. Will dug it out of one of his books where it was marking a page.

Tonka,

I'm writing this on the bus. You can probably tell by my handwriting that the goddamn bus hasn't moved in an hour. "Maoists Blocking the East-West Highway Blues" should be a Dylan song. I've got the window open, my shirt is unbuttoned, and I'm panting like the family dog. People from the Karnali River stop are holding USAID rice bags filled with live fish. I can see their shadows banging against the sides. Fish are so dumb. We're all fish today.

The Abu Ghraib photos are still in Nepali news. When they were first released, I remember feeling responsible in a weird way, having just come from the military. Some people even looked at me like I knew something, as if I could explain. Now, I'm too angry to be embarrassed.

I called my dad a few days after the scandal broke. The connection was shitty at the internet café, but I really wanted to talk to him, especially concerning the torture. He and I argued in the past about Iraq (he was in favor, I was not), so I thought A.G. would give us something to rally against. I was pretty blunt, saying that after what he went through in Vietnam (six years of torture!), he should be absolutely against what happened in Iraq, right? But he cautioned me from comparing the two and tried to change the subject. I kept harping on the point, challenging him to say that torture was never ok, and then finally he snapped and said "if some raghead has information about another attack, I don't care how we get it out of him!" I'm not sure if it was the connection, but I thought I heard his voice crack. I left it alone.

In 1996, when I was at the Academy, they called a surprise assembly during academic call to quarters, which was usually our untouchable time. Though we jostled in our seats, and most people were pissed off that they had to change back into their uniforms, we knew it was serious. "This better be good," we all thought. The Dean walked on stage in full service dress. He was tall and had all of his hair. He spoke with a Bronx accent in a somewhat high voice, and we were all scared shitless of him. He was old school—class of 1961—one of the first grads of the Academy. He knew my dad, who graduated a year after.

He held a book in his hand. We could hear him tapping it with his fingers: Robert McNamara's memoirs. He said that the former Secretary of Defense was amoral and flippant about the damage and deaths he was mostly responsible for in Vietnam. McNamara, he said, lacked even the basic capacity to practice ethics, which was something they drilled into us hard—just as hard as all the engineering. He talked about the classmates and friends he lost in Vietnam, and warned us to take seriously our decision to serve our country. And then he left the stage.

I had actually met the dean a couple of weeks before, under considerably worse circumstances, after I was recommended for disenrollment due to shitty grades and some other things. He retained me, but in his office he raised that high voice until I thought it would crack. He told me what a hero my dad was, and just as I was about to burst into tears, he said in a Bronx-ish DeNiro brogue, "None of that! There is *none* of that!" I walked out of there feeling like a pussy that had failed its pap smear.

I went back to my room afraid to feel happy that I wasn't kicked out. Did I deserve to stay? I knew others who were booted for much less than my infractions. I thought back to memories of playing catch in the back yard with my dad. When I was young and didn't know better, I got frustrated because he couldn't throw overhand. He'd just flip it and the ball stopped short of me, and I'd have to pick it up. One day, I asked in a snotty way why he couldn't throw the ball "normally," and he explained how the torture had permanently fucked up his arms and that flipping underhand was the best he could do. You'd think guilt like that would have made me a better cadet, a better person.

Sorry to unload all that. You were such a good listener when we were staging in Seattle, and I've never met anyone who could spout philosophy like you. I mean, I don't even know who High-digger or Vikkenstein are, much less what they said. I kick myself for not yet doing something courageous in life, something that would even the score with my dad, measure up, you know? But that's unrealistic. Is it also unrealistic to think we'll ever avoid flippant, amoral engagements like Vietnam or travesties like Abu Ghraib?

I hope you are well, my friend,

Trey

Reggie scurried to the internet café, googling as quickly as dial-up would permit, "Vietnam POW torture." As he read and clicked and waited for photos and accounts to load, dryness crept into his mouth to realize that he knew someone who was born to someone who underwent such things. He missed his bus and crashed with Tonka, who was happy to have him for another night.

In the hotel, Trey followed Reggie, limping in mimicry to the room where volunteers were de-stemming and seeding the weed they'd smuggled into the capital. From there, they smoked on the balcony of any empty room, which had been propped open by a towel muzzling the doorknobs. Trey stared at Reggie like a Cheshire Cat, his eyes dilating into the dusk. Reggie avoided eye contact lest he reveal to Trey that he'd read nearly every letter he sent to the other volunteers.

"Ok man," Trey began, "I don't know anything about you as a *primary source*, but people in our group, almost unanimously, think you're a saint."

"'And all the sinners, saints!'" Reggie sang.

"It's true. Tonka says you were a badass hockey player, that despite your slender frame, you were a bullish crosschecker and the fastest on the ice."

"I'm a hockey guy, yes."

"But your mom, again, according to Tonka, said you couldn't play anymore after so many concussions?"

"That's what happens when your mother is a nurse."

"So, I heard you turned your attention to music."

"I'm a music man, yes."

"But not playing it."

"True."

"Listening."

"And sharing."

"Yes! Iris told me your second suitcase is full of bootlegged concerts, many you recorded yourself all over Chicagoland—*saacho?*"

"True. Saacho. Yes."

"Half a *dozen* people in our group, no less, likely more, have gone on and on about concerts you played for them. You transformed them, Redge, I swear, to hear them tell it."

"Concerts can be such experiences."

"You played that REM one for me."

"El Salvador is a small country…."

"What I like is that you just stuck it in my Discman and walked away. And the way I was feeling at that time, it was what I needed. Some people want to be the ones to hold your hand through a concert. They want you to be thankful to them for the experience."

"You're welcome."

"I believe you. I also believe Jackie when she calls you Clark Kent."

"She does?"

"Yes. She says that you are a true teacher, born of something extraterrestrial, and when you step into that classroom, there is nothing to stop you, no speeding bullets or local motives."

"What about local Maoists?"

"Man, those Maoists! I want to hate them. But I believe in their cause." Reggie nodded.

In the Autumn dusk at the Yak and Yeti, Reggie relaxed in his rapport with Trey, which was a product of his imagination more than a state they'd cultivated over time. Reggie knew Trey by his letter writing, not in the flesh, which doubly excited him now that they were alone. It was as if Trey saw himself as a mosaic, and then jumped from a table, shattered, and couriered the shards to the others. Having read Trey's letters, only Reggie knew how the pieces could fit back together.

"It's a kick, Redge. These Euro trekkers in their *Crate and Barrel* body suits and yak wool feather boas, eating their electrolyte bars, stage here for the go-ahead to base camp. They're leaving, we're leaving. Sucks." Reggie nodded, Trey continued nervously.

"I'll bet they blow money in the *Thamel* bars, probably sleep with the *randis*, maybe some of the prostitutes Peace Corps works with. I met a girl in another group yesterday, a health volunteer, who ran a program teaching the randis how to put condoms on with their teeth. U.S. Government funding! Dig *that* George Bush!" Reggie laughed but stayed quiet. Trey licked his lips and continued.

"You know, maybe some dipshits in Congress are gonna read about these programs years later, and some guy—from the south, of course—is gonna be on CSPAN at two a.m., like, 'and, yes, Mr. Chairman, I have here documents from a *Peace Corps* program in Nepal in which volunteers taught teenage prostitutes how to affix prophylactics to their clients' *penises*!"

"With their teeth."

"I wonder if they need guinea pigs," Trey said, "You know, to practice with the condoms? Bananas can get expensive this time of year." Reggie laughed again, harder this time, patting Trey on the shoulder, guessing that he often made such jokes to keep from crying.

He didn't know how to tell Trey all he'd seen in the letters, how reading them felt like opening up a cavity to observe pumping guts, a pleural sheath, everything pink and vital. Reggie wanted to reassure Trey that he knew he was flawed, that he loved how vividly he struggled.

Reggie also feared that Trey was capable of leaving Nepal and never talking to any of them again. He was genial and full of energy, like a jukebox with a great collection of songs, but he could be easily unplugged and moved to another bar.

"Do you miss your students?" Trey asked.

"We rarely had school. There were strikes, local holidays. A lot of the time they didn't even show up. You?"

"We had a lot of strikes too, but I got to teach a fair amount, which was really hard. It was so hot in those goddamn classrooms, with all them kids. I won't ever forget one kid, Shiv. He'll likely symbolize my time here."

"What was he like?"

"He was a fourth grader, among the ninety in my class, crammed together, girls on one side, boys on the other, you know the drill. There was something 'off' with him. He kept blurting out, and the whole class would laugh. And shit, with 90 kids, I was lucky to teach one noun a day. 90 of them laughing sounded like road construction.

"I tried to roll with it. I brought him up to the board to do examples. I politely told him to 'chup.' One day, it's hot as shit, I've got sweat and chalk—goddamn, I hated that combination—sweat and chalk—running down my arms as I taught, running back into my armpits as I wrote on the board. He blurted again, and the laughter of the 90 in their light blue, government school blouses with their faces scrubbed so hard they looked like they had acne, trampled on my one noun for the fucking day.

"I marched out and asked my partner teacher for help with discipline. When he came in, half of their eyes looked down, the other half got as big as golf balls. He brought Shiv outside, and I am thinking to myself, 'finally, this will set him straight.' The teacher had Shiv point at a branch on a tree, then he ripped it down, and beat the shit out of him. I felt terrible!

"But the whole time he's catching this ass-whoopin,' he's still blurting—well, screaming now—the word that made the kids laugh: 'Khalo lado! Khalo lado!' over and over, only this time, the kids are not laughing, and Shiv is crying and sore as he walks back into class.

"Later, one of my better students, who spoke pretty good English, told me that Shiv was 'mad,' which was their way of saying retarded.   I did some research and talked to some of his other teachers, and I realized that he was severely autistic. So, fuck me, right? I'm the worst teacher ever. I'll miss old Shiv and his blurting."

"What does 'khalo lado' mean?" Reggie asked. "I don't recognize the phrase."

"Oh, it means 'black dick.' As in big black cock." Reggie laughed, snotting into his beard, and said, "Guess that was your noun for the day."

"Adjective too. It's funny as hell to think about as a curse. Apparently, it's the worst thing you can say in Nepali. I should have known, because every time I told the Nepalis where I was born, 'Colorado,' they snickered. I had no idea Shiv was special needs! Should have investigated, but he just seemed like a class clown. He had such a devious grin. It was so hot I couldn't think. I'm not a teacher like you."

Reggie relaxed, inviting Trey to ape his body language. The Shiv story got them closer to Trey the letter-writer, who Reggie hoped to coax out. It was an emotional trick to tell the sad tale of Shiv's beating, while also leaving room to laugh about a kid who blurted *black dick*. It was likewise a talent for Reggie to balance his laughter with a kind understanding, which conveyed to Trey a few things, that: teaching is difficult; it was an honest mistake with Shiv, and; corporal punishment is hard to accept, even as a guest in a foreign country.

As the weed took effect, Reggie could tell that Trey was not used to being high, noting how he compensated for his lack of experience by saying things in an exaggerated stoner voice.

"You know, man. Even this high, the Cubs are still shitty. Maybe that's how Harry Caray has such a good time up there."

"Remind me, please, how you are a Cubs fan?" Reggie loved having a favorite baseball team in common, but to meet fans from outside of Chicagoland made him curious; and with Trey, it seemed like a neat detail that he would have included in one of his letters.

"When my dad retired from the Air Force, we moved back to South Carolina, but Hurricane Hugo put a tree through our house. We were stuck for like two months in a hotel, and the only channel we had was…."

"WGN!"

"Channel 9, Chicago's Superstation!" They high-fived.

Reggie smiled, the idea of "the last night" still exciting him, as if he were on a stealth visit to Trey's site, a trip he never made while serving. No one knew or cared where they were: a small balcony looking across the courtyard of a hotel full of sad, stoned, nearly former Peace Corps volunteers. The man sitting before Reggie was not yet the writer whose letters he read over the last few months. Still, the filial draw was never stronger.

The duo coddled a long silence, passing the joint back and forth. Reggie's high made memories cascade, taking him above the smog of Kathmandu valley, past prayer flags whipping, nearly loosed from stupa frames, their colors like the icons—bell, cherry, bar—spinning at the Yak and Yeti casino. The sky changed from brown to blue, and the air blew hotter as he descended from the foothills feet first, his walking boot removed, landing atop a rainbow-painted *Tata* bus as it bumbled toward Dharan and Dhankuta, where he visited Daly City Jackie and Hammond Iris.

The *Tata* buses were never new. Like nursing home residents, they received just enough care to keep them running, to keep the money coming in. Their horns bleated swansongs at everything in the way, their unsleek chassis dust caked. Under the dust, paintings of gods and Devanagari phrases stretched the length and width, as taut as skin, as distinguishable as skin, identifying the bus as Hindu in the Hindu Kingdom of Nepal. They spewed bad gas, the smell of cities in films from the 1970s. It was the odor of a country without oil, without even the ability to refine it, dependent on a Southern neighbor, India, which was in many ways much poorer.

No one was more traveled on the *Tatas* than Park Ridge Reggie Plante. Besides standing out as usually the lone white person on the bus, he looked like an earnest John Lennon, a kind Beatle: the beard, glasses, and hair shoulder length, united by his soft eyes and softer voice. The Nepalis fawned over him, handing him their children, who tugged his hair and touched his skin, to whom he read simple English books during long trips. Out the window, Reggie interpreted a half-built, half-destroyed landscape peppered with trees haphazardly growing and partially slashed on the sides of washed-out, filled-in, washed-out roads. When there was a stretch of smooth highway, it was usually accompanied by a sign giving credit to either the Japanese or Danish development agencies. He spent time on his rides considering the volunteers he was visiting, some who knew he was coming, some were surprised when he arrived; all opened their rooms, and most gave him their beds.

Hammond Iris nuzzled Reggie at every opportunity, because he was kind and cool, because he was a teacher like her, and a Midwesterner who'd escaped. She was a self-admitted "fag hag," who tried to convince her soft male friends—Reggie included—that they were secretly gay. Reggie parried her provocations calmly, explaining that he was not attracted to men, which Iris accepted with disappointment. He remembered a bus ride during training in which Iris and Trey listened to music together, singing out loud at times, bringing her to such boisterous delight that she dramatically prodded him to "come out," to admit that he was gay. Trey quickly grew quiet and switched seats at the next bathroom stop.

"Ray-gee," she purred as he crossed her threshold.

"Hello, Iris," he said with a solemn smile, then gave a flat hug. Iris overcompensated.

"Oh, come on, Rage! Ray-gee, Rage, Ray-genald!" she yelled into his beard and nuzzled his neck. Her perfume was nice smelling after the bus. "Is this about Biratnagar? I wanted you to feel better! So I sent you to the bar. You're still sore?" Her face was frozen in a glad-to-see-you pose.

"Iris, my grandmother died, and I couldn't leave for the funeral. I invited you for company while I was grieving."

"Well, I thought you looked pathetic just laying in bed. You were too heartbroken to even listen to your music, Reggie! I knew it was serious!" More crushing than the actual death was the silly Peace Crops bureaucracy which forbade volunteers to leave during training, else be separated from the program. To Reggie, it was the ultimate evil algorithm, a garbage in—garbage out sentence of despair.

"You invited your host brother to *my* room!"

"Ugh, that was a mistake! He kept wanting me to go down on him." Iris made a sour face.

"Yeah, I came back to a locked door that *you* wouldn't answer."

"Like I said, a big mistake, Redge. I am sorry." Reggie knew she regretted inviting the brother, not locking him out of his room, but he hugged her again and they went out to the bazaar. He learned about her classroom (dark but adequate), her students (most great, some problem children), and her love life (non-existent).

"But I have been thinking about someone," she said slyly.

"Another host brother?"

"Nooooo…. someone in our group, someone I didn't think much of until he wrote me a letter." Reggie ignored her hint, knowing that he would have to if he wanted to read Trey's writing. At a café, he bought a couple *Tuborgs* and a plate of momos and led her through the familiar jokes all volunteers told each other: that the turmeric spice was turning their right hands yellow, while the Nepali toilets sans paper were turning their left hands brown. They discussed feces—theirs and other's for a solid half hour—before heading back to Iris' apartment, where she made tea while Reggie rolled a joint.

He told her about the masked teenagers with slung guns who shook down his bus every five kilometers, wondering if they were Maoists or just kids, or if it mattered. Iris paid vague attention.

"Tell me who else you've visited! I know I wasn't your first. Was I?!" she asked with a Betty Boop incredulity. He told her he'd seen Manitou Suzanne, and that she was serious with *her* host brother. Suzanne received a straightforward mailer from Trey, which talked about his love of Manitou Springs when he was a cadet, admitting that he was drawn to the "dark arts" despite being a regular churchgoer.

He also dropped in on Sugarland Vivek, who refused to share his Trey letter, though he mentioned it with bile in his mouth. He said he hated Trey, but would not elaborate, and he quit Peace Corps soon after. Iris was delighted with the gossip Reggie brought to her, as if it was a newspaper and he a creature who retrieved such things. She smacked her lips after swigging a water bottle full of half lemons the size of ping pong balls.

"I wanna get out West," she said, stretching in a half yoga pose.

"West? Super hot! Why?"

"To visit Trey."

"Trey Ciuri, the Air Force guy. Have you heard from him?"

"He's the one who wrote me the letter! I thought he hated me after that thing on the bus…." She stared into the sky to visualize the ride.

"What happened on the bus? All I remember is our back wheel hanging over the cliff when we took those mountain turns."

"That was freaky as hell, Rage! I thought we were dead! I knew it would be over soon!" She paused to suck some spit back into her mouth. "But it wasn't," she said sweetly. "And then I got this letter." She patted the fiber purse hanging around her neck.

"Good stuff?" he asked.

"I wouldn't call it *good*, but he *needs* me. He may even *want* me!" She lay flat on the roof, rustling minute gravel, then popped back up. "Do you want to read it?!"

"Well, it sounds intriguing," Reggie said with nonchalant poise. He imagined recording with electric eyes and then measuring it against the others.

Dearest Eye,

The man in the flight suit you saw at the Embassy is Walt Oneida. We were classmates at the Academy, and until I saw him that day, I had forgotten how well I knew him. But that's military school for you: a bunch of dudes huddled together for dear life while everyone yells at you. You learn a lot about each other.

Oneida is not his real last name. It's something Ukrainian, but his dad picked it from a town in New York, thinking it was Irish, more American (ironically, it's <u>Native</u> American). To emigrate, his family pretended to be Jewish, which he said a lot of people did to escape the Soviet Union in those days. His dad was trained as an engineer, but he had to drive a cab, and they grew up with very little.

Oneida was in fact one of the few lower middleclass cadets at the Academy. He dressed up nicer than the rest of us to go out to places like Chilis and Applebees, which guys made fun of, not realizing what a treat it was for him. He never used ATMs to avoid the fees, instead he stood in line at the cadet store and wrote checks for $5-10 over when he needed cash. Once, while we were listening to music, I yanked open the tray of his CD player, which ground the gears a bit, and he flipped out. The other guys made fun of him, but he was pissed because it cost him so much money, which to us wasn't that expensive.

He was from Neptune, New Jersey, by the shore. He bragged in a heavy accent about delivering pizzas in high school, "awl ovah E Street!" where Bruce Springsteen is from. He was racist in an immigrant's way, not like I remember from my youth in South Carolina. An immigrant doesn't trust or like anyone who's not part of their tribe, even other white people. In the South, they've rigged a system against blacks (some would say poor whites too). He actually had a fascination with black people, especially hip-hop culture. He used the N-word a lot, but it was "nigga," not the actual word. Again, the way he said it was different than I remember the rednecks in South Carolina using it. Perhaps you also heard similar things growing up in Indiana?

He was quiet with most people, but not me for some reason. He was uncool, not handsome, though very witty, and built like a tank. 6 feet 2 inches of pure muscle, but he wore clothes that were either too tight or too short. I had no idea why he liked me so much. I honestly didn't think that I was witty enough to keep up with him. I spent my time at the Academy skirting the rules and skipping class. My grades were horrible! Oneida, on the other hand, was an Instructor Pilot, and got near perfect marks in Mechanical Engineering.

Every time we hung out he dazzled and scared me with his insights, personal as they were. He complained about being a virgin, moaning that only "fat chicks" dug him. I'd say I was sorry, but I wasn't comfortable enough to admit that girls weren't into me at all. (I wasn't a virgin, but the circumstances of losing my virginity were sketchy, not sexy.) He talked about his "niggas" in Neptune who loved fat white girls (apparently New Jersey has a surplus). But they didn't love the girls themselves, only their asses. They'd discuss, almost academically as he retold it, the pros and cons of these obese derrieres. In a New Jersey accent, these were pretty funny accounts.

But he didn't stop there! He also knew many of the girls who'd been freaked by the black guys, and he impersonated them with wheedling noises: their disbelief that a man could pay so much attention to them, granted just one part, but still—until then they'd been ashamed of their figures. Whenever Oneida saw a girl with a fat ass (the Academy also had a surplus), he'd say TBM-WTTU (The Black Man Would Tear That Up), which we adopted as another military school acronym.

He told me that he sent money home from his paltry cadet salary (we made like $200/month), and that broke my heart, though he wasn't looking for sympathy. He shared with me that he had to go to prep school to get into the Academy, and again, I felt guilty because I got in on the first try. I wanted in turn to tell him that I was ashamed to have a father who was a war hero (whose name was written all over the Academy walls) which likely got me special treatment. But I couldn't say it. I hated it. I hated myself. I think he knew though, the way he'd try to hang out with just me even though we kept different circles of friends. I remember pushing him away multiple times, loosely promising we'd see a movie later or grab a meal at the dining hall, then doing something else. It hurt his feelings, which again pushed me away for some reason. But no matter what I did to Walt, he still liked me, still gave me the benefit of every doubt.

It was a total surprise when we saw each other here at the Embassy. Our loud reunion was genuine. I hugged him hard and asked silently for forgiveness. I mean, he's doing fine, of course. He doesn't need <u>me</u> for anything. He's an A-10 pilot (look up the plane if you're curious—it's a beast and their pilots are a lot cooler than fighter guys), and now he's been selected to work at the Embassy in Nepal after only 6 years on active duty? Pretty cool.

Me? I was an idiot missileer in the Air Force. Only the dumbest, least accomplished officers get nukes—that was me—and now I'm wearing Birkenstocks in Nepal, set to save the world. Oneida wasn't surprised at all to find me here, and I recognized a brotherly look in his eyes that seemed happy to find me out of the AF orbit, that I was cutting a different path now. I too was happy that he'd become so successful, that he likely didn't worry about money (or girls) anymore.

Whew. That was stream of consciousness. I hope it made sense.

I got a little flustered on the bus at your insistence that I *had* to have a favorite Tori Amos song (and that I come out of the closet). You were so in-my-face that I felt uncomfortable and had to withdraw. I am sorry that you took it so personally. Your disappointment reminded me a bit of Oneida when I would pull away from him. Now that I've had time to think about it, I do have a favorite Tori song: "And they say Marianne killed herself, and I said, 'Not a chaaaance, not a chance.'" I can see you smiling as you read this, then singing the lyric, and now playing it on your headphones.

Another aside: my best friend and roommate in college was a guy named Wade Herndon, a true renaissance man, but a fuckup in the eyes of the Academy, just like me. He was smarter than I was, more coordinated, a man with dozens of legitimate skills (fixing cars, playing piano, drawing), he was better with girls. I felt more confident when we hung out. We got into so much trouble, we barely graduated.

One weekend night, probably around three in the morning, I looked down from my bed unit to see Wade and his girlfriend going at it on the floor. I quickly went through the five stages of catching your roommate fucking:

1.   Irritation: It's 3 a.m. goddamnit!

2.   Curiosity: Jesus, he's really putting it to her. She was biting a t-shirt to keep quiet….I think one of mine;

3.   Arousal: This is better than porn!

4.   Deviousness: If I move my head to the right angle I can catch the show.

5.   Shame: When she opened her eyes to see me ogling her impalement, she spit out the shirt and screamed, "Face the wall!"

It freaked Wade out so bad he jumped up (all 6'5", 250 pounds of him), whacked his head on a chair, and puked all over my desk. The girl ran back to her room, and Wade started cleaning the puke (with my shirt), mumbling, "Sorry buddy, sorry buddy." I may have pretended to be mad, I can't remember, but I got dressed to go have a smoke (and escape the puke smell).

It was snowing in half the sky with a full moon in the other half, a uniquely Coloradoan beauty. I laughed to myself about Wade as I looked down from the terrazzo at everything being whitened. From behind, Oneida's voice surprised me. "Don't jump," he said. I wasn't thinking of jumping, but maybe I looked that way? Did he know that I struggled with suicide in the past? Who is this guy who can appear even in the middle of the night in the secret places I liked to smoke alone?

I still struggle with suicide. I wonder if everyone does. I don't want to talk about it because it's such a red flag for everything gainful in society. (I certainly would never have gotten a Top Secret security clearance had the Air Force known.) When it hits, a darkness overcomes me…. it changes life from an intriguing labyrinth with many paths into the linear desire to die. I am unable to please anyone, inept to help anyone, and I am disgusted to see myself. So, that's my long-winded way of sharing my favorite Tori Amos song. Sorry if it's too heavy. I am looking for peace here. Love, Trey

Reggie exhaled as if he had been holding his breath through the whole letter.

"Reggie, please forgive me," Iris pleaded. "I don't want to see you this way anymore,"

"Forgive you for what?"

"Sleeping with my host brother in your bed."

"You slept with him?"

"I had to. He wouldn't leave me alone."

"That's not what's bothering me. But it does now that I know. I would have changed the sheets."

"What's wrong then?"

"Trey. He sounds sad, maybe not sad at this very moment, but capable of great sadness."

"Aren't we all capable of great sadness?"

"For specific reasons, for a grandmother passing away, perhaps while you are trapped in a foreign country, and locked out of the only peaceful place you could find by a friend you hoped would comfort you, but instead is having sex with her host brother."

"That was sad, lemme tell you." She held up her pinky finger and made it move like a worm.

"But Trey seems as if he is capable of sadness at any time and for a variety of reasons."

"You're reading into it. We've all considered suicide, right?" Iris didn't wait for a response. "He was just all Tori-Amosy, that's all. He's gonna break up with that girl in America. He wants me, I can feel it." She grabbed her crotch.

"I wish I knew him better," he said. They sat on the roof until the stars came out.

In the morning, Reggie hopped a minibus to Dharan, where Daly City Jackie sang his name standing on one foot as she answered the door. He eyed her quickly, then tried to convince himself he was not attracted to her. The Nepalis said she looked too much like them to be an American, giggling and pretending to claim her as their own.

As giving as she was radiant, Jackie knitted clothes for her host siblings, and arranged for large donations from Northern California to be minor-miraculously greased through Nepal's hapless bureaucracy to the schools in her town: baseball equipment, eyeglasses, books and toys.

Reggie inventoried Jackie's host family, a standard middleclass unit, who lived in a concrete house of four rooms: a kitchen, a common area, and two bedrooms (one for Jackie, one for the family). The roof sprouted rebar, dripping like rusty dreadlocks from the four corners of the structure, and a black water tank with skinny pipes running inside and out to the garden where the *charpi* and the shower head were stationed. On the walls, Jackie's host father mounted two *khukuris*, crossed like Saudi swords; her sister hung posters of white babies making adult-like looks at the camera with badly conjured motivational captions; and on the front door, her host mother had molded a swastika out of cow dung. The TV was the shape of a moving box. It sat on a trunk covered by a shawl.

Jackie introduced Reggie to Dharan like she was the city's gracious girlfriend, noting that it was the fashion capital of Nepal, home to hundreds of retired Gurkha soldiers (including her host dad), who were rumored to be the best fighters in the world. Here they spent their British pensions on ice cream and their grandchildren. Though the town was a stone's throw from Biratnagar, a sweltering city of millions, Dharan seemed cooler in temperature and character. Her host father said it was because no Indians lived there.

They walked the bazaar, mostly in silence, then returned to Jackie's room.

"Reggie, I rejoice in your stealthing!" she said.

"I need the human contact. If I can't teach…."

"What are they like?"

"Who?"

"The other volunteers. Now that they're at post—are they the same as when we met?"

"Most are fitting into the stereotype: 'the toughest job you'll ever love, the longest vacation you'll ever hate.'"

"Do you think that makes it easier? Do you think I do that?"

"I think you resist through your kindness. I think Trey resists too."

"He scares me."

"What's frightening about Trey?"

"He fits in with all of us, but he's completely alone."

"Let me guess….he wrote you a letter."

"You too?"

"Not me. Not yet. May I?"

"It's over there. Yes."

Dear Jackie,

I'm ridiculously pleased at how many Californians (even NorCallies :) we have in our group! I think I freaked out Sandra and

Veena and Matt with my Golden State pride, but living so far away, I just can't hide it. Plus Nepalis love Hotel California! Why, I have no idea.

Maybe it's because I wasn't raised there. My dad's military career took us everywhere but San Pedro, the town where he and my mom grew up, met, married, and moved away from. It was always a mythical land, one we visited every summer, a place where my cousins wore strange but cool clothes: I remember Vans shoes and white socks of random lengths up their calves. My dad's folks (Papa and Grammy) still live there.… well, <u>lived</u>. Grammy died about a year ago. They kept us together, cooking pasta every Sunday, staying up with our lives no matter how far away we were.

Papa is a retired fire captain who cooked for his shift (pasta, of course). He has stereotypes for every ethnic group in LA, which are pretty offensive, especially in today's politically correct world. My dad blames it on the time in which he was raised—Depression-era—immigrants everywhere you looked. Without labels you didn't survive, he said.   Whenever one of my cousins brought a girl to pasta, Papa's first question was, "Is she Italian?" Statistically, the answer was usually 'no,' and he'd follow with "Is she Catholic?" The second question he asked on behalf of Grammy, who was much more devout than him.

One group of people he always admired was Filipinos. He said they took a beating when they came to California, but they worked hard and they went to Mass. More often than Italians! I confess that when I found out you were of Filipino descent, I liked you more than if you had been of some other background. At Mary Star, our church in San Pedro, we do Simbang Gabi every year! I didn't hesitate to ask you to go to

Mass with me on that first Sunday, though I know I surprised you with my forwardness. I'm glad that you went.

I'm an ok Catholic, but I've always battled a skepticism of the people who created the church: the gospel writers and the priests who followed. Sometimes I wonder if they created God as well—as if they were a bunch of Platos making up Socrates. Apart from that, I'm often worried about why some people have so much and most people have so little. It's made me angry with God, feeling unworthy of being so comfortable while everyone else struggles.

I saw it in South Carolina, where I grew up on the right (read: white) side of a near-Apartheid state (I'm dramatizing a bit, but it's seriously racist). In the Air Force, I served in Lompoc, which held so many people dependent on the prison industry that it reeked of stagnation, rot and regret. And in Cheyenne, the frontier poverty and loneliness really brought me down. I've always wanted to help to change things, but normal sign-a-check giving or volunteer hours charity didn't feel like enough.

Something happened to me when I was confirmed, when I became "an adult in the church." I was 16 years old, what did I know? But after that day, I noticed that in Mass, there was always a woman, a mother, definitely a caricature of Mary, sitting close to me. During the exchange of peace, she gushed, embracing everyone, saying, "Peesh be wiff you," like it hurt her to pronounce the words, like she had to really count out the peace she was giving away, as if it were finite (and judging by today's world, isn't it finite?).

English was not her native language, but where was she from? Her complexion was impossible to decode, the accent was like

Esperanto or Klingon. She looked poor, and I feared that she would die poor. I urged myself to ask her if that was ok, or if she wanted to improve herself financially, and that I could help. Or was God enough? I first saw her in South Carolina, and then in various churches in California, in Colorado Springs during college, and I expected to see her in Kathmandu the day we went to mass, but she wasn't there. I'll keep looking.

Grammy's piety and Papa's cynicism usually avoided collisions. Gram went to daily mass and perpetual adoration afterward, while Papa joked behind her back (usually to his male grandkids), "if you have to go to church every day, there's something wrong with you." He ushered on Sundays; he received Communion, went to confession once a month, pretty standard for his ethnicity. He sometimes alluded to the fact that what he saw as a fireman made him angry at God who let such things happen. But one day, Papa and Grammy switched places.

In the Fall of last year, my Auntie Donna, herself a devout Catholic and daily Mass goer, could not lift the gospel book during the opening procession. Her bone cancer was so advanced that doctors said it was a miracle she was walking, much less carrying a 15-pound book up the aisle every morning. When Grammy took the news, that Auntie Donna had less than two months to live, her all-trusting demeanor changed. She cried but no tears fell, they just boiled, Papa said, in the corners of her eyes, and she said over and over in what I imagined was a cold, Sicilian mantra, "Your children do not die before you, your children do not...."

Meanwhile, Papa began a Novena, and he even did adoration. He didn't make a big deal of it, he just went to church and stayed there for indiscriminate periods of time. After some intensive chemo, Auntie Donna miraculously went into remission. The cancer had claimed so much bone mass that she shrunk—from 5' 4" to 4' 8". Everyone in the family rejoiced save for Grammy, who seemed tired. A couple days later, she went to the hospital with abdominal pain, and less than a week later she was dead of previously undetected ovarian cancer.

Not long afterward, I had a chance to live with Papa before leaving for Peace Corps. We were like two sad bachelors, eating take out, watching TV, peeing with the door open. Though my dad and mom (who live on the East coast) were thankful to me for keeping Pop company, I had a nagging in my mind, which constantly filled me with doubt. Was I helping? Was I making a difference? All I did it seemed was live there. I went to work early and returned for meals. We watched reruns of Lawrence Welk and Dean Martin's "roasts" and went to bed. The voice told me I could do more, but what?

In the Air Force, I was a pretty good officer, despite being a shitty cadet at the Academy. It's actually a fairly common occurrence: there are many stories of slacker cadets becoming generals, even Senator McCain, they say, was badly-behaved at the Naval Academy. In my squadron of missileers, I took it on myself to improve everyone's morale. This I did by getting to know every single person, taking to heart their back stories, their wives' and kids' names, their plans for after missiles. (No one wanted to spend their lives in the nuclear deterrence business—those who did were honestly strange.)

One day, a squadron mate told me that his wife was forever endeared to me because I remembered her name when I ran into her at the commissary. Her kids too: I played with them and asked how their school was going, even helped them do some math while they waited for the cashier to ring up the groceries. My squadron mate looked like he would cry when he talked about how much it meant to her. It was winter in Cheyenne, when peoples' spirits were as barren as those frigid plains; and our job made us spend 24-hour shifts hundreds of miles away, a hundred feet below ground. As happy as I was that I seemed to help him and his family, the same doubting voice crept into my mind, telling me, "You didn't really help. You're just good with names, just like a politician. What did you actually give? Nothing." It was true. It was easy for me to remember names, to think of all these families serving their country, whose mission it was to aim ICBMs, which sat in silos as if in their own perpetual adoration, at "our enemies."

So, I guess what I want to say is that I am trying to find genuine ways to help people, beyond what comes easy to me. Even this letter, which I hope you take as a compliment, was easy for me to write. I don't want to give. I want to sacrifice. And I share this with you because you seem like you're figured that out, that people you engage with receive pieces of you that you can't get back, and yet you're happy to release. I feel like you have a soul that will float up to heaven when the time comes, once every last piece weighing you down has been given away.

Peesh be with you, Jacqueline, Trey

Reggie began reading in a chair, but ended laying on the floor, between paragraphs looking into the space under Jackie's bed, noting a spider web, wondering if it was inhabited.

"He thinks very highly of you. Were you close during training?" Reggie asked. Jackie blushed.

"No, we weren't. We went to mass, which *was* beautiful, but other than that one time we didn't talk. At all, really."

"He obviously noticed things about you, and I hope it doesn't bother you that I agree with him about your kindness."

"You, fine, Reggie. But not Trey! How dare he stereotype me through the lame filter of his grandfather! He probably pinned all of us down like that, probably you too. Did he write to you?" Reggie shook his head as a deeper worry wrinkled Jackie's face. "Jesus, my fobby mother says, 'Peesh' in Mass! How contrived!"

"I didn't know that could be offensive."

"It is! I knew he was trouble when he started nicknaming people."

"Oh, that was just….wasn't that harmless? A military thing? For camaraderie?"

"No. It's power! It's *Trey's* labels for people, not anything *we'd* choose. That's what people like him *do*—try to pin people like *us* down, like we're butterflies captured by Trey's genus and species. I was super happy when Veena went off on him."

Poway Veena, another Californian, took offense to Trey calling her "Veena, Warrior Princess" one night while the group drank *tumba*, which was warm, fermented millet. She embarrassed Trey in front of everyone, her voice reaching a pitch high enough to halt peripheral conversations in the small café in the hot evening. Trey ended up mumbling, "sorry" and left quickly. Reggie remembered laughing at the nickname, thinking it fit Veena perfectly as she was headstrong and thick, a rugby player at Berkeley.

"That was awkward, but I think Veena got a little too wound up. She admitted to me that tumba made her an angry drunk."

"Well, it obviously didn't stop Trey. What does he call you, "Park Ridge, Redge?""

"Yes," Reggie said with a smile. "And you don't have any pride in being Daly City Jackie? He called himself San Pedro Trey. It's hometowns. Benign, yes?"

"He's not even from Pedro!" Jackie belted.

"Is it really pronounced, 'Pedro,' with a long E?" Reggie asked.

"Yes, everyone calls it that, even Hispanics. So at least he didn't coopt *that*. He told me that it was renamed "Pee-droh" by the Italians and Croatian Catholics who settled there, after San Pietro."

"Well, that's interesting. I'm sure 'Chicago' is now pronounced differently than the way the Illini tribe said it. It's kind of American to happen that way."

"Oh Reggie," Jackie said in exhaustion as she lay her head in his lap.

"Can you describe 'Mass' to me?" Reggie asked. "I grew up kind of Methodist, but I haven't been in a church in a decade. I was even a bit thankful that I wouldn't have to go for my grandmother's funeral, as much as it hurt to be stuck here." Reggie noted that Trey sometimes capitalized the word "Mass" in his letters, sometimes not. Jackie moved her head closer to the exact middle of his lap.

"It wasn't like any church I've seen, even in the Philippines. Jesus' face was blue like Vishnu's, and Mary and the Saints leaned against each other like Krishna and Radha. The livestock of the nativity were blinding white like Govinda cows. It was stunning, it gave me such hope.

We sat on pillows, no kneelers, everyone lotus-style. There were dozens of gorgeous Nepali nuns, who looked so young and yet so faithful. There must be a convent attached to the parish."

Reggie returned from his memories as Trey stood with both hands on the balcony rail. He began to pace though it was a small space.

Trey said, "This morning I was reading in the Post—*The Kathmandu Post,* of course—a profile in the entertainment section on Shawn Kemp, the basketball player. I know you're a hockey guy, but you don't have to like basketball to appreciate how many kids Shawn Kemp has allegedly fathered—like sixteen. The article was badly written, of course, but they did print a picture of a Seattle-stoner-looking guy, a pudgy white dude grinning in a shirt that said, 'Shawn Kemp is my Dad,' which I thought was really funny." Reggie smiled, sensing the end of Trey's high. He was torn between suggesting that they eat or scare up another joint, maybe a trip to the casino.

"Seattle has such a grungy love for hoops," Trey continued. "It will always be a great basketball city, like Portland, more so than Charlotte, I bet. I mean, a band like Pearl Jam almost called themselves Mookie Blaylock. I know you're not a Pearl Jam guy, but every time I think of Eddie Vedder, I think of this girl I knew—kind of knew—in high school. After Cobain killed himself, she made it a point to say that Eddie would never have the guts to do it. She loved to juxtapose those two, Cobain and Vedder, and lemme tell you, she was not a Vedder fan. She said Cobain was born, Vedder was manufactured."

"Where is she now?"

"Dead, I'm sure. She may have killed herself. I never asked." Trey looked away from Reggie across the courtyard, his face shaped and head canted as if he'd caught the sound of an intruder or a child's cry.

"Cobain ripped off quite a few songs himself," Reggie said.

"Eh, I never got into them beyond what was on the radio. Seemed like enough for me."

Reggie sensed Trey's mood turning dark, so he said without thinking, "Peesh be wiff you."

"Peace, yes. Thanks Reggie. Kathmandu! And we're fixin' to leave. So, yeah, in *The Post*, they ran that *piece* on Shawn Kemp's kids, and I was thinking of how to stop stuff like that. All that kid-making. Not just for society's benefit, but for guys like Shawn. All he wants is unprotected sex on a regular basis with a variety of women. Now, for a couple of chumps like me and you—if I may call you a chump—that's unreasonable. The best we're going to do tonight in Kathmandu is a hairy-pitted volunteer chick. I call dibs on the one who knows how to put condoms on with her teeth." Reggie smiled.

"But Shawn Kemp? The guy was a legend, especially in Seattle. I'm sure hoes were shoveling the booty at him. Flingin' it! It was the least he could do to impregnate 'em. But all that procreation costs money, and you know those hoes would grab as much as they could get. Shawn's probably broke somewhere in Seattle. Probably the only place he can get in free anymore is the Sonics arena."

"How will you help poor Shawn and others like him?"

"So glad you asked. It's a new company that I'm going to start when this Peace Corps thing is done. 'Bust That Nutt.'"

"Isn't there too much nutt-busting already?"

"Yes! That's why at our company we will give these athletes, entertainers, and politicians vasectomies and freeze their sperm for when they *really* want kids. Like with a respectable woman, not these baller hoes. Hell, even if the sperm goes bad, a vasectomy is easily reversed.

But in the meantime, they can get up in them girls all they want, and above all, they can Bust That Nutt!!"

"Do you think girls will be less attracted to men they know cannot get them pregnant?"

"Who cares?! He doesn't have to tell her."

"When you see an attractive older woman, do you desire her in the same way as you would a young woman?" Reggie asked.

"Not exactly, I mean, there are some hot older ladies out there, but it's kind of a novelty to find them attractive. Like, 'you're great looking despite…you know.' I guess it's a backhanded compliment."

"Do you think they are less attractive because they are less likely to bear healthy children?"

"Maybe so. The idea of reproduction is so far from my mind right now. Plus girls aren't exactly lining up to sleep with me. I'm just glad that we age better than them."

"Politicians, athletes, and entertainers are fueled by their virility. I don't see too many of them signing up to get snipped."

"You're right, but they should! It's an outpatient procedure, just hold a bag of frozen peas under your nuts for a couple days, and you'll be back busting before you know it. Same nutt—no baby. And when you *want* a baby, here's your sperm. Or, we untie your vas deferens—there's a pretty decent success rate."

"Again, virility."

"Yeah, I hear you. If only there was a way to curb male virility—ha! It just makes me sad to think of all those half brothers and sisters out there, none of them likely to grow up with Shawn Kemp as their dad, at least not in the traditional role. Now that we're leaving Nepal, everything is making me sad."

"Just sadness you feel, no anger?"

"Well, I am angry at those girls for slinging the booty at Shawn so frequently. And mad at Shawn for falling for so many hoes so many times."

"No, here in Nepal."

"I can't say I'm mad at the Maoists. They're just fighting for what they deserve. This king is a tyrant who killed his whole family to get power."

"Anything else?"

"I'm sad for Kali. Did you know her well? We were in the same language class."

"Not very," Reggie admitted. "But I was sad to hear she left."

"She was unhappy, and she complained a lot. I actually hated her while she was here. She confirmed every stereotype I had of an Oregon hippie—totally well off but always moaning about gentrification and the plight of the 'global south.' Her idea of empowering Nepalis was convincing the neighborhood girls to dress more provocatively. She said it would give them power."

"Geeze."

"Yeah! She talked all the time about how strippers were so powerful because they held men on a string and made them throw away all their money, and I was like, 'what?!' She said she'd strip herself if she had a better body. Kevin overheard and said, 'If you had a better body, I'd *watch* you strip,' and that made her cry.

"At the heart of it, she had an eating disorder, and the carb-heavy diet was making her gain weight. She'd go to the bathroom at least five times a class to do god-knows-what. I tried to think of what it would be like to have such little control over my body. I imagined her in the shower, looking at herself with those little hand mirrors we use for shaving, feeling sicker and sicker. These disorders are serious business." Reggie nodded.

"She was actually very pretty," Trey said. "Those blue eyes and sandy hair, the way she bobbed it. I stared sometimes at the outline of her underwear beneath her kurta. She was far from a fatty. But you know how Nepalis played it up—they considered being plump to be a sign of wealth. Kali's host mom would 'compliment' her: 'You are looking so fat today!'

"Oh, this carb-heavy diet! These disorders!" Trey looked concerned, then impish. "But maybe she was prescient, Kali. She got out before the rest of us. Her cats back home were named Diego and Frida—so typical Oregon! I hope she's well."

"You cared about her."

"I did. I'm ashamed that I hated her. If I meet her again—even if she starts growing dreadlocks—God, I hate it when white people do that shit—I will ask for forgiveness."

"How's Rita?" Reggie asked.

"Have I mentioned her before?" Trey gave him a disoriented look.

"You told Iris all about her. Iris told me. Iris wants to jump your bones." Trey sat down again and looked between the rails across the courtyard.

"Jesus. I'm sure Iris is jumping someone's bones tonight, definitely not mine. She tried to convince me I'm gay."

"Me too."

"I can see that. What did you tell her?"

"I said I wasn't attracted to men."

"Good answer. Well, now that you ask, I broke up with Rita about two weeks ago. Over the phone. Christ."

"I'm sorry." Reggie saw that Trey's mood was now sullen, seemingly unsalvageable. While it made him sad as well, he was thankful to be able to see a darker side, the one he read in his letters.

"Yeah, it was impulsive. It was the night of Lord Krishna's birthday celebration, I forget what they call it in Nepali. Earlier that day, my best friend from high school, Tony Odette—he went in the Air Force too—emailed me that he knocked some girl up. During the Krishna parade, I was thinking about whether Tony would marry her, remembering our high school notions, how he used to say that he wanted to stay a virgin specifically because he didn't want 'to be a daddy.' Then I got sad to think that he and I don't see each other much. He's still in the Air Force, I'm here." Reggie said nothing.

"You know, Redge, it's so heavy, meeting and leaving people. When they need help, I sink to realize I'm not there anymore. I'll bet that people from my past don't even bother contacting me anymore, because I just move on, I just start over. Tony tried every year to get into the Academy, while I was there pretty much jerking off. He would have graduated and flown fighters like his dad, but instead he toiled through ROTC, then navigator training, and is only just now getting to fly himself. I know he's going to marry this girl he knocked up. I'll be at the wedding and I won't be able to shake the feeling that I don't see him much anymore. That I don't even know this broad who's going to be his wife, an *Air Force* wife. Sorry, I exported my heaviness to you. If you've spent your entire life in Park Ridge, Illinois, it must be hard to sympathize with my whining."

"It's ok," Reggie said as he patted Trey's shoulder.

"So, then in the middle of Krishna's birthday celebration, our police chief got shot. The Maoist bullet, fired by a teenager, split his head. This is the same chief I had to introduce myself to when I arrived at post. He died right in front of me. I saw his eyes change from a look of boredom to one of confusion, and it seemed like a minute went by before his skull came apart, before his body fell, and all before anyone heard the bang.

"The Nepalis just watched, even his family. Then everyone exploded like the parts of an atom—ran away. Rita flooded my mind, and I rushed to the internet café to call her, not to gush out my love, to tell her that we were done. Her love for me, her insistence that she'd wait for me no matter how long I was gone felt like barbed wire around my neck. She wanted so badly to marry me, she said…."

"Do you still think so?" Trey didn't answer. His face was fierce.

"The internet café was full, so I walked back to my host family's to use the phone, though it was five times the price. I sat in the hallway with the cord stretching from the TV room. The servant woman's daughter, Oshima— I called her O—climbed in my lap like she always did when I was on the phone. Sometimes she giggled like she was on a ride or something, and I would bounce my legs to make her laugh. Rita realized quickly why I was calling, that this was the breakup call. I stared into Oshima's hair. Rita was crying, but to me it was background noise.

"I thought of the servant woman's older daughter, Pratima, who years ago, 'left for Bombay' with a man who said there was a good job down there for her. Every year the servant woman received a postcard from her though Pratima never learned to read or write. My host dad, Jagdish told me one night that he feared the girl was gone or dead or worse, probably working in some truck stop brothel, nowhere near Bombay. He said it happened all the time.

"Jagdish told me how they traffic people—women at least. A well-dressed, well-spoken Nepali guy shows up on the fringes of towns like ours, where really poor people have too many kids, many of them girls. And he pretends to be looking for a wife, or he says he has a good job working in a *thulo manche's* home. He pays the family a small relocation fee, which is a double bonus for them because they were burdened by the fact that they were going to have to come up with a dowry to marry her off. From there she's taken to the Indian border where she is sold to an agent, and then poof! If the 'agency' is really good, they'll send postcards to her family, sometimes nominal sums. They'll say that life is good in Bombay or Lucknow or Delhi. I can't imagine being that poor, letting your children go like that."

"The girls especially. No one wants girls," Reggie said sadly, bowing like an old tree. He considered asking Trey what the servant woman's name was, but then he remembered that in most homes he visited, servants were discouraged from telling their names to volunteers. It would have been a violation of the caste system, which was technically illegal, but still very much alive.

"Jagdish says the Maoists want to stop all that. The same Maoists who split the police chief in half. I believe him."

"You are finally talking like you write, like in the letter you wrote me," Reggie said smiling.

"I hope you liked it, man. I put a lot of thought into it, more than most."

"I did. Does Rita know we're being evacuated?"

"I doubt it. I didn't finish my story about the breakup. So she calls me two days later, sobbing again, and I figured this is going to be the first in a long series of soothing, let-down calls. Oshima climbed into my lap, and again I let Rita's cries dissolve into her hair, thinking I would give the servant woman enough money to keep potential traffickers away, enough to get O married off.

"But Rita wasn't calling to feel better about the breakup. No! She was calling to let me know that she just *happened* to meet a guy at Mass—the day we broke up! One thing led to another and they made out. A lot. Go figure."

"Wow, what a coincidence. Sounds like you dodged a bullet."

"It was for the best, I guess. Still feels raw that she was sneaking around like that. And we were together for nearly two years. It's strange, though, I can't separate the image of the police chief dying from the idea of ending it with Rita. We were meant to break up just as sure as he was meant to die."

Reggie asked, "Why don't you refer to people by their nicknames while we're talking now? I thought it was a clever way to do it, and some of them have really stuck, like 'Tonka's.'"

"Aw, wasn't it a dumb idea to do that?" Trey asked. "Do people really want to be labelled?"

"It's a sign of affection! Like you're thinking about more than our names, like you consider us beyond letters printed on a form. We're your friends."

"Well, not everyone liked that idea. Were you there for tumba when Veena went off?"

"Yes," Reggie said. "She was just drunk, I think."

"Yeah, she's trying too hard to be an angry lesbian. She's so mad at the idea of coming out to her traditional Indian parents, little things set her off. I understand." Reggie raised his eyebrows.

"Is that true? How do you know?"

"I heard her talking to Buffalo James. Poor guy was earnestly trying to get with her, it may have been the tumba night, but the way she was denying him, it was in a gentle yet harried, 'you're not on my side of the fence' kind of way. Then I heard her talking to Sugarland Vivek about *his* strict Indian parents, and how hard it was to tell them anything beyond, 'my Peace Corps service will get me into a better medical school.' She's close to coming out."

"Sugar V!" Reggie exclaimed. "I wasn't as sad when he left."

"Yeah, that dude is smart but shady. He's not to be trusted."

"How so?"

"He lied about going to Rice for undergrad. He went to Houston, which isn't a bad school, but he had to embellish, I guess."

"How did you find that out?"

"I just kept asking him questions about Rice. I had a few friends who went there who talked about what a serious campus it was, that they prided themselves on having a shitty football team that JFK made fun of, that they reveled in their nerdom. The more I felt like he was making things up—he's a terrible liar—the more questions I asked him.

"Finally, he went off on me. He didn't admit that he went to Houston—I found that out at the internet café—but he looked at me real mean and said, 'You know, this Peace Corps *thing*? You're not doing it for *them*.' And he waved his hand dismissively at some Nepalis on the side of the road. You're doing it for *you*.' He might be right. I'm afraid he is, but it doesn't mean I'm dismissive of Nepalis, does it? Vivek joked more than once that Nepalis were 'our Mexicans,' referring to how Indians treat them."

"What a jerk."

"Sandra heard him one time and yelled, "what?!!!" in a real high voice, and he ran away like a bitch. Not surprised he quit."

"You're sure Veena is a lesbian?"

"Can't be positive, but it seems like she's leaning. I'll bet it's faddish for Berkeley people to be 'sexually fluid' or whatever they call it. You know, like the way Iris tries to cajole guys like you and me out of 'our closets?' I dated a lesbian in the Air Force—she was straight at the time, I guess."

"Tell me more!"

"Well, it's funny and sad. I liked her—ironically—because she wasn't like a typical girl. She played sports, like with guys, totally held her own. She wore no makeup. She was funny, like actually funny, not like, *I'll laugh at your jokes to sleep with you* funny. She only spoke when she had something to say—totally un-girl-like. Basically, she was a guy with a vagina."

"I can't imagine it! You guys broke up, I take it?"

"Yes, on Christmas Day. One hundred feet below ground on nuclear alert."

"It was just you two? All alone in a missile silo?"

"They call it a capsule, but yes. If we had still been dating, we would have scrogged all over that place—highly illegal. But she kind of came out to me. She said that it wasn't going to work, it just couldn't. And then she meandered in her speech with a lot of tangents and cul-de-sac segues—ironically, like a real girl—about her upbringing in a Navy town with a bunch of freaky evangelicals—though she called them "evan-GENITALS,' who tried to 'pray the gay away.' I had my suspicions, so I just cut to the chase and asked if we were through. She said yes, and cried, but I felt closer to her for it. She got out of the Air Force and is now a pretty successful stand-up comedienne. Most women comics are not funny, but she is—like Ellen a little bit. Anyhow, Veena seems to be going through this 'tough girl, woe-is-me' oscillation that I remember witnessing."

"Maybe you should share that story. Help her along?"

"Are you fucking crazy? Veena would eat my balls like gulab jamin."

"Mmmmm." They were laughing again, peaceful, and Reggie verged on telling Trey about the letters.

Before he could speak, Trey said, "I don't know, man. Maybe Sugarland Vivek was right. All these clowns creeping around Nepal, we included. We're just doing it to feel better about our wealth and health. Right? If we just read Howard Zinn and *Guns, Germs, and Steel,* everything will be fine, right?" Reggie wiped the smile from his face.

"I've thought about that. I don't want to describe it that way. I try to focus on the people I know I've helped. I'll never forget Shiv or Oshima based on what you told me. You shouldn't either."

"God, Shiv. I really helped him, didn't I?"

"I'll bet you recovered after you found out he was special needs. I'll bet you gave him extra instruction."

"I did. How did you know?"

"Fits your character. You helped the servant woman too, yes? Money for Oshima?" Trey nodded.

"Thanks Redge. I know that you say that Park Ridge is where Hillary Clinton is from, but I think one day that *she'll* be saying it's where *Reggie Plante* is from."

"Ha. She's a New Yorker now. I don't know anyone back home who would claim her today." Trey breathed deeply.

"A few months ago," Trey began, "I met this NGO guy in the Nepalgunj airport. He was cool beyond someone you would want to hang out with, like genuinely smooth, unflappable, smart, funny. He was half Ghanaian, half American, but no accent, no tribal clothes, just a regular Joe. He got to telling me—only after our flights were cancelled, and I let him share my car to the hotel, then bought him a drink—how much he loved Peace Corps girls because they were such 'easy lays.' I acted shocked and he slapped the back of my arm like we were buddies.

"He described himself as 'an educated black man' over and over, laughing out loud at how hard the white chicks tried to avoid saying how 'articulate' he was, even though they were thinking it. Or he would ask about the girls' fathers to bait them into assuming that his wasn't around. And he loved trapping them into commenting on affirmative action when they learned where he went to college.

"He'd say, 'I got lucky to go to Columbia,' and they'd reply, "Don't say that! It's important to have diversity, even at our best colleges!' And then he'd come back quick with, 'No, I meant because their acceptance letter got lost in the mail. I was ready to send Cornell a dorm deposit!'

"I have to admit that I laughed at his tales of slaying poon, but then I wondered: what if he was banging the girls in *our* group? They're like my sisters."

"They're grown women," Reggie said. "They can make their own choices." He looked at the crumpled joint and exhaled. "What are you going to do back in the states?"

"I hadn't thought about it. My parents just moved back to San Pedro to be closer to my grandfather. Probably move back with them till I get on my feet and let all this weed get out of my system, man." As Reggie thought about his own post-evacuation plans, a disoriented volunteer barged into the room. Reggie and Trey kept their heads down, hoping to be unseen on the balcony.

"Trachea Yuri! Is there a Trachea Yuri here?" he slurred. Trey and Reggie buried their faces into their knees, trying to hide their laughter. The volunteer, whom neither Trey nor Reggie knew, poked his head through the curtains to the balcony.

"Anybody know Trachea Yuri? The Embassy called." Trey cocked his head; his teeth began to chatter. Reggie peered at Trey curiously, then began to worry at the fear radiating from his friend.

"Yes, that's me." The volunteer handed him a piece of paper with a phone number, and said, "Your name is Trachea? Awesome. Call Captain Unitas, or something like that. I wrote it down, bro." Trey took the paper with trembling fingers, while Reggie raced to figure a way to ask about Oneida without giving away the fact that he knew all about him. The messenger left.

"You have to call Johnny Unitas?"

"I think he meant to say, 'Oneida,' my buddy from the Academy who works at the Embassy."

"Is it urgent?"

"I don't know. It *is* the middle of the night." Trey moved his lips and tongue as if his mouth was dry. Reggie put a hand on his shoulder and asked if he was alright. Trey shook his head.

Reggie grabbed Trey's head and revealed, "Iris told me about Oneida. She let me read your letter. Sorry if that makes you mad."

"Jeeze, that Iris has loose lips," Trey said trance-like.

"I'll say," said Reggie, laughing. "Oneida seemed like an interesting guy the way you wrote him. All that was true about faking Jewishness and his observations of fat bottomed girls?"

Trey laughed, "Wow, good memory from a letter that wasn't written to you. Yeah, Oneida is pretty funny. Whenever he'd see a fat girl, he'd drop into a Barry White voice and say, 'I feel no need to use the verb 'to be' when I say, 'She big." It sounds pretty mean to repeat it now, but I still laugh to think of him saying it." Reggie nodded.

"Walt had a ton of black friends, a lot of guys in the underground rap scene, back when Jersey was the stolen car capital of the universe. Lots of guys, he said, would use chop-shop garages to record their stuff. He told me a secret once, seemed sad to tell it too, that rap is absolutely terrible when performed live. It's the most produced form of music you'll ever hear, he said. If you want to hear rap live, don't ever buy the CD because it's completely different in a bad way."

"And he loved Springsteen."

"Well, being from the shore, everybody had to, he said. His dad was the real fan. He told a story about his old man, saving for months to take him to a show. Walt was embarrassed to go with his dad, who dressed up just for the occasion, even groomed his Hulk Hogan fu manchu. After the concert, they waited outside for Bruce to come out, but when he did, he completely ignored them.

"It was extra sad to hear Walt tell it because his dad was immigrant strong, showed no emotion. Walt talked about riding in his dad's cab, hearing the old man singing, 'Jungleland,' which Walt would impersonate with a Ukrainian accent. Half of him did it for laughs, the other half was genuinely bummed that his dad bought into 'The Boss' and all that working-class bullshit he used to sell records."

"So interesting," Reggie said.

"Yeah, Walt had a whole schtick. He lectured us on the *layers* of hypocrisy: that Springsteen wouldn't let Reagan use 'Born in the USA' for his campaign; that dumbass Reagan actually thought it was a patriotic song…he must not have read the lyrics. And even deeper, Walt shook his head at the fact that people believed Bruce was anything other than a limousine liberal—that he cared about 'the common man.'"

"Wow," Reggie said.

"Yeah, that was the beauty of old Walt Oneida. He could make you laugh one moment and cry the next. I had a drink with him the other night, when we first flew back to Kathmandu. He told me about his buddies in Iraq who pumped themselves up listening to Rage Against the Machine—said was the only thing that got them crazy enough to kill."

"Probably not the outcome Zach Dela Rocha had in mind," Reggie said as Trey stood up, smoothing the wrinkles from his shirt and pants, ready to go. He tried to think of something to keep Trey from leaving. "Why didn't you put that Springsteen story in your letter to Iris?"

"Eh, not her style. She's a John Cougar Mellencamp kind of girl." Reggie nodded in agreement.

"Why were you so open with her, so….giving? You gave her a lot. She cherished that letter."

"I told her some things I'd never told anyone. I guess you're in on it now."

"Your secret is safe with me."

"I think I wrote those things to Iris because I sensed that she needed it. She needed a secret, something I struggled with. Because she was struggling so much. That's why she tries to get all of us to become gay—because she's wrestling with a lot of demons herself."

"Hmm. Well, she said she felt needed, so that was perceptive and kind of you."

"I'm going to tell you another secret."

"I'm ready."

"When you knocked on the phone booth, I was talking with my host dad back at post. I told him about a shipment of guns coming to the Dhangadhi area. He's going to tell the Maoists that he knows, and there will likely be an ambush."

"How do you know that?" Reggie was at first floored by Trey's access to sensitive information, and then by his willingness to compromise it.

"Walt told me offhand while we were drinking. He thinks both sides of this war are clowns."

"What's going to happen?"

"I don't know," Trey said with slight haste in his voice, then he stood to leave. "Well, Mr. Plante, I sincerely appreciated our chat and the narcotics that facilitated it. I should give Walt a call. Maybe he wants to play some rap records."

Reggie hugged Trey and said, "T-B-M…."

Trey took a couple seconds to catch on, then smiled and mouthed, "W-T-T-U."

He returned to the phone booth in the lobby, noticing plaster flakes still on the floor. Oneida picked up before the second ring.

"Yeah, I know it's you, Ciuri," he said. Trey ground the receiver into his ear and jaw. "You know, Ciuri, this is you. This is just like you, same as at the Academy. You think you know who needs help, and you can break any rules you want because you see shit other people don't. If you get caught your dad will get you out." Silence passed, crackles on the line.

"I'd be surprised if he could get you out of this one, Ciuri. I hope you're still listening, because here's the most important part. That guy, the guy you told, who brought some of his terrorist buddies to the delivery? He's dead, he got shot. Think the rules of biology and physics don't apply? Go talk to his wife. If you really were a man you would have been there with the Maoists. You stay at the Yak and Yeti, I'm coming to you." Oneida hung up and Trey ran from the hotel into the deserted streets of Kathmandu.

Reggie followed Trey at a safe distance, as quickly as his walking boot would allow. For minutes at a time, he'd lose sight of his friend, then find him again as he crested hills. In an intersection near *Swayambu*, the monkey temple, he panned for Trey, but did not see him until he made a clatter atop a tall scaffolding surrounding a restaurant under renovation, from which he fell. The suspension between Trey's perch, his silent fall, and loud landing was interminable enough for Reggie to run through every word of Trey's letter to him:

Hey P.R.,

I know you appreciate a good nickname, hence my salutation. I've written to everyone in our group, no offense that yours was the last. It just worked out that way. I've not traditionally <u>been</u> a letter writer. I came of age, as an adult interested in wooing women and bonding with men (letters are good for such things!), when email was getting popular. But our group touched me. Not that I loved (or even liked) everyone; but the way we fit together, like particles, the 21 of us: we were the atom Scandium, if only for a short time. And when training was over, we scattered in a high-altitude-burst above a major city full of mostly innocents. It had to be done. We'll never be whole again, even if they evacuate us, for Kali and Vivek have already left. Letters were the only way to reconnect.

Now, about that evacuation. I had ruled out such an ending to our service until last night when I woke to find a rat sharpening his teeth on my bed post. How brazen he was, hanging by all fours, marking his territory. I lay paralyzed as my mind ran through the gamut of violent things I should do to the rat. I imagined him daring me, and I thought of my host dad, who found a cobra in the garden the other day—maybe she would swallow the rodent.

Suddenly, orange light rushed through my window from across the distance. A couple seconds later the sound arrived like a 4th of July canon. The rat scrambled and my host sister rushed into my room and pulled me to the floor just before the gunfire began. On every side of the house, as close as the rat seemed, Maoists and cops were shooting at each other. They'd have shot through us if they had to.

My cheek was pressed to the floor and I could smell my host sister's breath. I wondered if all 21 of us were going through this shit. Is this what it's like to do Teach-for America in the inner city? They sure describe it that way (though their descriptions drip with embellishments. Most of them are rich kids after all).

I remembered PC orientation, one of our first icebreakers in Seattle, back when we were feeling each other out, mostly trying to be impressive in subtly humble ways. Some folks started a side conversation about NPR. First someone said they loved Nina Tottenberg, and once that cherry popped, someone else said, "Oh, Anne Garrels!" Inevitably someone mimicked the intro "Steve Inskeep and Renee Montaigne," and another bleated "I'm Robert Sigel," then came other warm fuzzies: WGBH Boston, The John D and Katherine T MacArthur Foundation. For my part, I muttered Nic Harcourt's name, thinking no one would recognize him, but of course most did. Damn us, there wasn't an original idea in that room, just a bunch of parrots who would someday drive Subaru and Prius cars, that ironically shush away all ambient noise. We were just a murder of native English speakers who got lucky to be born in the United States! It reminded me of that REM concert you played in training….during the *End of the World*, Michael Stipe asks the crowd, "Right?" And we're the sheep who parrot it back.

9/11 and this "global war on terror" is how American guns are making their way into the hands of Nepali cops and soldiers! The Maoists are "terrorists?" The more I learn about the King of Nepal, the more I believe that America is yet again arming the wrong side. I guess we'll swoop in decades later to give aid and more guns.

I was on alert, a hundred feet below the plains of Sterling, Colorado on September 11th. My crew partner, Slim, happened to be a good friend, probably my best friend from those missile days. The attack changed our "state of readiness" to one not seen since the tenser times of the Cold War. Slim and I were like: "smoke 'em if you got 'em," literally lighting up in the capsule, which was utterly illegal. As we watched everything burn into the night, and the talking heads on TV began to repeat themselves, some making inane speculations about how and why it happened, I said to Slim, "Whoever they end up blaming for this, it wasn't them. At least the masterminds."

Most missileers would have been aghast at my insinuation, that the U.S. government would not truly reveal the methods and motives behind a national tragedy. Slim, who was smart and openminded, certainly for missiles, nodded and promised, "I'll find out for you."

Hope we can talk about this stuff face to face one day,

Trey

P.S.: I know you hate Bush—who doesn't? But I'm really scared of turning to only a slightly lesser cunt in his opponent. I can't believe we live in a world where Ralph Nader is the answer to a pub quiz question.

Chapter Four: Curtains

Trey decided to kill himself just after Slim revealed he was gay, though the two events were unrelated. Trey heard his friend's disclosure, and cared about it; however, he was in the middle of his own moment of truth, having unloaded on Slim through most of the night, the worst of his tales from firefighting. The goriest experience was just two weeks old, a car wreck in the early morning hours before President Obama's inauguration.

Trey knew Slim's partner, Jake, as "a dude from work," who seemed like a nice enough chap, but to Trey was one of many typical guys in the Washington DC area. As Trey worked once more through his algorithm, the one with "death" in the final line of code, it made sense to him that Slim and Jake were together. Trey would have been more curious—even happy—had it not been the moment he'd decided to suicide again.

As Slim explained himself on the metro platform, his guilt lost its heaviness; and Trey, while still listening, hopped down to grab the third rail. Slim was too absorbed in the moment to stop him, though he did get to the tracks quickly enough, with a plastic trash lid to beat Trey off the rail, and to drag his body to the platform before the train came.

Earlier that night, they watched college basketball at Nellie's, DC's best (and perhaps only) gay sports bar. Trey loved going there because he was guaranteed not to see any "typical District chicks," who he labeled "barely above average in every way." Slim agreed with Trey's choice of bar for similar reasons, plus one more. They got drunk, Trey much quicker than Slim, who wanted to be at least semi-upright when

Jake showed up for the second half. Trey's firefighting stories began as funny and noble accounts, then saddened as the night went on.

"Are there any girls in your firehouse?" Slim asked. "Are they all dykes?" Trey furrowed his brow at Slim's language, then thought of a girl he dated in the Air Force who turned out to be gay.

"We have one on shift, she's married. I had one in my recruit class. Definitely not a lesbian."

"Thank you for correcting my nomenclature. I would have figured they all ate at least a little pussy."

"There are a few lesbians in the department," Trey said. "It's legal, unlike the military. People treat them like guys because they can actually *do* the job, which is refreshing.

"Where is *your* girl tonight?"

"Michelle? Oh, we broke up a while ago, thought I told you."

"No! You didn't!"

"Did you care?"

"Yes, I hated her! Good for you! You can do a lot better. Maybe not in this bar, but in general."

"Thanks. It was for the best."

"Yeah, the best for *you*. I'm sorry dude, but she was a loser!"

"She was smart."

"Every white chick in DC is smart," Slim said. "She was a silver back, a shellback, a….what did Sandy call them? Girls who eat cupcakes and drink beer all day?"

"Sea backs."

"That's right, a sea back! Dude, you could see her gut hanging like a plumber. I think she was proud of it, like it was some feminist deal: 'keep your laws off my gut!' No intellect overcomes that."

"It's an interesting job," Trey said, switching back to the firehouse. "Good guys. Kind of reminds me of the Air Force with the camaraderie."

"Yeah, I miss that. It's lonely in the consulting world. Have you made any good friends?"

"A couple guys from recruit school, but we all went to different stations. Sometimes I feel isolated down by the river."

"Big money in Potomac," Slim said.

"Yeah, mansions. I took JFK's sister or cousin or some Kennedy to the hospital the other day."

"What was she like?"

"Old. Her house was hidden by a berm on River Road, and the ambulance had to go like half a mile on the driveway. Inside her place there was an old-fashioned elevator with golden gates you had to close to get to work."

"Fuck the Kennedys, I'm glad we killed so many of them."

"She was pleasant in the back of the ambulance. But there was nothing really wrong with her besides old age. Her nurse, who lived at the house, thought she should go in. We took her to Suburban Hospital, and as soon as we wheeled her into the ER, the nurse screamed, 'This is Blah Blah Kennedy! Please move aside!' And there were people who were *really* sick—shit, Suburban is the only trauma center in the county, but everyone shuffled to the side so a Kennedy could get a bed."

"Fucking terrible. I hope you poisoned her IV."

"She's not long for this world," Trey said as he ordered their second round. Slim looked him up and down.

"You look like you've been in training! Nice job, man! Be careful showing off those guns in a place like this."

"Yeah, the fire academy was pretty challenging….much harder than Air Force, at least physically."

"You think? I still remember you finishing your PT tests with a cigarette hanging out of your mouth."

"Remember when we used to pretend to pull each other out of the burning missile capsule? 'Save my tater tots! My chicken nuggets!'"

"I remember us smoking on 9/11. It's nice to see you quit, by the way. I mention this as I'm about to go bum one."

"Oh man, I quit back in Pedro." Trey paused. "I was quit when you visited, remember?"

"I guess it didn't stick with me. I was thinking of other things, like trying to save you."

"But I wasn't in trouble."

"You seemed like you were in a bad spot."

"Pedro was definitely a time of self-reflection," Trey mused. "That trip to see Sandy Ko still feels like a dream."

"All of L.A. is a dream, man. I'm glad you're here."

"It's funny. Most of my childhood I badmouthed my parents for raising me away from San Pedro, but living there I learned that it wasn't for me."

"How many jobs did you work, like sixteen?"

"Something like that."

"Seriously. Ambulance driver, 8th grade teacher, that shit you did at the labor union, newspaper reporter. Grad student. I couldn't keep it straight." Slim paused and put his hand on the bar closer to Trey. "I'm sorry again for all that shit I said. I was in a bad spot myself, and I wanted to see you succeed after your Peace Corps thing fell through."

"It's ok. I was a bit masochistic in those days. I wanted to be purified by the market. The Air Force was whacko. They paid us what? To do what? For how many years? It was a waste except for the books I read. I can't even remember the titles, only that they made me more curious and more rebellious."

"You were good for our squadron. For the base too."

"But I left," Trey said.

"Your time was up. Lots of us left. Who stays in missiles?"

"Well, Peace Corps was a big letdown too," Trey said. Slim went outside to smoke.

Two years earlier, during Slim's visit to San Pedro, Trey took him to his night classes at Cal State Dominguez Hills. Three hours later, as they waited on the corner of Avalon and Victoria for a bus to take them home, Slim complained about Trey's self-imposed shitty life, in which he worked multiple jobs, volunteered, went to school, lived with his parents, and rode the bus all over Los Angeles.

"These people are all stupid except you," Slim began. "Tell me you have them locked into some pyramid scheme that will get you rich and barely keep them alive."

"Dude, this is my life at the moment, and I was excited to share it with you," Trey said, absorbing Slim's frustration. "Some of the things I'm into here remind me of our times in Cheyenne."

"Yeah, when we were fresh out of college." Slim rubbed his bare arms. "You're better than this, that's all. I appreciate a diversity of experiences like anyone else, but it seems like you're punishing yourself for something. What? What have you done wrong that you have to ride the *bus* in L.A.? Jesus, ride double-deckers in London if you want to take public transportation."

"I feel like I'm getting on my feet, learning about the real world," Trey said. "Missiles was a video game to me. Peace Corps too was surprisingly scripted."

"I know I seem harsh," Slim said. "But you're not being challenged. At least not in an upward way. It's like you're lifting weights but building the wrong muscles. How will this 'education' from Domingo ever benefit you?"

"Through the people I meet, I guess. There's Austin, a Nigerian, who's trying hard to rap with these Long Beach and Compton chicks, who laugh at his attempts to talk 'black.' And there's Bunmi, who is Nigerian too. She has a crush on Austin and wishes he would stick to 'his own kind.'

"She called him out one day, 'Igbo man!' After class, he yelled at her, like straight up scolded her as a woman to embarrass him like that. I guess in Nigeria women don't do that. But he was embarrassing *himself* trying to impress these Compton chicks. They make fun of Austin's accent and that he wears his Bluetooth earpiece in class. But he got mad at someone from his 'tribe.'"

"Great. Write an article or a short story. Make some money off them."

"I can't," Trey said quickly, then went on. "There's Bekeshe from Ethiopia. She works for L.A. County in the Housing Office and she has some good ideas, but she can't get promoted without a check-the-box masters. Her husband picks her up with kids asleep in the back seat."

"At least she isn't waiting for the bus."

"There's Anya, a Cuban with orange hair, who told the class about her labor organizing days with 'the purple wave' of SEIU, where I work now. Did you know they were started by Italian janitors who were exploited because they couldn't speak English?"

"They *should* speak English!"

"There's Tom. He's white, you'll love that. He's a firefighter. And talking to him has made me interested in training for a department myself."

"Well, there's a goal. Wasn't your grandpa a fireman?" Slim looked across Avalon Boulevard.

"Yes. I haven't mentioned it to him yet."

"Well, tomorrow, when we see Sandy, please keep an open mind. I told him you're a great writer, and he sparked up that he's always looking for talent. He produces shows now."

"I appreciate you thinking of me."

"But…. I smell a 'but.'"

"But I was still describing my classmates, the ones you made fun of."

"Ok, I should have just made fun of your 'professors.' Good Jesus, they have PhDs? From USC and UCLA? Christ, are they *giving* them away? Those fools couldn't even speak in complete sentences. It was like listening to snow on T.V. They have no business in college! This college shouldn't even exist! Walking on that 'campus,' I expected to see a 'Checks Cashed' place and a burner cell phone store. These people are costing the state millions, sitting in class, while their kids are out spraying graffiti and robbing corner stores. I'm not a Fox News guy, but what I just saw—your profs and classmates—confirms every stereotype those clowns put out."

"Not everyone was born into as much as you and me."

"You can have sympathy for them, but do it once you've made something of yourself. It's like a plane crash: make sure your oxygen mask is on before you help others."

"Life is not a plane crash."

"And this….is not college! You're smarter than this, man! I feel like I'm watching a guy hooked on drugs. Yours is mediocrity."

"I've found challenges here much harder than the Air Force," Trey said.

"You're making it harder. These fucking mopes, none of them are *paying* for college, I know it. They're sucking the California teat. They aren't *saving*. They have huge credit card bills—not for necessities—for electronics and vacations, for gas in their SUVs! They watch TV, they don't read, and they blame others for their problems!" Slim paused as if to taste his bile. It wasn't jetlag making him ornery. It was something else, something that happened to him just hours before his plane took off.

"And here you are," Slim went on, "the only one who will amount to anything. I mean it, come back in 20-25 years—not one of your classmates will be notable— and you're paying *tuition*? Bleeding away *your* savings—cashing your IRA?! On Domingo?!"

"Dominguez," Trey corrected. "All I can say is that my classmates seem to be getting a lot out of this. They're genuinely challenged, and they see a college education as a way to a better life."

"Did you apply to UCLA?"

"Yes."

"Got in?"

"Yes."

"And?"

"And I don't want to be like those West L.A. chumps. They kept bragging that they get to take classes from Michael Dukakis."

"But you want to be like *these* people? Seriously?"

"I don't want to be like *anyone*. But my classmates, yes, I like them….a lot more than the Westwood tools. Most of my classmates had to go to terrible public schools, and English is at least their second language. I sit on my parent's balcony and drink coffee and listen to NPR."

"Ah, white guilt. Gets you nowhere. Gets them nowhere."

"I'm trying to not feel sorry for them, but it's hard. Same way it's hard to not hate the UCLA kids."

"At least the UCLA people will be successful. They're the ones who are going to be able to make change."

"I think some of my classmates are going to do good things," Trey said.

"No! These guys aren't making anything of themselves! They just want more money for less work. They are coopting the American dream."

"Was there ever an American dream?"

"I'd like to think so, at least for white people."

"Jesus, Slim."

"In the real world, Yuri, when you move out from your parent's house, you won't have the luxury of idealizing the pursuits of morons. I would say the "quixotic" pursuits, but they don't even have the lovability or determination to attain quixotism. They're the scratch and sniff generation. Scratch: 'College free? College get me more stuff? They owe it to me!' Most of them need to join the Army and die for my freedom. It would be much nobler than this shit." Slim paused to examine the hurt on Trey's face. He rubbed his eyes, then his arms, and travelled back in his mind a few hours to Washington, where he discovered an intruder in his house, a man sitting on his kitchen floor, waiting for him to come home.

Slim had money on the game at Nellie's, which changed how he spectated, often causing him to ignore his surroundings in favor of statistics running through his mind. During commercials he reconsidered Trey, his best friend from the Air Force, who'd changed in the years since they tended nuclear weapons under the frozen plains of Wyoming, Colorado, and Nebraska.

Outside, DC people lumbered by on the swiftly gentrifying streets. The Superbowl was over and there was a new President in office. Someone asked the barkeep to switch off basketball in place of a drag queen competition, which Slim vetoed with a growl.

Jake showed up as the second half began, and Trey greeted him with a man hug. Jake came around to Slim's barstool, nearly kissing him between his haircut and his ear but caught himself. Trey was too drunk and self-centered to notice.

Jake asked, "So tell me again—how you got to be friends with this scumbag."

"We were 'Guardians of the High Frontier,'" Trey joked.

"And what brings you to DC?"

"I live here now….partially thanks to this guy, I guess."

"Trey's a fireman, I told you, Montgomery County."

"Oh, that's right," Jake said as he pointed at Slim's beer for the bartender.

"But, being Trey, you can't just be a fireman. What else do you do? Guy's got like half a dozen jobs."

"Oh, on my off days, I substitute teach in the County."

"And."

"And I work at Trader Joe's in Bethesda."

"Bradley and Wisconsin," Jake said. "I know it well. I'm glad you could find time to come out."

"You too," Trey said.

"Why so many jobs? Money?" Slim asked.

"Gotta pay the mortgage," Trey said. "Can't believe I qualified, making 45K a year."

"Everybody is qualified these days….it's pretty ridiculous, actually."

"Yeah, my guy at Countrywide is balding with a ponytail, southern accent, and he starts most of our conversations, 'I don't tell all my clients this, but….'"

"Shady. And….tell Jake where your house is."

"Anacostia."

"That neighborhood has a bad reputation," Jake said offhandedly and then whispered something in Slim's ear. Slim looked nervously at Trey, then back at Jake.

"Old Trey is shuttling the Kennedys to and from the hospital."

"Just *to* the hospital. We don't do returns."

"What an interesting job," Jake smiled. "In my line of work I only meet other douche bags." He slapped Slim's shoulder again.

"Any other famous people?" Slim asked.

"I've had some good rides," Trey said. "I took a priest who fell in the shower at his nursing home."

"Did he invite you back to help him stay 'upright?'" Slim joked.

"No, he was lucid and friendly, seemed to genuinely appreciate that I was taking him to the hospital, even though it was my job. I asked him if he would hear my confession."

"In the back of the ambulance? Weird."

"What did you confess?" Jake asked.

"You're not supposed to ask!" Slim chided. "Sorry, dude, Jews don't grow up with such guilty routines."

"It's fine. I confessed that I was angry with God."

"That's it?"

"That and masturbation."

"Not a sin," Slim said, "if you think about priests while you do it."

"What did he say? About being angry," Jake asked.

"He said, 'God can handle it.'"

"What makes you angry?"

"Well, we'd just run a couple of dead kids. That did not endear my creator to me." Jake shifted on his stool.

"One kid we thought was a routine call. I was working a detail in Silver Spring, which is much busier than my firehouse in Potomac. It was the middle of the night and the call came out as 'parents need help with kid's inhaler.' I don't know how the dispatcher thought it was just an inhaler because the kid had a serious head injury, with pupils different sizes. He'd been vomiting all night, and when we got there he was unresponsive. The captain was working the kid in the back of the unit, and he looked up and said, 'lights are on but no one's here.'

"As unsettling as that was, the worst part was hearing the radio call from the original firefighter on scene. When he realized the situation was much more serious than the basic life support ambulance the dispatchers had sent. I know this guy pretty well, a real aw-shucks-Christian, has like seven kids, a steamfitter on his off days, too proud for food stamps, though he could use them. He got on the radio and said, 'Montgomery, this is ambulance 712. You should have sent….this pediatric needs help, advanced life….' And he trailed off. He did the best he could until we arrived on the engine. But the kid was far gone, 'circling the drain' as we say."

"That's tough," Slim said. Jake stared at the game but looked like he wasn't following it. Trey went on.

"The parents were immigrants, like from Hungary or something, Eastern European, heavy accents, young couple, reminded me of a couple from the movie *Casablanca*. They thought they were going to get out of there, but in reality…."

"Dude, you're tangenting," Slim forked over irritably.

"Sorry. They were food scientists, new post-docs, worked at FDA, lived over there in White Marsh. Their son was ugly to me. With his unequal pupils and no comprehension. Tube jammed into his trachea. But the couple was beautiful, their immigrant story shattered. All those thoughts made me hate a God who created me who could think that way."

"Deep," Slim slid in. "Comon 'Cuse!" he yelled at the T.V. He thought of Trey in California, and how contentious his visit to Pedro was; but he felt reassured that Trey moved to DC anyway. He still worked too many jobs to make ends meet, but he was a homeowner now, and he broke up with what's-her-face, both good things. Slim also remembered, as he looked at his partner, that he never would have met

Jake had it not been for Trey, but that was a back story he could never tell the full truth about.

"You said 'a couple' of kids," Jake said.

"Yeah, the other one was a 'walk-in.' As we were getting ready for bed, the tillerman—the guy who steers the back of the ladder truck—got on the intercom: 'Everybody get up and get to the engine room! Now!'

"Standing in the middle of the engine bay, a mother, covered in blood was holding her five-year-old daughter in one arm and a gas can dripping in the other. She had a cigarette barely in her mouth, and a little boy standing by her leg, away from the gas drip, thank God.

"The tillerman grabbed the cigarette, the captain took the gas can far away. Someone handed the little boy to me and told me to play with him. I gave him my helmet to try on, and then found some cartoons on TV. The other guys took the girl into the ambulance. She had the smallest gash near the top of her head, behind one of her braids, barely noticeable. Except for all the blood on her mom's shirt and jeans, we wouldn't have known there was an injury. I left the boy with a volunteer medic, and then got in the ambulance to help. We had to pretend that there was something to be done for the girl, though the other guys kept saying, like ghosts, with hollow sounds in their throats, 'This kid is dead, this kid is dead.'

"The ambulance went to the hospital with lights, no sirens, just a formality because they needed a doctor to pronounce the girl officially. The mom stayed in the firehouse with me while her son watched cartoons. The captain called Montgomery PD because there had been a violent death. It was standard procedure. I sat with the mom to get her story.

"When the police arrived, they didn't hesitate to handcuff her, just in case it was she who killed the kid, they said. I still had to get her story: She lived in Tobytown, which, in case you didn't know, is next to Potomac, right on the river, founded by freed slaves, where they still kind of talk colonial, like those island communities off the coast of Georgia and Virginia.

"As she told me her story, it was like she was stuck in a loop: they ran out of gas, went walking with the can to the station, it was dark. And just as she was about to say what happened to her daughter, she tried to use her hands to talk, but couldn't because of the cuffs. She'd let out a wail, half sad, half frustrated. I took a break and brought her water. On the way to and from the kitchen, I watched her son's face as cartoons flashed over his eyes, and sometimes he'd laugh involuntarily. Once, he let out a belly laugh, and one of the volunteer chicks started bawling at the sight of it.

"When it was all over, around one in the morning, the county sent over some social workers and a psychologist for a critical incident stress debriefing. Everyone shared how they felt, and I waited until the end when I said to the cops, "If that had been a white woman who lost her daughter, you never would have handcuffed her." Trey exhaled and ordered another beer.

"Jesus, what did the social workers say?" Slim asked.

"They just nodded. I think they were tired. But the cops piped up and said it wasn't true. Not sure I believe them. The way these guys talk, cops and firemen alike, they may not be Klan members, but they definitely believe that certain races act certain ways."

"Everyone believes those things," Slim said. "Even people who aren't white."

"That woman, why would she be so careless with her daughter?" Jake asked, looking into the bar's lights. "I assume the little girl was hit by a car while walking on the road. How careless."

"What was she supposed to do, wait in the car?" Trey asked. "I guess they could have walked in the ditch on the side of the road. They never found the guy who hit her."

"Some people don't care as much for their children as others," Jake said.

"Be careful with your sweeping summaries," Trey warned with a shaky voice. "There's a lot of factors here that make it more complicated than just how much 'some people' care about their kids."

"I'm very sorry," Jake said with his head bowed to where Trey couldn't see his eyes. Quickly he looked up and asked, "Did you touch the little girl in the back of the ambulance? Did you give emergency care, I mean?" Trey's face lost color.

"I can't describe what it was like to hold that little girl," he said with a timbre that made Slim stop drinking. "Whatever 'lifeless' is supposed to feel like, it was an absence of electricity, like when you go camping far away and your notice how maddening that sound can be. It was a pitch black with no stars. Or a loss of fluid, the faintest you've ever felt from giving blood, when you actually welcome a loss of consciousness. Or like when someone leaves you, how your mind recreates that car or plane or train that took them away. We all felt something in the back of that ambulance, and we strangely took turns holding her body, desperate to never forget. And I felt so guilty talking to the mother after holding her dead daughter."

Jake wiped his brow as he stood up, announcing that he had to go. A long silence passed as the game drew down. Slim's bets all panned out.

As they settled their tabs, Trey said, "What gets me more than the famous people who live in Potomac, is the fact that there are ten times as many *unfamous* people. Who the hell are they? How did *they* get their money? How could there be that much money in one place? On calls, I always look hard at their bookshelves, as if something there will explain it. Like when I was a teenager and I'd try to look down a girl's shirt or between her legs, trying to find 'the secret,' whatever it was making me so itchy. Of course, when I grew up, I realized there is no secret. Those girls I wasted my time paying attention to—it was just because of some dumb biology—not because they were interesting, smart, or kind. Probably the same with the Potomac-ites."

"Yeah, man, I'm not sure what you're trying to say about rich people," Slim offered, sounding fatigued.

"No, I just thought of it because it's weird for me to work in Potomac and live in Anacostia, where everyone is lower middleclass."

"I do admire you for jumping into that neighborhood so early," said Slim. "There's no obvious signs of gentrification, not even gay…." Slim stopped himself from saying "gay guys" who usually initiated changes in neighborhoods from black to white. He'd seen it happen in his own Northeast DC burg, where the H Street corridor was chasing longtime DC residents elsewhere. He felt exposed as both gay and racist. It was then that he decided he would tell Trey about Jake.

"It's been good," Trey said. "I love my neighbors, because they're actually from Washington. They watch football on rabbit-ear TVs, get drunk, and no one sleeps when the 'Skins win. They get in their cars and drive around the neighborhood honking at people on porches. Good thing for me the Redskins don't win very much."

"Yeah, their owner is a cunt," Slim said. "You haven't gotten harassed or robbed or anything? Surely you're the only white guy for miles."

"Yeah, it's funny. One of my neighbors, a nation of Islam guy, came over the day I moved in and gave it to me straight: 'Look man, people either think you a cop or you here for some drugs. Maybe some booty too.'"

"That's hilarious. How did you answer?"

"With my best white guy voice: 'Well, jeeze, I'm sure not a *cop*. And I don't use *drugs*.' He accepted my answer, but he seemed suspicious. Overall, everyone in the neighborhood has been very friendly. They have block parties every quarter to raise money for scholarships for kids from the area."

"That's cool."

"At the firehouse, there was a guy working a detail, black guy, another nation of Islam dude who grew up in Anacostia. The redneck dudes were making fun of me for moving there, saying it was just a matter of time before drug dealers would be slinging rocks from my front stoop. I went back to my white guy voice, and I said, 'Nothing violent or threatening has happened to me yet. It all seems ok.' And the guy who was from Anacostia looked up nonchalantly and said, 'Just wait till the economy get bad.'"

"I wonder if that's true," Slim said.

"I wonder why Jake left."

"Maybe he got tired of hearing your tales of racial inequality."

"The people in my neighborhood," Trey began. "They don't, I don't think they know how poor they are."

"Who cares if they do?"

"I mean, they talk about the material things they don't have, but I don't think they know about all the *other* things they don't have. I feel guilty about it. I know it's cliché."

"It's beyond cliché. You're not supposed to understand it, much less fix it."

"My basement flooded about two weeks after I moved in. It cost ten grand to fix the plumbing and clean everything up. I was able to borrow the money from my parents within a week. My neighbors don't have that kind of option. They'd either have to take on crushing debt or live with no plumbing and eventual mold."

"Not something you can fix. Is it?"

"Probably not. But I don't like being aware of these differences. It's like when I took you to Dominguez. My classmates had no idea the shitty education they were getting. Some of them were paying for it!"

"Dude, *you* paid for it too."

"It's like at the firehouse: people call us and we know the situation. We usually know if they are going to be ok, whether or not the call is bullshit. I'm riding in the back of that ambulance with a lot more awareness than the average patient. Even when I was confessing to that priest, I felt like I knew more than him." Slim sighed, his buzz growing heavier.

"You're not supposed to take it so seriously, Trey. You're going to burn out. You need to leave these people at the hospital or in the cemetery, wherever."

"One lady I used to take to the hospital at least once a week. She was a 'frequent flyer,' as they say. Lived in an expensive nursing home just down from the firehouse. We'd pick her up, take her to Suburban or Sibley and that would be it. She even had the decency to call during normal business hours."

"Ok, what was her name? I know you know."

"Miss Chris. Chris was her last name. She had Alzheimer's but she always remembered my name, that I was from California, and she'd ask in a kind of mischievous way why I wasn't married."

"Then you showed her the picture of Michelle's gut and she was like, 'ohhhh, *that's* why you're not married.'"

"Her husband died years ago, worked for the NSA she told me, and then told me not to tell anyone, said they always told people he worked for IBM. She'd ask me with a smirk, 'Do *you* want to work for the NSA? Just call your mom and tell her!' I knew the way she told the joke that it was something between her and her husband.

"Poor thing, Miss Chris, she had family, sons and daughters who lived in the area, but no one ever visited her, at least that's what she told me. There was an old sticky note, it wasn't even sticky anymore, taped to the picture of her daughter's family that read, 'Mom, this is your new home. You don't live in 'the Glen' anymore.' It broke my heart every time she asked me to read it to her.

"And in the ambulance, she'd weep about missing Mr. Chris and her kids. She wondered why they never came to see her, if it was because she had them raised by nannies. She asked me if it was karma. I told her I didn't know. I always held her hand, which was oddly half warm and half cold. Warm fingers, cold palm, vice versa. I can feel it now. Mind if I get another beer?" Slim nodded.

"So, what happened to her?"

"She died in the shower. For almost a full day she laid there, and by the time we got the call she was literally running down the drain."

"I thought she was in a nursing home. No one checked on her?"

"The orderlies took turns doing rounds, and they heard the shower and were like, 'Oh, uh, well, she's just in the shower, I guess.' and moved to the next room. Shit, she was probably alive for a long time after she fell. I guess it was justice that I got to pull her out of there and stick around till they pronounced her dead."

"That must have smelled awesome."

"I wondered if she was happy to die, if she knew what kind of misery it was to be trapped in a home like some factory-farmed chicken or pig. Her fucking family showed up, of course, talking lawsuit, suddenly so caring with money involved." Slim looked away from Trey. "Miss Chris broke her pelvis. Do you know how hard that bone is to break?" Slim turned back, shook his head. "Don't you see? The human body is not supposed to live long enough for the pelvis to break, but that's the number one injury in these nursing homes! They extend their miserable lives with drugs just to keep the money coming. Then finally they break under their own weight."

"You start too many sentences with 'Don't you see?' Trey. You've been doing it since Cheyenne, maybe before, and it's dangerous, man. It paints you into a corner and it makes me afraid to really talk to you."

"We ran a Central American kid the other day. He was probably in his twenties, but he seemed much younger. He got hit by a car up in Langley Park, crossing University Ave. Montgomery County put up a huge fence in the median, but it still doesn't stop these foreigners from jaywalking. I mean, they'd rather scale the fence than go to a crosswalk."

"It's probably easier than how they got to the United States."

"Probably. Do you really think Jake didn't like my stories?"

"No, he just texted me. He has a big project to finish. He could only come out for a bit." Slim thought for a second, then let his drunkenness talk him into saying more. "What do you think of him?"

"Jake? Normal guy, I guess. A little strange, like a guy who came to America as a kid and never quite fit in."

"That's true, actually. His parents were from Belarus. Now they live in Israel."

"Interesting. And you guys work together?"

"In the same building. Different contractors, different clients." Trey stayed quiet with a perplexed look, which was common whenever Slim talked about his work in the intelligence community. Slim mistook Trey's caution for curiosity and said, "We've been close for over two years now."

"Huh, that's great, I guess. How long have you and I been 'close?'" Trey asked.

"Since the days of missilin'," Slim said with a twang and ordered another beer himself, wondering if at any minute he'd spill his beans. Trey went on.

"The Salvadorian kid didn't speak English, and he didn't seem to understand my Spanish, or he was ignoring it as we went to the hospital. He had a goddamn bone poking out of his arm, just below the shoulder, and I had to hold him down for the medic to start an IV. I had all my weight on him, including on that snapped arm, plus he was restrained, and still I couldn't keep him down. The medic was shouting at me, calling me an asshole, and the Salvadorian's eyes were huge black bubbles, like a spider's."

"Dude, I know you probably have a million of these stories. This is just like at Sandy Ko's, remember? It's admirable how you remember so much, but don't curse yourself. Let some of this go, please."

"He knew, that Salvadorian, or at least he feared, that he would be deported if he went to the hospital. He totally knew the score."

"Did you get the IV in?"

"No. I had to hold that motherfucker down, practically sat on his chest while he faded in and out. He was all fucked up and we had to get him to Med Star in DC, which was the closest trauma center. I don't even know if he made it. I had blood all over me from tangling with him."

"That shit would make me sick, I'd figure they all had AIDS," Slim said, turning the heads of Nellie's patrons.

Slim thought of Jake, who didn't have a project so far as he knew and hadn't texted as he'd claimed. His manner and body language as he left made Slim nervous to think of the next time they'd meet. He turned back to Trey and said, "I'll bet you're good at firefighting. I'll bet your fellow firefighters admire you just like we did in the Air Force. But maybe it's not a good fit long term. For your sanity?"

"I did take the Foreign Service Exam a couple months ago. They're investigating my background," Trey said as he paid, swiping Slim's credit card out of the way as he tried to pick up the whole tab. They bundled up and headed to the metro.

"Why am I not surprised?" Slim laughed. "Was it like in *Spies Like Us?*"

"No, it was pretty bureaucratically boring. I passed though. The oral exam too."

"That's great, man, congrats!"

"Eh, I was just glad they didn't care about me smoking weed in Peace Corps. Hey, did you go to the inauguration?" Trey asked.

"Hell no, I wouldn't have been caught dead there. It was freezing. Jake and I just hung out at home." Trey gave Slim a strange look but went on.

"Yeah it was miserable. We had to stage from midnight on, just in case. DC let the bars stay open all night, remember? I only ran one call the whole day. An SUV full of drunks from Potomac. They were speeding back from Georgetown, and they hit a security guard head-on. Took the guy's head off, nearly. He would have used the American Legion Bridge to get to work, but it was closed for the event. All the drunks survived. I had to transport one chubby bitch, whose only injury was a burn on her back because the stupid cunt climbed onto their overturned car and laid on a pipe to stay warm."

"Dumb cunt."

"The whole ride, she's laying on her fat, seaback stomach, bellowing, 'Oh-bah-mah! Oh-bah-mah!' I've never come so close to wanting to kill someone." Slim took a long breath as they rode the escalator down to the trains.

"Yeah, Jake and I were glad to miss that whole thing. Pretty much just laid in bed."

"The security guard was black. The Potomackers were white. He was going to work the inauguration. They were coming back wasted from Georgetown."

"We've been together *over two years*, don't you get that? Since my trip to Pedro." Trey stared at the train tracks.

"Oh-bah-mah," he mimicked. "Oh-bah-mah."

Two years before the night at Nellie's, on the afternoon of his flight to visit Trey in Los Angeles, Slim had an unnerving encounter with a girl he'd hired a couple months prior.

At the time of her interview, Slim saw her as a minimally qualified applicant, fresh from a pricey liberal arts college, a child of upper-middleclass wealth: in DC, they were a dime a dozen. Her "work" as a consultant would gain her some experience before getting an MBA, which she'd likely never complete before meeting a guy who made thrice what she did, enabling her to "dabble" as she'd done all her life. She'd sleep with Slim for a while, and he would later transition into her professional network. She'd never tell her future husband the extent of their relationship; and she'd likewise never know that she was one of a long string of Slim's "hires."

During the interview, Slim served softball questions, pretending to scribble her responses into his notebook. Once on board, he put her on easy projects and brought her to happy hours, pairing his role as mentor with a pattern of compliments, and sooner or later she got drunk enough to ask to go home with him. In the office, Slim treated her normally despite the glint in her eye, which slowly dissipated as she understood they were not a couple. But if she texted him late in the evening, he picked her up, bought her drinks, and banged her just the same.

Sometimes Slim felt bad that he hired lesser-qualified women over suitable male applicants, but he steadied himself to think that if the rejected men were truly entrepreneurial, they would stick somewhere else and do good things, unlike the twits he strung out twice a year.

On the day he left for San Pedro, she cornered him in the office break room to ask where he was going.

"L.A.," he said, "Visiting an old Air Force buddy."

"Are you going *alone*?" she asked. "I've been there a few times." Slim looked at the others in the break room who were tuning to their conversation.

"It's a pretty quick trip."

"Were you a pilot?!"

"Nah, I was missileer, 'a guardian of the high frontier,'" he joked, borrowing the label higherups used with the rank and file to keep them motivated. Most onlookers in the break room departed save for one man, who was so good at being subtle neither Slim nor the twit knew he was there.

"What's your *friend* like?"

"Yuri," Slim said, mistakenly thinking she'd asked Trey's name.

"Is he Russian?" she asked.

"Kind of."

"What's he like?" Slim tightened his jaw and tried to think of a way out that wouldn't hurt her feelings. However, an urge came over him to keep talking, not for the sake of the twit's curiosity, but because Slim was nervous about visiting Trey, fearful that they were only best friends during the twilight zone that was missiles.

"He's a better man than me," Slim started. "I'd kind of like to be more like him, but I'm not sure which qualities of his I could copy. He's great with people, but he's that way because he really *likes* them. I have to force myself to like people. Trey has room to like almost everyone. If you were dating him, he'd never string you along like I'm doing."

"But is he good looking and successful?" she asked. Slim ignored her and continued further into his Trey memories. The man in the break room slowed his breathing and relaxed his muscles, still unnoticed by Slim and the twit.

"He does have his dark side, that's for sure. As much as he gives interpersonally, he can snap into some real hopelessness. Yuri has it in him to go dark for weeks at a time."

"And you two launched missiles together?"

"We didn't launch any, thank God. These were nukes, sweetie." She smiled and moved closer to Slim. He let the twit dissolve as his mind traveled back to Vandenburg Air Force Base.

"I heard about Trey—that's his real name—way before we actually met. When I started training in California, he was already a legend. The instructors hated him! The way they bashed this guy, you'd think he sold the launch codes to China, or drowned a bunch of puppies, or raped someone's sister. But all he did was ask his classmates, and a lot of the instructors, philosophical questions about launching nukes. He just wanted to understand why we developed and still had these weapons.

"They even slammed him for things he did in his free time. Get this, he took a poetry class at the local community college, at night, and they were beside themselves that someone would want to do such a thing while going to nuke school. The instructors even made fun of Trey for tutoring the children of inmates—Lompoc is a rough prison town, in case you didn't know. He volunteered at the base library and hid clues for scavenger hunts inside books. They say people are still finding them, and still looking for them."

"He sounds quirky," she said.

"He is. All his philosophizing and volunteering at Vandenburg took away from his studies—which I don't think bothered him—and he finished last in the class. By then, the instructor's badmouthing of Trey made him ten feet tall in my mind, but when I finally met him in Cheyenne, I was surprised at how disarming he was. Just a friendly guy with a funny walk. His hair was always almost out of regs. He wore his flight suit like a kid's onesie pajamas, like he was laughing at his parents: 'It's not bedtime, yet!'

"In the bottom leg pocket of his flight suit, where technically only your flight cap was supposed to go, he always had a paperback stuffed inside. Other guys from the squadron would come up and kick him in the ankle where the books were hidden to try to get him in trouble, and to make fun of him for reading so much. But he welcomed it and then told them what he was reading like a 5th grader giving a book report. It was like kicking a jukebox—he just started singing.

"The first day I saw him in the squadron, I was still orienting myself to missile culture, which is strange as shit, which is maybe what drove Trey to be such a looney. He was in the middle of telling a group of guys about a book called *Their Eyes Were Watching God*. He went on about how hard it was to understand the backwoods Florida slang, but he said he kept reading because the author, Zora Neale Hurston, once worked as a librarian on an Air Force base back East. He went on to say that Zora had an unrequited crush on Langston Hughes, and that maybe it was because Hughes was gay. None of these things any of us knew or cared about….except that Trey was so genuine about them. The guys in the squadron had never seen another dude who wasn't a teacher, or wasn't trying to sleep with some girl, talk about books like Trey. But he really cared that we got at least a gist of what he was reading, and even better if we read it too.

"I didn't recognize it then, and I probably wasn't comfortable enough in my sexuality to say so, but Trey reminded me of girls I knew at Northwestern, all English majors. They were so confident in their worthless degrees. It was probably because they came from money, but there seemed to be something else driving them. They knew they would be able to make it on their words. I would have read the back of a cereal box if they told me to. Trey, the same way, talked me into buying—and half reading—a couple of books. I realized after we grew to be best friends how intimate it is when someone talks you into reading a book."

"Which books would you recommend to me?"

"The Notebook," Slim said and laughed.

"I love that movie!" She wheedled. Slim continued.

"Because of Trey's reputation at Vandy, they crewed him with Bill Carson, the most hard core missileer in our squadron. Bill was from Texas, and Trey joked that if Bill had his way he would have replaced 'U.S. Air Force' on his name patch with simply, 'Texas.' Bill found out quickly that Trey knew his stuff and wasn't as big a fuckup as the instructors warned. And on a personal level, Trey talked football, sang Robert Earl Keen songs, listened to Bill's backwoods stories about hunting squirrel, and other such nonsense. They even had inside jokes about a radio show called 'Roy D Mercer,' which was dumb and redneck, but it made Billy laugh like a kid.

"Despite that, Bill was hard on Trey, still made him study all the time, and gave him mini-tests every shift. After a few months, they were on alert one afternoon, changing into their pajamas, when Trey went behind the curtain and came back dressed in a three-piece, mismatched suit he bought at *Goodwill.* He even slicked back his hair like Al Pacino. He just sat there manning the console like it was nothing. Bill processed it for about ten minutes and then fell out of his chair laughing. He'd never seen anything like it.

"He said, 'Ciuri's crazier than a shit-house rat! They should pull his clearance for being such a nutcase!' By that time, Trey had won over not only Billy Carson, but most of the squadron."

"So, your friend put on a suit while he was underground? How is that funny?"

"Well, it wasn't the suit. It was that Bill was this regimented Texan who loved missiles and the military more than life itself. Trey had such a bad rep coming out of training—mind you, only because he liked to tutor kids and read poetry—that he had to play from behind when he got in the squadron. But like I said, Trey's strength is people, even an old Texas bloodhound like Billy, and Trey reeled him in and then freaked him out with the Al Pacino thing."

"He does seem quirky."

"He used to organize trips to Denver to do pub quiz, which Trey was really good at. But he smoked so much that he'd miss questions because he'd be outside speaking Spanish with the burrito buggy guys. In the winter he stood on the steaming manholes and pretended he was Marilyn Monroe. Our teams always came up just short of winning within the number of questions Trey missed, and he'd laugh about it, and pretend to be a villain from Scooby Doo: 'I would have won trivia too, if it wasn't for you kids and your mangy dog!'

"He was like that. Just when I thought he was in it for himself, that he was looking for promotion, or attention from a girl, whatever—he'd say something humble, self-deprecating, cheesy, or generous. I was in awe of him. Despite my ego."

"I can't imagine you in awe of anyone," the twit said. "You barely notice me and we're sleeping together." Slim smiled, thinking they were alone in the break room while the man listened in the back, shapeless and invisible.

"He was one of the fastest people I'd ever seen to connect with others. Maybe because he was an Air Force kid, and he was used to moving all the time? He had such a variety of interests on the base. People would see him at the library and he'd remember their kids' names; he'd go to the gym on Friday night, when the rest of us were drunken idiots, to watch guys in our squadron play intramural basketball. On holidays, he drove out to the missile field to bring pizza to the people who had to work. And then he started writing newspaper articles about people on base that no one knew about—guys who organized the warehouses and cooked food for the missileers; cops who had been guarding missiles for four years with little recognition. One time he wrote about this guy who got a degree in biology and did well enough on the MCATs to get into med school. I watched this guy's wife reading the article—you would have thought she won the lottery. She kept sniffling and saying how she was going to send it to the guy's mom, and how she would cry too.

"Trey's articles endeared him to the commanders, because God knows they had a hell of a time keeping people motivated to be on constant alert for nuclear war. At that time, missiles was married with

Air Force Space Command, so conceivably people who did missiles could also do space tours, which were much more desirable. Trey started to recruit the officers who'd done space tours to give presentations on the different systems we have down in Colorado Springs, where most of our satellite squadrons are. He also connected F.E. Warren with the two bases that launched rockets, Vandenburg in California and Patrick in Florida, so we could learn about that. He bought books and software to learn French, Russian, and Japanese in case people in the squadron wanted to learn more about the space agencies in those leading countries."

"Wow, he must be a general by now." Slim ignored her comment, then took a breath and realized how free he felt to talk about Trey, how excited he was to reconnect with him, and how empty his pursuit of the twits had been.

"Yuri kept a *Pilot G2 .7* pen in his pocket, and he used to unscrew it before he left his apartment, checking the ink level like a cop checks bullets in his gun. He rarely drank and he smoked like a chimney. Girls liked him, kind of, but he didn't like them. Except for one chick in the squadron, who everyone knew was a lesbian—everybody but Trey. He said he dug her because she wasn't 'girly.' Now she hosts a standup show called 'The Dyke Mic.'

"He used to show up to the squadron an hour before everyone else, plug in his griddle, and have bacon and omelets smelling up the whole Ops building. It was a total fire code violation, but the commanders didn't dare say a thing because he raised the morale of so many would-be-disgruntled missileers.

"And the Colonels gave him leeway. One day, on a Monday in January, MLK's birthday, we were sitting in predeparture for the usual spiel, and at the moment when the Colonel asked, 'any questions?'.....no one ever had any questions....Trey stood up and asked if he could read something to the group. It was an OpEd criticizing the state of Wyoming for not making MLK day a holiday. No one had ever considered it, but to hear Trey talk about it opened a lot of our eyes.

"He helped us do our taxes, though we were all suspicious of how he learned to do them. None of us ever got audited—we probably didn't make enough money for the IRS to care—but it seemed fishy how Trey got everybody a refund. He also talked us into starting IRAs, which we later thanked him for.

"He showed us new music—The Mekons, Lifter Puller, The Meters, Creeper Lagoon. I still listen to that stuff—it's my missiles soundtrack. Trey was never a douche about it, either, when he'd introduce a new band. Most people, when you admit you haven't heard of their music, roll their eyes and expect you to bow to their coolness—930 Club types. Trey was happy if you liked his stuff, and he'd give credit to the guys who showed him—DJs at the Air Force Academy radio station, mostly.

"But the best thing maybe about Trey was that he accepted people who everyone hated. It was amazing how he could find something to like about nearly everyone." Slim stopped to notice how tenderly he was describing Trey, and how his tenderness glanced off the twit's face. "Even I felt unworthy sometimes, and we were best friends. Unless they crossed him, he loved everyone in the squadron like family.

"The worst person in our squad was this girl, Kat Schuster, a Space Captain who thought she was too good for missiles, always trying to kiss the commanders' asses while looking down on us, making us call her ma'am even though no one else at her level did it. Stealing credit from anyone she could. She was a twat in the truest sense.

"One day, Trey and I got back to base after a long alert. It was early afternoon and all I wanted to do was tie one on and go to bed. As we're dropping off the keys in the squadron, Trey got word that Captain Schuster had an emergency appendectomy while on alert, and was recovering in a hospital way out there, in Sterling, Colorado, which was a good two hours away.

"'Hey, Slim,' he said, 'Why don't we go visit Schuster? Bring her flowers?' It was so outrageous, I wasn't even mad at him. And I could see that he really meant it. Like, I wouldn't have brought Schuster a dead daisy, but Trey knew she was all alone out there and that no one would visit her dumb ass. So I said yes. And we didn't just bring her flowers. We brought pizzas to the guys at the missile facility nearby and cigarettes to the cops who were stuck guarding a site."

"Did that change Captain Schuster?" she asked.

"No way! She was still the same twat. In fact, I think she screwed Trey over a couple of times on alert, got him in trouble. How Trey got her back is another story."

"So, when will you be back from L.A.?"

"In a couple days," he said quickly. "Hey," he began and paused long enough to signal a change of subject. "We've had a good time together since you came on board, but today it stops. We both had fun, but we need to move on." She twisted her face in anger and then walked out. Slim followed.

The man in the back of the room was invisible, barely breathing. He'd hidden for much longer periods of time in more dangerous places. His shape had not changed during Slim's conversation, yet his ears drank in the words of a man describing another with love, humor and worry. Trey was not an easy man to be best friends with. But to hear it as if through a spy's bug, the man knew that Slim had allowed himself to be changed by Trey. He sensed in Slim a longing to being changed again. The man regained his shape, resumed normal breathing, and left the building, aiming to beat Slim to his house.

****

The night before they visited Sandy Ko, while Slim slept in the guest room of the Ciuri's San Pedro condo, Trey had a dream he'd had since early childhood.

He's around five years old, sitting in an airplane, his face pressed to the window's plastic sheath as it approaches Los Angeles. Trey's seat, a few rows in front of the wing, catches the engine's hum, routing it through his spine and out his forehead.

"We're lined up on final," says the colonel from the next seat. "Make sure and pop your ears."

"Century Boulevard?" asks Trey, knowing he's right, but seeking the colonel's praise for a correct answer.

"That's right! 100th Street!" The colonel peers over Trey's head. "Do you know why he's putting the flaps down?"

"Why?"

"To reduce the air flowing over and under the wings. The less air flow, the less...."

"Lift?"

"Yes!" The colonel musses Trey's hair and then says, "There's nothing prettier than a controlled descent, Trey. Well, your mom is prettier, right, Momma?" His wife smiles despite being compared to a moment in aerodynamics.

The dream usually ended there with Trey waking to a warm feeling; however, on the night before he met Sandy Ko, Trey's fantasy went on:

His father's tussling of his hair sent him falling from the plane. Fear shook his dreaming body, and in his mind he tried to hide the

216

suicides, to mask the fact that he'd decided on so many occasions to end his life. He deserved to fall now, his eyes blasted open, blaring unconcealable terror as he grasped at the nothing within his control.

Colonel Ciuri fell into Trey's view. He was Christ in a parachute, with arms outstretched into which Trey glided, allowing his dad to hold him, deploy the chute and float to earth.

Trey woke up with the same warm feeling, only this time he processed the dream as an adult, without wonderment. His dad *was* controlled descent: to glide to earth with him was to surrender, the alternative he'd run from all his life. It spurred him to seek other jobs, take on additional hobbies; to chat up and befriend strangers, to move and move and move again. He noticed with a strange joy that the feeling of surrender, though uncomfortable, was different than the desire to die.

At breakfast, before Slim woke up, the colonel tousled Trey's hair as he walked by.

"Slim still sleeping?"

"I guess so." He stared at the food he had once been eager to eat. He craved a cigarette, then remembered that he'd quit.

"You taking him to work with you?"

"No, I'm off."

"Where to? Hollywood?"

"Yeah."

"I'd figure a guy like Slim would have seen the place before. Flashy as he is. Nothing but kooks up there."

"Yeah."

"You give Slim one-word answers too?"

"How should I elaborate?"

217

"I'm trying to engage with you, Trey. We live together."

"Yeah, I'm sorry about that." Trey felt his face reddening.

"You think you're inconveniencing us? It's great to have you. We're in awe of what you're doing."

"Awe? Doing? I'm doing *nothing*, I've done nothing. That's why Slim is here—to introduce me to some buddy of his in Hollywood—to get me a better job than the four I have now."

"That's all part of the adventure."

"Adventures are for kids. I'm 28 years old for Christ's sake."

"You'll settle into something. Mom and I don't have any doubt."

"You always told me growing up, whenever I did something wrong that Papa would have kicked you in the teeth for this and that. Why weren't you harder on me? Why didn't you ever kick *me* in the teeth?"

"It was a different time."

"I think an ass kicking or two would have done me well. May have gotten me to study at the zoo and actually made something of my life."

"We didn't want to raise you that way."

"Why?" Trey noticed his dad's face reddening, and he had to look away.

"We didn't want anything to happen to you."

"Like what?"

"Like anything," his dad said from a dry throat. "We want you to live with us if that's what you need."

"A fool and a whore."

"What?"

"Just something I say."

"I've heard you say it, what does it mean?"

"It's a whole-life-is-fucked feeling."

"Please don't say that, please don't talk about life being worthless. It's not, Trey."

"Dad, are you ok? I was just….I was just trying to explain…."

"So explain it, but please don't be so harsh. So hopeless."

"I feel like that three-eyed fish."

"What fish?"

"The mural of the three-eyed fish down by Point Fermin."

"Haven't seen it."

"You've probably passed it a million times. The story goes that some guy painted it on his way back from a party. To protest toxic dumping in the harbor."

"Hmm. It doesn't seem to have been effective."

"But it's become a sort of symbol for Pedro. Three eyes, four dorsal fins, each eye pointing a different direction. He's from here, but he doesn't belong. No one understands what he means, a fool and a whore."

"I think you've just had a lot of time to think about things. And you're too hard on yourself. You went pretty quick from Air Force to Peace Corps, Grammy dying in between. Then you got evacuated. And teaching 8th grade? That's brave, Trey. But it's a lot. You're getting a masters, you're learning here. And you're with your family. We love it."

Trey swallowed to chase away the taste of his dad's praise.

"Yeah, that's what people tell me about moving back 'home.' They say it's like 'the prodigal son.'"

"There you go!"

"Prodigal means wasteful, dad."

"You're not wasteful." Trey sensed his dad's weakness: watching his son grind himself into nothing. He almost smiled to think that he had control over the colonel, that he could make him squirm.

"Here's another foolish, whorish example," Trey continued. "There's a famous writer, very up-and-coming. Everyone says he's writing 'great American novels.' Oprah tried to include one of his books in her club and he laughed at the idea, like his work was too good for the bloated twats who watch Oprah."

"Oprah does attract a certain crowd."

"She does! And they are likely a bunch of fat halfwits. But when you read this guy's stuff, you can just see him at a café with his NPR friends: a bunch of dolts who think they're better than everyone else when they're basically the same as the Oprah minions."

"Ok, that's literature and popular culture. You don't have to watch Oprah, you don't have to read that guy."

"Maya Angelou gets credit for that 'caged bird' line, but it was Paul Lawrence Dunbar who wrote it, and he was buddies with the Wright Brothers, and he died young. Of TB, I think. And Maya Angelou gets *credit*?! For *anything*?!"

"I don't know, Trey…."

"Norman Mailer said that aside from all the obvious reasons George Bush sucked, his disregard for the English language was his most egregious offense. I agreed, and I thought it had to be true if Mailer put so much thought into it, if he could zero in on how exactly Bush was such a yutz. But then I found out what a horrible person Norman Mailer was, the terrible way he treated people, and I felt like curling into a ball."

"Lit again. Politics. You can avoid that too and still help people."

"Where I work, at the union. We bust our asses to teach entry level folks to better themselves. It seems so noble to us. And then we see the bosses in their parking spaces with their hundred-thousand-dollar Mercedes cars, and they're just as bad as the CEOs they fight against. And the Democrats who take their votes! You think they care about the working class?!"

"I guess every organization has its hypocrisy."

"A guy at the *LA Times* the other day did a profile on the Bill Gates Foundation, and he found that the stuff they invest in actually causes the problems they're trying to solve. Like oil refineries that cause asthma in Africa—pay dividends to Gates who helps the ones who didn't die of it."

"You can still live your life. You can try to avoid hypocrisy. I'll bet it's hard."

"It seems like more than hypocrisy, though. In Peace Corps, I got really close to the people in my group, or at least I thought. I felt like we had bonded so quickly, that we were tight. I wrote letters—real letters—to all of them, but only three people wrote back and two of them were just complimentary replies. A fool and a whore has no idea who he's close with. And if those people really thought it out, that's how they would describe me, a fool and a whore. But no one can think."

"What about Wade? And Tony O? Slim in the other room here. How about that kid with the beard from Peace Corps who calls you from Nepal? You seem close to them."

"I'm glad you didn't mention Michelle."

"It doesn't take Oprah to see that you two are probably not getting married."

"I've tried to teach English everywhere I've lived. To people who wanted it. I don't think I helped at all."

"It's hard to measure. Look Trey, I don't want to be one of those sunshine blowers who says that everything you do makes a difference. That everybody should get a trophy."

"Ah, fuck it! My angst is just *American* angst! Oh, poor Trey Ciuri, how it weighs on his soul! So cute of him to care about the downtrodden! How he grieves for their toiling!"

"Jesus said the poor will always be with us."

"That's just something to keep them all in line, to believe that their reward is in heaven. Christ."

"It's all I had in prison."

"You know, I feel like I'm drowning when you bring up Vietnam. I know it formed you, and I am reminded nearly every day how hard it was to endure for that long, but I can't offer anything to what you just said. All my life, the mention of Vietnam has stopped every conversation."

"What would you add?"

"Remember when I was in fourth grade? When I brought the Big Gulp cups to show-and-tell, and showed the class the tap code?"

"Yes, your teacher called me right after, worried, wondering how much 'time' I'd done in prison."

"I still feel like that kid, proud, but not sure why. And continually unaware that I'm explaining it incorrectly."

"You seem to be aware now. How has your perspective changed?"

"Now that you're back. For 30 years now. Does it bother you that Vietnam was a mistake? That you never should have been there? That pukes like McNamara didn't care if you lived or died?"

"McNamara was a computer, and all his whiz kids punched cards. Even POWs were ones and zeros to him. Stats." The colonel paused. "He probably thought he was winning….killing three million Vietnamese, compared to our 58,000 lost."

"Is *that* our world? People who think that way get to run things?"

"I don't know, Trey."

"When I was in Nepal, it was early Spring, and one day I magically woke up an hour earlier than usual, at five am instead of six. I had no idea why until later, when I checked my email at the internet café and the website reminded me to set my clock forward. Nepalis don't do daylight savings. It was a simple thing, but I was overcome, and I ran out into the street and went into the first Hindu temple I saw and started praying."

"What does that mean? You prayed to Hindu gods?"

"Oh, I don't know. I wish you understood, Dad. I know it's too much to ask, but I wish you had the answers."

"No one does, Trey. That's a part of life. You know, maybe God says it's ok to be 'a fool and a whore,' if it means that you have to keep trusting that good things can happen; if it means that you never stop trying."

"That's what the politicians want! That's what the Catholic Church and all them *evangenitals* want! That's every dictator! Every union

boss, CEO, principal of a school! Trust! Never stop trying! Fuck that!"
Trey walked away and down the stairs as a sleepy Slim came up, joining
Colonel Ciuri for breakfast.

Slim had also dreamt the night before, a reenactment of what
happened just before his flight to Los Angeles. When he arrived at his
house, he found the door unlocked, the alarm echoing against the
walls. He should back away, call the police, he thought; however, the
idea of missing his flight, his ego driving him to take care of his own
business, and anger at whomever had broken in pushed him further. He
checked corners and closets, resisting the urge to pick up weapons: a
wrench, a lamp, small mirror from the wall. His instincts, honed during
years of wrestling, made him feel light, like he'd just made weight.
Whoever was in his house would submit to him or make him submit, and
though he hadn't been in a match since college, he liked his chances. He
imagined three kids from the neighborhood, scared and excited, trying to
remove the flat screen mounted to his bedroom wall. For a second, he
thought the twit had beaten him home and used her key.

As he stood at the kitchen island, he froze at the sight of clothing
folded neatly: a pair of khakis and a button up shaped in squares, military
style, next to polished, size nine shoes. Then Slim saw the figure in the
corner of his eye, just as he changed his breathing, increased his heat
signature, adjusted the angles of his body to no longer blend into the
shape and color of the dishwasher against which he sat. The figure's eyes
were open and sharp, a reptile's, looking upward but not directly at
Slim. It was Jake Aretz, a person Slim recognized from work, but always
tried to ignore. He barely made the flight.

****

They arrived at Sandy Ko's office after two hours on three buses. Slim and Sandy hugged, then caught up with small talk. Trey, who was piqued by the idea of meeting someone in "the industry," noticed that Sandy's head was as big as Slim's, but on a shorter, frailer body. His eyebrows were black and bushy, hair bleached to the roots, and he bore a baby face. Trey expected to see movie posters on the wall, perhaps a golden laser disc left by a predecessor, or signed memorabilia. He imagined that Sandy would be twitchy and call him "babe" or "baby," that he'd curse and throw things as if they were unbreakable props.

But most of Sandy's wall space was covered by either cork or white board, with thumbtacks hanging all shapes and colors of paper as if they were garments strung between apartment buildings. The grease boards were jumbles of brainstorming, each new thought competing with others in a collection of words and symbols that looked from a distance like vomit from which it was impossible to reverse engineer what the puker ate.

Sandy was sedate in a t-shirt and shorts behind a massive wooden desk that looked like a defect from a now-shuttered department store rather than an antique of any sort. There was a sink in the corner of the room on which a coffee cup full of lather, a shaving brush, and an old but sharp razor lay. A towel draped over a wooden chair in front of the sink, a small mirror hanging above it. The couch on which Slim and Trey sat had a folded blanket and pillow pushed to one side. Above them, three louvered windows with a view of the building across the street were cranked open, sucking up traffic noise a few stories below.

225

"I don't like going back and forth, like in a dialogue," Sandy started. "You have things to share with me and I with you. I'd like us to speak at length without being interrupted. If you are the kind of person we look for, I'll know it by what you say and how you say it. Sorry for the formalities, but I need to be clear. This is what someone said to me….shit, seven years? Seven years ago.

"So please tell me about your life here in Los Angeles, Monday through Sunday. Imagine your words on a long scroll, as unmolested Kerouackian prose that I will hopefully be able to bottle and sell. Get some water from the sink if you need it—no cups, sorry. And if you're going to do characters, please change your voice so I can see the difference between you and them. I'm going to record you. Be nasty, be racist, be unremorsefully violent. Nothing you say will offend me. There's only one thing you can't talk about, and I'll let you know if you're getting close to it. Start when you're ready."

Slim seemed unsurprised, almost smug at Sandy's invitation. Trey, though unprepared to step into the spotlight so quickly, felt a gentleness cover his shoulders. The opportunity to present his version of Los Angeles evoked images of traffic coughing ocean air through rusty exhaust pipes, the dust of a desert not formed to host so many inhabitants, ranchero music, chili and citrus, the loneliness of glamor, and a mass of people who needed help.

"The week begins in San Pedro at my Grandfather's house, whose front window faces the harbor, where ships with Chinese names slide by. They arrive full, leave empty. Between 2 and 3 pm, my relatives show up to a 1950s living room that smells of sauce cooking since the morning before. Papa keeps a banker's track of RSVPs and beats back hungry guests urging him to put the pasta in, bellowing that he won't begin until he sees 'the whites of their eyes.' The noodles scream like shellfish when they hit the water. We arrive empty, leave full.

"My cousins are Long Beach cool with Pedro dago roots. They have no reason to leave California, and even a trip behind 'the orange curtain' seems exotic. They either work or go to school. They date each other's friends, who they sometimes bring to pasta, who Papa excuses for not being Italian, so long as they're Catholic, which they usually are nominally. The cousins eat quickly and shake hands in hip ways when they leave.

"My aunts and uncles watch the Dodgers in Papa's living room, and in between innings they complain about Los Angeles, which annexed San Pedro solely for the harbor. 'We could be a rich city like Long Beach,' they moan. They talk about the factories that employed them after the war, the canneries that have since moved to Samoa, and even cry over the demise of *The San Pedro News Pilot*, which they nicknamed 'the fish wrapper' when it was in circulation. After dinner they have coffee and put in a Dean Martin roast.

"I'm not cool enough to leave with the cousins, but I'm too young to appreciate banter between Don Rickles and Nipsey Russell. I stick around and stare at the harbor, expecting to see Jack Nicholson's character from Chinatown zigzagging his way to the freeway, a blonde named Sharon Tate in the front seat. My aunts and uncles would say what a poor shame it was about Sharon, a San Pedro girl, who got caught up with that sicko rapist. 'She was pregnant,' they mention sadly.

"I walk home parallel to the water, about 12 blocks. I'm enamored by the semiarid climate that turns sidewalks into moonrocks, which are split into wrinkles as desert plants creep up. When I get back, there's an email from my editor at *Tongva Plume*, San Pedro's independent newspaper, asking me to interview Mike Watt, the famous bassist. I have 15 minutes before he opens for a band at The Whale and Ale.

"I borrow my mom's car and buy a funsaver at Rite Aid. The other reporters ridicule me for not having a digital camera, but those things seem so expensive; however, at seven bucks a pop, I may have already spent enough on disposables for two digitals—so fuckall.

"My very employment at the *Plume* is a ridiculous notion to everyone but me. The stringers and the editorial staff were taken aback when I stopped in on a random Tuesday, walking from the bus, looking for a job.

The publisher said, "'You're a Ciuri….and you want to write for *me?*' His paper is as liberal as my dad, San Pedro's returned war hero, is conservative. But I told him that my father reads the *Plume* and appreciates its reporting, even if he doesn't agree with the slant. 'Pedro is Pedro,' I said, which the publisher lapped up, even though he was raised in Palos Verdes, which sits behind private gates, and looks down on our port town.

"Most issues of *Tongva Plume* feature a photo of Charles Bukowski reading the paper next to a quote, '*Tongva Plume* makes me want to stop drinking and start giving a goddamn.' Perhaps that's what drew me to look there for a job—the quote from a famous resident. They put me on a dozen assignments, either as a writer or photographer. The Mike Watt piece was my last.

"I show up to the bar out of breath and look around for Watt, almost tripping over him as he sits against a piano, rehearsing unplugged. He has fierce blue eyes and a muscular physique underneath a cheap flannel. He's opening for a band from the UK called The Extremely Foul-Smelling Stools. They're drunk and mingling with the baby boomer crowd, hitting on men and women indiscriminately. I snap photos of The Stools and the boomers as I make my way back to Mike to ask for an interview, but just as I whip out my pen and pad, he plugs in and starts wailing. The boomers rush the stage, the Stools retreat behind it, I enjoy the show.

"Watt disappears after 15 minutes. The Stools go on almost immediately, and they're really good, better than the boomers deserve. I walk around the bar, searching for the only cheap flannel in the joint. It gets later and later, and I realize that I am probably the only one not drinking, and definitely the only one stalking Mike Watt. Just as I get ready to hang my head forlorn, I see the silhouette of a man carrying bass-shaped luggage across the street.

"I take a guess at where he's going, and zip through three alleys to get ahead of him. I flip the flash button on my funsaver and snap a pic of him coming around the corner. It pisses him off and he beelines a different direction. I don't have the guts to call out his name, to explain that I'm a 'reporter.' I haven't heard back from the paper since that missed opportunity, and though the job paid nothing, I feel a great loss for fucking it up. Maybe the publisher thinks it's my Ciuri blood that wasn't good enough to get the copy.

That's Sunday.

"Monday morning, I take the earliest freeway flyer bus from a parking lot under the Vincent Thomas Bridge. A bunch of boomers wearing tennis shoes over their stockings, high heels jammed into their purses—board in purple-colored, navel-level fog. Their perfume covers the scent of office supplies. I long for an outlier, someone different than us to get on; someone who would feel at home in Pedro and yet out of place on the fogged-in bus, someone like Bukowski, though he's been dead for a while.

"I get off at the edge of downtown, near Hotel Figueroa, and I imagine what it must be like to stay there, next to the Staples Center, so close to an inner city that hasn't gentrified but soon will. There's always a new Nike ad pasted on the hotel's three pillars, which all bus riders must face as we disembark. I walk to the next bus stop, in front of the library, where I can grab a copy of *The Onion*, and ride to East L.A. where I'll do a 12-hour shift on an ambulance.

"I've been on-and-off EMT certified since college, so I wanted to try ambulance work. But it was only after I got hired that I realized my company didn't run emergency calls, only dialysis transports—so fuckall. It's been an interesting look at the subculture, though, to hear the owners brag about how much money they make per call, blabbing about their network of clinics and doctors, and even people in the Medi-Cal offices. They giggle like Gargamel, which most of us line EMTs think is funny, even those of us who realize they are running a pretty large scam on the state. But, as long as we get our $10/hour and only have to work three 12-hour shifts a week to get health insurance, everyone seems happy. I work there one day a week, so it doesn't matter at all to me.

"For my orientation rides, they put me with Reyes and DeLeon, who man 'the Tijuana Wagon,' and spend most of their shift staged at MacArthur Park catcalling girls. They speak exclusively Spanish, but they switch into heavy cholo-esque English for me. They have nicknames for everyone based on their most pronounced physical characteristics: slanted eyes means you're 'chino,' a limp will get you 'cojo,' 'gordo' for a fat guy, 'culote' for a girl with a big ass. I'm sad that they haven't dubbed me yet. They call each other 'mija,' which means 'my daughter,' according to the Spanish I learned, and when I ask them why, Reyes adopts a professorial tone and says, 'Your literal translation of 'mija' is correct, however, when I say it to DeLeon, what I mean is 'my little bitch!' DeLeon answers something in Spanish that I can't quite get.

"The owners are happy to break up the Tijuana Wagon at least once a week, and I usually ride with DeLeon, who dials down his Mexican-ness—which is refreshing considering that he's Salvadorian. He still talks in a cholo cadence and ends every sentence with either 'bro' or 'dog,' which he pronounces 'dock.'

"I'd like to think he confides in me when he says his dream is to be an L.A. city firefighter— that he's been on the ambulance for five years to get experience. He also shares that he's intimidated by the written test, the oral interview, the background check. He says teachers told him since he could remember that he had a learning disability, though I notice no obvious deficit in our conversations. I ask him sample interview questions and he does fine. He later tells me that teachers in L.A. Unified branded nearly everyone he knew with 'disabilities' so they could keep their high needs status. It's funny to me that he knew their scam but didn't recognize how it could retard him.

"Every time I tell him he's smart enough, he comes up with another excuse: his prior weed use, the neighborhood he grew up in— Pio Pico—which 13 and some other gangs ran in. I did advise him to change his ring tone, in which a cholo voice set to a cumbia beat says, 'se me paró,' which means 'I have an erection.' It's all part of his obsession with being a man.

"And it goes far beyond machismo, or at least my understanding of it. Sure, there's the MacArthur Park *mama sita* moments, but DeLeon also 'dates' a lot of white girls, who he calls 'missy' on the phone, to whom he says his love has increased 'dramastically from day to day.' He explains to me, almost romantically, how much he enjoys ejaculating into a woman. He deplores anal sex, because it's 'gay,' because you can't make a baby that way.

"He woofs when LA City firetrucks go by, yelling, 'those the big dogs, those the big dogs!!' strangely pronouncing 'dog' with a 'G' instead of a 'ck' as usual. When he sees the recruitment billboards for L.A. City with a female in turnout gear, he screams, 'Fucking bitch! Get out of my department!' Then, when we spot a plume of smoke on the horizon, somewhere off the freeway, DeLeon yells, 'A lume up!' which is L.A. City patois for a working fire.

"We drive past a nondescript storefront in a strip mall on the edge of Monterrey Park, where DeLeon casually points out a bar for gay cholos. He seems perplexed that men so hardened by the street could want to be with other men. These guys would kill you for nothing, he says, but they love *la verga*. I see him processing what looks to me as hurt that such strong, determined men could opt out of reproduction, that they would not want to coax as many women as possible into bearing their children. Cholos don't live very long, he says finally, the few who do are called *veteranos*, and they just watch TV all day like vegetables.

"DeLeon is no gangbanger, but he knows plenty of them, some who rode the ambulance and got on with L.A. City so their gangs would have inside knowledge of the emergency responses system, access to hospitals, and the opportunity to steal knox box keys if necessary. He said gangs also sent guys to the military to gain skills to be used later on the street. 'Only the smartest, though, bro,' he tells me, 'go for L.A. City, dock.'

"He tells me about the time a gang kidnapped a rival member to 'practice on.' They took turns choking him out while the fire cadet tried to resuscitate him. 'Broke every bone in that fool's chest,' DeLeon said almost sadly.

"Tuesday, Wednesday and Friday I work at the Service Employees International Union, SEIU, as a workforce development instructor. I teach writing and math to surgical techs, nurse's aids, and phlebotomists who are studying to become nurses. My classes are a good mix of the county: blacks, Mexicans, immigrants from everywhere, even some whites. Sometimes they come to our place in downtown, other times I bus to Harbor General, USC, King-Drew, and Olive View. They're happy to be in class, thankful that the courses are free. And I think they like me.

"There are four of us at the union: me, Sadie, Buddy, and Lou, the lead instructor who hired me. Lou came to L.A. from Chile when he was a toddler, just after Allende was assassinated. His father was a union man too, a *troquero*, who raised his son on stories of Pinochet's henchmen rounding up the opposition, flying them over the sea, and gutting them like fish. He plays Latin beats on his computer and shouts at the other cubicles, *El que no salta es Pinochet!* Everyone who understands him does a quick hop. We're all suckers for that Che revolución shit.

"Lou brings us empanadas and homemade *pebre*, which he says proves he's a Chileno, but also admits that he hates *completos*—hotdogs with mayo and other shit—which proves that he's American. Lou joined the Marines after high school and broke his ankle on the third day of basic training. He ran on it for two weeks before they discharged him, which broke his heart. He finished UCLA three years later and tried to join again, but the recruiter said they didn't want enlisted men with college degrees. In a hush, he shows me a t-shirt underneath his polo that reads "Huevon," which I think means "guy with huge nuts" or something manly. He says he'd hate for the women in the office to see, especially the Latinas, because it's not politically correct, but he still wears it every day.

"Lou's wife is a doctor who sponsored many of her former surgical techs and nurse's aids into higher education, which attracted Lou to our union. He pep-talks us, saying, "our revolution arrives through education!" I notice that he rubs the *huevon* on his chest involuntarily before he speaks.

"Buddy Moreau, a New Orleans native, blames his wife and her daughter, who he refers to as 'the girl,' for his residence in Los Angeles. And though he complains, he drives his Prius around town like Leo DiCaprio, gloating about the free parking he gets for piloting a hybrid. He knows every Armenian bakery from Los Feliz to Larchmont. And he uses his USC alumni network as fruitfully as any former Trojan.

"At his first college, Ohio State, which lured him north with a free ride, he ached for New Orleans, telling his new mates about his *Picayune* delivery route, how he knew every building in downtown by how many papers they took. One night, some guys in his dorm had him over to watch a boxing match. As the fight went on, most of them were yelling "get that n-word!" and "beat that n-word down!" Buddy looks helpless as he tells me this story.

"I give him a look right back and ask, 'Buddy, did it shock you that dudes up in Ohio would be racist?' Before he can answer, I ask, 'People are racist everywhere, right?'

"He looks jaundiced and nauseous to recount it, and says, 'I was the only black guy in that room, man, and they say that shit?' I try to console him by again repeating my belief that everyone is racist. I don't mention that he looks white to me, that I would have guessed he was Hispanic before black, but as soon as I let that thought escape, he says in a southern, black accent, 'muthafuckas!' and laughs. Then he tells me that when he taught in L.A. Unified, black students would often challenge him, 'what the hell do you know, white man?!' He can't win, he says, being white or black.

"Sadie Jane tells me she's a lesbian before I learn much more about her. Then she corrects herself and says she's probably bi. She has a girlfriend, a live in, 'a sista from South Central,' she says with a jive accent while raising her sleeveless arm to reveal a hairy pit caked with deodorant. She corrects herself again, apologizing for mimicking black culture: the word sista, the area called South Central, which was renamed *South L.A.* to separate it from old gangsta lore. She says I need to get used to her saying things, then thinking about them, and rephrasing.

"She tells me she attended Smith College, then cautions me if I have any machismo, to leave it in the *parqueo*; but then she reorients and says that most girls at Smith are only feminists because they have enough disposable income to be that way. Even 'the manifesto that Betty wrote,' she says, was an informal poll of rich chicks who were tired of serving their husbands martinis.

"Sadie's real name is Sor Juana, but she changed it because it was too hard to live up to the namesake: a nun, scientist, poet. Sadie calls herself Latina, pronouncing it with an accent, but then she admits to me that being light skinned, she's been able to pass for white when advantageous.

"Sadie studied Thoughtful Feminism, a rare major at Smith, almost part of a secret society, she levels to me, bred by a counterculture that believed the Seven Sisters were perilously filled with the same types of girls: Betties, they called them—rich white chicks, who only fight to grab the power white men have. Thoughtful Feminism challenges current populist waves: it dispels the pay gap myth by using science and math, claiming that if women who complained about it were any good at science and math they would see the same thing. It blasts feminists for demonizing motherhood, for forcing two generations of girls to believe that raising their own children was weak. And it says that using one's sexuality to get what one wants is lazy and degrading.

"She did her thesis on an artist named Sheri Martinelli, who slept with dozens of influential twentieth century writers, from Ezra Pound to Charles Bukowski. She titled it 'Sister Sheri,' blasting Martinelli's behavior as the antithesis of feminism. Though most remembered Sheri as a 'muse,' she told me, what she actually was was a whore.

"After work we go to the roof, which faces the Hollywood sign, which we can see clearly once and a while. We drink beers and tell stories—it's like out of a movie. Lou and Buddy leave Sadie and me alone, and we trade song quotes, pointing at Los Angeles below, claiming that we can 'see the stars come out tonight, the bright and hollow sky, and the city's ripped backsides.'

"I compliment her teaching style, how she takes such time to get to know everyone in her class, and mails them postcards during the week, encouraging them on their journeys to become nurses. How she does role plays in the classroom, modulates her voice, brings in props, uses multimedia to teach dosage calculations. In that classroom, she *is* Sor Juana, I tell her. I whip out my high school baseball cap—St Jude—with an SJ moniker in faded green and gold, and I say it's for her. She then calls me 'Trey Fibonacci' because she says she sees me everywhere in nature, even in herself. She tells me that I am the first person to love her for qualities other than her beauty. She *is* a goddess, even with hairy pits. She says she's scoured literature, and never found a suitable male character who described a woman's beauty in other than physical terms. We kiss with beer lips, and I ask, 'what about the sista? She smiles and asks me, 'What about Michelle?'"

Trey stopped himself, awash in love with Sadie, ashamed to admit that he had cheated on his girlfriend. He teetered on the precipice of going on as Sandy leaned forward in his chair. Trey blinked Sadie away, took a deep breath.

"Where to from the SEIU roof? Once a week, I'm at the Paul Robeson Cultural Center, a ramshackle outside but a palace within. I imagine Robeson himself in it in the 1950s, his stolen passport nagging him like a phantom limb, the spooks tailing, nervous as they wait on Vermont Ave between Manchester and Florence. I get off the bus near the freeway, buy pan dulce, and sit with Oneil Cannon, a saint of a man, who tells the same story over and over, but it's the greatest story ever told, beginning in Plaquemines Parish over ninety years ago when, as a little boy, he met his great grandfather, a white man named Charlie, who came to America 'with a boot and a shoe,' and ending in South L.A. where he began a printer's union and fought for workers all his life. But you don't want to know about that.

 "Maybe you want me to impersonate a black guy placing an order to the Mexican cashier at the Popeye's on the corner of Manchester and Fig?" Sandy nodded. "Nah, how about a tale from the Wilmington Public Library, where I tutor this guy, Canneo, a Zaputeco from Oaxaca, who brings his daughter Lulu, who picks flowers growing in the parking lot, while we go through English lessons? They bring me grasshoppers covered with lime and chili.

 "Or maybe this: the Compton courthouse, right off the blue line, where I do my Americorps program at the Legal Aid self-help office? Wanna hear about men who come in with faces scratched into hamburger, ashamed to seek restraining orders from their wives because it's not manly? Want me to describe the look in a man's eyes when he understands that he's drawn a 'father unfriendly' judge, and he will lose his kids? How about the families who fill out, but don't understand at all, unlawful detainer paperwork, when their landlords try to evict them from the subdivided slum garage dwelling they've called 'home' for years? Surely you'd want to hear about Dalon, the paralegal who works there, who failed the bar exam 15 times, but is a wizard at the basic services offered in the courthouse. He shouts one liners appropriate to every legal situation: 'It's cheaper to keep her!' 'Mama's baby….Daddy's maybe!'"

Trey stiffened at the intensity in Sandy's eyes, then bowed his head to signal the end.

"Nice stories," Sandy said, pressing stop on the recorder. "There are characters and plots here. I love the cholo ambulance driver, gangsters infiltrating the military and fire department, the confused Latina dyke on the roof. The Pedro family thing could be a series. A bunch of light-skinned teachers who work for a union? Art house potential. Slim told me about your dad—definitely want to use the son of a POW thing. And didn't you teach junior high? Did Slim tell me that?"

"I don't want to talk about it in this context," Trey said. "It wouldn't make for a good story."

"Ah, but it would!" Sandy shouted, the most emotion he'd shown all morning. "That's what I'm looking for….your stories. Any twit can write. No worries, one day." The trio sat quietly until Sandy broke in:

"I can hire you, but you'll have to find your own health insurance. You'll be a private contractor to me. Everything you write becomes mine and then the studio's. Ok, now let's get to reality. Like I said, anyone can write, at least here—it's the stories you're selling— they're unique to you. Then the real trick is figuring out who to sell them to—that's what brings home the bacon.

"I deal in demographics. I'm a throbby-veined capitalist, and I chase the most lucrative demos—the people who watch the most television, and the people who buy the most crap that we advertise. The more TV they watch, the more they buy, the more I get paid, the more you get paid.

"Seabacks are far and away the top demo. 'Craft Beer and Cupcakes:' C-B-A-CK, as in what today's average white chick drinks and eats all day without a second thought. Seaback! I didn't come up with the acronym, but they're a goldmine. White women and the men who call themselves 'feminists.' You know, guys in skinny jeans who wear 'the future is female' t-shirts and follow their women into the living room, sit at their feet, and yield the remote control?

"We write for them. And we flog five narratives:

> 1. You can do anything a man can, probably better!
>
> 2. You've been systematically prevented from achieving everything you dreamed of! The patriarchy and the pay gap are real!
>
> 3. You can—read: should—sleep with anyone you want, anytime you want. Anyone who says otherwise is a slut-shamer.
>
> 4. You can eat anything you want—anyone who questions you is a fat-shamer.
>
> 5. Raising your own kids is for chumps.

"Upon those messages, we develop shows and sell advertising. Watch TV, buy goods, rinse, repeat. Craft beer and cupcakes. Seabacks are children, really, but with significant allowances, and we want them to spend their money freely. I'll give an example:

"We've got this one pig. Man! We didn't even have to groom her! That's the beauty of the YouTube generation. This heifer, she's a college kid, goes to one of those rich liberal arts places in the Midwest.

Knox? Kenyon? Macalester? Eh, I'll look it up. And on YouTube, she strips down, with no shame, to her disgusting underwear, with her gaudy, blubbery tattoos, and starts an interpretive dance in the quad! Entertaining? No! Talented? Not a chance! But it sold. Turns out, of course, that's she's a rich kid from the city, parents are connected, so lots of people want to sign her. And she'll do *anything*. *Say* anything. She's unapologetically gluttonous, which is perfect. After watching *her*, do you know how many seabacks *aren't* going to diet, who are going to *fuck* as many dudes as they can handle, who are going to binge through series after series? The money is beautiful even if they're not.

"And that's the young side of the spectrum. Seabacks have the older end too: the baby boomers, *Sex in the City* types, who control serious money. Real housewives, man! Truly candy from babies. They want so badly to feel like they're not old and used up. You don't even have to disguise the message! Just film a bunch of old, used up women who say over and over that they are not old and used up. Money in the bank.

"It's mindless, I know, and the narratives are unbelievable. As a man, there's a part of me that hates seeing such drivel on T.V. but I learned to accept—and you must also—that Hollywood is not a place to express yourself. We do not house and feed artists here. We employ psychologists, marketers, and businessmen. We are a bunch of Brian Epsteins. We sell bubble gum that loses its flavor, but before you know it, you're throwing your panties on stage. You'll watch our stuff, spend money, and remember it hazily, like you remember the names of your ex-girlfriends.

"The next best demo is minstrels—mostly blacks but it could be any minority who gets people to laugh at racial stereotypes. These roots go way back to the days of 'dance for them white people!' We got that guy who does that junkie character, talking about, 'I'll suck yo dick for crack!' Ha! We got guys who let us sell the N-word! White consumers pay a premium for it, you know. We got that one intellectual director who sells sneakers on the side—he's a slam dunk for the NPR crowd. And what about that boy, that rapper….we started him off bustin' rhymes about killing cops, now he sells insurance—total minstrel! We're also cultivating an offshoot: we call'em 'Uhuru Washingtons'—guys with African first names and slave last names—the pseudo militant intellectuals, hang out, talk smart, good potential for white crossover, for people who want to be even more enlightened. Honestly, it's the only way to get blacks paid and make whites feel ok about it."

"Don't look so sad, Trey! We're selling a stolen screenplay to boomer capitalists who only cared about civil rights in college, when it was convenient. Anyone with any integrity is getting his wrists sewn shut!

"I know that look on your face! It's the 'but what about art?!' whine! If you want to express your true self, you live in the wrong city. I came to Northwestern—you can ask this guy—as a self-hating, nerdy little Jew named Alex Kohen. I wanted to sleep with goy women and hang out with goy dudes. I wanted to fit in so badly I changed my name to Sandy Ko and pledged their wasp frat. Now, I'm out in Jew-land, and everybody thinks I'm Korean! Of course, you never really lose your J card, even if you change your name, and I made my mother happy by marrying a 'nice Jewish girl,' better known to the rest of us as a JAP, eh Slim-ee?

"Don't worry! Money is a fantastic balm. And when you get behind the curtain, my friend of Slim's, you'll learn some mind-blowing secrets! Here's one: pretty much everyone in Hollywood is gay. Yep, it's a long tradition: Catholics send their queer sons to the seminary, Jews send theirs to Hollywood. Another example: Bob Dylan is six people. There's the guy you see wheezing on stage, then there's his stand-in, and three writers—one of who is a woman—and a researcher. Bob Dylan! Six people! Many more secrets, far more shocking than these await, should you accept my offer. I can see it in your eyes—you want this!"

Sandy finished. He thanked Trey and hugged Slim, promising him he'd visit DC. Slim grabbed a cab to LAX. Trey bumbled home on the buses he'd grown to love. He watched a boy, battling sleep like a boxer who'd lost his legs, holding a baggy full of mango bathed in lime juice and chili powder.

Trey dropped in on Papa, who asked him to drive to the market. Papa still cooked, but had others, including Trey, take him from store to store to buy ingredients. It would have been simpler for Papa to send them with a shopping list, but he got such pleasure from comparing prices, discovering bargains, and complaining about the amount of time he spent waiting in line, that it became a daily field trip for John August Ciuri and his chauffeurs.

Papa delighted when it was Trey who could take him, and he praised his grandson for routine strokes of luck like finding a close parking spot or discovering a two-cent sale on tomato paste. "You're livin' right, Johnny!" Papa beamed and Trey basked.

As they unpacked the groceries, exchanging observations on the weather and the Dodgers' season, Trey told Papa that he wanted to become a fireman. Papa looked at the cans and packages, left them on the counter, and sat at the kitchen table.

"You have to fight to be a fireman, Trey," he said. "At least in LA City. I don't know about other departments, but it's not easy."

"Do you think I can do it?"

"You can do anything. Do you *want* to do it? Most days it's all bad news, and in LA, the kooks we have here, shit. They're terrible, the scum of humanity, most of them." Papa's face had changed from jovial grandfather to the grizzled captain Trey remembered from his younger years, the one who would curse every ethnicity and mock Grammy for going to church so often.

"What do I have to do to get in?"

"Take a test, I guess. I could call, no, I can't. I don't know anybody anymore. Maybe some kids or grandkids of my guys got on the job, but I don't know, Trey."

"What was the worst thing you saw?"

"Some coke head bitch in the Valley microwaved a baby to keep her warm. It was the early days of microwaves, thing was as big as my TV. Baby was warm, that's for sure. Coke head bitch."

"That's bad."

"Denise was a baby then. I couldn't separate holding her from holding this rubbery, microwaved kid. Your dad was stationed in Idaho, I think. Maybe the Academy, I can't remember."

"What can I do to get ready for the test?"

"Trey, I'm not sure this is right for you. You have to quit smoking. You have to get in shape."

"I quit smoking. I'm out of shape?"

"Well, let's see. Start doing pushups." Trey snapped to follow Papa's commands, sensing that his performance on the kitchen floor of his grandfather's house would be a quick test to see if he was serious. "That's terrible form," Papa said. "Your back is not straight, your middle is soft as tits." Trey started laughing, which further grizzled the captain. "I didn't tell you to laugh. I didn't tell you to stop. You laugh like that at Drill Tower, and they will kick your ass. Laugh like that on the fire ground and someone dies. Did you get away with that shit at the Academy?" Trey's face filled with blood. Everything in his life that came easy was illuminated by his weak pushups, his middle like a woman's breasts. He tried to think of a suitable excuse.

"The physical standards weren't that high at the Academy," Trey said.

"Why the hell not? They were when your dad was there."

"I guess because now there are girls?"

"Do they think war is like the *Olympics*? You think our women fight *Taliban* women? Jesus Christ! Well, there's no such thing as a *female* fire. Everyone, men and women, perform at the same level, the way it should be. And those pushups you just did looked like a goddamn girl's."

"I can keep doing them."

"No, flip over and start sit ups."

"I'm good at sit ups. Can you hold my feet?"

"Hold your feet? You better start doing sit ups now. If you can't do a sit up without someone holding your legs, don't even apply. Those wimps who hold feet aren't even using their core, it's all hip flexors. Girl stuff again." Trey looked down. Papa looked angry, and Trey imagined him deciding who he loved more, his grandson or L.A. City Fire. There was no answer. Papa wanted to protect them both.

"Look, Johnny, why don't you be a writer? Your dad tells me you're into that, that you're good at it. Do you really want to hang around a firehouse all day running calls?" Trey continued to look down. He was embarrassed that Papa's criticism brought him so low. He'd been yelled at in the past for misbehavior, which was something he could understand as a natural consequence to a childish action. However, as Papa looked down on him now, it seemed as if he'd been waiting for years to tell his grandson that he exercised like a woman.

"Look, Johnny. Look at me." Papa looked away when he saw Trey's eyes. "Remember when your dad recorded your basketball games? In high school?" Trey stayed quiet. "Answer me, do you remember?" Trey nodded. "Remember that one, against the redneck Academy, when you got into a fight at the end of the game?" Trey sniffed, nodded. "Your dad kept the camera rolling, even as that kid grabbed the ball and you went down. He kept filming. I don't know if I would have done that. If your dad was in a fight, I feel like I would first go sock the kid's dad and then knuckle the kid a couple times. But your dad kept filming. And I watched it, how you went down. It was without a fight, Trey. You let that kid bring you down and you gave up the ball. And then your buddy, Tony, the half Italian kid. He jumped in like you were his brother." Trey ground his teeth.

"You gotta fight, Trey. You can't quit. You can't give up." Papa looked at Trey for a second. "In the Fire Academy, back in the forties, they were working us out, and the captain said, 'If you quit on this, you *will* quit on a fire.' And I never forgot that. He was right. Guys who didn't give everything, some of them died. Some people died because of them. You can never quit, Trey.

"When your dad got shot down, I wrote him a letter every day. He was missing in action for the first few years. Grammy and I had no idea if he was alive. She spent more time in that goddamn novena room than she did at home. After some time, I had a dream, and a voice asked me if I would rather have a dead hero for a son or a live one who no one knew. I woke up before I could answer the question. A couple days later, we found out that your dad was in Hanoi with those goddamn gooks twisting him up in knots. Never quit, Trey.

"And I know it's hard to be someone's son. Shit, your dad went away from L.A. because he didn't want to be known as Captain Ciuri's kid anymore. So, if you go to Drill Tower, I have no doubt, mostly because you're a Ciuri, that you can do it. But you have to fight for that ball this time."

Chapter Five: Little Black Passport

The State Department was so riddled with rumors, most based on a speck of truth, that Linda didn't believe it when she heard Trey was getting married. It was a tale grown out of a game of telephone. It was disinformation conjured by her rivals. She compared the news with other gossips she'd processed in her 14 years as a Foreign Service Officer. Some were deeply concerning and likely true, such as when a slew of diplomats resigned after the invasion of Iraq. Others were catty and mean, like the time one of Linda's friends left the embassy bar in New Delhi with two Marines, and people said they held a *menage a trois*.

Regardless of its veracity, the thought of Trey engaged was to Linda more crushing than if she'd heard he'd been maimed, even killed. If he'd lost a limb or his life, Linda would hold it together as the stoic friend, rustling up donations and well wishes via google groups, social media, and her immense personal network. But an engagement fenced her away, made her another girl bemoaning a good guy off the market. Trey, so refreshingly un-State-like, was to Linda someone she could tease and still prop up, eat and exercise with, leave alone for hours and resume a conversation paused at a key moment; someone, in her Twin Cities speak, she could bring home.

They met two years ago in the parking lot of the Foreign Service Institute, a campus in Virginia where diplomats learned languages and tradecraft, which employees jokingly called the community college of the State Department. Linda happened on him as Trey helped a nurse change her tire. She watched as he circled the car like a cat around larger prey, his polo hung on the antenna, his torso beginning to sweat into his undershirt. He carried himself with an alluring lack of over-confidence, confessing to the nurse that he'd changed a tire just once before, kneeling at the jack to make sure it held, chocking the front wheels, rubbing gravel between his fingers.

Beyond fixing the flat, Linda noticed, he was *listening* to the nurse, who was at FSI for a fast course in Swahili before her next posting in Nairobi. She blabbed about her struggles with the language, (everyone told her it was easy), her State career, her divorce, and the nostalgia she held for her hometown, where she said her parents still lived very much in love.

Linda knew the sound of a woman speaking to a man she believed was really listening, how it coaxed out vulnerability, how it would curl the nurse's toes if Trey asked to see her again. He wore a kindhearted aura like a gown as he paced again around the car, this time counterclockwise. He told the nurse that her hometown sounded wonderful, that he'd served in the Air Force with a guy from Utica; and he had another friend whose mom taught at Fayetteville-Manlius High School; even another dude from the fire academy who had 315 tattooed on his forearm.

Linda felt ill at the cheesy rom-com circumstances: cute little nurse with a flat tire, on her way to Kenya, small town girl just wants what her parents have. How could Linda compete? Why would she want to? But something about the way Trey was listening kept her standing in the parking lot.

He lowered the jack clumsily and apologized; he kicked the spare and smiled into the sun, then lugged the tire to the trunk. One of Trey's classmates walking by kidded him, saying, "Nice job, fire man" at which he blushed, dabbing perspiration with his polo, catching sight of Linda, who'd set her bag down to watch.

"Um, sir?" Linda began. "There's a cat in a tree over here by my car. Are you free?" Trey smiled back, then grew flustered, checking the time on his phone.

"Oh, man," he said. "I have to be in DC in half an hour. How high up is it?" The nurse glared at Linda behind Trey's back, then tried to get his attention again.

"Thank you sooo much, Trey! I'd like to make it up to you. Can I buy you lunch tomorrow? Or a drink sometime?"

Trey turned back to the nurse and said, "Oh, that's ok. Just please be careful driving on it. Not too fast. And have someone put a new tire on as soon as you can." Linda stood with good posture, making sure to avoid eye contact with the nurse.

"Well," Trey said to Linda, "I'm parked over that way too. Let's take a look." The nurse ducked into her car and ran the AC before driving away. Trey fell in next to Linda as they walked. Linda felt mischievous and sexy, keeping Trey's outline in her periphery, listening for him, hearing nothing, smelling for him, catching some sweat.

"There's no cat," she admitted in front of her car.

"But you have a Replacements bumper sticker!" he exclaimed. "I didn't know they even sold these!'"

"They don't," Linda said. "I had it made. You like the 'Mats too?"

"My favorite! Did you see them live?"

"I'm not that old!" Linda joked. "I've seen Westerberg though."

"What's your favorite album?" Trey pleaded.

""Mats or Paul?"

"Both! Man! I don't meet many fans. Well, that's not true—lots of people in DC like them, but I think only because it's on their 'hipness checklists.' You must be from Twin Cities."

"I am."

"Like—Twin Cities, Twin Cities? Or like Edina?"

"Suburbs," Linda smiled.

"I had a buddy in Peace Corps from Minnetonka."

"Our archrivals," she grinned.

"Ugh, I'd love to talk music with you. You've probably walked in a skyway!" Linda nodded, bowled over by Trey's childish beam. "But I have to go," he said.

"What's your next post?" Linda asked like a big sister, a stepsister, she hoped.

"Delhi. First tour. I'm in Hindi now."

"Delhi was *my* first tour! Years ago." Linda said a rudimentary Hindi phrase and Trey answered. "We should have lunch."

"Yes, for sure," Trey said extending his hand, then pulling it back. "I'm Trey. I'd shake your hand, but I'm a greasy Eye-talian after that tire."

"It's ok, Trey. I'm Linda. I'll tell you all about Delhi." She opened her door and considered asking him if he wanted a ride to DC.

"Lunch would be great!" Trey said as he moved toward his car, then turned back. "Do you want to hear a quick story?"

"If it doesn't make you late."

"Eh, it's a going away party. I'll make it."

"Then I'd love to hear a quick story, Trey."

"Great. So, before the Foreign Service, I taught 8th grade."

"I thought you were a fire man."

"Yeah, before that."

"Peace Corps, teacher, fireman?"

"Yeah, I bounced around." Trey flashed a sheepish look. "I had an autistic student, Sabrina. It was a small Catholic school, we didn't have special ed. She was somewhere on the spectrum. Her parents knew, the principal too. They told me to integrate her the best I could. For the most part she was fine, but her classmates could be merciless in their teasing. Sometimes they excluded her. Typical junior high stuff, but hard on someone who has trouble relating."

"I'll bet."

"Yeah, it was a real challenge for me. When she was hurt, Sabrina would hug me and cry into my shirt. Other times, she'd stand on her chair in the middle of class and read something she printed out from Urban Dictionary: 'You cunts are a bunch of pussy-eating cock sniffers!'"

"Holy cow!"

"Sorry if the language offends you."

"It doesn't, I'm intrigued."

"I assigned each of them a major city in the United States. Twenty-eight kids, twenty-eight cities. They did reports on the history, industry, culture, etc.. The had to pick a song written about their town. Sabrina had Minneapolis-St Paul."

"Skyway."

"Yes! Sabrina brought the boom box to the front of class and handed out lyrics sheets to everyone. She was dressed so handsomely, even her hair was brushed. She looked like a little lady. She said, 'So, this song says exactly how I feel. Sitting on a cold bench with my stupid shoes and my stupid clothes. And I look up at the pathway that connects two big buildings and all of you are walking above me. You laugh when you notice me. And I just sit and wait for the bus. You're in the nice, warm skyway.' And she pushed play."

"Aww, that's beautiful."

"I was melting inside, nearly crying. But also praying that she wouldn't call them a bunch of cunts." Linda savored the filthy word, admiring how Trey could escort it into her mind, blending profanity into a touching story. As Trey drove away, she noticed his own homemade bumper sticker, which read: "Free Carthage."

When they met for lunch later in the week, Linda led Trey away from the FSI cafeteria, which was now over-crowded, built for a much leaner Foreign Service in the days when it was "male, pale, and Yale," to a bench under a tree near the field house. She shook his hand, joking that he was not greasy this time, then she said, "I'm glad I didn't lose you to that pretty nurse with the flat tire."

"Hmm. I didn't see her that way, I don't think. She needed help."

"You can't be attracted to people you help? She was attracted to you."

"I don't think so. I see them as weak, I'm ashamed to admit it."

"Everyone has weaknesses."

"But it's not my job to fix them. Their tires, fine." Trey paused. "Plus, she was divorced. I'm intimidated by women who have been married before."

"Wow. You must be intimidated by a lot of women."

"I can't imagine dating a girl who has so many backstories. Like she's lived an extra life. She met a man, dated him for months, maybe years! Then she had a wedding—you know how hard those things are to plan and pay for? Then, she got to a breaking point with a dude she promised she'd love 'forever.' Now she wants to start over with me? That's a lot to live up to."

"I have many friends who are remarried and perfectly happy. You don't always get it right the first time, do you? Shouldn't there be second chances?"

"It's not my job. Get a second chance with a divorced guy. You'd have more to talk about."

"Harsh. I suppose kids are a deal breaker too."

"There is no deal. To say so would be to say I'd even get into a relationship with a girl who had kids, which I don't think I could do. She needs a Brady Bunch kind of thing, not Trey Ciuri." Linda's ears perked to hear his full name.

"How do you pronounce it?"

"Kee-yoo-ree. They called me Yuri in the Air Force."

"You were in the Air Force too? How old are you? You look like you're right of out Georgetown."

"Georgetown? I didn't go there."

"Oh, it's just something we Georgetown ninnies say to each other. There's a million of us in the Foreign Service." Linda sighed, content with her surroundings, outside of the madhouse that was the FSI cafeteria. She knew so many people in the organization that she would have had to interrupt their conversation at least twice a minute to say hello or fake gab with people she hadn't seen in years. Usually she reveled in the Foreign Service social scene, but she wanted to show Trey these things after they had time to get acquainted. Other FSOs, Linda feared, would scare Trey with their pleasantries and pedantry.

"We had a few Hoyas in my A-100 class. For grad school though. Were you there with Iverson?" Trey asked.

"He left my sophomore year. I was there for Detrick Walker, who was supposed to be the next Iverson."

"Never heard of him."

"He was a DC kid. Even rougher than AI. Used to bust into parties, yelling, 'Who's gonna suck this dick?!' Strangely, when he asked, there was a lull during which a number of people considered the question. He walked around campus asking everyone for condoms, explaining that he was about to 'pop that ass.' He got in trouble with the law, lost an eye, I think. Ended up on the street."

"Yeah, I heard a story about when Georgetown was recruiting Grant Hill, they gave him a Dick and Jane book to see if he could read it. Hill was so offended he went to Duke."

"I'm sure that's true. Half of us at school bought into the 'Jesuits give everyone a chance' myth, and the other half hated how important basketball was, at any cost."

"It was the same with football at my college," Trey said.

"Hey, who was the first Ciuri?! Who are you and your dad named after?"

"Very good! Most people don't ask."

"I have a 'Trey' for a cousin. Harold Sven Pearson III."

"Best to go by Trey with a name like Harold Sven. My grandfather, he recently passed away, was named John August Ciuri."

"Very evocative. He sounds wiry, strong," Linda said, surprising herself. Trey was wiry and strong to her. What did she know about his grandpa?

"When he was young. He got pretty round in his later years."

"What did he do?"

"Firefighter." Trey smiled before Linda could.

"He must have been proud."

"Yeah, he gave me a lot of advice when I was applying to departments. It's so competitive, I was flying all over the country to take tests. And the rule is: you move to the first place that hires you. I was living in Los Angeles, but I moved here to take the job."

"And then you quit the fire department to join State?"

"I did." Trey paused, making Linda more cautious, then continued. "And as I sense a 'why?' coming on, I'm realizing that I've given different people different reasons for why I left."

"Which reason are you going to give me?"

"One I haven't given anyone else." Linda smiled.

"In A-100, I told my classmates that I applied for Foreign Service because every call we ran at my firehouse was to a home that spoke a different language. I'd talk to patients in the back of the ambulance, all the way to the hospital. They taught me words and talked about where they were from. Their countries were so fresh in their minds—so legitimate—it made both of us forget they were sick or injured.

"I didn't tell my classmates this part. During my first fire—it was far from an inferno—we were pulling ceilings down afterward, looking for traces of embers behind the drywall. It's exhausting work—jamming a pike pole into the wall, pulling down, dodging plaster, squinting through the dust, over and over. In the idle of this routine, with chunks of drywall piling on the soaked carpet, I thought of the poor residents who lost everything—not because of any fire, but because we hosed the shit out of their home. I caught the smell of burnt wood and plastic, and I saw on the far wall a large Brazilian flag, and the words 'Ordem e Progresso.' I stared at it through the dust, recognizing the crest from flip flops and soccer games. And then one of my mates ripped it down and threw it in a pile with the rest of this poor family's shit."

"That's an image, for sure. So, you quit because you were interested in Brazil?"

"No, I quit because this poor family lost everything because monkeys like me and my mates soaked their apartment, stripped their walls and ceilings, and then threw all their goddamn furniture out the window. Marauders couldn't have done a better job. And the fire wasn't even in their place!" Linda smiled at Trey's animation, his hands reckless yet caring, adding texture to his words.

"When I was in the Fire Academy, an old, grizzled Chief gave us a presentation on the Tokyo Fire Department: some history, a couple stories, and one 'fact.' He said that despite being one of the largest cities in the world, Tokyo had only a few hundred firefighters.

"'Do you know why?' he asked us. Most people could have cared less about Tokyo, but I was intrigued. He said, 'Because in Japan, if your house catches on fire, it's *your* fault. It's your *neighbor's* fault for not holding you accountable. Everyone is in it together.' Then he asked us, 'Why do you think we have so many firefighters in American cities?' In Montgomery County alone, we had a thousand paid guys and a thousand volunteers. None of us had an answer. I was thinking that maybe it was because the Japanese were so efficient, they could do the same job with a fraction of the manpower.

"'Because we are diverse!' the Chief yelled. 'Those Japs are all the same. Look the same, think the same, they all do the same shit when a bell rings. Try getting half a city block of Americans to work together in an emergency.'"

"Was he proud of American diversity or apologizing for it?"

"I think he was trying to be proud of it. Montgomery County is a socialist utopia. There's so much money, and everyone is pretty much a foo foo liberal, myself included. But the County tried to pile-drive it into us—and firefighters aren't exactly 'progressive' as a general rule. The kicker was that most of us couldn't even afford to live in the county we 'protected.' And we believed in diversity—we just didn't trust their contrived focus on it."

"How do you know it's contrived?"

"I have trouble believing rich people when they talk about peace and inclusion and all that shit. I'm sure the Chief was told by some MoCo lackey to fire up the new cadets with a 'good ole diversity story,' so he did his best. I looked up how many firefighters they had in Tokyo, by the way, and it's over eighteen thousand. I'm not sure where the Chief got his information."

"Why don't you believe rich people?"

"They're only 'nice' because they have the disposable income to be that way. I ran so many calls in Potomac and Bethesda, and lemme tell you, when someone calls 911, that's when you see who they really are. The majority of the residents I met were horrible. 'Liberal' as the day is long. Miserable pukes though. They can't even call themselves 'left wing' because lefties actually work. These MoCo clowns—I have no idea what they do.

"And I didn't just *fight fires* in Montgomery County. I substitute taught their kids on my off days and rung up their groceries at Trader Joes. You know what's it's like to share political and social values with someone and then discover that they really don't care about the people they fight for, and that they are just as bad—or worse—than the people they fight against? It makes you feel like you're a fool….and a whore."

"Maybe that's the reason you quit," Linda suggested.

"Maybe. I've got a million of these stories and rants, so push the 'change topic' button whenever you get bored."

"I am far from bored. But I don't want to make you late for class. Do you want to hear about Delhi?"

"Sure," Trey said. Linda blinked a few times, grabbing deep breaths to get into India mode. She remembered how many of her colleagues were jealous of her posting, a feeling she savored until she lived there for two years and nearly broke. On the bench, she examined Trey more deliberately than she had in the parking lot, deciding that he was almost traditionally handsome. His nose was a tad too large for his face. He was in good physical shape, but his clothes didn't fit him just right. And the way he walked, she remembered, with that lack of overconfidence, it was as if he learned to stroll by watching arrogant men and decided to parody them.

"They're going to tell you India is 'a land of extremes,' which is true if you want to look at it simply. One moment, you'll catch the whiff of jasmine in a beautiful girl's hair. And the next thing you know, you'll be slapped silly by the aroma of seven hundred million people pooing outside. You'll eat curries that will tie your taste buds in knots. And then take a blender to your guts. Beware the Delhi Belly, John August, beware. You'll notice herds of mindless 'eat, pray, love' idiots seeking 'peace.' Probably more than a few from Montgomery County. You'll realize what a sham it is, how avaricious even the yogis—especially the yogis—are. Yes, Trey, you heard it here first: Yoga is bullshit. It's a Sanskrit word that means, 'expensive stretching.' In fact, it's like you describe Bethesda people who can afford to be nice. Poor people don't do yoga."

Linda paused to see how Trey was taking her jabs but didn't give him time to ask questions. "Delhi was a hard place to live. I'm sure it still is. I can't tell you how many times I was groped in the bazaar by packs of young men who waited for the instant my back was turned— chicken shits! My second tour was in Latin America, and they catcalled me all the time, even by name, 'Linda! Linda!' You know, like the word for 'pretty?'" She smiled at Trey who kept listening. "But I thought about it in contrast to India and said to myself: 'at least the Latinos have the 'guts' to do it in my face.' Indian men have no such courage. Of course, you'll be fine as a man. A white man to boot."

"Have you ever been harassed like that in the States?" Trey asked.

"Once. I was with my boyfriend at the time. Had I been alone I wouldn't have thought anything of it. I was back from college and we took a trip to 'the city.' Chicago, I mean. In the Midwest, it's our New York. We call it 'the city.'

"We were riding the El, and we stood watching some boys shooting dice. One boy looked me up—from my toes to my eyes—what a gaze. I was eye fucked, or at least eye fondled. Then I felt guilty as a white chick, trembling before this 'urban savage.' In my mind, I recited the poem, *We Real Cool*—do you know it? It's about Chicago black boys doing whatever they want. And I felt like he wanted me, that he could have taken me, so I repeated the poem to make myself feel like I had some power in the situation. Then the boy pointed to a seat as if he owned the train, and he asked me if I wanted to sit down.

"'I'm fine,'" I told him.

"'Yes you are,'" he said like a grown man. I acted offended, but my boyfriend was oblivious. And yet I felt kind of ravished. My boyfriend never commented on my looks with such confidence, and I wondered if that was the real reason I was offended. But then I felt like a racist, thinking that this dice shooting kid had nothing to lose by saying what he said. I replayed Margaret Atwood's *Rape Fantasies* in my mind as I leaned closer to my clueless beau. Sorry for all the literary allusions, I was an English major.

"Me too," Trey said.

"Did you imagine me being raped by the boy?" Linda asked.

"No. I saw you in a consensual act. But it was hard to imagine you in college. Young."

"Young?! *Younger*, you mean! We're probably the same age, Trey!"

"Oh, sorry. I meant it as a compliment to your experience. I'm new at this State Department thing, and I could sit here and listen to your stories all day. Plus, I never knew girls in college who could keep Gwendolyn Brooks and Atwood straight in their minds. And most people don't have the courage to admit they're racist. The college girls I remember were super insecure."

"Yeah, well I probably wasn't as collected as I am now. College guys aren't exactly sure of themselves either, you know."

"Did you join the Foreign Service right out of school? I mean, Georgetown?"

"Ha, yes. Well, almost. I travelled a bit. My A-100 class was the first after a long spell. They hadn't hired FSOs for years before us."

"When did you graduate?" Trey asked. Linda looked through the branches above them, then wiped her brow though she wasn't sweating. She usually acted offended when men asked questions that would reveal her age, but she was content with Trey's curiosity. She wanted to compare this moment with the previous times she'd enjoyed getting to know someone, and she tried to remember the last time she cared about what came out of a man's mouth.

"It was the time of the Monica Lewinsky blowjobs," she said wistfully. "I chose Georgetown because I was Catholic, and I hated everyone I met who went to Notre Dame. Of course, once I got there, I realized that Jesuits were wiser than God, and by the time I graduated, I was like god-who? I'm still like that. Does that offend you? Are you religious? I'm guessing no."

"Um, I still go to Mass. In my younger years I used to pray to be able to help people. I got mad at God when I failed. Now, I just pray to meet a nice girl and settle down."

"That's sweet, Trey. Well, you met me while you were helping someone. Boom! Lightning bolt!"

"Boom."

"So, at the time of the Clinton scandals, I was like any liberal girl: 'What's the big deal? Monica—what a slut.' But then I looked in the mirror one morning, and I was like, '*I* am a 23-year-old girl! I wouldn't know the first thing about seducing a 50-year-old guy, let alone the President!' I suddenly felt mean, inhuman, an enabler.

"And you had all these journalists—led by their snouts by Hillary and Carville—calling her a slut. I remember this one ginger spinster—with the *Times* or the *Post*—she won awards for basically being a mean girl. They set feminism back a generation because they let Bill do whatever he wanted. Guy's still lionized—why?"

"Be careful with Hillary—she's our boss now."

"Yeah, I'm trusting you to not tell her."

"I don't know what to think of her," Trey said. "I thought she'd leave Bill after all that humiliation. Go her own way. I thought that's what being a feminist was about."

"No, Trey. Feminism is whatever a 'feminist' decides it is, and *you* don't get to comment on it, straight white male!" Linda smiled wickedly, trying to read Trey's face. "Anyhow," she added. "I'm glad that Obama won, especially in the primary."

"Me too. I'm happy the way things are turning out," Trey said. The sun hit him in a way that had he been facing Linda, she'd have kissed him.

"You're happy with what? Our country? Your life? Are you happy you met me?"

"Yes, I think Obama represents a lot of what most of us want."

"That's so vague. But I feel the same way. And your life?"

"We'll see about life. I still can't get used to the idea that I'm a 'diplomat.' It seems so hoity toity, like cuff links and bidets, something Europeans do."

"You'll get used to it quick. Especially in Delhi. They'll kiss your *ghora* ass all day long."

"Ghora?"

"Oh, right. They don't teach that one at FSI. It means 'whitey,' can be derogatory, depending on how it's used."

"Geeze. Was there *anything* you liked about Delhi?"

"The food. From the neck up. No, I mean, there is a certain allure to the chaos. The way auto rickshaws weave in and out of traffic. It would be dangerous if they could go any faster than 15 miles per hour. But then they try to rip you off, even after you agree on a price before getting in."

"Again, it's easier for a man, a white man. You're a symbol of the highest in social strata: they want their daughters to marry one of you, they want to do business with you, they speak your language better than you. They even sell whitening *cream*! Their women buy *genital* whitening cream! The white man is god."

"Nepal had similar dynamics. Some of my girl Peace Corps friends got approached by Nepali dudes—who'd only seen white women in porn movies. They asked in all seriousness, 'We will have sex now?'"

"I think I'd prefer that to shady Indian guys. The world is going to learn someday about all the rapes that take place there. My colleagues who worked in the political section talked to NGOs, who were reporting astronomical stats on violence against women, human trafficking, child labor, you name it. But because of the business lobby, they had to dumb down their reports back to Washington."

"That's troubling. President Obama will change all that."

"Yeah, maybe," Linda said, letting out an exaggerated sigh and putting her palm on Trey's cheek as he turned toward her. He flinched and took a drink from his water bottle, coughing after a swallow. Linda took her hand back. "While I was there, I had to drive an Indian friend to a back-alley ultrasound to find out the sex of her baby. Know why?"

"Something to do with reveal parties?"

"Because for every thousand men in Northern India there's 920 women or something like that. Feticide is so common when parents discover it's a girl, the government made sex determination illegal."

"Shit. What am I getting myself into?" Linda's eyes turned devious and playful, and before she could say it, Trey hollered, half smiling, "I don't care if I'm a white male! It doesn't mean I want this shit to happen!" Linda laughed and pretended to lapse into deep thought.

"Ok, one good thing that happened was Narendra Modi."

"Who?"

"Hopefully you'll never learn who he is. Hopefully we took care of him. He's the Chief Minister of Gujarat."

"Where?"

"Ah, your *Delhi-wahlay* Hindi teachers are probably all Punjabi— they don't care about anything outside of Northern India. Gujarat is a southwestern state, near Bombay."

"Don't you mean 'Mumbai?'"

"Only Hindu nationalists call it that. Modi, speaking of which, is a terrible Hindu nationalist. While I was there, he did nothing to stop anti-Muslim riots which killed thousands in his state. Everyone we spoke to said that Modi knew exactly what was happening, and let it pass." Trey seemed unfazed, but added:

"There were anti-Muslim riots in Nepal when I was there. Some Nepali guest workers were killed, one of them was beheaded, after being sent to Iraq through a corrupt manpower organization. They thought they were going to the Gulf." Linda went on.

"In the three months before I left Delhi—when was that? '02, right. Spring of '02, all I did was work with the political section to firm up a visa ban for Modi, making sure that he couldn't travel to the United States. And you know, when that pig tried to come in '05, he was rejected. Bush never got any good press for standing up for Muslims— in many cases, rightly so—but his guys stuck to the ban based on violations of religious freedom. Of course, what Modi did and does is so much worse than 'violations' of religious freedom."

"This seems to have affected you pretty good. The whole India experience."

"India tests every conception you have of humanity," Linda said, arching her back, gazing again at the branches, remembering the urge to kiss Trey, realizing the moment was gone. "Toward the end of my tour, I was walking home from the market, freshly ogled, freshly groped. Three different vendors had tried to rip me off for vegetables. I thought of other diplos who never exited air conditioning during their tours: they had drivers and cooks and cleaning staff who basically experienced India for them. I thought they were missing the real deal, the smells and sounds, that chaotic allure. I spoke Hindi pretty well, wore traditional dress, learned the customs. But after two years of consular work, and thousands of visa interviews in which people brazenly lied to my face, I decided that it was better to be air conditioned and ignorant than to know the real India. To Indians I was just another corrupt official who they needed to get past to get what they wanted. That feeling made me cry for a long time.

"The basest human impulses are to eat and to reproduce. India took care of the first one with the green revolution, which our agri-scientists helped them with. Now pretty much everyone in India can eat. And because women have no rights, men screw to their heart's content. They've created an incredible underclass, so uncountable that even people of extremely low means can have 'servants.' In America, we were coy on the human cost of capitalism. We wrote it into and out of our constitution! In India, they're damned proud of layer after layer of exploited classes.

"But you know what's even more primal than the food and sex drives? It's the stripped-down humanity that treats kindness like a weakness. It's what children do if they never learn any better: they take every advantage they can without a second thought of others or the consequences.

"It's like—and maybe this is a post-colonial thing, but I doubt it—I am sure the Indians were horrible to one another long before the Brits got there…. It's like the Indians have devolved below charity and selflessness. They are sub-sympathetic: In India, kindness is a weakness! And it's not just a 'scarcity' thing. I've seen horrible acts of common meanness from billionaires to Dalits. Before my tour I thought Churchill was just being uppity when he said something like, 'India has no more right than the equator to be a country.' But he was right—not for any geopolitical reason—but for the inhumane one I just shared with you."

"Well, that's harsh," Trey said, cleaning his sandwich wrapper and other rubbish from the bench.

"Don't worry, white man," Linda smiled again.

"Seriously, please stop that. I live in a black neighborhood. I hear 'white man' stuff all the time.

****

Weeks passed, the weather changed, and one day near Thanksgiving Linda received a text from Trey, inviting her to his home: "Would you like to help me make a lamb and a Smurf?"

She waited a day to respond, feeling slighted by the long lapse since their lunch, though they did see each other often on the FSI campus—flanked by friends—both taking time to introduce everyone to everyone else. When they'd part, Linda looked back on her way to the Russian department as Trey moseyed toward the South Asian language wing.

It was difficult for her to admit that Trey did not chase her with reciprocal vigor. She'd been as forward as she'd ever been with an interest—but also more vulnerable—a combination of emotions which she hoped would attract this man she chance met. And though she considered herself relatively young, 12 years as an FSO was more than a third of her life. And in that way, amid eager-eyed millennials now scurrying through FSI, talking about international relations in the same cadence they discussed boy bands and bloggers, she felt tired and aged.

Linda had never been to Trey's neighborhood, Anacostia, or "East of the river" as DC gentrifiers coded it. In her borough near Capitol Hill, she was often invited to "neighborhood meetings," which were trumped up affairs, designed to "include" long-time residents, all of them black, while newer homeowners, who were never black, made patronizing speeches about the windfall profits stood to be gained once they sold their "beautiful houses." The mention of Anacostia, however, still struck fear in the eyes of whites. Aside from a tentative repurposing

270

of St Elizabeth's mental hospital for Homeland Security's new head-quarters, not even Linda's gay friends had heard of the neighborhood as a potential place to live.

"Glad you found the place!" Trey smiled.

"The Corolla with the 'Free Carthage' bumper sticker stuck out like a sore thumb."

"Yeah, another homemade."

"What does it mean? Is it 'Carthage,' as in North Africa?"

"Yeah, like a country that doesn't exist anymore. I wanted to make fun of those idiots who talk about 'free this place' and 'free those people,' when they have no idea where these countries are and wouldn't know….let's say….a Tibetan or a Uyghur if they bumped into one in the street."

"There certainly are a lot of 'Free Tibet' types."

"I got the idea years ago, after an Air Force friend introduced me to a frat brother of his in Hollywood—a producer. He was in many ways the anti-Hollywood: he wasn't an entertainer, cared less about 'the arts' and all that. He just wanted to make money."

"Sounds pretty Hollywood to me."

"He let me behind the curtain. He told me that the Beastie Boys were created—fabricated in the early eighties at the advice of market researchers who found that rap was too dangerous—read: black—to enjoy mainstream commercial success. They needed a 'white bridge' as they called it. So enter these rich kids from Manhattan and Brooklyn…."

"I don't believe it."

"I was skeptical too, but when I think of what the Beastie Boys actually did musically, it kind of makes sense. I mean, all they did was sample songs and shout the rhyming words at the ends of sentences. But suburban kids—read: white!—loved it. When those kids grew up and started listening to NPR—and yes, I resemble these remarks—they brought in the whole 'Free Tibet' shit. I think one of the Beasties even became vegan or tantric or something to keep their appeal."

"Created?"

"Just like our bumper stickers. I mean, they obviously know how to play instruments and make records, but their emergence was far from a ground swell of mid-Reagan-era rebellion precipitating a rock-rap explosion of expression. It was the right product at the right time."

"I spent half my seventh-grade year memorizing the lyrics to Paul Revere," Linda said sadly, still not believing Trey's fantastic account, yet warming again to the "Eye-talian" way in which he illustrated things. She thought for a second. "Wait, The Replacements weren't created, were they?"

"If they were, we should just kill ourselves right…." Trey stopped. Linda detected the change in his mood.

"Yeah, not even Hollywood could imagine those guys."

"Do you want a drink?" Trey asked.

"Only if you're planning on taking advantage of me."

"Ok, let's hold off until these cutouts are done." Linda studied the cardboard on Trey's living room floor, noticing the outline of a cartoon lamb and Papa Smurf, each design about four feet high.

"What on earth are these for?"

"You're going to think this is so cheesy!" Trey grinned. "But you know at FSI, how they put cardboard cutouts of wolves all over campus to keep geese from congregating on the green?"

"Yes. I don't think they are scaring many geese away."

"No, they're not! So, I was thinking that we could put this lamb—note the scared look on his face—and Papa Smurf on the lawn. We'll either scare geese or make diplomats laugh."

"Probably the latter."

"Sadly, I don't think anyone will care. Chuckle maybe. But care not."

"Why should they care?" Linda asked.

"Exactly. I feel like that's the attitude at State. Sometimes it bums me out. It seems like a bunch of people in their own world, scurrying to their next assignments, networking. It looks like other organizations, but there's a detachment that rubs me raw. I mean, in the Air Force, there was a guy whose additional duty was to prevent idiots like me from planting Papa Smurf on the lawn."

"You haven't even started your first tour yet. Give it some time. Am I really here to help you paint Papa Smurf? Can't we just get drunk and listen to the Beastie Boys?" She kissed Trey.

"Thanks," he said. "I'm serious about this cardboard though. Can we make out after?"

"That's the sexiest rejection I've ever gotten," Linda said, warming further to Trey, admiring his eccentric commitment to a harmless cardboard rebellion, not to mention the promise to make out later. She squeezed a tube and started on Papa Smurf's hat, taking breaks to look around Trey's rowhouse and ask him about the pictures on his wall: a drawing of Paul Robeson mid-speech, a Library of Congress photo of Zora Neale Hurston, an arrangement of beer coasters he collected in Germany around the time the wall came down, a painting by one of his 8th graders.

Trey opened the bottle of wine Linda brought, and they painted and drank, their hands brushing as the cardboard came alive. Linda grew giddy imagining the first wave of diplomats on their way to class, conjugating verbs in their next languages, and then….lamb, wolf, Papa Smurf…..hmmm. She leaned into Trey's gravity to let him smell her hair, looking away as he smiled with purpling teeth, noticing how he adjusted his pants. Her stomach boiled, driving her to her feet, facing her middle to his face, which was focused on the last touches of the lamb. She began to move her hands down her stomach into her hips, as if she were smoothing wrinkles in her shirt, her jeans were humid.

As Linda braced herself to grab the back of Trey's head as he moved toward her mouth, she was overcome by a desire to know more about Anacostia. Her body wailed, pleading her to not inquire about the neighborhood at such a moment. She feared, though, that if they fell too quickly into a physical act, she would forget that Trey was the only white man for miles, that he wasn't a typical DC gentrifier. The stories he could share with her about his neighbors would make their future affection more satisfying.

Don't ask him! she heard at full volume. Linda considered how she described her sexual impulses today—as her "needs"—whereas when she was younger, she acted on them without much thought. She wondered what this was, a ravenous need to pepper Trey with questions that would reveal even more of him, which she imagined as consuming as a multilayered orgasm. As their lips approached, Linda's previous partners dissolved into one stereotypical dude who struggled to make eye contact. Trey stood a head above her, his jeans pocket full of arcade tokens. Linda ignored her loins.

"Can you tell me, Trey," she began. He seemed sloshed smiling down at her. She wondered if he was a lightweight or if he hadn't eaten much that evening. "Can you tell me about Anacostia?"

Trey snapped into sobriety and said, "I thought you'd never ask!" pointing to the wall between his house and the next one on the row. "Next door is Miss Millie, a Baltimore Catholic raised in the same neighborhood as Thurgood Marshall. She said he used to bring her family apples from his yard. Awestruck, I asked her, 'What did you call him?' Silly me, I was thinking there was some neighborhood nickname or something. Miss Millie smiled and said, 'Mister Marshall.'

"She moved to Anacostia in the mid-fifties, when this was a white neighborhood, and got a job at St Elizabeth's, the insane asylum just down the road. In 1957 she was assigned to a ward called Chestnut, where her first patient was Ezra Pound, who nicknamed her 'Mille Occhi,' 'a thousand eyes' in Italian, because she wouldn't let him get away with anything. She was so strict, Pound's lady friends would only visit on Millie's days off. She called him Mr. Ez.

"She was sad when Pound was released in 1958. But as she told me that, her mood changed, and she noted that 1958 was the same year Paul Robeson got *his* passport back, and everyone in her old Baltimore neighborhood was happy about that. Miss Millie's dad used to play a record of Robeson singing at the Canadian border. It didn't matter what the government did to Paul, Miss Millie said, his voice went all over the world. She told me that if I listened to him, I would be a better man."

"Pound was a fascist, Robeson was a communist," Linda noted. "Funny they got their passports back at the same time."

"Miss Millie ended up as John Hinkley's nurse. She used to take him to Mass at St. E's, and his mother, every Christmas would palm her a hundred-dollar bill for taking care of her son. Millie was fond of Hinkley, and it made me think about how people in the medical profession have to separate what their patients did from their right to receive good care."

"Don't you think it comes natural? Like in the heat of the moment, someone in need, no time to think about what they did before you encountered them, right?"

"I had a hard time with it. With the people in Potomac. Maybe because no one I treated was that sick. I had time to study the books on their shelves, to see the way they talked to their household staff, to listen to them in the back of the ambulance."

"You still provided good care, though? You didn't leave them on the side of the road, did you?"

"No, but I wanted to."

"That's just an impulse. That you didn't shows you're human."

"We're ignoring some pretty strong impulses right now," Trey said, kissing Linda. Electricity zoomed down her shoulders and into her arms, which pulled Trey closer. But again curiosity dulled her lust.

"I'm sorry to do this....again....because I want you. But can you finish talking about Miss Millie?" Trey caught his breath and smiled. He seemed amused, but Linda wondered for how long.

"Whenever I'm cooking, Miss Millie beats on my door with her cane. 'Traaaaay?!' she says, 'That smells good. Bring me some, please.'

We eat together on the porch and she tells me about DC in the 80s, how Marion Barry lived just down the street, and how everyone loved him, even after the crack and all that. She told me about Chuck Brown and GoGo music, and a preacher named Sweet Daddy Grace, who seemed pretty shady."

"Can't get that from a history book! Probably not even on the internet."

"When I leave for work, Miss Millie leans out her bedroom window and says, 'Traaay. Don't die in no fire.' I don't have the heart to tell her I have a different job now."

"Ah. 'Traaaaay.' I love it," Linda said. "I'm ashamed to be fascinated by this—that you're a white guy here! I know you're not one of those 'pioneers' just trying to flip the neighborhood."

"It's ok. My buddies at the fire house, even black dudes from Anacostia, thought I was crazy. I'm very comfortable in African American communities, though. The best thing about my neighbors is that they're actually from Washington. I'm from nowhere."

"Welcome to the Foreign Service. We're all from nowhere. The neighborhood hasn't been dangerous at all? Driving here I passed a lot of guys hanging out in front of a liquor store."

"Not that I've seen. I mean, twice a week someone tries to break into Jimmy's Escalade down the street. But my neighbors say, 'Well, he shouldn't have an Escalade around here.' At first, I thought that was unfair. You should drive whatever car you want, right? Whatever you can afford. But this is a lower middleclass neighborhood and Cadillacs are luxury cars. That causes a disturbance in the force. You go flashing an Escalade around here, and it's simply market forces that are going to get your ass robbed."

"That's logical," Linda said, rolling her eyes. "I imagine no one has tried to steal the Carthage Wagon?"

"Just the damned Romans. They put sugar in my tank." Linda laughed and then gave a serious look.

"You wanna put sugar in *my* tank?"

"That would be nice, Linda." They moved to the couch, kissing hard, but keeping clothed. Again, Linda fought the urge to know more about Trey and his life here as she looked over his shoulder, his mouth on her neck. She saw through the front window a tree-lined street, though neglected, different from white neighborhoods, with stray wires and old mylars hanging from the power lines, and one huge streetlight as tall as a rocket boring light into the lonely road, like a shower left on.

"Who else lives here? Who do you know?" She asked as he moved to the other side of her neck and burrowed around her ear, his hand palming the outline of her bra. She pulled away from Trey with a worried look. "Agh! I want to do this! But I'm so curious! About you. About here. You must think I'm some ninny white girl tickled to be on the other side of the river with her big strong escort."

"I believe you, Linda," Trey said catching his breath. "I don't think you're a white tourist, though we do get plenty of them here. It's made for some funny moments. A couple times people have come up to me like they know me, saying, "Hey Fred, what's up man?!" And I'll apologize and say there must be some mistake. And they'll apologize saying I look just like a white guy they met the other day. And to myself I say, 'We don't all look the same!'

"That's a reversal, huh?"

"Another time, I was at the post office, and people used me as a landmark to fight over a place in line. One lady said:

"'I was two behind that muthafuckin' white man!'" And another lady was like:

"'Yeah, well, I was *one* behind that gott-damm white man!' And I just stood there, humming a stereotypical white melody, pretending it was completely normal."

"That is hilarious!"

"I got to the window and I asked the clerk….I must sound like Jimmy Stewart to them, 'Uh, yes, hello, can I please have some of those Marilyn Monroe Forever stamps?' And the whole back of the line started dying laughing, like belly laughs, and then the clerk lost it. She had a huge gold tooth. And then I started laughing. People were shaking my hand, introducing themselves. It turned out most of them knew Miss Millie. But they got that suspicious look and were like, "I didn't hear about no white man moving in next to Miss Millie."

"Ah, what a satisfying way you have," Linda sighed, filling her glass. Their eyes held for some time and they kissed again. Trey ran his hands along Linda's ribcage, then down to her hips, tucking his fingertips between her jeans and her middle. "Oh, Trey," she wheezed and pulled back once again.

"If you don't want to do this, it's ok," Trey said. He looked at the cardboard on his floor and Linda emptied her glass.

"Noooo, I do. I want you," she crooned. "I just want to know a little more, please?" Trey sat up straight, readjusted his pants. For a moment, Linda considered giving him head as he continued, but decided that it would cheapen their engagement.

"Ok, there's Andrew. Miss Millie calls him a hustler, which I guess he is. He shouts my name from the street, probably twice a week:

'"Trey!'

'Hi, Andrew.'

'Trey! Lemme wash your car, man!'

'You washed it on Tuesday, Andrew.'

'Comon, Trey!'

'Ok.'

'Thanks, man! Hey, Trey….'

'Yep.'

'Hey man, you got a bucket?'

'Yes.'

'Hey Trey.'

'Yes.'

'You got some dish soap and a sponge?' And so he washes my car with my supplies, and I pay him ten dollars that I probably shouldn't. Miss Millie growls at him as he half-asses the job. I feel taken advantage of, but I don't know how to cut him off. I don't want to be some heavy-handed white guy, explaining to Andrew that he should have his own supplies, that he shouldn't be so dependent on my softie nature.

"I have another neighbor, Miss Doris, who worked in DC Public Schools for 30 years in the cafeteria, first doing 'pots and pans,' as she called it, and then in the front. She told me offhandedly that there were kids in her school, little ones, who thought their names were 'muthafucka' and 'bitchass' because it's what they were called at home. My heart shattered to hear that. I was in her house, it's the same model as this one, built after World War II for laborer families. I looked at her wall and saw she had framed certificates of her food service training. The certificates were yellow, made by a dot matrix printer, but they were dustless. I knew she was proud of what she did." Trey took a long pause. "And I tried to be proud too."

"Why did you have to 'try?' Weren't you proud of her?"

"I got stuck on all the advantages I had in life."

"Start hanging out with foreign diplomats, especially in the IFS—Indian Foreign Service. You won't feel so privileged."

"Is that the secret?" Trey asked. "Search out people who have it better than you? To feel better about those who have it worse?"

"It depends on how aware you want to be. Most people don't care to go into their neighbors' homes and ask about the awards on their wall. Most people in my neighborhood, if they heard about a kid named 'bitchass,' would look back at you like a cow with a cud."

"I don't want it to be a predicament. I just want to interact with people I like, avoid people I don't, and help everyone I can." Linda looked away from Trey and rolled her eyes.

"Anyone else? Anyone our age?"

"Andrew is our age. And there's Rico. His name is actually Ibn, a Nation of Islam guy, but the neighborhood calls him Rico, 'because that's what his mama named him.' He's pretty enlightened, but not politically correct, a union electrical worker. Wife left him with two kids: Bakari, who they call 'Kari, and Dimitry, who they call Meetree. He's warm toward me but still suspicious. We talk football—Redskins of course—and I ask him why he sticks with them after all the bad shit the owner has done to the team. He says, 'Maaan, it's the Rett-skins!' and he slaps my back. Then I ask him about Obama. Most people around here love him, obviously."

"Be careful with saying 'obviously,'" Linda laughed.

"Yeah, I know. But they do. Miss Millie wears a t-shirt with him all blinged out. I swear, whoever made it just pasted Obama's head on Jay Z's body."

"Yeah, they sell those on the mall. Too funny. Even funnier, I'll bet Obama's like the whitest dude in real life. Like he would totally stand in line for Marilyn Monroe stamps."

"Maybe. I assumed Rico, being a big leftie and a hardcore Nation guy, would be an Obama guy too. But he got serious when I asked him and he said, 'We'll see.'"

"I wonder why."

"Rico's pretty involved. He rolls up his sleeves, I mean. He runs the neighborhood association that cleans up and gives scholarships to kids to go to decent elementary schools in better parts of the District. He's been interviewed on WPFW a few times, he told me."

"I haven't heard of it."

"Leftie stuff." Trey paused. "You know, you can always come back here in the daytime and meet some of these people."

"Yeah, I know," Linda said sleepily. "Would you like to come home with me for Thanksgiving? I'll buy your ticket."

"Thanks. A buddy from the fire department invited me over."

"Ok," she sighed, pouring the last of the bottle into her glass, instinctively looking at Trey's kitchen. "Are you sure you're cut out for this life, Trey? I mean, by yourself?"

"Well, I don't plan to be alone forever."

"That's a good plan."

"You seem comfortable by yourself," Trey said, standing to take the bottle and cork to the trash.

"I've got my moments," Linda admitted. "Who were you closest to in your A-100?"

"Oh, man. There were 94 of us, a lot of them. They're hiring so many FSOs these days!"

"Yeah, some old timers say we're 'diluting the pool.'"

"Well, I'm certainly atypical. I have a hard time keeping a straight face when I hear people break into 'heated discussions' on foreign policy."

"Why?"

"Because it sounds so amateurish. The theories are like horoscopes, like they could be true in a lot of cases. Or not."

"Who are you close with, Trey?"

"I'd like to say all 93 of my classmates. They're all great in one way or another. During A-100, I used to compare our class to a plutonium atom—you know, atomic number 94? And there we were about to explode all over the world."

"Spreading democracy like fallout, love it!"

"Something like that. I think we'll represent America well. We had a lot of former teachers in our class. I felt close to them, especially because I didn't last in the profession."

"They didn't last either."

"One girl I connected with immediately. We sat next to each other on the first day. She taught English in Philly, like the actual city, public."

"Where is she going?"

"Somewhere in Latin America."

"I know you know exactly where she is going," Linda said, wondering why he would withhold the name of the country. She feared that he held many more secrets.

"She loves literature. She loved her students. The way she spoke about them, I could listen to her talk for hours: books and kids. She was brilliant and yet unpretentious, much smarter than me. I'd get embarrassed sometimes when I'd make a connection and she'd be three steps ahead of me in the discussion. But she always smiled, waited, made me feel like I was on par."

"She probably liked you. Like I do," Linda said and quickly bowed her head as tears fell quietly into her lap. They dropped so quickly Trey mistook them for a more malignant discharge, his EMT reflexes kicking in.

"Linda! Are you ok?!" She inhaled loudly and looked up, puffy, a half-hearted grin became a sour-mouthed grimace.

"You don't know as much about me as I do about you!" she cried, now sobbing more regularly.

"Comon, Linda. I mean, we haven't spent that much time together. I really enjoy your company, though."

"I feel more curious than you."

"Curious is good, right? I'm really sorry to see you so sad."

"Why haven't you asked me if I've ever been married?"

"I don't know."

"How many other people did you ask to paint cardboard before me?"

"I sent a blast on the list serve to my A-100. No takers. I'm glad you were up for it!" Linda wiped her eyes, stood, and pointed up the staircase with an inquisitive look. Half of her was asking for the bathroom, the other half was curious about Trey's bed.

"Yes, top of the stairs," Trey said. Linda creaked up the wooden steps and disappeared for 15 minutes. Trey cleaned and set Papa and the lamb against the couch. Linda returned.

"Are you ok to drive?" he asked.

"Are you seeing other girls?"

"Are *we* seeing each other? I didn't invite you over expecting that we would mess around." Linda realized how drunk she was, how sober Trey was. She considered apologizing for putting him on the spot but doubled down instead.

"Comon, Trey, this isn't the 1950s! You invited me to your home!"

"This wasn't a pretense," Trey said pointing at the cardboard. "I'll be on the FSI lawn tomorrow before dawn."

"Well, I'll be there closer to nine when class starts." She said good night and walked to the door.

"I'm sorry," Trey said. "I am not used to being pursued like this. I don't think I've ever met someone who likes me as much as you seem to." Linda stiffened, letting the cold air sober her up. White chick rolling through Anacostia, she thought, no chance a cop pulls her over. She looked grimly at Trey.

"In Russian, they have a saying: 'Only Americans believe in coincidences.' And their word for 'coincidence' is Sav-padeniah, meaning 'to fall together.' I'm feeling pretty Russian about us, that it was no coincidence we met, and I want us to fall together." Linda looked away as she said the last part, but Trey put his palm to the side of her face, kissed her, and then pulled her back inside.

A year and change later, Linda, who had moved on to Moscow, heard through a friend that Trey had asked his girlfriend to marry him while he was back in the States on R and R. The news wasn't as painful as her unrequited affections at FSI, but she felt a sting, some anger, and then a deep sadness. She resumed writing him letters, around one per week, which chronicled her own love affair with Moscow, the Russian language and the Russian people. When the thought of trying to win Trey back crept into her mind, she beat it away with the pathetic realization that she was experiencing a typical female reaction.

Professionally, Linda was rolling. As a midlevel Public Diplomacy (PD) officer amid the Obama-Medvedev "reset" era, there seemed to be nothing beyond the capacity of Russians and Americans: they cooperated in Space, on energy, trade, even in Afghanistan, where the countries now could compare bruises. Russia was an active member of the G8, and on its way to joining the World Trade Organization.

Every week, Linda spoke before hundreds of young, talented, eager Russians who wanted to start businesses, support civil society, study in the United States and return to help their country. The price of oil was high, as was Russian sentiment toward America. Even amid the petro-windfall, Russians didn't seem content, 'sitting on the oil needle,' especially youth, who demonstrated for government accountability, transparent elections, and a more diversified, open economy.

As the months went by, however, she noticed Russian security services following her to meetings, sometimes sitting blatantly at nearby tables with recording devices aimed toward her conversations. Her contacts in the democracy sector were reporting harassment and surveillance, some were detained and questioned randomly, and a few were roughed up. By September of 2011, Linda and her colleagues were working under a pressure not felt since the Cold War. She set up tripwires in her apartment to check for break-ins. Most nights she drank herself to sleep. One evening, as she cried in her winter garden, she remembered the calendar and Trey's mention that he would be married in a couple weeks. It was late in Delhi, but she called him anyway.

"Is something wrong?" he answered sleepily. Linda breathed, loud enough for him to know she was there. He said her name and waited.

"How are you?" she creaked, feeling hungover though she was still drunk.

"Worried about you. Are you ok?"

"I don't think so," she said and started crying.

"How can I help?"

"Can I see you? Please?"

"I don't know if that's a good idea."

"I won't try anything," she said and made herself laugh.

"It's not that, Linda. I'm not worried about us 'doing anything,' but would it help our friendship if we saw each other before I left?"

"I don't know. But I'm really doing horrible here. Things are changing in Russia. Again. Like they used to be, I'm hearing."

"Soviet stuff?"

"Worse. I don't know. I feel like Putin himself is watching me."

"Probably listening, that's for sure."

"When do you fly back? For the wedding."

"In a week."

"Nonstop?"

"Through London."

"Can I meet you? Can you schedule a layover? Fly out a day earlier so no one knows?"

"Putin knows."

"Fuck him."

"It won't be good for us."

"Please Trey, I won't try anything. I just want to wish you well in person. Please." Trey stayed quiet for a minute.

"Ok."

"Thank you, John," she said.

"No one calls me that," he snapped. "My grandfather called me Johnny sometimes," he said more softly, like she remembered.

"I'm sorry. I'll be there. London. Tell me the day. I'll book two rooms."

They rallied up in Marylebone at the Hyatt Churchill, where Linda had stayed so many times, the staff half recognized her. She smelled Trey in their initial hug, her old feelings rejuvenated, her loins primed. His hands were the same on the small of her back, his forearms against her bra, his chest on hers. In their embrace, she ran through how she'd breathe near his collar, daring him to pull away and face her eyes. She saw exactly how she could get him fed and drunk and comfortable and sympathetic, how to get him to sleep with her, how she would cry afterward.

"I thought you'd appreciate South Asian food without feces in it," she began.

"Ha, you were right about Delhi Belly. I think I've gotten used to the constant rumble and nausea. Certainly the loose stools."

"Mmm, let's eat!"

"You look well," Trey said.

"Thanks, but I feel terrible."

"Because of the wedding?"

"No! Because of Russia. Putin and Medvedev are going to castle again."

"Switch jobs? People saw that coming, no?"

"It doesn't make it feel any better."

"Sorry. You're still doing good public diplomacy work, though, right? I loved reading about those Russian students. I can't wait to do it myself."

"Well, you need to get a Facebook account, and probably Twitter, if you're going to do PD 'in this digital world.'"

"That's what Alex Rosen in the Department says, I know."

"Alex Rosen is a twat. It's what *I* say."

"Ok."

"Seriously, PD or no PD, you *need* Facebook. I found out about your engagement from my spies in Delhi."

"I would change if I was on Facebook. I'd be suckered into sharing everything. I'd fall for all the click bait. I'd never see their suggestive advertising coming."

"You sound like you know yourself well, Trey Ciuri. Time to get married."

"In a week!"

"I heard about your bachelor party too."

"The road trip?"

"No, in Delhi."

"Oh, yeah, that was so….Indian. Like a poor imitation of quality."

"Where did you find the strippers?"

"Whoa, *I* found no such individuals. I also *requested* no such individuals. My suggestion was to play poker and get drunk. The political guys 'invited' two young.….I guess I can call them 'ladies,' but….whoa."

"Figures POL guys knew where the strippers were. Gone are the days when their cables were anything other than a report on the news. At least they could furnish your party with 'entertainment.'"

"They meant well, I guess. I should have explicitly said, 'no strippers.'"

"What's this 'road trip?'"

"Oh, that's the real bachelor party, the one with my best friends from way back. We're starting in L.A. and driving to Baltimore, picking up dudes on the way."

"You're doing that in one week?"

"Sheeeit! We could do it in three days! A week gives us time to sightsee."

"Doesn't sound like much fun to me."

"Well, you're not…."

"Invited, I know," Linda said and looked down.

"Sorry. Sometimes our banter encourages too much honesty."

"Is that why we didn't work out?"

"I'm sure there were a lot of reasons, Linda."

"None of them we discussed in DC. You just left."

"I thought it was understood that distance would be hard in this line of work."

"Oh, but it was so easy with your fiancé? What's her name?"

"Millie."

"Your neighbor?! From Anacostia? St E's?!"

"Ha, no. But she's invited. She asked for a few other invites for some of her Baltimore peeps. My Millie was cool with it." Linda peered around Trey's shoulder toward the hotel bar, then quickly locked his eyes in a serious look.

"Why was that night in Anacostia not our culmination?"

"I think we culminated pretty well, no?"

"Yes."

"I thought that was what you wanted," Trey said.

"It was! You wanted it too?"

"I did, yes."

"And the way you held me, the way you told me as we were making love, how interesting and wise and funny I was."

"I believed all those things. Still believe them."

"You didn't once say how pretty I was!"

"Sorry, I must have gotten caught up in the moment."

"No! I *knew* you found me ravishing! You didn't have to say it!"

"Geeze, Linda. Like I said, I value your friendship and I'm lucky to know you in the Foreign Service. You've taught me a ton. We had a great night making….cardboard."

"But?"

"There's no 'but.' No conjunctions. That was two years ago. I am getting married in a week."

"Why did you pull me back inside?"

"Because I thought it would make you happy. And you were pretty drunk. You would have killed someone, maybe yourself."

"I feel like killing myself."

"Why?"

"Because I've been on birth control for 15 years and my uterus is twice the age it should be. Even if I found a guy to get pregnant with, it would be a long time to take and the baby's health would be in jeopardy."

"I'm sorry. Have you thought about IVF, doing it yourself?"

"I'd rather adopt. Why create another life in a pre-made broken home? There are millions of kids who need good homes. I read to kids at an orphanage in Moscow every week. I've learned more Russian from them than I did at FSI, I think.

"Don't kill yourself, trust me."

"The more Russia tightens the screws on us, the more cynical I get about America. The more hopeless I feel."

"Well, I understand feeling hopeless. And I understand wanting to give up."

"You don't seem so. You're one of the most positive, creative people I know."

"Behind that is a long history of darkness."

"I think you're trying to talk me down."

"I wish I was."

"This is so dramatic! We haven't even started drinking yet! Shall we go to the bar?"

"I'm ok, actually. I have to stay ahead of jetlag for this trip. Drinking really messes me up."

"Well, I hope you don't mind if I medicate."

"Be my guest," Trey said, walking to the bar.

"Oh-k," Linda said, tasting her cocktail. "I know alcohol is a drug, but wow, right to the brain! Like I can trace it in my veins. I feel right as rain. I have a problem." Trey smiled uncomfortably on his barstool. "What?" she asked. "What?" she asked again, nearly finishing her drink. Trey shifted in his seat and looked hard at the bartender. Linda ignored his discomfort, continuing: "What….is this road trip all about? Who's going? Who are the men in the Ciuri party?"

"There's four of them. From different times in my life. Tony is my best friend from high school. He's a C-17 pilot in the Air Force, lives in Tacoma, married, three kids."

"Impressive you've kept up. I lost track of my high school friends after college."

"Tony and I were supposed to go to college together, but he never got accepted to the Academy."

"Oh, where did he go?"

"CU Boulder, just up the road, so we saw each other a lot. Though sometimes it was uncomfortable for me. A lot of guilt."

"He really wanted to go there, huh?"

"Yeah, it still haunts me that I got in and he didn't. It feels like one of those stories where one friend gets drafted and dies, and the surviving friend is left to anguish over it."

"Except it has nothing to do with war, no one died, and he made it in the Air Force anyway."

"There's that, yes. Tony actually gave me my first lesson in foreign affairs. He's half Haitian, half Italian, so he has this strange olive-ish complexion, which is hard to place, but is without a doubt 'not Anglo-Saxon,' which in Boulder was very popular among the rich chicks who went there. His freshman year, when Rabin was assassinated, Tony pretended to be a grief-stricken Palestinian or Israeli, yearning for peace, and banged like a dozen Jewish American princesses before their birthright trips."

"That's shady. But effective, I imagine. There were a lot of girls at Georgetown who would have at least blown a guy for being ethnic. That's why so many of them entertained Detrick Walker's 'who's gonna suck this dick?' question."

"Tony stretched it as far as he could, spending hours in the library, combing the back pages of the Herald Tribune, memorizing phrases in foreign languages, nuances of different cultures. When there was a nightclub fire in The Philippines—he was an anguished cousin. War in Chechnya, he was half Dagestani. The snow bunny bubbleheads at Boulder didn't much care—they were going to bang *somebody*. Tony just gave them a warmer feeling of social justice."

"It is hilarious that women believe that giving a guy sex is doing a service. Like, a lot of guys we *do* feel sorry for. It's certainly not as enjoyable for us as it is for you."

"Why is that?"

"Because you guys work so hard for it. Well, I take that back. You, Trey didn't work that hard for it."

"Well, you were a rarity. Thanks."

"See! You're thanking me, like me fucking you was some gift. I didn't want it to be a gift!"

"Maybe we should talk about something else. Moscow sounds like an awesome city. I'm sure it's better-run and less polluted than Delhi."

"There are places in sub-Saharan Africa better run and cleaner than Delhi. There is something special about Moscow, yes. Something special about Russian people. They're so….funny….their humor, I can't describe it, maybe because it hits close to home with my Minnesota roots. The way they wrap up babies at the slightest hint of a chill, how a babushka will nearly kill herself running across the road to pull an ear flap down on an exposed child. I think Russians like Americans too—our adventurousness and naiveté, our strange obsession with being generous, with charity. They can't figure out if giving is part of our culture or if we just throw money away because we have so much of it. They laugh at how we use Tchaikovsky in our redneck Christmas commercials—Santa leaving a Dodge Ram under someone's tree set to *The Nutcracker*. They're so smart, but unless they are in the intelligentsia, they're embarrassed by their education." Linda looked up and day-dreamed for a few seconds. "I love the Russians. But I hate their oligarchs and politicians." She ordered another drink.

"Another thing in common with America."

"What?"

"Our people are generally good. But our politicians and oligarchs represent the worst of us."

"Well, there is 'the chosen one.'"

"Obama?"

"'Child of promise,'" Linda said, rolling her eyes.

"It *was* pretty cool when he came to Delhi. He like literally glowed. I've never seen a human being exude that kind of aura."

"Did you have to work with any staffers?"

"Unfortunately, yes."

"Aren't they the fucking worst? Jesus, Obama is so saintly, but he surrounds himself with these demonic cherubs who worship him." Linda downed her drink and flagged the bartender. "Why should it surprise me?! I'm sure Barry's been doted on by hairy-pitted liberal-artsy chicks since he was a toddler."

"I've actually heard that Republican staffers are much nicer and more knowledgeable. It's a shame about their political beliefs."

"Yep. It's a deal with the devil. Would you rather work with a decent, smart person who does not share your views, or an arrogant idiot who does?"

"'Little pink houses for you and me.'"

"You said it. Agh! Does it matter that no one except ninnies like us know that's an anti-American song?"

"I don't think it does. Same way it doesn't matter that Obama surrounds himself with some of the most slimy, low-integrity sycophants. As long as people have 'hope.'"

"How 'audacious' of you to suggest, John August."

"You need another drink."

"I accept. But please don't let me try to seduce you. Because after a few of these I most certainly will."

"It's ok, I don't find you that attractive," Trey said and smiled.

"Ahhhhh!! That's funny! But dangerous. Seriously, I'm going to come at you with everything I have before your flight tomorrow. Be strong."

"Since we're talking about it now, don't you think we can just avoid it?"

"Without alcohol, yes."

"Well, Millie has always been curious about you, and she wished us well on this detour: that we could tie up loose ends, if there are any, and that I could make you feel better."

"Jesus Christ, she knows we're here?! Is she watching us?! I feel like I'm back in Russia!"

"She's fine with it. Like I said, I told her everything about us. I consider you a good friend, Linda, a mentor. I almost invited you to the wedding. But I figured it would hurt your feelings."

"I would have come. It's open bar, right?"

"Oh-k. Another drink for Moscow's Assistant Cultural Affairs Officer."

"What a title. The Russians, of course, think we're all spies."

"Even PD people? Man, *that's* a stretch," Trey said stretching his arms and fake yawning.

"Ok, tell me about the next best friend."

"Wade Herndon, from the Academy. Guy can fix anything. Except his marriage. Man, as I said that, my body just yearned for a drink."

"Have one!"

"If I do, you'll take advantage."

"You'll resist if you're committed."

"Orange juice please. Wade and I almost got kicked out of the Academy a million times. But it was for sensical stuff, like attending poetry readings and art openings, watching plays, going to Denver."

"Contrarian cadets. Did you ever put a smurf on the lawn?"

"No, but we did have a pet snake. Started off as a little guy, a ribbon snake, but it got pretty large on feeder guppies. One day, he turned out to be a she when she gave birth. The babies escaped into the squadron. Most of them got stepped on."

"So sad."

"We also had a four-foot statue of the Virgin Mary that we used to leave outside the door whenever one of us was masturbating. To let the other guy know not to come in."

"How charming."

"Well, I felt guilty doing it while Mary was in the room. We weren't even supposed to have stuff like that—no furniture except government-issue, but Wade was able to convince our officer in charge, Major Brazier, that it was a religious thing. And if there was one thing the Academy promoted, it was Jesus and all his accessories."

"Such a good Catholic, ashamed of masturbation."

"My mom haunted me with it. She said, 'Just pray away the urges, God gives us strength.' But when I did hold off on 'self love' for a while, I'd have the most erotic, nasty wet dreams. I never told my mom, but I was like, what's the difference?"

"Only a Catholic would debate masturbation versus wet dreams. 'Which one will send you to hell faster?' Didn't Flannery O'Connor write about that?"

"So, the snake was belly-up, post-partum, and we were kind of freaked out about what to do, but we were rushing to class, so Wade just threw a couple of fish in her bowl, figured she'd munch on them like afterbirth or whatever. We left her in the middle of the floor to get some air. While we were at school, she ate the fish and puked 'em both out— stunk up the hallway. Major Brazier followed his nose, opened the door to find this poor grieving mama snake with a belly ache, puked fish splattered everywhere. And above it all on the desk, the Virgin Mary watching over. He was like, 'What kind of hellacious Satanic ritual is going on here?!'"

"In real college, no one cares if you're a Satanist. At Georgetown, I think they even had a club for devil-worshippers, at least devil-*verstehers*."

"We would have gotten in more shit, but Wade told Brazier that the snake was from Biology class, and they didn't have enough room in the lab. That was our existence at the Academy—try a bunch of strange, illegal shit and then skate past disenrollment."

"Is he still in the Air Force?"

"Yes."

"Married, kids?"

"Divorced, kids."

"Well, I guess marriage isn't for everyone. Especially female FSOs."

"I've heard that. But I don't count you in that category."

"I didn't either until recently." Linda grimaced, took a long swig, continued. "My second tour I had an Ambassador— never married, no kids. She sat a couple of us girls down and talked about when she was coming up, how hard it was, blah, blah. She said that when she was a midlevel officer, a DCM of hers offhandedly remarked, 'Eunice, if you want to be successful in the Foreign Service, what you need is a wife.' As in, someone to take care of your business at home so you can hobnob and pursue your career.

"She used that as motivation as she rose up. My friend and I rallied around her success and resolve, but as the tour went on, we saw how deflated and lonely and bitter she was. She would end meetings by telling people, just like Eeyore, 'Well, try to have a good day.' At receptions, she'd let her yap dog out of the kitchen about an hour into it, and the thing would nip at guests until they got the hint to go home. She retired right after that tour and lives alone in some beach town. I'm sure that dog will survive her. Foreign Service was all she had. I don't want to be like her, but I fear I'm on my way."

"You have too much energy, too much personality. You'll be ok."

"Some ladies from the older generation married gay FSOs who weren't allowed to be gay. They've had kids and long careers. I don't want that either. I'll kill myself before…."

"Again, don't say that. It's serious, not something to say offhand."

"Oh, sorry Dr. Compassion." Trey looked at Linda gravely, and then ordered three shots of good vodka, which he dumped into his orange juice. He then told her in meticulous detail about his suicides. And while Linda didn't believe him completely, she didn't once interrupt his narration, and she stopped drinking to process his feelings. This time, it was not she badgering Trey for information about his life; it was he sharing things that were intensely personal. She felt even closer to him, but less sexually drawn. When he finished, he ordered another drink, a true screwdriver.

"So, I'm not going to ask you what you think," Trey said. "Just know that I've never shared this with anyone—not my parents, the groomsmen, not in confession. Just you. If you tell my background investigators, I will hunt you down."

"Promise? Was there ever a time….when you didn't….do it?"

"You mean, like, on the verge, made the choice, and then backed out?"

"Yes."

"Near the end of my firefighting time. After I told my Captain that I was going to quit, I overheard him talking to the other guys: 'Ciuri. Nice guy. But I wouldn't want him on the fire ground.' That's like the worst insult you can get in the fire service. It means that you're pretty much worthless, that your guys don't believe you can save them in the heat of it. Had I not been so excited to join the Foreign Service, I would have probably made moves."

"Well, I'm glad you didn't. We'd have never met."

"Sure we would have."

"Whatever you say, Trey. Any other times?"

"While I was teaching. It had been an up and down year, and I wasn't sure if it was for me. Half of the time, I could get those 8th graders excited and curious; the other half they ate me alive. Near the end of the year, I wrote the famous Hemingway quote on the board. He called it a six-word novel: 'For Sale, Baby Shoes, Never Worn.'"

"I love that story," Linda said, warm and drunk as the bartender signaled last call. She didn't look up but knew it was raining. She dreamed of sex with Trey to it.

"I challenged the class to write their own six-word novels. And they came up with:

'You did not teach us anything.'

'You still live with your parents.'

'You need to get a girlfriend.'

'You won't be back next year.'

"On and on they went on. They aimed straight at my heart! I left school nearly crying, holding it in until I could find someplace to be alone, hopefully with a mechanism that would end my life. But as I walked up the street, I passed a first grader from our school, dragging his father back to his classroom for an open house or something. The kid's hair was recently washed and he had a mouth full of silver teeth—lots of immigrant kids have silver teeth—and he was babbling on about a story of a brown bear to his father who couldn't comprehend a word, but he was beaming at this kid as they rushed to the school. The dad was a workingman wearing his dress clothes. It's an image that warmed me and broke my privileged heart at the same time.

"I kept walking, fully crying now, took a left and ran into the SEIU building, which I saw every day from my bus route. SEIU is a labor union in case you were unaware."

"I'm aware. Andy Stern and Barry O are thick as thieves."

"I bust in and scared the receptionist with my bloodshot eyes. I told her that I knew the story of SEIU, that it was formed by Italian janitors in Chicago who were exploited because they couldn't speak

English. I said I wanted to volunteer to teach their members English who needed it. I must have told it to half a dozen people—and one of them hired me. The following day I told my principal I wouldn't be back next year."

"And you decided you wanted to live?"

"I wonder if that's what it was. I definitely decided I didn't want to die. There's a difference, I think." Linda shook her head to test her sobriety. Trey called for the tab by holding up his palm and signing with his finger. Linda was feeling warm and ornery.

"Well, I don't want to minimize what you shared with me just now, but you, Trey Ciuri, have nothing to be hopeless about. I don't fall in love with fools and whores, or whatever you call yourself." Trey continued to stare at the bartender as he brought the check.

They paid and headed toward the elevators on wobbly legs. In the lift, Trey gazed at the ceiling, his hands folded like a penitent. Linda slowly inched toward him, breathing, like the big bad wolf, she imagined. They walked toward their rooms.

"Ah, well, I guess it's time," Linda said with a leer. She couldn't feel her face very well but guessed it was in a mean shape.

"Yeah, well I'm glad I stopped here." Trey grabbed her shoulders and held her at a distance. "You are a wonderful person, Linda," he said. "You believe that like I do and you'll be fine." Linda pretended to ignore him.

"I have two Tesco bottles of wine in my room. Let's play the 'Mats until the sun comes up," she slurred.

"I can't," Trey said, smiling. She scowled.

"In Russia, they say that only fools and Americans smile."

"You know me." Linda stepped into his space, her mouth dry and open. She stumbled on purpose, and Trey caught her by the shoulders, then spun her away and held her from behind.

"Trey," she said breathlessly, her eyes closed.

"Yes."

"Trey, be careful of the other FSOs….they're going to smile in your face and write great emails to you, but they're going to slander you in the next second. Be careful, Trey."

"I will, Linda."

"Traaayyyy," She said, growing limp, collapsing into his body.

"Yes."

"Beware of the little black passport. Don't let them make you a useful idiot."

"I won't, Linda." Trey picked her up like a bride and opened his room with the electronic card.

"Trey. Trey! The FSOs are gonna complain about their free housing! And their maid asks for too much money! And about the nannies who raise their kids. And that the locals just don't 'get it.' Gonna tell you what a pay cut they're taking to 'serve their country.' Watch out…."

"I will, Linda." He took off her shoes as he stood over the bed. He looked at the window, she stared at his face.

"Are you sure you know what you're doing?" Linda asked. Trey turned down the sheets and laid Linda on her side. He unbuttoned her skirt from the bottom.

"Does anyone?" he asked.

"Most people are nervous before their wedding. Have you thought of everything?"

"No." Trey took the dress off her left shoulder, then her left hip. He reached under her body to get the other side, leading her right arm through, then folding the garment at the foot of the bed.

"Is that ok?!" she asked. He unhooked her bra and led her arms free.

"Yes, it's ok, Linda" he said as he tucked her in and grabbed his toiletry bag.

"You're headed for another suicide, Trey Ciuri," Linda said, shutting her eyes, "….if you keep up with that attitude."

Chapter Six: Luckenbach, Texas

(In the voice of Waylon Jennings): Now, I don't know about y'all, but when I see grown men crying at a wedding, I know somethin's up. And I'm not talking about the father of the bride. There he is, happy as a pig in slop, and pretty drunk too. No, these weepers are groomsmen, and you know every one of 'em. They should be happy. It's Trey's big day. But still they're crying, all four of 'em, wearin' those silly orange bow ties that Millie picked out.

There's Wade, rubbin' his throat, tryin' to hide it, but a tear's comin' down. Tony O's Italian half is mannin' the waterworks—he's on one knee! Reggie's got snot bubbles in his beard. And look at sweet Slim, he's chokin' on blubber, drinkin' straight whiskey to stiffen up.

Well, maybe those are tears of joy. But you're gonna have to wait to find that out. I'm gonna drop y'all at the beginning of the road trip, in San Pedro, where Tony and Trey started across the country. Five days till the wedding, y'all, and some surprises on the way.

"Hey man!"

"Yuri."

"Thanks for coming down."

"For this? Wouldn't miss it. Nice minivan—you sure you're not married already?"

"Ha. I just wanted to be able to fit Wade's big ass."

"Where's he these days?"

"Divorced."

"No, where's he stationed?"

"Oh, C-Springs. Cheyenne Mountain, I think."

"We're picking him up first?"

"Yeah—if we can drive straight—it's about 16 hours. You got what it takes?"

"I took a week off for your wedding. If I can sell that to my wife, I can drive the whole way to Baltimore."

"When's the last time you saw Wade?" Trey asked.

"Not since you were still in. He came to Cheyenne, right?"

"A couple times. We kind of had a falling out after Vandenburg. And then he met what's-her-name in Montana."

"She go to the zoo?"

"Yep. Psychology major. I warned him they're all crazy. Literally—that's why they study it."

"She wigged out on him?"

"Worse. Left his ass, took the kids, went lesbian."

"Like 'dyke' lesbian?"

"Is there another kind?"

"I don't know. How do you become a lesbo after having kids?"

"No idea. She was cute too. Before she weed-whacked her hair."

"Dykes are so fake. They just want to be dudes."

"You sure about that?"

"We've got a bunch who are crew chiefs and load masters. The way they talk, it's like a kid trying to be like his older brother. They hit on the same girls we do.…er, did, when we were single."

"Well, I don't really care why she left him, it sucks. And I know I shouldn't be so derogatory in the way I mention Adrienne's sexual orientation.…"

"Yeah, I was just about to tell you how offensive you are.…"

"But in a weird way I'm thankful because Wade and I reconnected. One day I got a text as I was walking out of the grocery store: 'Adrienne's leaving me.' I dropped everything. Got work subs at the fire department and flew to see him."

"Dropped everything huh? You and I haven't seen each other in *years*, Trey!"

"And here you are, in my time of need."

"You *need* me? You've never needed me."

"Well, I tried to minimize my neediness."

"Is that healthy? It made me afraid to reach out to you."

"When? Why?"

"When I wanted to talk. When I had decisions."

"What decisions? Like with Carrie? When you emailed me, you'd already decided to have the baby. Before I knew it, I was at your wedding. You've got three kids now. What decisions?"

"Never mind."

"Wade never *needed* me before. In our whole friendship, since we were 17, he was always in control, always the guy who fixed things. I felt like a freeloader, like some idiot kid watching a movie in the other room while his parents talked about important stuff. When I had a chance to 'be there' for my best friend from college, I jumped at it."

"Were you able to help?"

"We hung out. Caught up. I got to see the girls. It was the last weekend before Adrienne swooped in."

"What a crock."

"You'd think the courts would look at her drastic change in lifestyle and say, 'Hmm, maybe that's not the best environment for two little girls. While their mom is finding her inner KD Lang."

"Shit's all rigged."

"No shit. Wade had just gotten back from Afghanistan too. One day he gets a call from USAA: 'Good morning, Major Herndon, we're sorry to hear about your divorce....' And he's like, 'My *divorce?!*' He'd only been back a few weeks. Hell, he missed Janie's birth while he was over there. It was all he could do to drag Adrienne's ass to counseling, which she got credit for in the custody proceedings."

"That's terrible."

"While I was visiting, Wade and me and the girls were eating at a diner in downtown Denver. Adrienne was coming soon for the handoff. Wade's oldest, Riley, noticed that the flower on the table was real. Then she walked around to the other tables—smiling at everyone—checking out their flowers. She came back and asked Wade how they could get 'real live flowers' in the winter. Usually Wade lived for moments like those: to explain the whys and hows in the world. You remember the 'Wade factor?' When he'd exaggerate?"

"Yeah."

"This time his face lost some excitement. He didn't seem as adventurous. The wheels weren't turning. 'Look at this flower,' he told her gently, but he was watching the clock, nervous about Billie Jean King coming to steal his kids. He said, 'Look at the pattern on the petals.' And he drew it on a napkin, gave Riley a pen, and told her to go to another table and draw the pattern she saw.

"'They're the same!' she yelled across the restaurant, half confused, half delighted. And Wade's face too was half kind, half anguished. He said, 'These are grown in greenhouses. They control the light, the temperature, and the water. Everything. They're all the same and they end up here.' Melissa Etheridge came a few minutes later and he brought them out to the parking lot. Came back inside. He was rubbing his throat."

"Why was he rubbing his throat?"

"Because he was sad. He sat down and I asked him, 'Do you ever think about….

And Wade said, 'Killin' her? Yep.' I laughed my ass off. He stayed pretty serious, though I knew he was joking. Kind of."

"That's a bad place to be in."

"It was a little scary to hear him say that. It reminded me of a story he told about Philmont—Boy Scouts. One night, a bear came into camp, overturned a latrine, and was eating food particles out of the shit."

"Sounds delicious, when do *we* eat?"

"So, Wade and a couple other guys had to track the bear down and kill it."

"For eating shit? Seems excessive."

"Because it was no longer scared of humans. Shit today, a Tenderfoot tomorrow. 'He had to die,' as Wade said. And now with Adrienne, and the way Wade thinks, it's a little scary how logical he is, and precise, and I would say, fair and kind. If he's at all entertaining the idea of killing Adrienne, one: she probably deserves it; and two: he has a good plan for getting away with it."

"Well, let's hope not."

"I can't imagine what it feels like, to lose your kids. I had a glimpse, though. When I worked an Americorps program at the L.A. County courthouse. I was in Legal Aid Self Help—helping people fill out family law paperwork. When fathers realized that they were going to lose their kids, like if they got a 'father unfriendly' judge….a light went out in them. Something very dark, very scary. These were decent dads so far as I could tell. Certainly Wade is a good dad. Society fucks up when they don't try as hard with dads." Tony let a grimace hang on his face.

"There were times when *I* needed you, Yuri. Maybe not divorce level. But best friends should be there for each other."

"I feel bad now. Dude, do you know how much I admire you for charting your own path? As bad as I felt at the Academy—it was just guilt for being such a fuckup."

"You *were* a fuckup at the zoo."

"I was! It should have been you there. Me at CU."

"God has his plan."

"Who?"

"You heard me."

"So *this* is what I missed all these years? You're a Bible beater?"

"I wasn't a very serious Catholic in high school or college, no."

"Dude, I copied a lot of your one liners that made fun of the church."

"Maybe you'll change when you have kids. When I started deploying, I was so alone without them. First time we did a video call, Johnny peeked behind the computer to see if I was there. The look on his face killed me. I hung up and ran outside. My crew was coming back from dinner, laughing and tipsy. I wasn't that emotional ever—not when I didn't get into the Academy four years straight, when relatives died, not when we lost games, when girls broke up with me—not our graduation."

"Yeah, I pussed out on that speech. It's still a regret."

"It's the past. That night I was looking up at the sky, and I remembered how I used stare into the nozzle of my dad's jet. I never told you this in high school—which is strange because I told you everything—but one of my dad's guys died right after takeoff. There was a big wind gust and he overcorrected, winged over into the ground. Dad took it harder than anything I'd ever seen. The guy's kid went to Thomas Sumter. A couple weeks after, dad came to our baseball game against TSA. It was the only time he showed up."

"I remember that. We were scared shitless of your dad."

"He sat at the top of the bleachers, quiet as usual, but every time the kid came to bat, he leaned forward. You were pitching, I was at short."

"We lost that game. I don't remember him. Was he good?"

"You struck him out every time."

"Shit."

"Except the last inning. Dad stood at the gate to the field. Kid was up and dad put out his hand, like a blessing. Kid got a hit past me in the hole."

"That's it? That's God?"

"It's a lot of things. It's personal, Yuri. I can tell you're not there yet."

"I believe in God, man. But there's a difference between God and the church, right?"

"You'll find him there. In the sacraments."

"Let's hit the 'change topic' button. Please. Things good with Carrie?"

"Well, she's not coming to the wedding."

"Oh, that's ok. We don't really know each other. She's gotta watch the kids, yeah?"

"She could have come. My parents were ready to fly down."

"That's nice of them. Is it me?"

"No, she only knows you through my stories."

"Then she hates me."

"No."

"Are you guys ok?"

"We're not going to get divorced. She won't be a lesbo when I get back."

"Well, that's positive! Hey man, I feel off balance. You have news? You hiding something?"

"Yuri! This is hard, man! I loved….you like a brother. But you disappear a lot! We went how long without talking?!"

"I'm sorry, man. I never forgot what you did for me. And I'm super proud of everything you've done in your life. I mean, fuck the Academy! I'm living proof that it doesn't make men or leaders or whatever. You're self-made. I hope I'm not insulting your belief in God when I say that every time you faced adversity, you reached within *yourself* and drove harder. Always getting better, never quitting. You're so much better than me."

"It's not about me, Trey. It's about you. I can't wait to meet this crazy broad who locked you down. But mostly I'm glad you're ok. I've prayed for you every night—even when I didn't believe in God—since the day we graduated."

The Ciuris were tickled to see Tony. The colonel talked to him about flying and Mrs. Ciuri doted on pictures of his kids. Trey ate and watched them reunite. When Tony asked about Millie, the colonel and Mrs. Ciuri admitted they'd only met her once, but that she seemed like a nice girl, and they were excited for the wedding. Toward the end of the meal, Tony asked if he and Trey could be excused to shoot hoops, and everyone laughed. They toasted Grammy and Papa. In the morning, Trey aimed the minivan East, toward another Ciuri family favorite, Wade Herndon, who met them at an old haunt of Trey's near the Broadmoor Hotel.

"I can't believe you made me come here," Wade said, hugging Trey.

"Come on, man! It's the statues! Remember?"

"I live here, Trey. I can see the goddamn statues anytime I want."

"Is now one of those times?"

"Nope. What's up, Tony O?!"

"Not much, Wade. You?"

"Same old shit. 'Cept I'm divorced. Dee-vorsed."

"Sorry to hear that. How are your girls?"

Trey interjected, "I'll bet they miss their dad, livin' with ole KD Lang, eh Wade?"

"Somethin' like that."

"Do you ever think about…." Trey continued, smiling.

"Killin' her? Yep."

"Haha. Trey told me that one already," Tony said. "No killing, ok? So, you two know about these—what are they, wind chimes?"

"These were built by Starr Kempf," Trey said.

"Oh, *that* explains it. Who's he?" Tony asked, looking at Wade who was shaking his head.

"He's dead," Trey started. "Suicide," he went on, looking away from his friends. "It was a rainy night in 1997. I was drinking coffee at a little spot down the road from here—Montague's. Wade, is it still open?"

"S'far as I know. Haven't been there since….a while."

"Well, it was a nice coffee shop. Tony, you know this already but….at the zoo, we were always searching for enlightenment outside of all the military, football and Jesus…."

"And when Trey says 'we,' he means 'I,'" Wade said with a grin, which Tony mirrored.

"I don't remember twisting your arm, ya big sonofabitch. Anyhow, Montague's was a good place to hide—away from the zoo and away from all the other dipshits who were searching for artsy shit like us, the Colorado College types."

"Why ya gotta go after CC? Their girls were hot and their hockey team kicked our ass."

"All girls were hot compared to the zoo. Not everybody enjoyed the CU smorgasbord like Mr. Odette."

"Somebody had to do it, er, I mean them."

"That night I was facing my third disenrollment board. What did they call it, 'a hard look?' That was it…. 'POW Daddy' or not, nothing was going to save me, so Braz-wah said."

"That cocksucker."

"So I was mopey and I snuck out to drink coffee and smoke in the rain. I picked up a copy of *The Independent*, and on the cover was a picture of what you're looking at right now. I decided I had to find the statues that night. Turned out they were only about a mile from Montague's. So, I made my way."

"They are impressive," Tony said. "Surprised his neighbors didn't sue him."

"I think they did," Wade said. "Even after he was dead."

"I stood at that gate, smoking until dark. Rain was dripping from my hat, and his widow came outside and said, 'You can see these tomorrow, please come back then.' I told her, probably in a pathetic way, 'I won't be here tomorrow.' So she said I could stay and went back inside. I thought hard about his suicide, probably harder than anyone who ever laid eyes on those statues, I told myself. I pretended to be some CC chick staring at the statues in the rain, wondering, 'How could he exit a world into which he brought so much beauty?'"

"I'm sure that's how CC chicks sound," Wade said.

"Naturally!" Tony beamed.

"Anyhow. I knew the answer, I knew exactly how Kempf could make his choice," Trey said.

"Well, that's swell," Wade said. "If you're done, now, Starr, y'all can get in your minivan and follow me back to the house."

"I just wanted to share this with you guys," Trey said sheepishly.

"Well, great," said Wade. "Wish you woulda just picked out a titty bar or something. Normal bachelor stuff." Tony nodded with his head bowed.

****

Trey wept with nostalgia on the drive from Colorado Springs to Chicago. The freeway numbers, names of the towns, a truck stop in Salina, and all the cops in Kansas itching to give tickets to out-of-staters. A Bob Evans every hundred miles. The casino in Kansas City where Trey once wasted two hours and his money for gas while Wade slept in the parking garage. The I-70 semis, Wade's surgeon hands drafting between flocks of them. Sunset in the rearview.

"I can't believe you're a diplomat," Wade began. "I thought only dickheads from Connecticut did that shit."

"Sheeit," Trey countered. "There's a guy from Murphysboro with me in Delhi. He almost passed out when I started talking about Anna and Makanda and the Cobden Appleknockers."

"No shit?"

"No shit! State Department is hiring like everybody now. Didn't you hear that quote from Secretary Gates? He was like, 'Why the hell are there more military band members than Foreign Service Officers?'"

"I didn't hear that. I like Gates. Can't believe Obama kept his ass."

"Obama's smart," Trey said.

"Yeah, that's about it," Wade said.

"Isn't that all you need?" Trey asked. "After Bush, I mean."

"I don't know, Yuri. How far have your brains taken you?" Tony asked.

"Touché."

"Don't speak that diplo shit with us," Wade warned.

319

"Sorry," Trey said. "I thought it was a kick that Gates started off in a missile squadron. He was an Intel officer, undercover though."

"Really?" Wade asked. "Where?"

"Whiteman. When they had nukes."

"They still have nukes," Tony said.

"I know, I meant ICBMs. You guys ok? I sense some hostility."

"I just can't separate the image—scratch that—the images of you beating off in my truck, and then think of you doing diplo shit."

"Dude, it's not as sexy as it seems. I interview 120 Indians a day for visas."

"Right. You date any of them diplo gals?"

"One. Before Millie, obviously."

"I bet she talked real nice."

"Actually, she cursed more than me."

"Why'd y'all break up?"

"Eh, it just wasn't right. She was older than me."

"What's wrong with older women?"

"I want to have kids, man! After 35 there's serious health risks. And this chick was on BC for like half her life. You know how bad that messes up their plumbing?"

"It's true," Tony said. "I love it how chicks tell you that shit and expect you to feel sorry for them, like, 'oh, you poor thing! All those bad men who forced you to get on the pill and have sex with them!'"

"Ha, they do kind of make it into a victim thing. I always thought birth control was a feminist pillar, like liberation or something."

"It's whatever's convenient for them—just like all women."

"Whoa, Tone. Wade's the divorcee here. Why are we getting bitterness from you?"

"Call me after you've been married a few years."

"I will."

"Yuri, you're not really with State, are you?" Tony asked. "You're working for the Agency, right?"

"I'm not good looking enough." Trey said. "What about you, Wade? What are you doing in the Mountain? Secret squirrel stuff?"

"Lotsa 9/11 still. Air Defense. Lotsa shit on China."

"China? I didn't think they were a worthy adversary yet."

"We want them to think so. Makes 'em cocky, then they cut corners. No country in the history of the world has ever stolen more fake plans."

"We bait them?"

"Those clowns will follow anything with bright lights and loud noise. It's like opening a casino and setting up the Pai Gow table. The chinks swarm like rats."

"And you let them steal plans of shit that doesn't work?"

"Better. The shit works but they copy it—that's what they're good at. So there's not much R and D….they're rote memorizers anyway. There's so many back doors we fuck with 'em anytime we want. We can change the imagery on their satellites or juke 'em into a funky orbit. Sometimes we just leave the dome light on in their birds, so to speak, and drain their power."

"Wow! That sounds much cooler than visa interviews."

"Who's this guy we're picking up in Chicago?" Tony asked.

"Reggie. He looks like Jesus, you'll love him," Trey said.

"I'm scared of Peace Corps people."

"Don't be scared. We beat off in automobiles like everybody else."

"Reggie? Is he black?" Wade asked.

"No."

"Thought I'd have some company for a minute," Tony said.

"You still pretending to be black?" Trey asked.

"Hey man," Tony warned.

"Sorry."

"Sorry for what?" Tony challenged.

"I'm sorry I didn't call you after the earthquake."

"That's fine."

"Does your dad still have family there? You went down there, right?"

"Three times. Twice with the Air Force to fly in aid. Once on my own."

"What was it like?"

"Worse than you could imagine."

"Was it good, though, to be back to where your….your roots?' Sorry, I'm asking like a chump."

"It's fine. Most people didn't believe I was Haitian, given my complexion. I should have known anyway. My dad and his people are all light skinned. They always passed when they needed to. I never understood that as a kid, that white Haitians were pretty much just French. They owned everything, lived on the south shore, away from the madness you see on Nat Geo. *Grand blancs* are probably going to come out of the earthquake better than before, with all the aid money. I never told my dad about all this."

"You still helped people, though, right?" Trey asked.

"I wrote a check. I landed a plane on a dirt strip. I talked with other light skinners and halfsies like me. When I tried to hang out with the locals, they weren't shy about telling me to stay with my own kind."

"Sorry, man. If it makes you feel any better, before Papa died, I asked him why he never visited Sicily. He said he'd never want to go back to a place they had to leave. He talked about how his parents weren't even allowed to go to school, that it was like that all over Southern Italy. 'I have nothing in common with those Europeans,' he said."

"It's ok. Better I learned it myself, so I can tell the kids someday. There are light skinners now, some of them famous, who are writing articles about how 'their heart breaks with the people in Haiti' and all that shit. Makes me sick. They were probably, historically the source of a lot more misery than any earthquake."

"What does Colonel Odette think?"

"My dad? I'm not sure if he ever thought about that stuff. He just focused on flying and the Air Force, stayed out of politics and race and all that."

"Does he like Obama?"

"No way, man. Talk about a light skinner. What a fake. Obama couldn't set foot in Lemon City or even Sumter without faking it." Tony paused, then stuck his head into the front seat between Trey and Wade. "Trust me, I know all about faking it. That dude *had* to marry a black girl. He *had* to hire a guy with the blackest name around: Reggie Love? Gimme a break. I know a fake like I know myself."

"What did Pop think of 'little Johnny' becoming a fireman like him?" Wade asked.

"He was proud. He knew that stuff didn't come easy to me. I told him about staying in the engine bay by myself, memorizing every tool and piece of equipment on the ambulance and the truck, tying knots over and over until it was second nature." Wade looked forward and smiled.

"You sure 'Reggie' ain't black?" Wade asked.

"Positive. His dad just liked the name. If anything, he's Nepali. He stayed there after we got evacuated, married a Nepali girl, comes back to the States about twice a year."

****

Park Ridge was ideal, more Ferris Bueller than Wonder Years, save for the constant drone of planes landing at O'Hare. Every third house in the neighborhood was being torn down and remade a McMansion by bicoastal transplants, who Reggie's mother welcomed with homemade jam and something from the garden.

Wade, Tony, and Trey slept in hammocks in the back yard while Reggie finished burning CDs for the last legs of the trip. The sun went down, stealing the day's warmth, waking Trey first, who shuddered at dusk pooling on the flatness of Illinois. Into his mind danced the suicides, like snaps of electricity, and then the throbbing heads of matches, people about to self-immolate for Tibet, for Palestine, for whatever. Trey stared at Tony and Wade and at the light in Reggie's window. Millie's face appeared and he was consoled.

Reggie helmed the minivan like a dad, earning silent respect from Wade and Tony. The music on his CDs was esoteric, hopeful; nothing agonizing on the ears, but nothing anyone in the car had heard before. Indiana's highways were full of fog and semis, and along the sides of the road electric eyes and lights warned of deer crossing. Trey took responsibility for the quietness in the car and sang a lyric he knew Tony would not resist finishing.

"I remember the first time I drove through Indiana."

"Watching fences in the distance fade away."

"Once there was a girl I knew there, she was pretty…."

"Iris?" Reggie interrupted, making Trey laugh.

"Who's Iris? Peace Corps chick?"

"Yes," said Reggie. "What song are you singing?"

325

"The Samples."

"They never came to UIC."

"They're more of a Carbondale band."

"It's nice that we're talking," Reggie said.

"Well, we weren't sure about you, Peace Corps," Wade said.

"Should I masturbate in the car to prove I'm legitimate?"

"Christ, Trey told you about that?! And you're still friends? You're legit."

"The Corps brings you close to your comrades," Trey said. "Semper high, man."

"Right."

"Funny Trey stories….go," Reggie said.

"Jesus, this is going to be good," Trey mumbled.

"I got one," Wade said. "The shit machine."

"Ugh, that was tragic, not funny at all."

"Trey had this girlfriend. The way he acted, she was his first, even though he told us he had a few in high school."

"Gotta call bullshit on that one," Tony said.

"It was so long ago! Who can remember?" Trey asked laughing.

"She started out cool—like they all do—and then she got to complaining about everything that made Trey Trey."

"She didn't make him stop beating off in the car, did she?"

"He did that on his own. It's amazing what the occasional blowjob'll do to a man. No, she made him stop wearing all his crazy clothes, his Velcro shoes, made him listen to Tori Amos, told him to quit smoking, made him feel bad for going to the Waffle House. Shit like that."

"That sounds pretty normal."

"And then she started getting fat."

"Gotta drop her."

"He didn't. He tried to save her."

"Save her from being fat? He put a padlock on the fridge?"

"He'd invite her to go running with him, and she would start complaining about shin splints or something. Then she'd go do yoga and wonder why she didn't lose weight. He'd talk to her about nutrition, simple shit, like 'maybe an éclair before bed ain't such a good idea.' But she'd get all emotional, and—Trey, what was her go-to CD? What she always told you to listen to if you wanted to know how sad she was?"

"City of Angels," Trey said with fatigue and embarrassment.

"Trey and I were on probation so much, and Braz-wah, our officer in charge was always prowling for us…."

"That cocksucker," Trey said, imitating Wade.

"…..all we could do most weekends was watch movies on our computers. And Trey tried to make it romantic for her. He'd sneak in a bottle of cheap Andre Brut, a couple strawberries, and they'd spoon on the bed. One time, we're watching and she sits up—she's got a mouth full of bon bons—and says, 'Oh my God, Gwyneth Paltrow's so skinny! Look how unhealthy she is!' And Trey's laying there like, 'oh fuck, oh fuck,' lookin' over at me while…..what was her name again?"

"Penny. You called her 'nickel' after she plumped up, remember?"

"That's right, Penny. Penny's looking at Trey like he's supposed to agree with her about Gwyneth Paltrow, and Trey's like, 'I'd throw your fat ass out the window if Gwen walked in!'

"Another time, Trey tried to convince her that the health shakes she was drinking weren't actually good for her. And she was like, 'What do you know?! These have every vitamin and mineral I need!' But Trey was trying to say that the natural process of digestion: chewing, swallowing, lubing up the food to get ready for the stomach and shit, was what your body needed naturally. When you down one of those shakes, he said, you miss the key parts of digestion. She was like, 'Whatever. Listen to City of Angels, gimme those bon bons.'

"So Trey snuck into the Biology lab for a few weeks every night, and he spun up a bunch of enzymes, procured a bunch of acids, and then had me rig up this test tube system to simulate the digestive tract. It was one of the only times he actually applied himself at the zoo. When it was all finished, he told Penny he had a surprise for her. He set up every stage: used a pair of joke teeth to chew the food, added enzymes in a dish, sent it through a glass pharynx with a hand pump, then a rubber esophagus, added lube, mixed it with acids and other enzymes, all that shit. He even used real bile and bilirubin….made himself throw up to get some!"

"That's fucking sick," Tony said. "What was the point?"

"I wanted to show her that I cared about her health."

"I'm not finished!" Wade yelled. "So, Trey's getting ready for the finale, pumping it through the intestines….and I *maaaaay* have strung up the tubing a little tight for the rectal simulator."

"Yeah, just a little too tight, asshole," Trey said.

"It *was* an asshole! That's what you hired me to make!"

"Ok, I'll finish the story," Trey said. "So, I'm standing there at the back, and I had already decomposed a cheeseburger a couple days before, so conceivably it was all broken down and ready to shit out of this pucker tube Wade made. But he put a series of kinks in the intestines that created a ton of pressure, and as soon as I released the asshole valve, splat! Homemade shit all over me." Wade jumped back in.

"And all over her! Lab shit is much nastier than the real thing. It's like baby shit: 'part toxic waste, part Velcro.' The bitch ran her fat ass into the hallway, and Trey was covered in shit, yelling 'shhhhh!' and laughing, and I'm over at the eyewash station, like, 'we gotta hose'r fat ass down!'"

"Again, you proved what?" Tony asked.

"He wanted to show her that he took her eating disorder to heart," Reggie said. "She probably struggled with her weight. Trey tried to encourage her to exercise. He made suggestions on nutrition. She likely resented his concern because she was not ready to admit or discuss her condition. Trey, for his part, probably enjoyed the frequent blowjobs she gave, and she used them to stave off any substantial criticisms he would have of her. When her childish referral to the City of Angels CD became too much, Trey was driven to more grotesque methods of caring."

"Thanks, Obi Wan," Tony said. "But avoiding exercise is *not* 'a condition.'"

"Where is she these days?" Wade asked. "Must be half a buck by now."

"Dunno, I never kept track of her. She was a Psychology major."

"Christ, that explains it. You could look her up on Facebook."

"I'm not on that shit."

"Yeah, Yuri, but that's just it….you *should* be on it, because then you wouldn't miss out on so much," Tony said. "We wouldn't have to take a weeklong road trip to catch up before your wedding."

"I'm scared of all that social networking stuff."

"Tony, it's your turn," Reggie prodded.

"I don't have any stories on the spot. And I don't really feel comfortable with you calling the shots."

"Well, I'll tell mine, then," Reggie said. "It was on a road trip, just like this one, four years ago, when Trey got hired by the fire department in Maryland and had to pack out from his parent's house. He rented a car—significantly smaller than this one. All he took were books and clothes. Things were so strange, the way we left Nepal, that he and I were silent except for our music, until Hobbs, New Mexico, wherever that is. Trey stopped to use the bathroom. I watched the sunrise. Ten minutes later, he ran out of the convenience store like he'd robbed it, yelling, 'Drive! Drive!'"

"What did he do?" Tony asked.

"He clogged the toilet. He wanted to dramatize the moment, to feel like a bandit."

"Another shit story, that's all I'm good for," Trey grumbled.

"The rest of the trip was more open between us, and I think that's why I made the cut to be a groomsman. I mean, the other guy is from the Air Force too, right?"

"Slim. Yes," Trey said. Reggie continued.

"Trey has a thing for small businesses named for their proprietors: Chet's Auto Body, Jake's Pizza, Tina's Nails. And he thinks it's the most hilarious thing when the proprietor answers their own phone. So, whenever he passed such places on our trip, he did his phone voice and said, most times in a southern accent, 'Chet's Auto Body, Chet speaking. Bonnie's Laundromat, Bonnie speaking. And so on."

"Side splitting," Tony said.

"He's also fascinated by American-style marketing, so much so, he likes to make up products and pitch them in a variety of voices. On our trip, he spent probably 150 miles, honing in a British accent, 'The 2007 *Whirlpool* Buttfucker….Buttfuck those dishes.' Over and over. 'Buttfuck those dishes.'

"Then he'd impersonate the consumers of the *Whirlpool* Buttfucker. Trey, could I have some help? A southerner, please?" Trey laughed and contorted his face to do voices:

"Shit, these dishes ain't gonna buttfuck 'emselves! I gotta get one-a-them-there buttfuckers!"

"A black preacher."

"The Bible cautions against buttfuckin', I know….but baby, the dishes!"

"A flamboyant gay man."

"Mmmmm, I do dishes by hand, but I'll take two of those Whirl pool boys!"

"An Eastern European."

"My wife. No good. She no fack butt on deeshez."

"Latino gangster"

"Yo dock! I ain't no culero, but I'll like buttfuck those platos y cuencas, bro." Wade and Tony laughed hard and long.

"You didn't do the Jersey voice?" Wade asked. "In the Springs, whenever the *Sleepy's* mattress truck drove by, he went into his New

Jersey asshole voice: 'Thank you for cawling *Sleepy's*….where I slept with your mother!'"

"I really clogged that Hobbs toilet," Trey said. "I remember that sunrise too. We drove straight into it."

"And got a ticket in Texas."

"Yeah, the cop was like, 'California?! Where'r y'all goin' with all them books? Got any drugs in there?'"

"I couldn't tell if he was asking because he wanted to get high or if he was doing police work."

"He even asked about Redge's beard and long hair. He was like, 'Y'all musical performers?' And I told him, 'Well, sir, we are on our way to Luckenbach. I've always wanted to see it.'"

"And he smiled and gave us directions. Even though it was six hours away."

"Waylon and Willie and the boys," Wade half sang.

"What song is that?" Tony asked.

"Somethin' Trey and I used to sing at a bowling alley in Lompuke."

"It's kind of a farce, actually," Trey said. "No one lives in Luckenbach, and Waylon Jennings didn't write the song, and I read that he didn't even like singing it, but the crowd wanted it, needed it. And people from the area don't like it because it has nothing to do with the town."

"Ain't nuthin' gets 'em goin' at the county fair like Waylon and Willie, though."

"I guess that's all you need. That and Jesus."

"Amen," Wade said.

"Trey had a girlfriend named Michelle when we took our road trip."

"That was a lead balloon."

"Did I meet her?" Tony asked. "Oh, no, that's right, I never met any girls you dated, right Trey? Didn't even hear about them until you'd broken up."

"Ree-lax, Oh-dette. You're gonna meet the only one that matters."

"She looks cute in her pictures. And if she locked you down, she's better than all of us put together."

"I think highly of her, yes."

"Well, good, I hope the honeymoon never wears off. Maybe getting married later in life will spare you a lot of the bullshit."

"Like what?"

"Like all the shit you wished you would have told each other when you were dating. Compatibility shit."

"So, pardon me for getting personal, but I can only assume that you're talking about you and Carrie. And you don't mind discussing it in the car?"

"What the hell? I've known Wade almost as long as I've known you. And Obi Wan here seems like he's a wise man."

"So, what does she say to you now that she didn't in the beginning?"

"That I ruined her life by getting her pregnant. That she shouldn't have 'wasted her virginity' on me. That I deploy too much and miss all the important moments in my kids' lives. That she has to defend me when they cry all night when I'm gone. That it's getting harder and harder to defend me. That I'm still stuck on not getting into the Academy, and then not getting a pilot slot out of ROTC, and then not getting fighters like my dad. That I ruined her career by 'making' her stay home with the kids, shattering her identity. That I chained her to the Air Force, made her move every three years, left her for months at a time, shattered her identity, that I'm not man enough to fly fighters…." Tony caught his breath and found that he was teary and hoarse, the other men in the car silent. Reggie pulled off the highway and put his hand on Tony's shoulder as he was looking down.

"I think it's your turn to drive," he said. Tony switched places with Reggie, adjusted the seat, and ejected the CD.

"Sorry, man, I'm gonna try the radio. What was that we were listening to, anyway?"

"Zappa," Reggie said, patting Tony's shoulder again.

After a few quiet miles, Tony said, "Schöne Wochenende" to no one in particular.

"What's that?" Wade asked.

"My funniest Trey thing, I just thought of it. 'Schöne Wochenende,' he used to say when he'd see a girl with a nice ass."

"What does it mean?"

"It means literally 'good weekend,' like 'have a nice weekend' in German, but Trey was nerdy and sneaky about it: 'Schöne' means beautiful. 'Wochen' he pronounced like 'walkin',' and 'ende,' as in 'rear end.' Schöne Walkin' Ende. It was our code for a girl with a nice butt."

****

The quartet pumped through Ohio and West Virginia and ended at a campground on the northern edge of Montgomery County, Maryland. Trey hopped like a sprite out of the back of the minivan, muscling a large tent from the hatch.

"Well, here's your Thursday night special!"

"What the fuck is that?" Wade asked.

"What does it look like?"

"It looks like something a motherfucker who never goes camping would buy. That's like a tailgating tent. For the fucking summer. It's October goddamnit."

"Well, I had to get something that would fit four normal-sized motherfuckers and a sasquatch."

"Dude, Baltimore is up the road. Let's just press through," Wade said, looking at Reggie and Tony for support.

"Slim is meeting us here, man. I'm open to going to B'more, but I'll be honest. I envisioned us around a fire the night before the rehearsal dinner."

"Goddamnit."

"What's Slim's story?" Tony asked. "I don't think I met him in Cheyenne."

"None of you did. We were close in missiles, but we got closer when I moved to DC. He's a consultant now. And there's something else I need to tell you about him."

"He black too?" Tony asked.

"No, he's gay."

335

"Whoa, was he gay in the Air Force?" Wade asked. "How many alerts did y'all pull together?"

"He was pretty darned straight in the Air Force. It's a new development. But, hey, I don't know how 'out' he is with strangers, so don't ask, don't tell, ok?"

"Whatever. Hopefully he's prissy and won't wanna sleep in a goddamn tent."

Slim pulled into the campsite faster than the speed limit, kicking up dust and gravel. He bolted from his Jetta and hugged Trey.

"Jake's not coming!" he wailed into Trey's shoulder.

"I think he's pretty 'out,'" Wade said, making Tony laugh. Reggie introduced himself.

"Hi everyone," Slim said, regaining his composure.

"I'm sorry to hear that, man, Trey said awkwardly. "Let me introduce you to the party." Slim shook hands with Wade and Tony, who both said, 'what's up."

"Well, I brought booze and food and firewood," Slim said.

"Guess we're camping," Tony muttered to Wade.

"Why is Jake not coming?" Trey asked.

"I'll tell you guys over drinks. You want a beer? Scotch? I got cigars. Good ones."

"I like this guy," Wade said. "Who's Jake?" he asked.

"My…." Slim stammered, "My, ok….my guy," he said sadly.

"Well, my wife's not coming either," Tony offered. "What about you, Reggie? Where's your better half?"

"In Nepal. She met Trey a few times in Delhi."

"Oh, in Delhi, of course," Tony said.

"I'm divorced," Wade said. "But I hear a wedding's a great place to get laid."

"I'll help you with that, big guy," Slim said. "I'll reel in a fag hag and send her your way."

"My man!" Wade said. "It's ok that I call you 'man,' right?"

"Don't make me show you how manly I am," Slim warned.

"I'm really trying to imagine it," Tony said, "Doing another guy and being 'manly,' really, I am."

"Well, it's better than what straight men these days are becoming: politically correct sissies who can't say what's on their mind for fear of offending everyone. You all look like that Gotye guy—shaved legs, skinny jeans: soccer floppers. Be gay and you can say anything you want."

"It's true," Trey said. "There's this dude in Delhi—kinda has a crush on me—which is weird, because I never believe even girls when they find me attractive. After a few drinks at the Embassy bar, with no fear of who hears, he's like, 'your cock, my mouth, let's go.' Total sexual harassment!"

"That's what I'm talking about," Slim said.

"Jesus, that's nasty," Wade said.

"But imagine it," Slim said. "Someone whose only dream is to have your dick in their mouth. I guarantee you've never met a respectable girl who's happy to do it. She thinks she's doing you a favor. In 'the community,' we daydream about it."

"That's sick," Tony said. "But fascinating."

"But seriously, fellas," Slim continued. "There's a civil war brewing between men and women, and you are going to want us on your side. We humor women, but we're more loyal to you."

"As long as we let you suck our dicks?"

"As long as you don't mind that we fantasize about it. There are plenty of them to service without yours joining the cause, trust me."

"You gonna suck a dick at the wedding?"

"If the opportunity presents itself, I don't know. Jake," Slim sniffed.

"He's right about the civil war," Reggie broke in. "That's why marrying a Nepali girl was so important to me."

"How is Drupata?" Trey asked. "I wish she came along. But I think she'd be overwhelmed by all the dick sucking."

"It's not overwhelming," Slim said, "Just take it inch by inch."

"She's ok back home," Reggie said, and then turned to Tony. "I was thinking about what you told us in the car."

"That was just a release, it's ok."

"No, you made good points. And you have a right to be hurt."

"Who said I was hurt? I was just warning Yuri of what lies ahead."

"There are three lessons you need to learn. Your wife is white, I assume. Am I right?"

"What the fuck is this? Yes, my wife is white and she married a half-Haitian. I check all those interracial boxes for my kids."

"I'm asking because the battle Slim is talking about is with white women, who have evolved into quite possibly the most worthless subset of humanity we've ever known."

"Shit, Redge, we haven't even started drinking yet," Trey said. "I don't remember our Peace Corps conversations getting so heavy. Or harsh."

"Let me get us started here," Slim announced and started pouring scotches.

"Jesus, 18 year," Wade moaned happily.

"Nothing but the best for our missileer turned volunteer, teacher cum firefighter cum diplomat."

"Stop talking about 'cum' now, ya hear?" Wade joked. "I really like this guy."

"Let him suck you off," Tony said.

"'Like' is such a strong word. Can I turn my head and pretend he's a girl?" Wade arranged newspaper and kindling in the fire pit. Reggie went on.

"White women have followed the allure of money to the point that they have evolved out of usefulness to the human race. They didn't invent anything, build anything. They organized nothing. All they did was forsake motherhood and maneuver via whining for the spoils men won. During the next war, they will be specifically targeted."

"Ok, Terminator," Tony said.

"Joke if you like, and I know this is supposed to be a light-hearted celebration of Trey's wedding, but I will say three things, Tony. Feel free to leave them here like the hangover you'll have tomorrow, but here they are:

"One, Carrie needs you more than you need her. Believe it. And let her know in explicit terms that that is how it is. No man, a provider for and protector of his family needs his wife more than she needs him. If he does, then he ceases to be a man.

"Two. Turn to porn. A regular routine is the best defense against white feminism: it's anonymous, it's anything you can dream, and it doesn't require your wife. No more pussy on a pedestal, because it can't possibly rival what is buried deep in your psyche. As long as it's legal, pursue it and jerk off to it. Your wife can't compete with the heroin-like endorphins of a masturbatory release. It's true biology. And you'll find, the more satisfied you are with yourself, the less she'll be able to manipulate you with sex.

"Finally, understand that men created this problem. We gave them the disposable income to begin white feminism, which only seeks the material things that white men have. We let them get away with being lazy and uncreative. We permitted them to attach dollar values to motherhood, rendering it unprofitable and therefore unpopular. We put dollar values on promiscuity, encouraging them to behave according to men's' worst impulses of consumption. And we let them personify our racism, with their advocacy for abortion only to keep racial breeding down, their patronizing charity toward minorities, and their sexual objectification of men of color. The white feminist never cared about a better tomorrow, a better world. She just wants to buy better shoes than the next white chick without working for them."

"Well, that's a thesis I haven't heard before," Trey said, scanning the faces of the others for their reactions.

"Living in Nepal with a wife who cares for me and our children has made me hyperallergic to western culture, which is dominated by a weak, white female whine. Trey, I hope that Millie is thoughtful, kind, that she complements you, that you support each other."

"Here's to that!" Trey toasted, noticing that every man raised his glass save for Slim, who sat withdrawn, drinking and refilling, becoming a silhouette as the fire grew and the sun diminished.

"It's funny, Obi Wan. I think I believe everything you're saying. But I feel like a zombie. Maybe it's the booze. I don't think Carrie would tolerate me telling her how much she needs me."

"Be resolute. Be a man. The next time she tries to passive aggressively suggest that your deployments let down your kids, tell her, in front of your kids to stop being hurtful. Then start documenting every verbal insult she throws at you. Everything she uses to bring you down. You'll be outraged when you actually compile how many times Carrie emotionally abuses you. And to think she does it in front of your children? Unacceptable.

"It's ironic in this anti-bullying culture, people selectively ignore the toll women have been able exact on men through verbal abuse. But we're taught to bear it like donkeys. Words are weapons. A photo of a woman with a black eye is worth a thousand words. But what if those words were carefully strung out over years of verbal abuse, designed to degrade the man who finally lost it? I'm not saying you should hit Carrie. Never hit her."

"Carrie would leave me in half a second if I started 'documenting' her insults."

"Let her. But before you do, look at her straight and say, 'you will never see me again.'"

"But she *would* see me again. In court for custody and all that, which I wouldn't get."

"No, you have to be resolute. Be a man. She gets *none* of you! She will *never* see you again. That means you are willing to never see her or anyone who has a drop of her blood, including your kids. If you are a man, you've been a good father, and deep inside she knows that, and her instincts will be to keep your influence on the kids, even though her emotions, the weakest part of women, tell her to hurt you by keeping them away from you. Be resolute. If she is a woman, she will not be able to stomach the reality of single motherhood, no matter how much money she squeezes out of you, no matter the custody arrangement."

"Reggie, man, are you sure you're ok?" Trey asked. "Your nose is running into your beard. Maybe you should blaze up a j?" Reggie put up a hand like a stop sign, which Trey heeded.

"Never break for a creature, a white woman! that is so inherently weaker than you. She is *nothing* without you. You provide and protect. And while society feels sorry for her—only because of marketing—not because she actually deserves sympathy—you cannot. And if you have to write off your kids, that's what *men* can do. No woman gets to hold you hostage. She's the one with all the complaints. She's the one who has so many things to 'figure out.' Is it the fault of your kids? No. And, yes, there will be some gut-wrenching emotions as you appreciate what this separation would mean. Think of it as a long deployment. But stick to your guns: she will never see you again. This kind of resolve will break 98 percent of women. The other two percent are not women."

"What do you mean, 'not women?' Of course, they're women."

"They are women so long as they behave as they should. Today, we're seeing plainly the great fallacy of American feminism. For generations they've been pushed to behave just like men. Though most of them, as I said, don't have the gumption, composure, or analytical abilities to compete. They end up ham-handing it, and their men— including their sons—get crushed in the process."

"Betty Friedan did say that the goal was not to be men or to demonize them," Trey slurred.

"Shut the fuck up, Yuri!" Wade yelled, imitating *The Big Lebowski*. Reggie continued with Tony rapt, Wade amused, and Slim darkening.

"In sports, a woman who pushes herself to compete at a truly high level begins to see interruptions in her cycle and eventually will stop menstruating. She's become a man. In business, a woman who puts in 16-hour days, schmoozing, developing professionally, must forgo any thought of being attractive to the opposite sex. She must forget about having a family. She is a man as well."

"Wow," Tony said.

"It goes on. In Tech or STEM or whatever you call it. If a woman chooses, like millions of men do, to stay up all night coding in her pajamas, eating stale pizza for weeks while puzzling over the algorithms that rule our world, she is a man. If a woman is trained to fight on the battlefield alongside men, she'll be killed unless she…."

"Becomes a man. This is interesting, all this switching." Reggie went on.

"The man who leaves the pot on the stove which catches the building on fire is a woman. The woman who enters the burning building and puts the fire out is a man."

Trey broke in. "What about if a man takes on traditionally…."

"I know what you're going to ask," Reggie interrupted. "There's society and there's biology…women who shun motherhood are breaking with their DNA….they are…"

"Are men?" Trey asked in disbelief. "No, man, what if a guy wants to stay at home and be a house husband?"

"He's not a man. His family will be weaker." Trey shook his head.

"So how does this apply to me?" Tony asked.

"Just be a man, which means being appreciative of your emotionally fragile wife. Understand that she is a child who wants a hug, that's it. She may be trained academically and professionally but academic questions don't keep her up at night. Whether or not you truly love her does."

"Of course, if academic questions *did* keep her up at night…." Trey said sarcastically.

"She'd be a man!" Tony exclaimed.

"You're getting it," Reggie said, sucking snot back inside.

"This is super sexist," Trey said.

"Well, biology is sexist and thank God. These differences have kept humanity going. American feminism is trying to fuck it up."

"'Stronger women' is not a good thing? What are you going to tell your daughter when she wants to become a doctor?" Trey asked.

"Strong women *are* important. But if they choose to have children, their first duty is to them, not to working an unfulfilling job to pay for daycare and buy consumable crap made in the third world. My daughter will be able to be anything she wants. But if she has children, she'll have her priorities straight. She won't try to 'have it all,' as Western women are fond of saying. On the same note, my son will cherish his wife's dedication to the family. Her service will make him prouder than any paycheck, even if they—quote-unquote—need the money."

"Shit, Redge," Trey said. "Shangri La done changed yo' world view!"

Wade tossed another log on the fire. The wedding party was into their third bottle, their backsides numb on sitting stumps. Other campers filled out the site, some families, some groups similar to Trey's, who used headlights to illuminate their area before bedtime.

"Did you bring sleeping bags?" Wade asked.

"Oops."

"Goddamnit."

"Don't worry baby. You can spoon up on me"

"I'd rather stuff my big ass in that minivan."

"Do you miss India?" Reggie asked. "Is Millie excited to live there?"

"I miss the food. From the neck up. Millie visited the last two summers, so she knows what's in store. She's been groped at the market like every white chick who discovers 'Incredible India.' I told her to smack any dude who touched her, but she said, 'Then I'd be a man!'"

"Haha," Reggie said. "In all seriousness, it's been my experience that an Indian man, especially if he's in a pack with his friends, wouldn't think twice about smacking a woman back. Or worse. I hope she's careful."

"She is," Trey said, taking a quick look at a light from another campsite, then reorienting to his mates. "You know, the eat-pray-love fools talk so reverently about Indian curry being good for you—they say it prevents cancer. But the food is so choked with ghee and the water is so ridden with feces that no one there *lives* long enough to get cancer. They all die of dysentery or heart attacks." Trey's mates' eyes looked like ping pong balls and their fingers moved along their cigars like guitarists' between frets, finding the tip, avoiding the cherry. Their bodies hummed to the frequency of a buzz on good booze as leaves made brittle sounds crashing into the site.

"When I was bagging groceries at Trader Joe's," Trey continued, "a lady bustled up to our manager and asked him to open another checkout line because—get this—Chief Justice Roberts' wife was in *her* line. The manager's name was Hobbes—like the guy—like the tiger named after the guy. He went to NYU film school—used to whisper in my ear how despicable TJ customers were, especially in Bethesda. At least Whole Foods people were unabashed in their assholery, he said. Trader Joe's customers pretended to care about their fellow man, which was worse.

"So this girdled Bethesdite demanded that Hobbes open another checkout line! And Hobbes didn't think twice about accommodating that fat bitch and her friends. But he went straight to Mrs. Roberts and hugged her and rung her up himself. Later he told me that 'his film' needed characters like the ones who didn't want to stand in line with Mrs. Roberts." Trey again looked for a reaction from the wedding party.

"Odette! Tony O!" Trey trumpeted. "Remember 'The Sink?'"

"I worked there, Yuri."

"One time, when I was up there….man, for a cadet at the zoo to see a real college town like Boulder?! It was like a dog tasting meat for the first time. They gotta lotta street dogs in Delhi, and sometimes I throw them a piece of ham, and they almost convulse to death to taste it, that feeling of carni-vor-ating they've never known. That was me looking at those CU girls with their perfectly fitting clothing and their expensive bras. And the thought that you were banging them, of course. I excused myself that night to go to the WC, and as I was jerking off in the stall, I looked up at a spot of graffiti, written like a Bible verse: 'No matter how hot she is, someone, somewhere is sick of her shit.'" Tony nodded as if to a bass line in a rap song.

"Redge! You sexist teacher! Namaskar, mero saathi!"

"Namaste, saathi."

"After Peace Corps, I got on with this Catholic school, 8th grade. It was '06 around May Day, which is a huge holiday in L.A., and Congress was debating some kind of legislation that would have sent like every undocumented immigrant back. Half my students were in favor. They said that their parents 'came the right way.' The other half were scared because they knew someone who would have to go. One of my quietest kids, Ana, stood up to the 'right way' immigrant kids and said, 'My mom cleans toilets to send me here. She doesn't do anything wrong. Some people should go back, but not her!' That shut us all up.

"With Mother's Day around the corner, I had the class read *Charlotte's Web*. To me, it was the perfect example of an unsung mom's love, giving essentially her life to save a schlub like Wilbur, right? Ok, I had my doubts. I mean, maybe it was a feminist book that said schlubs like Wilbur win all the prizes while the women behind them give their lives and are the real creative ones. I mean, shit, what kind of literary universe is it where E.B. White is a *man* and S.E. Hinton is a *woman*?! But that's beside the point. I got one foot in 8th grade memories and the other in your anti-feminist creed." Reggie nodded.

"So after we read Charlotte, I gave them envelopes and a stamp and had them write Mother's Day letters. And what happened next was a weird mechanism: they had no idea where to write the address, or where to stick the stamp! Even the idea of dropping these crude items into a metal box gave them no feeling of excitement like it did when we were sending letters as kids. So, they wrote letters to their moms, never expecting that they would actually make it to their destinations. They wrote honestly and at length! Their mothers were bowled over. The kids came in the day after, shaking their heads, even the roughnecks: 'Man, Mister C, that letter trick was sick.'" Reggie smiled. Tony looked at the sky. Slim was almost invisible.

"I mean, these kids….you remember when we used to have to call the radio station to request a song? Or like, when you'd key up your blank tape and get ready to push record when you thought they'd play it? Tony, remember WNOK? We'd call and they'd be like, 'N-O-K, you're on the air, don't curse.' And some dipshit would always yell, 'Fuuuuuck!'" Tony looked at Trey warmly.

"Wade! Wade, you remember Dudley? God rest his big ass soul." Wade nodded. "Remember how your brother used to give him a raw egg? How he protected it?" Wade nodded.

"Slim! Clinton Chandler Ralston the fourth! You remember Rico, my neighbor in Anacostia?" Slim stayed quiet. "One time he got in my face. We were drinking. Not like this, but we were getting pretty friendly, pretty honest, and he says, 'Trey, I want you to tell me the worst black joke you ever told. Not *heard*, Trey. TOLD. He looked me dead in the eye, dead serious. I was like, 'Comon, Ibn'….I used his Nation name. 'That ain't cool, man!' But he wouldn't budge. He was like, 'It's ok, Trey, I just want to hear you tell it. It don't mean you racist. I know you don't tell them jokes now.'

"So I told him. I was ashamed. I couldn't believe I still remembered it. And Rico kinda just sat there and rolled it over. Poured himself and me another drink. And he said, 'You wanna hear the worst white joke I know?' I was like, 'Hell yes!' He said, 'What's red, white, and yellow, and funny as hell?' I was like, 'I don't know.' He said, 'A busload of white kids going off a cliff.' At first I was like, 'That's it?' And he was like, 'That's all we got, man. When you ain't got no power base, you ain't got time to be witty. We just want y'all to die!'" Slim kept quiet. The others too were docile.

"Hey man," Trey continued, "I'm really sorry about Jake." Another long pause. "Hey dude, you ok? It must be tough. Bad timing with the wedding. You've been together, what, four years?" Tony, Reggie and Wade shifted their attention from Trey to Slim.

"He would kill you all," Slim croaked.

"I'm sorry?" Trey said.

"He could kill you all and nothing would happen."

"Hey man, no killing, ok? What's going on? Join the fireside, will ya? We can help you get through this."

"You want to help me get through this?!" Slim yelled, his eyes darting from the fire to the groomsmen.

"Yes, we do," Wade said. "Calm down, man. Let's talk about sucking dick again."

"If you want to help me, you'll put your phones in the van."

"What are we in a SCIF?" Wade asked.

"Dude, my kids are going to call any minute," Tony said. "What's with this phone shit?"

"Listening device, throw it in the van! Throw it in the van or I'm leaving!"

"I'll call Carrie in the van. You guys can give me your phones if you wanna hear what he has to say. Fucking weird." Slim opened the last bottle and looked dead at Trey.

"I better not, man. I'm pretty pickled."

"You," Slim said to Trey with malice. "He's going to do it just like *you*. He's the only one I ever told. Just jump down and grab the third rail, easy as that." Trey's face lost some color, which was imperceptible to the others. "You, Trey. I told him how it haunted me, how you kept chanting 'Oh-bah-mah, Oh-bah-mah!' That word never escapes my head. And then I watched you go down, and I dragged you back up. And I told Jake about it and now he's gonna do the same thing."

"Slim! Do you need to call the police to help Jake? Is he considering suicide? Why? I don't understand. What happened?"

"You play dumb, Yuri. You playing dumb with Millie too? Am I the only one of us who's met Millie?" The groomsmen nodded. "She's great! She loves Trey! But she doesn't know what I know! What I did, what *he* did!" Slim's hand popped from his windbreaker, fingering Trey with a theatrical point.

"Slim, let's talk about Jake. What happened?"

"Boycott, Divestment, Sanctions. That's what happened: BDS."

"That stuff? What about it?"

"Jake doesn't work for CACI or BAE or whoever he told you. He works for his government, and his government will do anything overt and covert to kill BDS."

"So, what did he do?" Wade asked impatiently.

"It all goes back to that night, Trey, when you did what you did in the Shaw metro."

"What did *Jake* do?!" Trey yelled. "Jake! He's the one that has you all fucked up! Talking about BS-whatever. What did *he* do?!"

"That night matters, fucker, so listen. All you guys listen. It's best that you know, and by the looks on your faces, I can tell you don't know what I'm about to tell you." Trey looked down, resembling Slim from the last two hours. "It was February '09. Obama was brand new. Everybody was ecstatic. DC, the country, the world. Fuck, they gave him the Nobel prize less than a year later, for nothing. In four months he would make the Cairo speech—look it up if you don't remember. It should have been a gamechanger. Jake's government went to great lengths to make sure nothing came of it.

"But BDS kept going. It was grassroots momentum. It had a precedent with South Africa—that was how they helped end Apartheid. So Jake's government targeted effective but unknown people working on it. Jake was assigned to a Swedish diplomat posted in DC. He had been working the issue for years and he was starting to meet people close to Obama. Had he gotten those meetings it would have been much harder to stop.

"First, Jake did it upfront. After weeks of surveilling and studying the diplomat, he grabbed him on the street from behind in a wrestling hold. Jake whispered in the Swede's ear: 'No more BDS,' and he pushed the Swede down and ran away. The next few days, he tapped the Swede's phone, heard him telling his bosses, talking to DC police. The Swede kept going with BDS. This made Jake angry.

"He broke into the Swede's apartment while the Swede's wife and kid were there. He went from room to room, undetected. It's what he does. And in the kid's toybox, Jake left an empty gun and some stray bullets. He listened to the phone calls the Swede's wife made: frantic, scared to death, the kid crying, not understanding why this 'new toy' had gotten in his room, why his mother was taking it away. Jake sent an SMS to the Swede, which disappeared after he opened it: 'No BDS.' But the Swede persisted.

"Jake went back to their apartment building, one of those classy mid-rises with a fancy elevator that runs up the stairwell, where you have to close three sets of doors to get it to operate. The Swede's kid, he was probably about five, loved to watch it come up to their floor. He pressed his face to the plexiglass and marveled at the gears. His parents encouraged him to be an engineer. So, as the Swede was going to work one day, descending the elevator, he saw a black trash bag on the stairs with a blond-haired head sticking out. The Swede freaked, stopped the elevator, ran to the bag, and found that it was a child mannequin. Again, the SMS. But again, the Swede persisted.

"That night, Trey. February. Jake left Nellie's. He was out of his mind angry at this obscure Swedish diplomat. No one knew this guy. No one would ask many questions if he got mugged and shot in Woodley Park. Why so fervent in his pursuit of BDS?

"Jake cut a hole in the plexiglass between the elevator and the stairwell and rigged a jagged piece of metal to pop out as it got to the Swede's floor. The next day, the kid was in the hallway, waiting as usual, and the metal, which was supposed to just cut his face, got him in the neck. The Swede and his wife had only about a minute to hold that kid before he bled out. Swede left DC. Obama did nothing with BDS. Jake's government was successful. But he carried that inside and didn't tell me until your wedding was getting close.

"I spilled my guts to Jake that night, how scared I was, how I had to beat you off that rail, how I thought I was going to get zapped too. I told him how betrayed I was opening up to you, and yet, you, you who were going through a lot too, couldn't open up to me. You just did it in front of me. You haunted my dreams. And you got lucky. I don't know how you started breathing again, but I thanked God. But Jake, who'd just killed a kid….said nothing. Maybe he held it in because he saw how fucked up I was? Maybe that Swede kid gave his life for you?" Trey held his face in his hands. He made no sound as he rocked.

"This sounds fuckin' familiar," Wade said. "I remember pulling this motherfucker out the surf on Jalama Beach after he told me to drop him off. It was a miracle I came back when I did. I had no idea you'd try it again. What's wrong, man?"

"It's ok now," Trey said quietly. "Not something I bring up. I'm sorry, Slim. That you had to see it. Wade, I didn't intend…."

"Fuck your intentions. Lucky-ass motherfucker. You better love life now—do that shit twice and live to tell?"

"Three times," Reggie spoke up.

"What?" Wade asked.

"In Nepal, he did it from a scaffolding, I saw him fall."

"How did you see? I thought I was…."

"I followed you. Cleaned you up. You must have hit something that absorbed the impact. You just had some bruises that I blamed on the weed."

"No, no," Trey said, "No, that's not what....happened."

"I didn't drag you out of the ocean and do CPR on you?" Wade asked, rubbing his throat. "You didn't wake up in your bed the next day and just leave for Cheyenne without saying shit to me?"

"No, I did, but....I went to another place. Another life. Another chance."

"I find it sadistically funny, Trey, that you did this so many times and didn't talk about it with any of us," Slim said. "Don't you *want* to stop doing it? It's one thing to have a near-death experience and not talk about it, but what you're doing now....this whole denial thing...makes me not want to be around you anymore."

"I prayed for the third rail to be my last, I did. But just like all the rest, I got another chance. I ended up looping back into myself and starting at a different point."

"Yer fulla shit," Wade spat.

"What do you want me to do, apologize? I'm here, that's my punishment. You know how hard those decisions were to make? You think I just gave up? Got lazy? Pushed restart on the goddamn Nintendo game?"

"Yes, that's exactly what I think."

"Me too."

"And me," said Redge. Tony got out of the minivan, looking happier after a call with his kids, then perplexed at the Picasso-like distortions on the faces of his friends.

"What's wrong? Slim still think the Gestapo is coming?"

"Tony!" Trey yelled. "I've struggled! With feeling low!" The men looked around suspiciously, suddenly realizing how loud they'd gotten and how much quieter the rest of the campsite had become.

"Yeah, no shit, Trey," Tony said. I've known you for almost 20 years. But I'm still here for your wedding."

"Trey's tried to kill himself, it turns out, at least three times," Wade said. "You got any stories, Tone?" Tony dropped his phone and looked again at the sky.

"One thing is for sure, Yuri," Slim said. "You've come clean with us tonight and that's it. Any talk about you starting again, getting some new chance, 'looping back into yourself' is just you trying to feel better about this shit. You fucking say that shit again and you'll have two black eyes in your wedding pictures."

"Well, I don't know how to explain it, but doesn't it seem a bit fishy that this has happened at least four times…."

"*Four* times?!"

"Yeah, in high school, the day I graduated. I took a bunch of pills in my front yard."

"I was at the hospital with your dad," Tony said. "He kept praying, 'Johnny, come back! Come back!' He lost his voice, holding your hand, and you came back. And we tucked you in and told you the next morning that you drank too much at the grad party."

"I *did* drink a lot at the grad party!" Slim swung at Trey's ribs, belting him below the heart. He puked on the fire.

"It's true," Trey cried.

"It's not true," Slim said. He grabbed his phone from the minivan and rang Jake. Trey stayed on all fours.

"I guess it's time for bed," Reggie said. "I wish you did have a joint for me, Trey. Whatever's the truth, I'm glad you're alive, and I am excited to meet Millie."

"Slim beat me to it—knockin' yer ass off—but you deserved it," Wade said and caught himself. "We're all here for you. You got no reason to do this again. And no reason to just be thankful you *did* get so many chances. Good night." Tony stood over Trey.

"That's why I keep telling you to get on Facebook, asshole." he said. "You would have seen Prudence's last message."

"Prudence Diehl? I thought she died a long time ago." Trey rolled over and stared at the branches above, smelling the seared puke rise, squinting tears into the now-cold air. He could barely hear the interminable ring of Slim calling Jake.

"Yeah, that's what you miss when you isolate yourself. Prudence lived out a long life considering the CF. She was 33." Tony picked up his phone, summoned the webpage, and read:

'My disease never bugged me as a kid. I was happy go lucky and my parents liked it that way. A few trips to the hospital? Lollipops and balloons. Coughing fits that seemed to never end? It was sure nice when they did. Every symptom I had, everything that made CF so difficult to live with, I always had people in my life who would help me along and make me feel better about living. Until high school. Then people starting getting sad. They read up on Cystic Fibrosis behind my back and they treated me differently than other people. I got into the rut of feeling predestined for a miserable death.

'My first year at USC, Kurt Cobain killed himself. And instead of feeling outraged or sad or confused, it gave me hope. Here was someone that millions looked up to, who could come to terms with his pain and make a choice. That's what I was going to do too, I decided. Until I met Trey Ciuri. It was sunrise at Swan Lake when I told him that I would be ending my life soon. Trey put out his hand and it was like he slowed the dawn. It must have stayed sunrise for a good two hours while he listened to me and told me how funny and smart and kind I was, and that even another hour on earth would make a difference in his life and hundreds of others who loved me. I came down from that ledge, and now, as even the most optimistic doctors tell me I'm on borrowed time, I remember Trey's kind face, and how he told me he would pray for me, even though I didn't believe in God. Thanks Trey. See you around.'"

The next morning, Reggie sat next to Trey as he drove the last leg to Baltimore. The other three either slept or pressed their faces against the window.

"How did you know Millie was the one?" Reggie asked.

"When I saw her teach. Baltimore City schools are so shitty, I felt like a journalist embedded with the Special Forces, covering a war. But there she was, a little blonde, teaching history to kids who either didn't give a fuck or didn't have the aptitude to give a fuck.

"Baltimore City is so terrible that the heat goes out like every winter. And Millie has to buy her own supplies! I've gone with her to Walmart to mule boxes of copy paper back to her apartment. Copy paper! It ain't because they don't have money. They spend more per student than most districts in the country. It's because they're corrupt! Those goddamned North Avenue bureaucrats—they all make six figures—while my girlfriend has to buy her own shit."

"Chicago has similar schools. But only in the poor sections."

"I'm sure it's the same in every major city. You can't get a good public education in this country unless you have the money to pay for it or the money to live in a district that pays for it. But either way it ain't free."

"What about her teaching convinced you that you wanted to marry her?"

"Oh, her discipline. She stays after every day until her lessons are planned and her papers are graded. No exceptions. Even when we had a date that night."

"I wish I had that kind of discipline. I'm afraid that I've become more Nepali in my approach to deadlines."

"Ke gar-nay?" Trey asked, which meant, "What can you do?" a common Nepali phrase expressing apathy.

"What's her style in the classroom?"

"I don't know, but it's effective. I was in awe, but I tried not to be too impressed—didn't want to scare her away. It was hard not to gush, though, when compared with my classroom management failures. When Millie was teaching they were rapt. But when she left the room, they resumed being the fucking nastiest, loudest, most threatening bunch of kids I've ever seen. Girls loomed like grown-ass men, who the boys deeply feared, but still said filthy sexual things to, inviting fights. The boys were so unengaged it made me furious! These boys were the most emasculated, don't give a fuck guys I'd ever seen.

"But Millie walked back in and they straightened up. Not in a military sense, like when the colonel walks in you come to attention. It was like, 'ok, it's time to learn.' One day, she assigned the tables group work, and from time to time she'd walk around and check on them. Most of them called her 'Miss,' which I loved. Millie stopped at one table and had to lean over to read something. Her shirt rose up and everyone could see her thong riding halfway up her back. My eyes bugged out of my head. I figured that was it. These kids, the boys especially, would start whooping and laughing and making sex jokes. I know *I* would have in high school. But they looked at me with my surprised—and probably aroused—face like *I* was the bad kid. Others pretended they didn't notice. Still another kid engaged Millie so she would stand up and be covered again. The way they protected her, I knew it was a reflection of her character, and how she protected them."

"That does sound special that they would shield her like that."

"Well, part of it was their oblivion. I mean, when she told them that she was engaged, they were like, 'You have a boyfriend? We thought you just slept at the school.'"

"That's funny. How kids, even the poorest, still think they're the center of the universe."

"Diplomats too."

"Is Millie ready to fit into *that* lifestyle?"

"I think she understands it. But here's another thing I love about her. In Delhi, there were some girls, wives and girlfriends of the other guys, who were bragging to her about how cheap 'the help' is in India, and Millie just said politely, 'I've always cleaned my own place and cooked my own food. I'm not going to stop just because I move someplace where it's affordable.'"

"Atta girl! Although I will admit that we have a few servants in Drupata's family home."

"Hard to avoid in that part of the world." Trey said as he saw Slim awake in the rearview.

"Hey Slim, how are you?"

"Ok. You?"

"A little sore, but I deserved it. Did you get a hold of Jake?"

"Yes. He'll be at the reception. He's not so big on church."

"Fuckin' J," Trey joked.

"He doesn't like synagogues either."

"That BDS stuff is crazy. I knew people were against it. I just didn't know to what extent."

"They know that it would make them give back the Palestinian's land. But they also know that the way they're going, they're going to fail. You just can't keep up this kind of Apartheid and succeed for very long, even with our military aid."

"Is that what Jake believes?"

"Yes, he's more pro-Palestinian than me after all that has happened. He says it himself, 'Palestinians are Semites too.' Enough politics, though. Why the hell did I have to buy an orange bowtie?"

"The Orioles, baby!"

"It did seem like a familiar shade. Jake said he's going to wear an entire suit that color, if he can find it before tomorrow."

"That'll be swell. I'm so glad he's ok. Sorry again."

"That's ok."

"Millie has this daydream of us with our kids at their first Orioles game. We watch them out of the corner of our eye for that moment during the national anthem when everyone screams, 'O!!!!!!' We laugh at their surprise. And we promise them that the next game they'll be ready to scream it too."

"That's cool. You know, they do the 'O!' thing at Nats games still? Stupid unoriginal bureaucrats."

"What did you mean last night when you said you 'looped back into yourself?'" Reggie asked.

"I don't know, I think it was the heat of the moment."

"Because there seemed to be something different about you after you took a dive in Kathmandu."

"Dent in my forehead?"

"No, like you were a different person. I never asked you, obviously. What did Oneida say to you to make you want to…."

"He just reinforced things I hated about myself."

"Do you think you're beyond that?"

"Well, yeah, I wouldn't get married if I wasn't."

"Does Millie know?"

"No. But she's the reason I can even talk about it with you guys. She's the reason I wouldn't consider suicide again."

"Her classroom stuff again?"

"No, the looping I was talking about. You know, I described it as another chance, but maybe it was just dreams while I was in and out of consciousness. I'd return to times in my life and I would be aware that I'd lived it before."

"Like when? Any time specifically?"

"Pretty random, it seemed. First time, I went back to Germany in 1987, a couple weeks before the Superbowl, Redskins—Broncos. The Broncos were favored, which really bummed my dad out because he hated John Elway. And I said, 'Don't worry, Dad, the Redskins will win 42-10. And when they did, he was impressed but unmoved. 'We should have bet on it,' he said.

"Other times, I went back in college, high school, right before 9/11. I was aware of the suicide that got me there, and I found that I could predict some future events. But then everything kind of folded into itself and life just went on. There were people to talk to, things to look forward to."

"Must have been daydreams."

"What happens when you struggle again, man?" Tony asked. "I mean, God forbid, but what if you start 'feeling low' again? Have you thought about getting help?"

"Help? You're not allowed to talk about stuff like this, right? I mean, why didn't any of y'all bring it up to me over the last 20 years?"

"That's a good point," Tony said.

"If the feelings return, I guess I'll have to tackle them as they come. It's surely not going away. But last night, laying in my own puke, I was thinking that before I met Millie, and before I came clean to you guys about this stuff...."

"You didn't come clean. We had to beat it out of you."

"Fair enough. Before Millie, the only things that would stop me from descending into 'the death spiral' was if I had something to look forward to: a new job, a trip, a project, something. Millie's the first person I've ever got that 'looking forward to' feeling from, in general. The idea of not seeing her tomorrow is enough to keep me from getting low.

"I was talking to her the other day, getting worried, asking her, 'Aren't you worried, Millie, that public education is a cruel joke? That no matter how hard you try with your kids, they're still fucked? No matter how much money they throw at these schools, your students are never really going to have a chance at success?!'"

"Hopefully she told you to shut yer hole," Wade said.

"No, man. You know what she said? She said, 'Of course they're fucked. Of course public education is a joke. Of course the kids have less than half a chance. But that's why I'm here. And that's why you're here for me.'"

"Do you go to Mass together?" Tony asked.

"Ah, you know me, I go, but I have my struggles with the church."

"What does she think about that?"

"She tells me to just think about St Francis. He was Catholic as can be, but he wasn't a priest. He was just Christlike." Tony smiled out the window at Baltimore coming into view.

"She sounds like a beaut," Wade said.

"Wait till you hear the song she picked out for our dance, fellas. Won't be a dry eye in the house."

Afterword

More important than the timeline of this story—from Desert Shield through most of Obama's first term—is the span in which it was written: between the deaths of Freddie Gray and George Floyd. When Mr. Gray was killed, I was living in Baltimore, commuting to DC; while my wife taught in a public high school not far from the CVS that burned in the subsequent riots. Earlier in the day, her students pulled her aside and warned, "Miss, you better leave early."

But we lived in David Simon's neighborhood, far removed from the scenes depicted in *The Wire*. The only evidence I saw of unrest was during a game at Camden Yards in which police held us in the stadium until a disturbance could be quelled. At the State Department, one of my duties was to monitor Russian media. I saw a clip of a journalist from RT chasing a young man who'd stolen her handbag as she covered the Gray protests. Should I report it as disinformation, I wondered?

Six years later, I was living in Riga, Latvia when Mr. Floyd was killed. Earlier that day, a woman named Amy Cooper encountered a black man in Central Park, and according to CNN contributor Van Jones, she "weaponized race like she had been trained by the Aryan Nation." Had she not been filmed, would she have joined the Floyd protests, crying for justice with the other hipsters? Would the upper middle-class people marching in Twin Cities have called the police if, a year earlier, George Floyd walked through their neighborhoods? Better yet, would they send their kids to the schools Floyd's had to attend?

Watching these events unfold from abroad was tough. As a public diplomacy officer, explaining them to foreign audiences was further daunting. But behind these "difficult" scenarios lay an even more sobering realization: I and most of my upper middle-class peers had no skin in this game. That we would probably be fine emboldened our reactions, whatever they happened to be.

To realize this felt like a snare similar to the situations in the book that drive Trey to call himself "a fool and a whore." For even the awareness of such entrapment seems like an infinite ruse, a tasteless joke, a no-win affair. "Oh, poor Trey and his American angst!" he moans to his father who is just trying to keep his son alive another day.

Are fools and whores bad people? They're sensitive and caring and yet safe: risk averse and risk free. They want to affect change, but they don't know how, and they don't *really* have to listen when people show them. If they start "losing," they can unplug the video game and start over. Trey fails many times to unpack all of this, perhaps most honestly in his letter to Daly City Jackie in which he describes the difference between giving and sacrificing.

In the days after Freddie Gray, sitting in my neighborhood bar, I puzzled over what I could do to help someone, anyone. I started to feel sorry for myself, thinking of my mistakes, my privilege and curse to be the son of a POW, my privilege and curse to be able to watch everything from a barstool. The sad spiral and alcohol depressed me further, and I thought that maybe my life wasn't worth living.

But I thought of the people to whom this book is dedicated— three died too soon, one lived almost a hundred years. It felt to me like the first step to sacrificing was to consider others instead of myself. Maybe it requires the belief that thought and caring are as finite as bauxite, and that when you decide to give some of yours to someone else, you are sacrificing your own well-being. I don't do it often enough, but when I do, it feels much better than self-pity and American angst. Maybe sacrificial thoughts lead to sacrificial actions. Maybe those actions inspire imitation and then a better world.